Other *Leisure* Books by Ellen Tanner Marsh:
THE ENCHANTED PRINCE

TILL DEATH DO US PART

Much as Jewel tried to deny it, she was unable to ignore the bare inch or two that separated her from the naked body of her husband; a body that had, in the past, pleasured hers beyond all imagining. Tor had awakened a passionate side of her that she could not control, and now she lay there and yearned for him no matter how hard she tried not to.

She choked out his name. In an instant, he was gathering her against him with an urgency that left her breathless.

"What is it, lass?"

"You know perfectly well."

He withdrew instantly. After a moment, in a strained voice, he said, "I have to do what I must, Jewel. There's no way out of it. My people depend on me."

"I understand," she said. Her sense of duty was just as strong. "But you could be killed."

"I'd think that would make you happy."

"Go to hell!"

He tipped up her chin with a finger and stared at her piercingly through the darkness. "Tears?" he said wonderingly. "Do you grieve for me, Jewel MacKenzie Cameron?"

"No."

He chuckled sadly. "Stubborn to the last, my wee witch. Well, come then. If I'm to die tomorrow, love me one last time tonight."

ELLEN TANNER MARSH

THE ENCHANTED BRIDE

LEISURE BOOKS **NEW YORK CITY**

A LEISURE BOOK®

September 1996

Published by

Dorchester Publishing Co., Inc.
276 Fifth Avenue
New York, NY 10001

THE ENCHANTED BRIDE

Chapter One

Glasgow, Scotland
Late spring, 1762

Rumbling down the length of High Street in the direction of the waterfront, an elegant coach with darkened windows turned the corner and splashed through the gutters beneath the hulking stone gates of Cowcadden Prison. Halting the team of soaking horses in the deserted courtyard, the coachman scrambled down to open the door.

"Mind your step, miss. The footing's bad."

A cloaked figure descended to the cobblestones, trim boots squelching through the mud. Bright red curls flamed beneath the wide hood of her cloak, which partially concealed a heart-shaped face of breath-catching beauty. Heavily lashed blue eyes that tilted at the corners framed a nose that was slim and straight and a little bit haughty. A red mouth with an unusually full lower lip was set beneath it in a determined frown.

"Do ye really wish to go in, miss?" the coachman asked, casting a nervous glance up at the prison. No lights shone from the windows set deep amid the shadowed embrasures although the afternoon was gray and gloomy. A rough-looking sentry slouched near the iron-studded door, paying no attention to them. The rain hissed on the stones, and a dog barked from somewhere amid the crumbling row houses crowding the prison's lichen-covered walls. There was no one else about.

"Of course I do," the girl answered. "That's why we came, isn't it?"

Her voice was firm and clear, with only the faintest hint of a Highland accent. No one hearing her speak could have guessed that she was from the north, although she had traveled south for more than two days in order to reach the medieval city of Glasgow and its notorious prison.

"Besides," the girl went on, "I've Tykie to protect me. What could possibly go wrong?"

As if to underscore her confident words the coach sagged as an enormous man with a barrel chest and muscular arms descended to the street behind her. His long black hair was tied back from his craggy face with a ribbon, and a single gold earring dangled in one ear, giving him a very dangerous look.

Although he was certainly capable of inspiring fear in the hearts of all law-abiding citizens with barely a glance, Tykie Ferguson seemed surprisingly unsure of himself at present. Studying the looming walls of the prison he shook his head and gestured nervously for his young mistress to get back in the coach.

"Oh, for heaven's sake!" Jewel MacKenzie exclaimed impatiently. "I've told you before that my mind is made up! Now are you coming with me or shall I go alone?"

Tykie shook his head in alarm. Pleading words clogged his throat, although he could not utter them. Fifteen years ago, after the Highland clans had been defeated in their civil war against the British, vengeful English soldiers had cut out his tongue. Now, seeing the stubborn tilt of his mistress's chin and knowing full well that nothing on earth could sway her, Tykie hung his head in defeat.

"Come on, Tykie," Jewel coaxed, smiling sweetly. "I promise I won't let them hurt you."

But Tykie was in no mood for her teasing. The task that had brought them here was simply too dangerous, and admittedly far too daft. Though he burned to tell her that they'd be wiser to turn heel and hurry home, he merely lifted his hand and motioned her forward.

"Come along then." Daintily picking up the hem of her cloak, Jewel started toward the great oak doors of the prison. If she, too, was feeling even the slightest doubt about the wisdom of her mission she certainly wasn't going to let the hulking man behind her catch wind of it. Climbing the uneven flight of steps to the massive doors, she lifted the heavy knocker and sent it crashing against the wood.

Apparently no woman so young or lovely ever sought admission to Cowcadden Prison, for Jewel's unannounced appearance on the doorstep caused quite a stir. Without delay she and Tykie were ushered down a long, torchlit corridor to the cold, bare office of the prison warden. Here, the thin little man sitting behind the desk combing ink-stained fingers through his greasy wig looked up in astonishment as Jewel was shown inside.

"Oh, my goodness!" he squeaked. "What's all this?"

Halting in front of him, Jewel swept back the hood

of her cloak and shook free her bright red curls. Planting her hands on her slim hips, she regarded him boldly. "My name is Jewel MacKenzie, sir, and I've come—"

"Barrows!" the gaoler interrupted, recovering himself sufficiently to shout for the guard. "Have you taken leave o' your senses? Why the devil did you let her in? I'm sorry, miss, but you'll have to go. No visitors allowed."

Jewel felt Tykie's big hand on her arm, but she shook him off. "I haven't come to visit anyone," she said coolly. "Mr. Ferguson and I would like to settle the debts of one of your prisoners."

The gaoler gaped at her, looking rather ludicrous with his wig askew and his mouth and eyes wide. While it was not uncommon for mothers, wives, or sisters to bail out their errant menfolk whenever they could scrape together enough money, it was indeed unusual for one of them to be so finely clothed or in possession of such obvious breeding.

Cowcadden Prison incarcerated brutal murderers, seasoned criminals, heavy drinkers, and gamblers unable or unwilling to pay their debts. To the gaoler's mind none of the riffraff currently stinking up his prison cells could possibly qualify for salvation at the hands of this glorious angel. Nevertheless, she seemed quite determined, and the ferocious fellow behind her was scowling in a manner to suggest that courtesy and haste in resolving the matter would be in Allen MacInnon's best interest.

Sighing, he scratched again at his wig, hoping to dislodge a few fleas, then reached for a well-thumbed ledger on the desktop before him. "Very well," he said reluctantly, "who is it you've come for?"

There was a sudden gleam in Jewel MacKenzie's tilted eyes, and for a moment MacInnon could almost believe she was enjoying herself. "I'm not sure. Perhaps you would be so kind as to tell me."

The jangling of keys outside the iron-barred door was followed by the screeching of rusty hinges that echoed down the stone corridor. Torchlight flared in the darkness and the scowling face of a guard peered into the black depths of the cell. "Cameron? Ye're wanted."

No response from within. Moisture dripped from an unseen source but otherwise there was silence. The guard with the torch gestured to another man standing behind him, who entered cautiously with his pistols raised.

"Cameron, do ye hear? Ye're wanted outside."

"Go away," said a deep, annoyed voice. "I'm sleeping."

The guards exchanged weary glances. This one had been impossibly insolent ever since his arrival six months ago. Neither flogging nor starvation had served to cow him, and every last one of the guards had been looking forward with relish to his imminent departure. A ship bound for the colonies was due to sail from the river Clyde any day now and these two guards in particular were highly impatient to see it go.

Now the taller of the guards gestured with his pistols. "Outside, Cameron. MacInnon wants ye."

A lazy yawn sounded from within. "What for? Is my ship due to sail? I hope you've secured a decent cabin for me."

"I'll secure a crack to yer skull if ye don't come away now!"

"I'd rather finish my nap, if it's all the same to you. And mind the rats on your way out. I won't have you crushing them with your hobnails. They're pets, you know."

The guard in the doorway growled low in his throat and lunged forward, only to be halted by the one with the pistols. "I'll handle 'im, MacTavish. And you shut yer trap, Cameron. There's a lady out front askin' for ye and ye'll no keep her waitin'."

"A lady, is it?" came the deep voice from the darkness, sounding amused now. "You wouldn't know a proper lady from a pig's ass, Sligo."

The guard named Sligo tightened his fingers around the triggers of both pistols. Twelve years of guarding insolent prisoners like this one had taught him the wisdom of ignoring their taunts and keeping a rein on his temper. Angry men made mistakes. He was still alive. Plenty of others who'd worked alongside him over the years weren't.

"Cameron . . ."

"Oh, very well," came the bored voice from the darkness. "I admit you've made me curious. I didn't think a soul in Glasgow knew I was here. Might as well take a look at her, hmm?"

And with that, prisoner Tor Ban Cameron stepped into the flickering torchlight. He was a tall man, taller than either of the guards, and very broad-shouldered despite the fact that he was very gaunt. Dark blue eyes burned in a thin face made angular from insufficient food. A black beard bristled on his square jaw, and his tattered shirttails hung from his long, wiry frame. Nevertheless there was a suggestion of strength about him, and it was obvious that both guards knew better than to turn their backs on him for even a moment.

Single file they proceeded down the dark corridor, MacTavish in the lead, the prisoner next, Sligo bringing up the rear with one of his pistols pressed into Tor's spine. Their passage was accompanied by shouted oaths or cries for mercy from the cells on either side, where countless other prisoners huddled in the icy darkness. No one paid any attention, neither the guards nor Tor.

After negotiating the seemingly endless twists and turns of the foul corridor, Tor was led up a long flight of worn steps into a bare room with a single, barred window high on the wall. The patter of rain came from outside as did a chill wind reeking of the gutters. To Tor, who had seen and smelled nothing but the inside of his prison cell for the past six months, the scent was unbearably sweet.

There were others in the room, all of them fellow prisoners although Tor recognized none of them. Cowcadden Prison was a warren of tiny cells so black and airless that a man could barely make out the hand in front of his face, let alone discern the features of his neighbors. All of these men were rail thin and in tatters, bearded, filthy, some of them scarred or pockmarked by illness. Tor supposed that he looked little better.

There was movement in the doorway just then and a sound Tor had not heard in many a month: the silken rustle of skirts. His head snapped up and his eyes narrowed attentively.

"Here you go, miss, they're the brawniest of the lot, free of disease and mental sickness as you asked. Mind you stay behind the guards now."

A woman appeared in the arching doorway, standing on tiptoe to peer over Allen MacInnon's shoulder although the gaoler wasn't much above average height himself. Tor saw at once that she was barely older than a girl, the skin of her pretty face smooth and in the bloom of youthful health. Dark lashes framed eyes of robin's-egg blue, but it was her hair, set free of the hood of her cloak, that caught Tor's attention and the gaze of every man present. Like moths to a flame, their eyes were drawn to it, for it seemed to glow in the gloom, illuminating a dank and musty place that for centuries had been starved of all light.

If Jewel MacKenzie was aware of the intensity of the masculine gazes turned upon her she gave no sign. In truth she was using every scrap of self-control to appear as outwardly calm and aloof as possible. She wanted no one, least of all these motley prisoners, to know how disconcerted she was to find herself face-to-face with them at last.

Not that they weren't just as awful as she had imagined, even though the requirements she had given the gaoler had been intended to weed out the worst of them: no murderers, no one convicted of violent crimes—especially toward women—no one who displayed the least indication of aberrant behavior. Literacy was a must, as was a physique that guaranteed the ability to perform hard physical labor. And for God's sake, she wanted no one who showed any tendency to rise above his lowly station!

Slowly her eyes swept the gaunt faces before her. In the silence Jewel could hear Tykie grunt his disapproval as he, too, studied the lot. Deep down she had to agree with his assessment. Every last one of the ten-odd prisoners MacInnon had assembled looked as though he had just crawled out of a filthy pit of unspeakable horror. And the smell of them! How could MacInnon stand it?

For God's sake, Jewel! she scoffed inwardly, what did you expect? They're criminals, they've spent months, even years, in gaol! Of course they're going to reek to the high heavens and look as if they'd strangle their own grandmothers!

"Well, miss?"

Jewel had originally intended to narrow the choice to a mere handful, then speak to each one of them privately before making her decision. Now, studying one ugly, depraved face after another she could feel her heart sinking into her toes. Perhaps she had been mistaken after all in convincing herself it would be easy to marry a convict.

Alternatives crowded in on her, but she pushed them fiercely away. She had agonized over every one of them often enough in the past year, with no hope of a workable solution. This was the decision she had made, and this was the decision she would stick with, by God!

Once again, slowly, she let her eyes travel over the silent men. MacInnon had done as she asked and brought her only tall, able-bodied ones, but oh, how some of them made the hair rise on the back of her neck!

Except for that man in the corner, the big one who stood with his hip propped against the wall and an almost bored expression on his bearded face. Jewel hadn't noticed him right away, and now she looked at him again carefully. His dark blue eyes held hers without faltering, and the expression in them wasn't vacant or haunted like the others', although perhaps it was a little too arrogant for her liking. On the other hand, he was tall and very broad in the chest and shoulders, which meant that he should make a good worker once the meat was back on his bones.

Jewel took a deep breath. "You there," she said, nailing him with her eyes, "what was your crime?"

"Assault on a nobleman," Allen MacInnon told her contemptuously.

"Shall we say a difference of opinion?" Tor countered.

Jewel frowned at the insolence of his tone. She certainly didn't want a man who was too full of himself. On the other hand, he spoke as though he was somewhat educated, not a simpleton, and she certainly had no intention of burdening herself with a half-wit, either. She turned to the gaoler. "Can he read and write?"

"I can answer for myself," Tor said curtly.

"Ye've no been spoken to!" snarled the guard named MacTavish, and slammed his balled fist into Tor's gut.

For one awful moment Jewel thought that the big prisoner intended to hit back, but he was prevented by the guard named Sligo, who cocked both of his pistols and aimed them straight at his heart. Briefly Jewel saw something flare in the prisoner's eyes, something she could recognize and, regrettably, understand: pride, anger, and a fierce self-loathing brought about by one's own helplessness.

"Can you read and write?" she repeated, addressing him directly.

"Of course."

"Can you work with your hands?"

He looked down at his palms, which were callused after many years of labor, hard calluses that even the long, idle months of prison had not erased. His lips twitched into a humorless smile. "I should think so."

"Figure sums?"

"Aye."

Jewel chewed her lower lip, thinking. As she did so, ten pairs of male eyes watched that soft, sweet mouth and yearned—all except Tor Cameron, who had grown weary of the little redhead's questions and was wondering if he shouldn't take advantage of this unusual situation by attempting an escape.

Even as he looked around him to assess the possibilities, Jewel turned to MacInnon. "I'll take that one."

Tor raised his head to see that she was pointing her pretty little finger straight at him.

"If you're sure, miss—" MacInnon began doubtfully.

There was no mistaking the arrogance in Jewel MacKenzie's tone. "Aye, I am."

"What the devil does she mean?" Tor exploded.

No one answered him. Instead, MacInnon ushered the redhead outside, followed closely by the hulking brute with the earring who had been hovering protectively over her all this time. The guards were left behind to return the men to their cells while Sligo prodded Tor with his pistol.

"Get movin'."

"Where?"

"The well. Ye're to wash an' put on a coat."

Tor scowled at him, annoyed by all this secrecy. "What for?"

Sligo grinned a brown-toothed grin, enjoying himself hugely. "Can't get married without a proper coat."

Tor stood still, his angular face wiped free of all expression.

"Aye, marriage," Sligo went on sweetly. "T' the wee redhead. Though why she chose the likes o' ye is beyond my ken."

Tor stared at him, blue eyes burning in his thin face. "Do you mean," he said slowly, "that yon poison-haired bairn chose me for a *husband*?"

Sligo gave a guttural laugh. "Bairn? I'd no exactly call her that! Did ye no see her breasts beneath that fancy cloak? Firm and high and strainin' at her corset?"

"Just tell me what she's after," Tor snapped.

Sligo shrugged. "MacInnon says she trotted in bold as brass demanding a husband, one with brains and muscles braw enough for hard work. For some daft reason she chose *you*." The last word was emphasized with a jab of the pistol into Tor's chest.

"And you expect me to agree? Just like that?"

Sligo snorted. "What makes ye think ye've got a

19

choice? Once she pays the fine on yer head she'll own ye free and clear."

But there was no indentureship levied with his fine, Tor knew. No one could buy him, by God, least of all a red-haired snip with some daft scheme on her mind!

But as his initial shock faded and he began to analyze the unbelievable situation he quickly came to see the advantages of having the price removed from his head. He'd be a free man from that moment on. Free to walk out of this stinking prison, free to go wherever he pleased, speak with whomever he chose, to do as he wished—and, by God, he wished to do plenty!

For the first time in many months a slow smile curved Tor Cameron's sensual lips. All right, then, let the wench buy him off, let them clothe him and bring him up into the anteroom that served as Allen MacInnon's office. From there it was only a matter of a few steps out into the street and freedom. In no time at all he'd be away, before the silly girl, or MacInnon and his bastard guards, knew what he was about.

"All right, then," he repeated, this time aloud, "I'll clean myself up a bit. But MacInnon'll have to give me more than a coat. I'll need a clean shirt and trousers if my bride isn't going to pass out from the smell."

Led out into the dank sideyard that housed the prison's single pump, Tor insisted on being permitted to shave. A man with clean clothes and a bare jaw looked far more respectable than one with a beard and tattered attire, he knew. After he escaped into the Glasgow streets he wasn't about to be branded a criminal by looks alone and be brought back to Cowcadden in chains. He'd kill any man who tried.

Rain pattered on the shingles as he stood outside

in the cold scraping at his jaw with the dull blade of a tiny penknife. It was a barbaric way to shave, but MacInnon had refused him the use of a proper razor, which could easily be turned into a weapon. Mac-Innon, sniveling coward though he was, was not a fool.

While shaving, Tor made a seemingly nonchalant study of his surroundings. Crumbling row houses crowded around the prison yard, their windows dark, their rainspouts awash with dirty water. In the distance he could hear the rumble of traffic and the moan of a foghorn somewhere on the river. To him it was the sound of freedom. Every nerve in his body seemed to tingle.

Aye, he'd head for the water, he thought, and he could feel his gut tightening as he considered the distance from Cowcadden to the river. No matter. There'd be plenty of places to hide along the way, and men willing to help him once they found out who he was running from.

Having shaved as best he could, Tor now stripped off the tattered remains of his shirt and began to wash. The icy water, though brackish, felt like a benediction against his skin. A steady gush spilled over him with every heave of the pump handle, reminding Tor that elsewhere in the world water was available in an endless supply. He himself hadn't been rationed more than a pannikin a day for six long months.

God's blood, it was heaven just to stand unfettered in the filthy yard and let the rain beat on his shoulders while the fetid air of the Glasgow slums filled his lungs! It was the air of freedom, Tor thought, and as such doubly sweet.

By now Sligo and the other guards who had accompanied him outside were beginning to grow impatient. Nudged none too gently with a heavy boot,

Tor toweled himself dry with a piece of burlap and then shrugged into the worn shirt he had been given. The oft-laundered fabric felt almost sinful against his skin. Never mind that the muscles of his broad chest and arms had melted off his frame during the long months of incarceration so that the shoulders of the shirt hung bunched and baggy, the sleeves far too long. It was soft and clean and, best of all, no longer stamped him a prisoner.

"Come on," Sligo growled, giving him another swift kick with his hobnails. "Ye're pretty enough."

The other guards laughed, but Tor's expression never changed. Only his full lips thinned a little at the corners. Perhaps there'd be time to teach this one a lesson before he fled into the street.

Without another word he went back through the arched door, ducking his head as he stepped into the darkness and crossed to the front of the building, where, deep inside the thick stone walls, his tender young bride awaited him.

Chapter Two

Jewel MacKenzie almost didn't recognize the tall, gaunt man who was shoved through the door of Allen MacInnon's office. He had shaved off his beard, revealing an angular jaw and a cleft chin that might have been attractive but for the fact that it was crisscrossed with cuts, thanks to a very dull knife. His long hair had been drawn off his shoulders and into a queue that was tied with a ribbon. A worn lawn shirt and breeches that were too small, hugging his narrow hips and long legs, completed the transformation from scruffy convict into—well, perhaps not a gentleman, but at least someone a bit more civilized.

Unfortunately there was nothing civilized in the dark blue eyes that nailed Jewel's the moment the prisoner entered the room. Jewel saw the savage animosity in his gaze and wondered fleetingly if Mr. MacInnon hadn't been mistaken in assuring her that this prisoner—what was his name? That Tor Cameron, while insolent and a troublemaker, was not at heart a murderer.

"Believe me, Miss MacKenzie," the gaoler had said, discussing Tor as they waited for him to be brought in, "I know what lies inside every one of 'em. You can't help but learn after thirty years at Cowcadden. Some men are better off hanged, others might as well be transported, others be here that don't deserve it. Some'll come out broken and lost, others won't be out long before they're sent back. But that one there, he ain't no killer, though that's about all I can guarantee."

Tykie had scowled when he heard this, and Jewel had tried not to look as though she was having very serious doubts about her decision. But then she had reminded herself that without a husband she'd end up losing Drumcorrie, and that was something she wasn't about to tolerate.

"Supposing I don't consent to this?" Tor Cameron demanded as he strode inside, his words intended for MacInnon although his burning gaze never left Jewel's.

MacInnon shrugged. "You'll be transported as scheduled."

"I'd take the wench," the guard named MacTavish advised with a coarse laugh from the corner, although he was instantly silenced by a warning glance from Tykie Ferguson, who stood a full head taller than he at the opposite end of the room.

"I suppose I'd be a fool to refuse," Tor agreed, raking Jewel up and down with a gaze that made her feel as if she were being stripped naked.

She forced herself to stare back at him, her pointed chin boldly tipped. "It's your decision, Mr. Cameron."

"Oh, is it?" He gave a cynical laugh, and was startled that he could still do so, for his life had been so starved of laughter that he had come to think nothing would ever amuse him again. "Come on, then," he growled, annoyed. "Let's get on with it."

"Keep your breeks on," MacInnon snapped. "There's much to be said first."

"Oh?" With seeming nonchalance Tor crossed his arms over his chest. "Such as . . . ?"

"Such as you'd better not even think about escaping once you're wed," MacInnon said ominously. "It'll mean the gallows the moment you're caught."

"I appreciate the warning," Tor said politely. "Is that all?"

"Oh no," MacInnon went on smoothly. "That fellow there"—he jerked his head in Tykie Ferguson's direction—"has volunteered to, ah, look after you. He'll notify the authorities the moment you try to do anything the least untoward. But I warn you: Miss MacKenzie has given me to understand that he has something of a temper, so ye'd better think twice before misbehaving, hmm?"

Across the room Tor's eyes locked with Tykie's. For a moment both men measured each other with cold hostility. Inwardly Tor suspected that MacInnon was right. This fellow would bear watching.

"I hope he'll allow us some privacy," Tor said dryly, "especially in the bedroom."

A low growl from the corner warned him that he had gone too far. Unconcerned, he bowed in Tykie's direction before turning back to Jewel. A satisfied grin curved the corners of his mouth as he saw the hot color that had rushed into his young bride's cheeks. For a madwoman she certainly blushed easily.

"Well, then," Tor continued lazily, "I'm more than ready to pledge my troth. Where's the priest?"

"Shut up," MacInnon snapped. "I ken you're no Papist."

"Then who's marrying us?"

"I am," MacInnon said coldly.

Tor rubbed his chin, trying not to laugh. "I might have known."

"Fortunately for Miss MacKenzie," MacInnon continued, ignoring him and turning his back to rummage through a dusty cabinet in the corner, "Scotland's marital laws are extremely lax. She won't have to be cried at kirk or post the banns aforehand."

And thus escape the uproar when her people found out who she was marrying, Tor thought wryly. For the first time he considered the implications of this. His brow darkened. What in hell were the girl's motives anyway? A woman didn't just walk into a notorious prison like Cowcadden and choose some unwashed criminal for a husband, by God!

And where in hell was her bloody family? From the way she was dressed in that fine woolen cape with a glimpse of a rich velvet gown underneath she had to have money, which meant that her family must be important enough to possess a name they cared to keep untarnished. Didn't anyone other than that brute in the corner object to this lunacy?

Allen MacInnon had withdrawn a yellowed book from the depths of a musty drawer and turned to set it on his desk. "Now then," he said, licking his thumb and leafing carefully through the brittle pages, "what's your full name, Miss MacKenzie?"

"Jewel," she said calmly. "Jewel Elizabeth MacKenzie."

Just by chance she happened to glance at Tor as she spoke and caught his look of surprise. Once again her chin came up and she fixed him with a baleful stare. "Do you object, Mr. Cameron?"

Oh, no, Tor did not. In fact, he found her name astonishingly apt. Jewel. Well, why not? One certainly had to admit that her hair was as lustrous as a ruby, and her eyes the translucent blue of aquamarine. And the delicate bones of her face were as cleanly cut as the facets of any diamond, weren't they?

Tor gave a harsh laugh, disgusted by such ludicrous thoughts. Instead of waxing poetical about this simpleminded wench, shouldn't he be deciding how best to make good his escape? What the devil was wrong with him anyway?

The answer was there, of course, stirring hotly in his loins. Lust. Simple male lust. How long had it been since he'd bedded a wench? Or clapped eyes on one quite so beautiful? The air in MacInnon's office was cold, so she'd kept on her cloak, but Tor had already seen glimpses of what looked like a very delectable body wrapped in the blue gown beneath it.

Sligo, simpleton though he was, had been right in insisting there was nothing girlish about the high, firm breasts straining against Jewel MacKenzie's bodice, or in the lines of her willowy waist. Nor did it seem likely that any man would dismiss as childish that mouth, which was certainly made for kissing, with its silky upper arch and full lower lip.

Desire flared again, insistently, but Tor forced himself to master it. Not only were his breeches far too tight for that, but once unleashed, he couldn't guarantee that his passion wouldn't turn him into some mindlessly lusting animal. If he had no thought of anything save sex, then how on earth was he going to make good an escape?

On the other hand, a devilish voice suddenly whispered in the back of his mind, what was the hurry?

Tor's thoughtful gaze dropped to Jewel MacKenzie's soft mouth as he considered this. Supposing he delayed his escape for just a little while, until he'd bedded the chit and had a decent meal somewhere miles removed from Cowcadden? And wouldn't it be easier to overpower just that black-haired beast with the pirate earring as opposed to a cadre of prison guards?

Further, Jewel MacKenzie had money, and plenty of it. How else could she have managed to pay the price on Tor's head and grease MacInnon's palm well enough to get away with this madcap scheme? Money meant luxury: good food, a soft bed, a pampered girl in a silken robe waiting to welcome her bridegroom into her bed. Where was the harm in enjoying a wee bit of that before moving on?

Careful. Tor could feel the blood coursing through his loins as he pictured Jewel MacKenzie, dressed in nothing but that clinging robe, beckoning to him from amid the soft, clean sheets of a four-poster bed. Any moment now he'd be giving himself an erection huge enough for all of them to see.

The thought was like a dash of ice water to Tor's feverish brain. Damn these tight-fitting breeches! Satisfy your cravings later, he told himself sharply. Play your cards properly now and you'll have all you want in an hour's time.

And that was exactly how it went. Quietly, calmly, giving no hint of his inner turmoil, Tor Cameron repeated the vows that bound him to this slim, red-headed girl in what had to be the most bizarre ceremony the walls of Cowcadden Prison had ever witnessed. He gave no thought to the fact that he was making an oath he had no intention of keeping, invoking the name of God in what was purely a sham. None of that mattered to Tor Ban Cameron. Like the pale, silent girl beside him, he had his own reasons for pledging his troth.

Then it was time to bless the ring. Tor was about to make a disparaging remark to the effect that, as a lowly prisoner, he couldn't be expected to provide one, when Tykie Ferguson stepped up behind him.

Looking down, Tor saw that he was cradling a delicate gold band in his massive paw. There was no mistaking that the ring was old and very valuable, and for a brief moment he hesitated, frowning. Where had the chit come by it? Was it some sort of family heirloom?

"Cameron!" MacInnon prodded impatiently.

Instantly the moment passed and Tor smoothly slid the ring onto his bride's slim finger. Tor Ban Cameron and Jewel Elizabeth MacKenzie were now officially wed.

With a grim smile Tor looked down at his wife. Startled, he saw a moment's anger and, aye, tears, blaze in her brilliant blue eyes. So, he thought, intrigued, the chit isn't entirely happy about this.

His curiosity deepened. What in bloody hell were her motives for taking a husband if she had to shed tears because of it? Had something beyond her control coerced her into marrying him?

"Under the circumstances," Allen MacInnon intoned at that moment, "we'll forgo kissing the bride."

Jewel's sigh of relief was not lost on anyone.

"I think not," Tor interjected easily. "A man's got every right to seal his vows with a kiss."

"Then get on with it," MacInnon snapped.

Grinning, Tor put his hands on Jewel's shoulders and turned her toward him. Beneath the woolen fabric of her cloak he could feel the delicate curve of her collarbones. For the first time he was able to look fully into her face, and he took his time, enjoying the pleasure.

Up close she was even more beautiful than he'd realized, with skin as flawless as a rose petal and entirely devoid of freckles, a rare thing among redheads, Tor knew. Her eyes were fringed with dark lashes that served to emphasize the maddening tilt at their corners, and her cheekbones were high and classically lovely. She was indeed a gem of exquisite rarity. What in God's name was she doing marrying a convicted prisoner in the dank gloom of Cowcadden Prison?

"Here, we ain't got all day!" MacInnon growled.

Tor looked back at Jewel. Her eyes had begun to flash with what could only be described as disgust while her tauntingly lovely lips were pulled into a grimace.

Heart thumping with what he convinced himself was anger, Tor lowered his head to capture those lips between his own, but Jewel was too quick for him. At the last moment she turned away so that his kiss landed harmlessly on her cheek.

When he drew back his eyes were dark with fury. "You'll not escape so easily next time," he said for her ears alone.

"There won't be a next time," Jewel shot back between clenched teeth.

For a moment they stared at one another, steadily and hatefully, as enemies might. The challenge had been given—and readily accepted.

"Should I handcuff 'im for ye, ma'am?" MacTavish inquired hopefully as Jewel straightened and stepped away.

"That won't be necessary," she told him coldly, pulling up the hood of her cloak to cover her bright red hair. Instantly the gloom of the cavernous office seemed to press closer, as though she had taken away some of the light. "I imagine Mr. Cameron is wise enough to realize on which side his bread is buttered. But I am anxious to leave now, Mr. MacInnon," she added to the gaoler. "Would you see to it that my . . . my . . . husband's belongings are brought outside?"

No one missed the way the term seemed to stick in her throat. Tykie Ferguson scowled while Mac-

30

Tavish snickered and Tor's lips thinned to nothing.

"Naturally I have no belongings save the clothes on my back," he said coldly.

"And even them is borrowed anyway," MacTavish reminded him.

It was a cruel blow for a man of Tor's pride, which had already been brutally hammered after endless months of incarceration. Without looking at anyone he crossed to the door and stepped out into the hall. Down the uneven steps he strode, gaunt shoulders squared, and no one tried to stop him.

Outside the rain had stopped, and cold, salty air was rolling in from the river. Drawing it deep into his lungs, Tor was overwhelmed for one wild moment with the heady urge to run. No one would catch him, he knew, not MacTavish or Sligo or that silent, hairy giant of a bodyguard belonging to Jewel MacKenzie—no, wait a moment, it was Cameron now, wasn't it?

The thought was enough to make Tor stop dead in his tracks. Jewel Elizabeth Cameron. Mrs. Jewel Elizabeth Cameron. His wife.

As though caught in the grip of some bizarre dream, Tor turned slowly to watch her coming down the prison steps, with her bodyguard and the Cowcadden contingent following behind. Her head was bowed against the wind and she was holding aloft the sweeping hem of her cloak to keep it from dragging in the mud. He saw the dainty half boots that covered her slim ankles and his gaze traveled higher, past the tiny waist and lovely breasts to the hood of her cloak, which revealed only the pert tip of her nose and a glimpse of that flaming red hair.

No, he'd not run yet. Only a fool would do that. If he abandoned her now, he'd never know the truth about her, and that fact, along with those slimly turned ankles, was much too intriguing a thing not to explore further.

Looking deliberately away from her, Tor took note of the coach waiting on the cobblestones before him. Not as grand as he would have liked, but well sprung and in good repair nonetheless. With approval he saw that the horses stamping in their traces were of fine English breeding.

Footsteps halted on the wet stones behind him. Without turning he could feel Jewel's sudden hesitation as though it were a physical thing. Apparently only now, as she prepared to board the coach in his company, was she becoming aware of the enormity of what it was she had done.

"Up you go, ma'am," Tor said before she could change her mind. Taking her elbow he led her to the door, but in the next moment he was deliberately shouldered aside by the coachman, a wiry little scrap of a fellow Tor could have crushed with his bare hands.

"*Miss,*" the annoying fellow corrected, bowing low in Jewel's direction.

For a moment Tor contemplated giving the man's satin-clad backside, perfectly exposed by the exaggerated bow, a good, swift kick. Instead he said coldly, "I'm afraid you're mistaken. It's Mrs. Cameron now."

The look that was turned upon him was searing in its scorn. No lowly vermin could have been more thoroughly ignored as the banty little coachman stepped around Tor to help Jewel into the vehicle and then solicitously lift the trailing ends of her cloak in behind her.

"Mr. Ferguson?" he inquired, bowing again.

Grunting, Tykie Ferguson climbed in as well, though by rights it should have been the bridegroom's turn. The coach rocked dangerously as he settled himself inside and the door was slammed behind him.

With his nose thrust haughtily in the air, the coachman walked around to the front of the vehicle. Before he could climb aloft, however, he was frozen in his tracks by the coldest voice he had ever heard.

"Admirable, how devoted you are to your mistress. Perhaps I should caution you to keep a close eye on her from this day on. She doesn't know it, but I've killed a number of men in my day."

The coachman, whose name was Piers MacInnis and who had known Miss Jewel since she was a baby, whipped about in genuine alarm. He swallowed as he found the big prisoner grinning down at him, his eyes glinting with what Piers felt certain was a hint of madness.

"K-killed a number of them?" he squeaked, praying he hadn't heard right.

"Aye. And all of them were coachmen."

Piers went pale, then reddened, then scrambled quickly onto the boot. Taking up the long reins he cracked his whip and set the team galloping away so wildly that Tor had barely enough time to wrench open the door and fling himself inside to avoid being crushed.

"Your servants are very loyal," he observed somewhat breathlessly, taking a seat opposite Jewel because the big, hairy fellow named Tykie had deliberately claimed the one beside her. Now Tykie sat glaring at Tor with unconcealed animosity, one ham-sized hand in his pocket where, Tor felt certain, his blunt fingers were wrapped tightly around the handle of a dagger or a pistol.

"They're my friends," Jewel told him stiffly. "And I won't tolerate your being rude to them."

That said, she turned her head deliberately away, giving Tor the full benefit of her contempt—and the lovely view of her profile. Clasping his hands behind his head he studied her at leisure. Her throat was silky smooth, her jaw slim, her nose turned up quite haughtily at the tip, a warning from Mother Nature, Tor felt sure, that her character could be equally as imperious.

Tor had the urge to laugh at the snub she had given him, but instead he leaned back even farther and propped his crossed legs onto the opposite seat, nearly brushing the hem of Jewel's cloak with his boots. Beside her Tykie tensed threateningly. Tor turned lazily to look at him, but Tykie said nothing, only scowled blackly until Tor reverted his gaze back to Jewel.

"Your bodyguard doesn't say much, does he?"

"That's because he can't."

Tor waited for an explanation, but when she said nothing more he scowled impatiently. "What's that supposed to mean?"

She looked at him hatefully. "It means he hasn't got a tongue. Sassenach soldiers cut it out after the war."

Tor sat back, speechless despite himself. Sassenachs—the contemptuous term that Highlanders used for all Englishmen. That meant, of course, that Tykie Ferguson had fought in what everyone was now calling the '45, that tragic, misguided attempt in 1745 by Prince Charles Edward Stuart—Bonnie Prince Charlie to his adoring followers—to reclaim the British throne for his father, King James I, who lived in exile in France.

Poor sod! No one had to tell Tor Cameron how brutal the English soldiers had been as they reaped their terrible vengeance on the Highlands after Scotland's defeat in April of 1746, sweeping through the glens and across the mountains slaughtering innocent men, women, and children and setting fire to their homes. Countless Highlanders had been murdered, countless more driven away, and those who remained had suffered intolerably beneath the harsh new laws forced upon them in order to subdue their spirits forever.

The heavy sweep of England's vengeful fist had broken up families, scattered the clans, and banned all things that made the Highland Gael what he was: the wearing of the kilt, the playing of bagpipes, the singing of those blood-stirring songs about a land and a people that Tor, too, had once fiercely loved.

Whoa! The ferocity of his thoughts annoyed him. What on earth was he thinking? Instead of waxing nauseatingly poetical about a country he no longer cared about he should be demanding answers to a number of more immediate questions. Like where in blazes were they headed? Why on earth had this stuck-up little snippet of a lass marched into Cowcadden Prison to marry him? Who in hell was she anyway?

"I was wondering—" he began.

"Then please do so quietly," Jewel interrupted. "I should like to rest."

"Oh, excuse me," Tor growled as she closed her eyes and leaned her head back against the seat. For a moment he was tempted to take that little white throat between his hands and squeeze until her neck snapped in two. Did she think she could treat him like the mud on her shoes simply because she had freed him from gaol?

Oh, no, my dear, he thought grimly. In that I'm afraid you're sorely mistaken. All things considered, Jewel MacKenzie Cameron was in for an unpleasant surprise when they finally reached their destination. After all, she wouldn't be able to hide behind Tykie Ferguson's broad back forever. Sooner or later Tor intended to get her off alone and then, then, my wee pretty, he thought grimly, there'll be hell to pay!

Chapter Three

Good God, what have I done?

Even though she had shut her eyes tightly, Jewel found that she could not drive the image of Tor Ban Cameron's brooding face away. She could feel his anger like physical heat radiating from the seat opposite hers, and she wondered again, as she had so often in the last hour or more, if maybe she shouldn't have fled that stinking prison while she still had the chance.

Too late, too late, too late.

The words thundered in her heart in rhythm with the rumbling wheels that bore her ever closer to Glen Chulish.

Tears stung Jewel's eyes as she thought of her home. There had been MacKenzies in Glen Chulish since the early fourteenth century. Back in those distant days, the MacKenzie clan had spread like wildfire across the Scottish mainland from its holdings on Kintail. With fierce raids and shrewd ingenuity the clan had grown powerful, establishing more than thirty-five clan branches and increasing its territory tenfold and more.

Glen Chulish had been a small but plum jewel in the expanding MacKenzie crown. For centuries now, the same family had tilled its rich soil and remained fiercely loyal to its land. This was especially true nowadays, after the MacKenzies had paid so dearly for Bonnie Prince Charlie's disastrous defeat at Culloden. The victorious English had been swift in their punishment: two of the most powerful MacKenzie clan chiefs had been executed, while seventy-nine others had been transported. Worst of all, Jewel's distant uncle, Kenneth MacKenzie, the Earl of Cromartie himself, had been stripped of his title and lands and sent into exile.

Because of this, there were few MacKenzie strongholds left. Small as it was, Glen Chulish was now vastly important to the survival of the dwindling clan. Since infancy, Jewel had been made to understand that Glen Chulish, like the other strongholds that survived, must at all costs remain in MacKenzie hands.

That was why she had taken this admittedly desperate trip to Glasgow: for no other reason than to keep Glen Chulish safe. Never mind that marital law proclaimed her a Cameron from this day forward. Jewel had been born a MacKenzie, and as a MacKenzie she would live and die. No matter what her signature in that silly Bible in Cowcadden Prison might read, and no matter what that ill-mannered lout across from her might think, she was a MacKenzie still.

Scowling, Jewel stole a glance at her new husband. The Gaelic word for the Cameron name was *Camshron*, or *crooked nose*. Well, Tor Cameron's nose certainly fit that description! And as for the cleft chin beneath that long Roman beak . . . More than once Jewel had been heartily tempted to punch it flat.

At that moment Tor turned his head and caught her staring, even though Jewel could have sworn she had kept her eyes so near to slits that anyone else would have thought she was sleeping. She saw the way his big body became still, as though he were well aware of her thoughts, and as though he were assessing her in turn.

It was an embarrassing moment—or would have been for anyone else save Jewel. As was her usual way, she met such unpleasantness head-on. Sitting up, she tossed her head and glared at him.

"I hope you'll put some meat on those bones right quick, Cameron. I've a feeling you can't work very hard looking like a skeleton."

"Then I certainly hope you intend to feed me well."

"You can be assured that whatever you get at my table will be better than Cowcadden fare," Jewel told him tartly.

To her surprise, she saw him swallow, a purely reflexive response that was not at all in keeping with the harsh rejoinder she had anticipated. Now what awful memory was responsible for that? she wondered. Just how bad was the food at Cowcadden anyway?

To her great annoyance, she found herself suddenly pitying the gaunt man across from her. What had they fed him there in that terrible place? Certainly not enough, from the look of him. When had he eaten last? Was he hungry now? She hadn't even thought to ask.

And that made her feel deeply ashamed. Jewel had never meant to be unkind. She had just been too wrapped up in her own misery to consider Tor Cameron's needs. Well, then, the least she could do was make up for it now.

"I've got something to eat here," she said, rummaging beneath her seat. "Leftovers from this afternoon. 'Tisn't much, but if you're hungry . . ." As she spoke, she pulled a wicker basket onto her lap and opened the lid.

There was a bottle of wine and some cold fowl wrapped in cloth. A half wheel of cheese and a few slices of oat bread also remained. She smiled kindly at Tor. "Would you care for some?"

Tor didn't answer. Instead he turned his face away.

Jewel felt her temper stirring, but its heat was quickly squelched when she saw the muscle leaping wildly in his jaw. "Tykie," she said quietly, "please uncork the wine."

As he did so, she set the chicken, bread, and cheese on the seat opposite, close enough that Tor could reach it without effort. Then she made a great show of settling herself in front of the window and pretending vast interest in the scenery outside. She would not humiliate the starving man by watching him eat.

She didn't have to. She had only to listen, her heart squeezing, while he chewed and swallowed in almost desperate haste. Backhanding his lips, he reached for the bottle and gulped the wine.

Not until he sat back, sighing deeply, did Jewel steal a glance at him. Unexpectedly, quite by accident, their gazes met. There was a long silence while they challenged each other with their eyes.

"Better?" she asked softly.

But Tor wasn't about to yield an inch, not even after Jewel MacKenzie had provided him with just about the best meal of his life. He merely looked at her with hooded eyes, his expression unreadable, letting her know that Tor Ban Cameron wasn't the sort to soften just because the wee chit who was his wife had given him enough food to fill, for the first time in months, the hollows of his innards.

Jewel took his meaning immediately. Her long lashes fluttered down over her eyes, masking their vivid blue. So he was going to play the proud warrior, was he?

To cover her sudden, inexplicable disappointment, she reached again under her seat. Tor watched her without seeming to do so as she drew out a dark green bottle and uncorked it herself. The splash of liquid into a glass was accompanied by a scent that filled the coach like heady perfume.

Tor swallowed convulsively. Whiskey! Ye gods, she was pouring him whiskey!

He couldn't help it. His hand shook as he took the glass from her.

Jewel pretended not to notice. In silence she watched as he swirled the contents beneath his long nose, like a connoisseur, and closed his eyes in bliss.

Not until the glass was empty did Tor look at her again.

Obligingly she handed him the bottle.

" 'Drumcorrie Single Malt,' " he read aloud, studying the label with its border of deep purple thistles. "I've never heard of it. But I have to admit, 'twas outstanding." He scowled at Jewel. "Where did you get it? Where was it made?"

"Glen Chulish."

"I'm afraid I've never heard of that, either."

"Well, you're going to soon enough."

His head came up. "Eh?"

" 'Tis my home."

Tor's eyes narrowed. "Your home? You live in a place that makes this kind of whiskey?" His tone suggested that he considered the matter highly improbable.

Jewel glared. "That kind of whiskey, Mr. Cameron, is known as Drumcorrie of Glen Chulish. And I don't just live in a place that makes that kind of whiskey. As a matter of fact, Drumcorrie is my distillery. And what's more, Mr. Cameron, you're going to help me run it."

For the first time in his life, he found himself rendered completely speechless by another's words. Like the hulking mute in the corner, he could only stare at her while a suitable response failed him altogether. So that was it, was it? The chit needed help in running the place, and she'd come down to Cowcadden to buy herself an indentured servant! Tor had no idea how whiskey was made. But he had a hearty suspicion that it involved hard physical labor, with long hours spent slogging across drafty malting floors, stirring huge, smelly vats of bubbling brew, and rolling heavy barrels and hoisting cumbersome sacks—all the things that no man in his right mind would consider doing for the rest of his natural life!

He opened his mouth to tell the haughty redhead that he had no intention of becoming her slave and that she might as well head straight back to Cowcadden to find someone else who did. But at the same moment he discovered that it had become deuced difficult for him to talk. Not because of the shock, mind, but because both the whiskey and the food had done something odd to his brain. His thoughts seemed to be twisting around in a nonsensical fashion, muddling his senses and making him decidedly drowsy. As the carriage swayed and the warmth in his belly seemed to spread to every limb, he found his eyelids growing heavy. After a moment, he realized that he had no choice but to close them. Without being aware of it, he drifted off to sleep.

How his face changed when he did, Jewel thought, watching him surreptitiously. How unguarded it became, and so much younger and less severe!

She exchanged a troubled glance with Tykie.

"We'll have to feed him. Build him up. I don't want him getting sick on us."

Tykie snorted. It was obvious that he felt none of the compassion for the man that Jewel did.

"I know what you're thinking," she countered coolly. "A healthy prisoner is a dangerous one."

Tykie grunted his assent.

"And you expect he'll try to escape the moment he's strong enough."

Scowling, Tykie made a slicing motion across his throat.

"But not before he kills the two of us first."

Tykie nodded darkly.

Jewel laced her fingers together because she didn't want Tykie to see that they were trembling. "I have a feeling you're right," she agreed in an unexpectedly small voice.

Tykie didn't look at all pleased to hear this admission, but he had learned over the years to be philosophical about these things. Young Mistress Jewel had made her bed, and once again it would be up to Tykie to help her lie in it.

Heaven help us a', he thought glumly.

Tor Ban Cameron awoke with the furious urgency of a man expecting ambush. One moment he had been slumbering peacefully on the carriage seat; the next he came bolt upright, tensed like a panther ready to spring.

Sure enough, there was an arm around his neck and the prick of a knife against his throat, just as there had been so often at Cowcadden. Reacting instinctively, he let out a roar and seized his attacker.

"Stop it! Both of you!"

A woman's voice with the bark of a field marshal came from behind him, the sound so unexpected that Tor froze in his tracks. Shaking his head like a dog coming out of deep water, he looked around and saw a flushed, angry face directly before him. It took a moment for him to recognize her. Jewel Mac-Kenzie Cameron. His wife of scarcely a day.

Slowly Tor sank back in his seat. At the same time, Tykie loosened his hold around Tor's throat and did the same, although he made no move to pocket his knife.

"What was that all about?" Tor demanded furiously.

"You made an unexpected movement, Mr. Cameron," Jewel explained.

"I was dreaming," Tor retorted. "My muscles twitched."

"It seemed threatening at the time."

"My apologies. Perhaps you should tie me up the next time I fall asleep."

"That may not be a bad idea," Jewel agreed thoughtfully.

Tykie nodded vigorously.

To hell with you both, Tor thought furiously.

Scowling, he rubbed his eyes and peered from the coach window. Dusk. A lonely moor with a wind-swept lake lay before them. The lights of some unknown village winked in the distance. How bloody long had he been sleeping? He wasn't used to dropping off that way. Then again, he wasn't used to whiskey or such rich, bountiful food, either.

No, he wasn't used to them at all. And the belated thought occurred to him that maybe he should have paced himself while eating and drinking. Already his long-neglected stomach was protesting such abuse, and Tor cursed aloud as a warning rumbled through his bowels. He couldn't afford to get sick right now, by God!

"There's no need to take offense, Mr. Cameron," Jewel said curtly. "Tykie was only doing his job."

"Tykie can go to hell," Tor retorted, his eyes squeezed shut, his breath coming harshly.

"Mr. Cameron! I insist that you refrain from addressing—"

"And I insist," Tor interrupted coldly, "that you stop this bloody vehicle. Right now!"

"So you can escape?" Jewel mocked.

"So I can spare those dainty booties of yours. Unless you'd prefer to have me vomit all over them?"

Jewel turned pale and quickly called to the coachman.

Tor had been hoping to conduct his exit in a dignified manner, but it was all he could do just to stumble outside and lose every bit of the whiskey and that glorious dinner right there on the roadside.

It was the last, humiliating straw. His earlier euphoria at finding himself free was gone. His elaborate plans and his dawning hope for a future as a normal human being were but ashes in his mouth. Through all the bitter months of incarceration, of being beaten, starved, and grossly tortured, he had never sunk quite this low.

Intolerable that it should be a fragile little redhead who ended up humiliating him. Intolerable that with such a simple act as feeding him a decent meal she had brought him to his knees.

Worse was the fact that she didn't even seem to realize what she'd done. Through his agony, Tor became aware of the unbelievable fact that she had descended from the coach and was actually kneeling in the mud beside him. Dimly he realized that she was offering him a pannikin of water and a scented handkerchief, and calling up to Tykie to fetch a clean shirt from his trunk. What in God's name was wrong with her? Only a half-wit would refuse to turn her back on such a disgusting scene!

At least she had enough sense not to say a word to

him, although Tor could hardly be grateful for that. When his bout of nausea was over he leaned back against the carriage wheel, ashen faced.

A moment later he felt the touch of a blessedly cool hand upon his brow. Opening his bleary eyes, he found Jewel bending close, trying to discern whether or not he had a fever. Did she look relieved to discover he didn't?

"Go away," Tor rasped.

But she wouldn't. Instead she offered him another sip of water. Tor longed to refuse, to push the pannikin aside and curse her to the edge of hell and back, but he was simply too weak. And thirsty.

He drank greedily while she held the pannikin to his lips. She had to hold up his head because he simply couldn't do it for himself, but by now Tor was beyond caring.

When his raging thirst was quenched he tipped back his head and closed his eyes. Jewel washed his face with her handkerchief, and Tor let her. Never mind that her touch was unexpectedly soothing, and that for some stupid reason it was making him feel a little better. His humiliation was complete.

"Can you stand, Mr. Cameron?"

"I suppose I can."

"Mr. Cameron?"

Tor realized that his response had been an unintelligible mumble. With an effort he pried open his eyes. He saw Jewel's face, pale and very young, floating before him. It was much too pretty a face, God curse her, and at the moment it was filled with something that Tor was not about to tolerate.

"For God's sake," he raged, staggering to his feet, "stop feeling sorry for me!"

Shouldering Jewel aside, he made his way back to the coach. Collapsing onto the seat, he turned his head to glare at Tykie.

"And you! Keep the bloody hell away from me!"

Tykie glared back, then turned his reproachful scowl on Jewel.

I know, I know! she mouthed back, furious herself. If she hadn't needed him so badly, she would have gladly left the foul-tempered Mr. Cameron lying by the roadside, puking his guts out without a wee bit of help from anyone! As it was, she had no choice but to signal the coachman onward and wish to hell that she was home again in Glen Chulish—alone!

Chapter Four

They stopped for the night at an inn on the outskirts of Carlisle, in a quiet section of the town where they could be assured a measure of privacy. While Jewel vanished wordlessly up the stairs with the innkeeper's wife, Tykie and Tor were shown to a room just off the kitchen. It was a stark little cubicle, stuffy and unwelcoming with its chipped enamel washbasin and narrow iron cots. But at least the straw mattresses were clean, the floor freshly swept, and no evidence of vermin was visible in the hearth.

The innkeeper's boy laid a fire while Tor collapsed on the cot closest to the door. He had just closed his eyes when Tykie shook him savagely.

"What?" Tor snapped.

Tykie shook him again, and indicated that Tor was to occupy the bed in the corner, away from the door, where Tykie could keep a better eye on him.

"Leave off," Tor growled. "I'm not going anywhere tonight."

And it was true. He felt bruised and beaten and unutterably weary. Forget the ambitious escape plans he had laid in the warden's office at Cowcadden. They'd have to wait. Right now he didn't even have the strength to pull off his boots.

Eyes closed, he lay there without moving. He heard the splash of water as Tykie washed himself at the sink. He heard the fire beginning to crackle in the grate. A murmur of voices came from the kitchen while a coach rumbled past outside on the road.

Normal sounds, everyday sounds, which no one but Tor seemed to hear. He wondered how long it would be before he, too, took them for granted again.

The door creaked open. The smell of oat porridge wafted inside. Tor could hear the thump of wooden bowls hitting the table. Leaning down, Tykie shook him roughly.

"Go away."

But Tykie wouldn't. He shook Tor again.

"Bloody hell," growled Tor. Shoving himself off the cot, he crossed unsteadily to the table and sat down.

The big mute settled himself distrustfully in the opposite chair. Eyes on each other, the two men began to eat.

"Faugh! I've had better gruel in prison!" Tor snarled.

But not nearly so much. Even bad gruel was heavenly, Tor supposed, when there was enough of it for once to completely fill one's belly. And his belly was certainly pinched after having lost that earlier meal in the coach.

"What's your mistress doing traveling without a lady's maid?" he asked between mouthfuls.

Tykie shrugged and stared at the wall beyond Tor's shoulder.

"Left her home?" Tor pressed. "Or hasn't she got one?"

Tykie stared.

"Maybe you're the only one willing to put up with her, eh?"

Tykie ignored the taunt. He kept on chewing.

"Ah, well. I won't get any answers out of you. Even if you could talk, you'd not betray her, hmm?"

Tykie glared a warning.

Tor was amused. "Loyal, ain't you? And I suppose you've seen it all, riding herd on that red-haired virago. Wish you'd enlighten me. After all, she is my wife now, and a soldier should always be briefed before going into battle, right?"

Tykie's lips thinned, but he kept on eating. Tor chuckled. He was feeling remarkably better. Unlike that last meal, the porridge was giving every indication of staying put. He wondered if he dared risk another whiskey. That Drumcorrie stuff was true nectar of the gods. He wondered if the hulking monster across from him would fetch a bottle if he asked. Tor doubted it. Tykie's unswerving devotion to his fair young mistress was one thing. Fetching whiskey for her objectionable husband was another.

Without warning Tor's expression changed. His eyes widened and he bolted to his feet. Even as he started toward the door, Tykie was upon him, the knife appearing with lightning speed from his pocket.

"Put that away!" Tor snapped. "I'm not going any damned where!"

Tykie halted, confused.

"The chamber pot!" Tor grated through clenched teeth.

Tykie looked around, uncomprehending. Then understanding dawned. Obligingly, he set it in the corner of the room, then watched distrustfully as Tor wavered toward it and fumbled with his breeches.

"Do you mind?" Tor bellowed, becoming aware of

the mute's unblinking stare. "I'd like some privacy! That bloody stuff has given me the runs!"

Tykie backed away, obliging. But not before Tor saw him throw back his head and give vent to great gusts of laughter.

When Jewel came downstairs the following morning she was surprised to find Tykie sharing a pot of tea in the common room with her coachman. There was no sign of Tor Cameron.

"What did you do with him?" she demanded, halting in the doorway with her hands on her hips. "Tie him to the bedpost?"

"Don't ye fret, miss," the coachman answered for Tykie. "He willna be goin' anywhere on his own. He's ill."

"Ill?" echoed Jewel, scowling.

"Aye. Mayhap 'tis the plague." Piers MacInnis sounded downright hopeful. "Mayhap we should leave 'im here."

Tykie nodded his heartfelt agreement.

Jewel ignored them. With an angry swish of her skirts, she retreated down the corridor. Oh, this was wonderful, simply wonderful! Yesterday had been bad enough, in all good conscience! But this? She was not about to delay her return to Glen Chulish even for another hour because that difficult, foul-tempered piece of prison trash was too lazy to get out of bed! God knows she'd been gone from home too long already! And as for Tykie, shirking his duties just because the man complained he was ill . . .

But he *was* ill. Jewel realized as much the moment she stepped into the room and heard Tor's shallow breathing. Crossing to the cot she found him flushed with fever and barely conscious. Piers was right: he obviously didn't have the strength to stand, let alone make good an escape.

"Bloody hell," Jewel muttered to the corpselike form of her husband. "I suppose I'll have to nurse you now, on top of everything else!"

"You c-could leave me here to d-die," came a difficult whisper from the cot.

"Nonsense," retorted Jewel, hiding her surprise by energetically rolling back her sleeves. She'd had no idea that he was awake and listening. "I've too much invested in you already."

"A b-bad investment, 'twould seem. I've always known that w-women have no s-sense for business."

"Mr. Cameron. 'Tis bad enough that I have to delay my return home by playing nursemaid to the likes of you. As long as I'm doing so I'd appreciate it if you kept your bloody comments to yourself."

Water splashed in the bowl and her angry footsteps swept away toward the door. Tor kept his eyes closed because it hurt too much to open them, but he could hear the exchange of heated voices in the hallway. Jewel was requesting, quite forcibly, the services of a doctor and a lengthy list of medical supplies.

A moment later she was back, pulling up a stool and seating herself at the head of his cot. Tor wanted to tell her that he refused to be seen by a doctor. He had no intention of being bled by some drunken poltroon passing himself off as a man of medicine, but when he tried to speak, his voice was little better than a croak. Worse was the fact that Jewel paid no attention.

"Be still, Mr. Cameron. Save your strength."

For what? Battling his raging fever so that he might recover and spend the rest of his life as the indentured slave to this tart-tongued Highland wretch? Better to die peacefully here in Carlisle with at least the memory of his few hours of freedom to brighten his passing!

But the tart-tongued wretch didn't seem willing to let Tor Cameron die. Living in as remote a place as Glen Chulish, Jewel MacKenzie knew a thing or two about doctoring; everyone who lived there did. She knew that the fever must burn itself out, but that she must bring down its terrible heat if she wanted to keep her patient from weakening or damaging his brain. And this man's brain, Jewel decided grimly, had better remain intact or he'd be of no use to her at all.

"Wh-what are you doing?" Tor croaked as she began undoing the buttons of his shirt.

"Be still," she snapped, and drew the garment from him.

His skin was hot to the touch, so hot that Jewel couldn't help feeling a twinge of fear. And pity, when she noticed the scars across his chest and shoulders where he had been beaten—often, from the look of it. She didn't doubt that there would be scars on his back as well. Tor Cameron must have been very strong once, if the span of those shoulders was any indication, but he was pitiably gaunt now, and racked with fever.

Jewel bathed his blistering body with the icy water in the pitcher. She swabbed his face and neck, then his shoulders and chest. Dipping and wringing out the rag, she repeated the process while Tor lay unmoving, his eyes closed.

Again Jewel couldn't help feeling the tiniest twinge of fear. If she lost him now, she'd lose Glen Chulish. That in itself was enough to stiffen her resolve to save the man's life. That and the fact that she was well aware that he would never have fallen ill to begin with if she hadn't dragged him out into the chilly air of Glasgow when he obviously didn't have the strength to withstand the rigors of travel.

Now why should I be feeling guilty? she asked herself furiously. Better for him to die out here, a free man, than to waste away to an agonizing end in the stinking hold of a ship bound for the colonies!

But he's not going to die! she reminded herself stubbornly. I'm not going to let him!

With renewed determination, she dipped the cloth back into the water. Agitated though her thoughts might be, her hands were gentle as she bathed her husband's burning brow. Not for a moment would she let Tor Ban Cameron think that she was in the least bit worried, or afraid.

He lay there so still that Jewel was sure he had lost consciousness, but Tor was awake. Even though his fiery misery he was well aware of her gentle touch. Oh God, how long had it been? Women had touched Tor Cameron in the past—more of them than he cared to remember—but not like this.

No, not like this.

Never in his life had Tor been touched by a woman whose sole intent was to ease his pain. Why, there was something almost motherly in the patient way Jewel MacKenzie sat beside him, bathing away his mounting fever. Tor had long since forgotten the loving touch of a mother, but for just this once he allowed himself the luxury of drifting once again beneath the gentleness of ministering hands.

He felt a catch in his heart, and wondered how such a haughty, self-absorbed creature as Jewel MacKenzie could possess such a tender side, a surprisingly welcome side. He was burning up with fever and racked with pain, but her cool hands upon him were like a benediction. He clung to them without realizing that he did, seeking their strength and their healing.

By the time the doctor came, Tor was resting easier. The fever still burned, but not as fiercely as before. Jewel was instructed to wait outside while the portly little man made a brief examination. She did so reluctantly. Like all Highlanders, she had a hearty distrust of the medical profession, and she had taken an instant dislike to the overweight fellow with the soiled waistcoat and unwashed hands who waddled in to care for her husband.

Her husband. It was the first time Jewel had thought of him that way without having to be reminded. The thought was disturbing. She told herself that he was an investment, nothing more. An investment in Drumcorrie's future, and a good one—no matter what Tor had said about her woeful lack of business sense.

And just to make sure that her investment was well protected, she sent Tykie into the sickroom to make certain the doctor treated him properly. But Tykie didn't stay long. Less than a minute after she had sent him inside he reappeared in the corridor, looking pale and nauseous.

"What is it?" Jewel asked, pushing herself away from the wall. "What's he doing in there?"

Tykie pointed to his forehead and his neck, then made a wiggling motion with his hand.

"What?" persisted Jewel, not understanding. "What is it?"

Tykie spread his thumb and forefinger several inches apart, as though measuring something, and again wiggled his fingers in a wormlike fashion.

Jewel's eyes widened. "Leeches?"

Tykie nodded miserably.

"You mean that idiot in there is *bleeding* him?"

Again Tykie nodded. Like his mistress, he had an abhorrent distrust of modern medicine, especially when it came to the awful practice of using leeches for the purpose of drawing blood—and presumably bad humors—from the patient's suffering body.

Tykie could well remember the fact that Mistress Jewel's own mother hadn't lasted half a day after a famed English doctor had insisted on bleeding her following the difficult birth of her second, stillborn child. And bleeding hadn't helped when, years later, the master himself had taken to his bed and, swollen with gout, had been thoroughly bled. That very night he'd turned up his toes and died. So much for the healing power of bloodsucking worms!

While Tykie hadn't thought much of Jewel's hard-living father and didn't give a damn about Tor Ban Cameron, he knew quite well that trouble was brewing by the way Mistress Jewel's chin came up as she started for the sickroom door. And since he had labored all his life to keep her out of trouble, he moved quickly to block her path.

"Get out of my way, Tykie," she commanded.

Tykie shook his head.

Her chin went up another notch. So did Tykie's.

Jewel's lips thinned. She knew from past experience that she'd never be able to budge that mountain of firmly planted flesh, but she wasn't about to let that doctor in there bleed the life out of her husband, either.

"All right, then," she said, planting herself just as firmly in front of Tykie's immovable hulk. The top of her head barely reached his coat buttons. "*You* go in and make him stop."

Tykie went pale.

"I mean it, Tykie. Either you go or I do."

Looking pained, Tykie went. But he hadn't gotten two paces into the room before Jewel came tumbling after him, puffed up like a wildcat and ready to claw the very eyes out of the unsuspecting doctor.

Fortunately Tykie was prepared for that, for he knew his young mistress far too well. Without so much as turning around or breaking stride, he

55

caught the angry girl by the collar and tucked her beneath his arm as though she were little more than some weightless package. Crossing the room, he halted in front of the startled doctor.

Even though he was mute, Tykie Ferguson had never had any trouble communicating his wishes to others when he meant them in earnest. In fact, a few threatening motions were all it ever took to convince most folk that it would be prudent to retreat. Dr. Horatio Hubert proved no exception. No way on earth was he about to continue his treatment while being confronted by this gesticulating giant and the wild redhead struggling furiously beneath his arm. The leeches were hastily returned to their jar, the leather straps removed from his patient's limbs, the satchel snapped shut. Sweating profusely, Dr. Hubert hurried out without even giving a thought to the compensation owed him.

Not until the doctor had gone and the door was firmly shut on the curious coachmen gathered in the hall did Tykie set Jewel down. He was spared no more than a furious glare before she turned her attention to the man on the cot.

The bleeding had taken its toll. Tor's face was ashen and his breathing barely perceptible.

Jewel's frightened gaze swept up to meet Tykie's. "Do we dare move him?"

Tykie shrugged. It would suit him just fine if the fellow up and died. Better for Mistress Jewel as well. Daft it was, this whole affair!

"He'd be better off at home," Jewel added, chewing her lip indecisively. "Annie could care for him."

Annie would have a fit, Tykie thought. The last thing Drumcorrie's overworked and crabby housekeeper needed was a dying prisoner to nurse to his grave!

But was he dying? With growing hope, Tykie studied the sick man's face. Looked bloody awful, didn't he? Long as it wasn't the plague and he died before infecting the rest of 'em . . .

Making up his mind, Tykie jerked his head in the direction of the door. His meaning was clear. He would fetch the coachman, and they would load Tor Cameron into the coach and take him to Glen Chulish.

But Tykie couldn't help feeling a stab of guilt as he saw the relief spread across Mistress Jewel's worried face. He turned away quickly so that she wouldn't read his real intent in his eyes. Not in a million years did he agree with her that the fellow's chances were better at Drumcorrie. In truth, he was hoping that the journey would finish him off. If their luck held, the fellow might even expire before they reached the Glenaird Pass. Then they could conveniently toss his corpse down into the ravine. 'Twould save 'em all a lot of grief and the expense of a funeral, it would.

But Tykie wasn't about to let Jewel know that.

Chapter Five

Unfortunately, Tor didn't oblige Tykie by dying as the Drumcorrie coach rumbled across the Glenaird Pass. Nor did he die as they crossed the last, rocky peaks of the Aird mountains, and the Chulish valley appeared below them through a blanket of evening fog. In fact, he was still clinging stubbornly to life by the time the coach halted in the stableyard and the barn door opened to spill its welcoming light upon them.

Alerted by the frantic barking of the dogs, Drumcorrie's few servants and distillery workers hurried out to meet the mud-spattered vehicle. In recent memory, no one from Glen Chulish had ever made the long journey to distant Glasgow and lived to tell the tale. A few of the servants had privately believed that the travelers would never return.

But there was Tykie, as hale as ever, swinging out of the coach and turning to help his mistress alight. Expectancy lit every careworn face. No one but Annie had been told the nature of Mistress Jewel's visit to Glasgow. Everyone but Annie was agog with curiosity to know what Mistress Jewel had brought back from that great, distant city.

A collective gasp went up as Tykie and Piers lifted the unconscious Tor out of the coach on a board. The crowd parted like water to let the sick man through. Furtive whispers followed his passage.

"Whot the de'il be a' this foolishness?" came a sharp voice through the mist.

Everyone froze, including Jewel, as Annie Brewster marched across the cobblestones from the direction of the house. A Scottish terrier with a bright red collar scurried along at her heels.

No one moved. Tykie and Piers obligingly lowered the stretcher to give Annie a better view.

There was a long silence as Annie studied the unconscious man, then glanced sharply at Tykie. Her look told him clearly that she considered him to blame.

Tykie blushed and bowed his head. In Annie's eyes, he had failed miserably.

"He's had a fever," Jewel piped up, dancing around the stretcher with the nervous energy of someone gone too long without sleep. "Can you help him, Annie?"

"The lord kens," Annie snapped, sparing her mistress little more than a chilling glance. "Bring him in."

Awed, the crowd moved aside to let the stretcher pass. Rain was falling, and Annie walked beside it, shielding the unconscious man's face with her shawl. Through the kitchen they went and up the back stairs with Annie in the lead, the black terrier racing along behind. All but forgotten, Jewel brought up the rear, her expression set and anxious.

On the landing, Annie unlocked the narrow door

that led to the attic, where her own rooms lay.

"No," Jewel said at once. "The Jacobite suite."

"But that be your father's old room!" Annie's voice was sharp.

Jewel said calmly, "This man is my husband, Annie. He'll have the Jacobite room."

"I was afeared o' that," Annie muttered grimly.

With the housekeeper still in the lead, they moved down the dark-paneled corridor. The servants listening in the hallway below exchanged stunned glances. No one said a thing. No one had any idea what to say. Once again Mistress Jewel had behaved in a manner to suggest that she had taken complete leave of her senses.

Tor Ban Cameron awoke to the drumming of rain on the roof. He felt so absurdly weak that for a long time he could do nothing but lie there and struggle to remain conscious. But after a long, long while he could feel his strength returning. He found that it was no longer an effort merely to draw air into his lungs. He could open his eyes without feeling as though his lids were made of stone. He could turn his head and take in the dark oak furnishings of his room and the rafters supporting the ceiling above.

He realized dimly that he was lying on a real bed. The mattress beneath him was sinfully soft, the linens clean and sweetly fresh. He lacked the strength to do more than savor such luxury, but that was all right with him. At the moment it was more than enough.

Exhausted by the effort of wakening, he drifted back to sleep. For hours that ran into endless days he slept, unaware of the comings and goings of the household, of the woman named Annie who tended him, of the Scottish terrier that never left her side, and the curious maids who, though terrified, stole upstairs now and then to peek in on him and whisper among themselves.

Nor was Tor aware of his wife, who came only at night, when the house was dark and still and no one would see her. Annie had taken over every facet of Tor Cameron's care, and Jewel had not been permitted back into the Jacobite suite lest she catch the fever herself. But she came nonetheless, if only to see for herself that Annie's terse assurances were true, and Tor Ban Cameron had not as yet died.

She would do little things for him whenever she was there, things that Annie never dreamed of doing: smooth a lock of tumbling black hair from Tor's feverish brow, or tuck in a stray corner of his woolen blanket against the bite of the evening air. And she would sit and talk to him, even though she knew he couldn't hear, because she didn't want him to think that he had been abandoned.

She was determined to see that Tor did not die. While she might loathe him because his presence here at Drumcorrie was a constant reminder of the depths to which she had been forced to sink, she was not about to have her journey to Glasgow end in disaster. Annie and Tykie would never let her live it down.

Fortunately, Tor did not die. Every time another dawn broke over the mountains he was breathing still, and his heart continued to pump blood through his veins. And when he opened his eyes at long last, he knew right away who he was and why he had been brought here, although he had no earthly idea where *here* might be.

He remembered the raftered ceiling and the dark, unwelcoming furnishings of the room. He'd seen them before, the last time he woke up. But he was no nearer knowing where they were—or where he was—than that last time either.

61

As he lay there considering this, the bedroom door opened. Tor turned his head on the pillow, expecting Jewel, but this woman was much older, and far more sour faced, with a severe chignon of prematurely gray hair knotted at the back of her head. She was carrying a tray in her work-worn hands, and a scruffy black terrier trotted alongside her.

As she set the tray down at Tor's bedside, she noticed he was awake. Instantly her expression took on a strong likeness to a prune. "So ye've decided to live." She sounded more sorry than pleased.

Tor cleared his throat. "Have I?"

"Eat," she countered, and was gone.

Exhausted, Tor closed his eyes. He thought about going back to sleep, but the smells emanating from the covered tray were impossible to ignore.

It took him a long time to struggle upright, but he managed at last. The tray held a bowl of barley broth and a basket of oat bread. Simple fare, but so delicious that Tor finished every bite. And once he'd eaten, he actually felt more alive than dead. Perhaps he really was going to live after all.

From outside the window came the sound of voices and the ringing of hooves on stone. Dragging himself out of bed, Tor parted the drapes and found himself looking down on a courtyard. The big brute, Tykie, was hurrying through the pouring rain to seize the bridle of the ugliest horse Tor had ever seen. It was some sort of draft animal, as fat as a sausage and wildly unkempt, and Jewel was sitting on its enormous back like the proverbial bump on a log.

She looked tiny and wilted to Tor, her feathered hat drooping, her emerald cloak running with water. Her boots and the hem of her habit were spattered with mud. Only her hair remained undimmed, shining like a scarlet beacon through the gloom. She was saying something to Tykie and gesturing in the direction of the mountains behind her. Where on earth had she been? What was she doing outside in such bloody awful weather?

By now thoroughly exhausted, Tor waited only until Tykie had led Jewel's mount through the wide barn doors before dragging himself back to bed. There was much he wanted to think about, but the moment he lay down again he drifted back to sleep.

He didn't stir when Annie returned for the tray, and was certainly not aware of the muffled oath she uttered when she picked it up and saw that he had eaten everything.

"Aye," she told the little dog panting at her heels, "he'll live."

She didn't sound at all happy about it.

The next time Tor awoke, the endless days of rain had passed. A watery sun shone through the millrace of clouds beyond his window, and the dinner tray was gone. Tor had no idea how long he had been sleeping. He had no idea what day it was, or the hour. Disoriented and irritable, he tossed aside the blankets and started to get out of bed.

At that moment the door opened. A face appeared through the gloom, all eyes and pointed chin.

Jewel. Tor hated to admit it, but he was glad to see her.

"Oh, sorry," she said cheerfully, stepping inside. "I didn't know you were up. Otherwise I would have—"

She broke off, staring at him so intently that for one awful moment Tor thought that he was standing before her stark naked. Looking down quickly, he was relieved to see that only his feet were bare, while the rest of him was covered with a respectable nightshirt.

Respectable? Far from it! Tor realized all at once that the nightshirt was some absurd, knee-length thing with embroidered sleeves and pale blue stripes, a horrible affair that he'd sooner die than wear, especially in the presence of his wide-eyed wife!

"What in hell is this thing?" he roared. But his roar had lost its power during his illness, and sounded no better than the feeble bleating of an old, old man. Embarrassed, he clamped his lips together and stood there glaring.

Jewel glared at him just as fiercely, her hands clasped behind her back. Still, Tor could have sworn that she was trying hard not to laugh.

"Well?" he demanded. "What *is* this thing?"

"It belonged to my father," she said innocently. "He always wore a nightshirt to bed. Don't you?"

"No," Tor snapped. "I always sleep in the nude."

If he expected to shock her, he was mistaken. She merely crossed the room and halted in front of him, hands still clasped behind her back, rocking on her heels like a naughty child. She was dressed in a gray woolen frock with a touch of lace at the collar. A maidenly thing, far too simple for so dramatic a creature, Tor thought, and yet she still managed to look alluring, with her auburn hair tumbling down her back and secured away from her face with heavy combs.

Tor grudgingly admitted to himself that she would look beautiful even in rags. Jewel MacKenzie Cameron was one of those rare women who could shine in anything, in any situation. God, how he resented her!

There was something different about her, too. Something definitely at odds with the wide-eyed, uncertain creature he had first encountered at Cowcadden. Even though she seemed a little flustered to find him up and about, she wasn't acting the least bit chilly and hateful toward him. Now why was that?

"Annie says you've been eating. She seems to think you're going to live."

"Does that please you?"

"Aye." Jewel's blue eyes regarded him solemnly. "I need you at the distillery, Mr. Cameron."

Suddenly Tor knew what was different about her. That self-assurance, that hint of gaiety lurking in those tilted eyes, could only mean one thing. She was happy. Why? Because her *investment* was going to live? Or because she was glad to be home?

Scowling, Tor turned his head to study his surroundings. It was a grand room, this one in which they had installed him, but much too dark and overly furnished for his taste. Heavily carved armoires and chests of drawers filled the empty spaces between the windows and the doors. A sitting room or something similar in function opened off to the right, the floor covered with a rug of somber blues and greens. The corner of a huge writing desk and a tasseled brocade hassock were visible behind the partially opened door.

"This is the Jacobite suite," Jewel explained, following his scowling gaze. "We call it that mainly because of the furniture. My father loved all these dark, heavy things. Awful, aren't they?"

For the first time, Tor found himself agreeing with her. His lips twitched as he looked at her. "You're very honest, aren't you?"

"Always."

"I thought as much. You've certainly made no bones about why you brought me here."

At least she had the good grace to blush at that. And even to turn her back on him and stroll with seeming nonchalance over to the window. Tor watched as she traced a slim finger along the sill.

"I take it your father's no longer living." Why else

would he have been given the fellow's room?

Jewel's jaw clenched visibly. "No. He died last year."

"Ah. And your mother?"

Her shoulders went up and down. A flippant shrug. Too studied, Too thought, watching her closely.

"I never knew her. She died when I was a baby."

Ah, now that explained a lot. A mother whose absence had obviously been keenly felt in this young woman's life; a father whose presence had obviously brought out the worst in her. Tor suspected that that boldly clenched jaw spoke volumes about the way Jewel had felt toward her father.

Feeling fatigued all of a sudden, he backed up to the bed, knowing better than to turn his rear end on her when he had no idea just how much of his backside the infernal nightshirt covered. Settling himself comfortably against the bolster, he drew the blankets modestly over himself and gave his wife what he hoped was an approachable smile. For the first time ever, the chit seemed willing to answer his questions, and he was determined to take advantage of that no matter how exhausted he might be.

"So you live here alone." He gestured around him. "I take it we're in Glen Chulish, and that this is Drumcorrie."

"Aye, but I don't live alone. I have Annie and Tykie."

"Annie?"

"The housekeeper." Jewel's lips twitched as she spoke, for the term was woefully inadequate for describing Annie Brewster.

Tor had a dim memory of some sour-faced creature with rough hands and a sharp tongue who had poured noxious swills down his throat and nearly burned him to death with a hot and smelly mustard plaster. "Ah, of course. The woman with the dog. A wee black one, shaggy as a rug."

"That's Goat. We all despise him."

"So you live here with a dog you hate, your housekeeper, and your mute friend Tykie. But no flesh and blood."

"No."

"No maiden aunt horrified to find you orphaned and alone after your father died, who moved in with you to make the situation respectable?"

"I have plenty of aunts," Jewel assured him, turning to stare out the window, "but none of them were willing to come."

Because of her, or because of Glen Chulish? From the stark, uninviting view lying beyond Tor's window, he could well imagine that the place wasn't exactly hospitable. And neither, apparently, was this volatile redhead, if her own kith and kin had all but refused to take care of her once her father passed away!

"Why didn't you move in with one of them?"

Jewel shot him a look of scorn. "And leave Drumcorrie?"

"In England," Tor said, "your situation would be considered scandalous. And probably illegal. You wouldn't be permitted to live by yourself before you came of age."

"This isn't England. You should know that, Mr. Cameron. Because I very much doubt that you're English either, with a name and an accent like yours."

"My accent?" Tor was amused. "Does it show after all this time? Faith, I've not been home to Scotland since the war."

"Did you fight in the forty-five?" Jewel asked in surprise.

But Tor had said enough. He was tired now, and cranky. While he certainly enjoyed trading words with Jewel MacKenzie Cameron, he didn't have the strength to continue doing so at the moment. And he had absolutely no desire to answer questions about himself. Besides, it was none of her business. She might have brought him out of prison and married him to boot, but that didn't give her the right to pry into his private life.

"Go away," he said irritably. "I'm tired."

"Of course," Jewel retorted stiffly. "I'll send Annie in to give you a bath this evening."

"Fine, fine." Tor waved her away without another thought.

Evening brought a renewed bustle to the house. Even though Tor had never left his rooms, he had come to know the rhymes and rhythms of the place very well. In the morning there was always the sound of far-off doors closing as the maids went about their cleaning. There would be smoky smells drifting up from below as the kitchen fires were lit, and livestock bawling out in the barn, impatient to be fed. Mid-morning always brought Tykie from wherever it was he spent the early hours, his unmistakable step booming across the floors below. Then dinner would be served and the clinking of silverware would drift up to Tor dimly above the patter of the rain.

And then, for a few blessed hours every afternoon, the house would be still. That was when Tor always slept most deeply. Nights were restless times for him, when every joint in his body seemed to throb and ache and his rest was disturbed by bitter dreams.

Unfortunately, those blessed afternoon hours were never long enough. Soon the evening's cooking would begin and the pots would clank and a woman's sharp voice could be heard giving endless orders in the kitchen below. There would be a lot of bustling about and murmured conversations in the hall, and the courtyard below Tor's window would be filled with activity. That was when Tor would lie in his bed and wonder at the capricious ways of the fate that had brought him here to this place, and how long it would be before his strength returned and he could get the hell away from it.

Not surprisingly, he slept fitfully that afternoon, for Jewel's visit had disrupted his calm, familiar routine. When the sun sank behind the mountains and the cooking fires were lit in preparation of the evening meal, Tor awoke feeling just as tired and irritable as he had earlier.

Restlessness compounded his irritation, and his mood was nothing short of foul when the expected dinnertime knock finally sounded on his door. Tor knew it would be that infernal woman, Annie, with her smelly dog and his supper. At the moment he wasn't exactly appreciative of her company, or anyone else's.

"Put it down and go," he snapped.

"Excuse me?" came the frosty response.

Tor's head whipped around. Jewel, not Annie, was marching purposefully toward the bed, and the tray she carried didn't contain his supper but a washbasin and a towel and a bar of milled soap. Behind her scurried a saucer-eyed creature of no more than twelve, struggling with two pails of steaming water. The girl stared at Tor as though expecting him to sprout horns, and when Jewel's back was momentarily turned, Tor made a terrifying face at her.

Oh! but that sent her scurrying outside, the pails left behind and her mistress abandoned.

Jewel didn't seem to notice. She was stirring up the fire with a poker and did not turn around until the flames were leaping brightly.

"Now, then," she said calmly. "Time for that bath."

Bath? What bath?

Tor watched, uncomprehending, as she snapped

open a neatly folded apron and tied it about her waist. Next she rolled back her sleeves to reveal her slim, lovely wrists, and then filled the washbowl from the buckets that the maid had left behind.

"Wait a moment!" Tor pulled himself upright. "What the devil are you doing?"

"Fixing your bath," Jewel answered calmly. "I told you this morning to expect one."

"Aye, perhaps you did. But I thought—At the time, I didn't realize—"

Jewel was working up a lather with the soap and washcloth. She seemed deeply intent on her work. Her head was bowed, her eyes downcast. "Annie was supposed to do it, but she, ah, she's busy downstairs."

Silence.

"You mean she refused."

"No! She—she had other things to do. Besides, you and I are . . . are married."

"Which makes it proper for you to bathe me," Tor guessed shrewdly. "Or so Annie said, hmm?"

"She's being spiteful," Jewel said with a shrug.

Tor had to hand it to Jewel: she was doing a heroic job of appearing utterly uncaring, but looking at her shrewdly, he could easily see the blush that tinged her cheeks even though she still refused to look at him.

Doing his best to hide his twitching lips, he leaned back and propped himself comfortably against the pillows. So the lass thought she had the nerve to bathe him, did she? Thought she would show Annie that there was nothing to the task, that bathing a sick man was just as simple as bringing him a meal or taking away his chamber pot, eh?

Outspoken, outrageous little thing, Tor thought, grinning. He'd never doubted her courage—or was it her madness? But just how far would she carry through with this?

In one easy motion, he drew the nightshirt over his head and tossed it aside. Whistling beneath his breath, he settled the blanket comfortably to his armpits. He had been wearing nothing under the absurd garment, and both of them knew it.

Tor's amusement deepened as he saw the blush climb higher into Jewel's cheeks. To give her credit, she kept right on lathering the soap. Deciding to be helpful, Tor pulled the blanket down over his hips, leaving his upper torso bare. That way the chit could bathe most of him without having to uncover him. The rest he'd do himself, after he'd chased her from the room. But he definitely intended to make her squirm a little first. Ah, lord, he couldn't remember when he'd last enjoyed himself so much!

The room was silent save for the crackling of the fire. Jewel had worked up enough lather to shampoo half a dozen horses.

"Well?" he prompted. "I'm waiting."

Up came her haughty little chin. Eyes the color of a crisp autumn sky flashed in the firelight. Before Tor knew what she was about, she had slapped the soapy rag onto his chest and began scrubbing away with enough vigor to strip off his skin.

"You'll feel much better after this." Her voice was firm and cool. MacKenzies never showed fear in the presence of their enemies. "You'll smell better, too."

" 'Twill make you happy, I suppose," Tor growled.

"Oh, believe me, it will."

He tried to think of something to say that would reduce her to quaking jelly. But Jewel had apparently decided she wasn't going to let him intimidate her anymore. Worse, Tor had to admit that the warm water and silky lather felt too cursed good, and that the scrubbing motion of Jewel's skillful hands was extremely invigorating. Closing his eyes, he lay back and let her soap and rinse his chest and shoulders, his arms and face and neck.

God, but he was hairy! Jewel kept her lips compressed as she scrubbed away at one armpit and then the other. Did all men have so much hair furring their chest and everywhere else? As for that rock-hard jaw, she'd have to get Annie to shave it in the morning. One more day and he'd have a full-fledged beard.

"There!" she said with a goodly measure of relief as she rinsed off the last of the soap and plopped the washcloth back in the basin. "All done."

Tor leisurely opened his eyes. "What about the rest of me?"

She scowled. "The rest?"

"Why, lassie, take a look. You've only washed the upper half."

So she had. And been damned disconcerted doing just that. She wasn't about to take on the rest of him!

"Well?"

Even though her face was flaming, she bravely lifted her eyes to his. That was when she saw that he was laughing.

Oooh! Above anything else, Jewel hated being laughed at! All her life people had refused to take her seriously. Her stepmothers had always teased and goaded her, her aunts and cousins had thought her mad, and Tykie had often despaired of seeing her safely out of childhood. Annie, grimly unamused, had always predicted that one day Jewel would meet a disastrous end. But it was Jewel's father who had been the worst of the lot. All his life he had humiliated her, criticized her, and roared out his rage whenever Jewel refused to marry first this eligible suitor and then that one. At least he'd given up beating her long ago, when Tykie and Annie had drawn themselves protectively around her, but that hadn't stopped him from letting her know in cruel and cunning ways that she would never be good enough, *man enough,* to take over Drumcorrie.

He thinks I'm too cowardly! Jewel thought now, seeing in Tor's amused expression the same taunting look that had always been there in her father's. I'll show him I'm not—and make him bloody sorry, too!

In a frenzy she lathered the washcloth once again, then jerked back the covers and slammed it down upon him.

Tor yelped. Not only had he believed her incapable of this, but here she'd caught him smack in the testicles! And, bloody Judas, the water had gotten damned cold!

"Lie still, Mr. Cameron. There's naught to be afraid of."

Oh, how that haughty tone infuriated him! Thought she'd regained the upper hand, had she?

"Be my guest, ma'am."

His smug tone made Jewel grind her teeth together. With enough energy to peel off his skin she washed his feet, his thighs, his rib cage and belly. And then there was nothing left but that awful, hairy thing between his legs, which Jewel had studiously avoided looking at until now.

"Well?" prodded Tor.

While she had stubbornly been refusing to look at *it,* he had been looking at her, and reading her every thought right there on her face. Jewel didn't have to look back at him to know that he had issued her a challenge, one that he didn't believe for a moment she'd actually accept.

Well, he was wrong. She'd show him.

Rinsing out the washcloth, she took a deep breath. Cameron was her patient and he needed a bath. That . . . that manly part of him wasn't any different from

73

anything else she'd washed so far, right?

Oh, but it was. The moment Jewel touched it something odd happened inside her. Her heart started to gallop and her throat squeezed so tight that she could hardly breathe. She had never seen a naked man until today, let alone been expected to touch one, and here she was holding the very essence of a man's *maleness* in her hands.

Worse was the fact that now Tor's maleness was undergoing subtle changes, responding to Jewel's touch by shifting and lengthening in a manner that she had never dreamed possible. Up swept her shocked eyes to meet his hooded ones.

"Sorry," was all he said. "Reflexes. The same thing would have happened with Annie."

For some entirely illogical reason, Jewel was suddenly furious. Down splashed the washcloth into the basin, up came the sheets to cover Tor's quickening body, off came the crisp white apron.

"Is that it?" Tor taunted. "Just a few swipes with your cloth?"

Jewel was already heading for the door with the tray in her hands. Now she whirled to face him. "Of course it is. What else would you expect for something so small?"

The door closed forcibly behind her.

Groaning, Tor fell back against the pillows. At any other time, he would have roared with laughter at such a clever rejoinder. Unfortunately, there was nothing remotely amusing about the situation. He had lied to Jewel, because if that shrew of a housekeeper had dared touch him the way his wife had, he knew that his testicles would have shriveled clear into his body. Whereas Jewel, with her gentle hands and rose-petal skin, had aroused him to heated torment with a simple touch.

Tor groaned again and closed his eyes, aching for

her and not knowing how to save himself. He had gone far, far too long without a woman, and it was a curse to find the one closest at hand a crimson-haired seductress who also happened to be the one he'd dearly love to strangle.

Chapter Six

It was Annie who brought Tor's breakfast the following morning. The terrier was not with her, and his
remark concerning the animal's absence brought the
first glimmer of a smile to Annie's sour visage.

"He's stalkin' wi' Tykie."

"Stalking? But 'tis April."

"Na deer, rabbits." But Annie seemed pleased to
discover that Tor knew something about hunting.
"I'll be servin' rabbit stew on the morrow. 'Twill gie
ye strength."

"Believe me, I'll need it," Tor said grimly, thinking
of the long journey away from Glen Chulish.

Voices sounded in the courtyard below. Tor recognized the hoofbeats of the big, ugly drafter Jewel
always rode. He gestured toward the window.
"Where does she go?"

Annie didn't pretend to misunderstand him. Her
lips thinned. "That be no business o' yours."

"I'm her husband," Tor snapped.

Color flamed in Annie's gaunt cheeks, but she, too, could be stubborn. "Eat. I'll be back later for the tray."

Disgruntled, Tor watched her sweep to the door. There she halted and turned to face him. Her expression was cold, as was her tone. "This ain't Cowcadden, Mr. Cameron. There be no locks on these doors."

Then she was gone.

Tor lay there, glaring after her. Thought she'd done him a kindness, had she? Thought she'd make up to him for whatever evil her mistress was plotting by hinting that he was welcome to leave his bed and join the household now that he was well, eh?

Interfering bitch. Now he'd no longer have an excuse to continue lying abed. If he didn't appear downstairs soon, people would begin to wonder why. They might even start suspecting that he was afraid.

Tor's shoulders slumped. Aye, damn it, he was, and it was galling to realize as much! He'd been imprisoned for so long—endless weeks during his trial, and then those hellish six months in Cowcadden—that he'd almost forgotten what the real world was like. And of course that made it far easier to lie up here in bed and allow himself to be fed and looked after like some invalid than to actually go downstairs and confront a household full of strangers.

Where was the bravado that had shored him up on the journey here, before he'd fallen ill?

Making up his mind, he ate his breakfast, then rummaged through the armoire for his clothes, only to find that they were gone. No doubt Jewel had burned them. Her father hadn't left much in the way for him to wear either. He must have been a very short and overweight man, and his taste in clothing had run to the ridiculously ostentatious, judging

77

from the forgotten garments still folded away in the drawers and chests.

At the very last Tor was able to fashion together an acceptable outfit from a yellowed shirt and embroidered waistcoat that he found in the bottom of a trunk. An old pair of riding breeches belted at the hips fit not too badly, although they ended nearly even with the tops of Tor's boots, which he had found stored behind the sitting-room door. Whenever he moved, a goodly length of his hairy legs showed where the boots ended and the breeches began.

Looking like a fool and knowing it, Tor opened the door and stepped outside. He had no recollection of being brought up the dark stairs that confronted him, nor of entering the hall below. Weakened by the descent, he collapsed on the bottom step with his hands dangling between his knees.

After a time, when his strength returned, he lifted his head and looked about him. The MacKenzie stronghold, the one Jewel so proudly called home, was not particularly grand. It had more the look of a medieval hunting lodge than a castle. Old weapons and a threadbare tapestry woven in the colors of the MacKenzie tartan covered the stone walls. Daylight flowed in through old, leaded windows set deep amid stone embrasures. The hall was apparently used for nothing more than receiving vistors, for there were no chairs nor a table upon which to dine.

There were portraits hanging near the rafters, but Tor was too weary to examine them just yet. Rising, he headed for a doorway below the medieval minstrel's gallery. At its juncture with a long, gloomy corridor, he turned left without hesitating. After endless hours lying abed and listening to the comings and goings of the household below, he knew that the kitchens lay to the right. Since he had no wish to run into Annie, he avoided them altogether.

To the left lay a series of doors, and the sound of voices, both male, drew him to what must have been the former MacKenzie chieftain's study. Here, several impressive trophy bucks were mounted along the wall. Worn books lined the shelves and a thick fur rug covered the oak plank floor. A skinny little fellow was standing with his back to the door when Tor came in.

"She's gone for the day, Master Ruan. Did Annie no tell ye?"

"No, Sinclair, she didn't. Annie never tells me a bloody thing. Ah, well, pour me anither dram, will you? 'Tis harsh outside and no mistakin'."

The speaker was a young man in possession of incredible good looks. Eyes as blue as Jewel's blazed in a face of classically perfect proportions. He must have just come in from riding, for he was windblown, and sat sprawled perfectly at home in the big leather armchair with his muddy boots propped on the desk. When he saw Tor come in, however, he straightened with a jerk and quickly swept his feet to the floor.

"Sorry," Tor apologized. "Didn't mean to startle anyone."

"Bloody balls! I thought 'twas Annie!" The handsome fellow sounded greatly relieved.

The skinny one named Sinclair had whirled at the same time, and was now gaping at Tor in utter astonishment. Tor had to fight the urge to step up and snap his mouth shut for him.

"Who the devil are you?" the young god named Ruan inquired.

"Tor Cameron," Tor answered coldly. For some reason he had taken an instant dislike to the young dandy, and now Ruan only made matters worse by taking a long, assessing look at him and bursting into laughter.

"You?" he howled when he could speak. "You're Jewel's latest weapon? Ha ha ha! Sorriest-lookin' excuse for a man I've ever seen, and that's the truth! Ha ha!"

Tor turned to the skinny one named Sinclair. His eyes were shards of flint. "Where is Mrs. Cameron?"

"Mrs. Cameron?" echoed Ruan. "Lord help us a'! Gone tae find me, she has, though I'm the one what's found *her* out! Ha ha ha!" Tears were streaming from his eyes.

Tor coolly debated the wisdom of snapping the younger man's neck in two. But since he was still too weak, he did the next best thing under the circumstances. Reaching across the desk, he grabbed Ruan by the collar and hauled him up and out of his chair. "May I ask what you find so amusing?" he asked coldly.

"Now, now, laddie," Ruan squeaked, dangling several inches off the floor. "No harm done. Ye took me by surprise is all." And he grinned his most charming grin to show that there were no hard feelings.

Tor set him down none too gently, although he would have preferred beating him senseless. Ruan took his time shaking out his rumpled clothes and trying to collect himself.

Tor, meanwhile, helped himself uninvited to the bottle of whiskey that Sinclair had left on the desk. Both men regarded him openmouthed as he drained nearly every drop, then backhanded his lips and belched before lowering himself into the chair Ruan had vacated.

Neither man knew it, but Tor was close to collapse. As well, the whiskey had his head spinning. But he'd be damned if he let either one of them suspect.

"Well," he said, exhaling what seemed to him a breath of pure fire. "Would you mind telling me who the devil the two of you are?"

"I-I'm Sandy Sinclair," the skinny fellow squeaked. "I-I run the d-distillery."

"Oh, stop your stuttering, Sandy!" Ruan said irritably. "What are you afraid of?"

Tor regarded him lazily. "And you?"

Ruan drew himself up to his full height. He really was a pretty fellow, and it only made Tor dislike him all the more. What was he to Jewel, anyway?

"I am Ruan Fifemain Dubh MacKenzie, the Black MacKenzie," Ruan announced proudly. "Chieftain of the Fionnala sept of the Glen Chulish MacKenzies."

Tor's eyes glinted. "You'd be a popular fellow in prison, handsome cockerel that you are."

Ruan reddened. "I suppose you'd ken a' aboot that, eh?"

Slowly Tor set down the whiskey bottle he had just raised to his lips. He was a little unsteady coming to his feet, but neither Ruan nor Sandy noticed.

"W-wait a moment!" Sandy gasped. "Please consider—"

Fortunately, any pending violence was interrupted by a disturbance in the hall outside. An outer door slammed and voices were exchanged, one of them high and breathless, the other unmistakably Jewel's. A moment later the study door burst open and Jewel hurried in. She looked ravishingly beautiful, all windblown and redcheeked with flashing, ice blue eyes. The skirts of her dove gray riding habit whirled about her as she moved and she carried a whip in her slimly gloved hands.

"What are you doing out of bed?" she demanded furiously of Tor.

Rage packed Tor by the throat. He wasn't in prison anymore, by God! No one had the right to speak to him that way, least of all this wee scrap of a lass who was far too lovely for her own damned good! He came swiftly around the desk, intent on slaughtering all three of them with whatever weapon was closest at hand. But the moment he moved, the floor seemed to buck beneath his feet and his stomach gave an ominous heave.

Oh, God, the whiskey! Before Cowcadden, he could have tossed off an entire bottle and not been the worse for it. But now—

Without a word to anyone he fled from the room. Somehow he made it back to the hall and up the stairs without falling. His head was swimming and the warnings that had begun sounding in his gut were growing alarmingly insistent.

At the very last moment he made it to his room. Groaning, he collapsed on his knees in front of the chamber pot and lost all that remained of Annie's fine breakfast. The blood roared in his ears. Another spasm turned his stomach inside out. He choked and coughed and was promptly sick again.

Then, through his agony, Tor became aware that he was not alone. Dimly he could sense the presence of someone at his shoulder. Without having to turn his head, he knew that it was Jewel. She had followed him up the stairs and now she was kneeling beside him. She was saying something to him, but he couldn't understand what. He felt her hand on his brow, wonderfully cool and soothing. Groaning, he leaned forward and was sick again. Closing his eyes, he fought for breath. His humiliation was complete.

When he awoke, the room around him refused to swim into focus. Stubbornly he shook his head and rubbed his bleary eyes. Gradually his dizziness faded and his vision returned. He saw that the drapes had been drawn across the windows to hide the coming night. A candle sputtered by the bedside. The filthy chamber pot had been replaced with a clean one. His soiled clothing had been removed and sweet-smelling sheets had been drawn across his chest. A flagon of ale stood nearby.

Tor reached for it and took a long, unsteady drink. His stomach made no protest. Groaning, he rose to his feet and crossed to the basin. There he washed his face and rinsed his mouth. Bleary eyed, he raised his head and suddenly saw his own reflection in the mirror.

He went still.

Small wonder Ruan MacKenzie had laughed at him. Small wonder the fellow had clearly thought Tor an illiterate savage. This hollow-eyed beast with the sickly pallor and stubbled jaw could not be Tor Ban Cameron! Why, he didn't look remotely human anymore, did he?

Straightening, Tor stepped back and took a long, hard look at his naked body. Once he had been fit and strong, a mercenary soldier with a deadly aim and an arm powerful enough to wield the terrible, two-handed Highland claymore in a single grip. He'd earned himself a deadly reputation for that, but nowadays he doubted he'd be able to do more than drag the heavy weapon behind him. Worse, there were scars from brutal beatings all over him. His ribs showed. The slabs of muscle that had once spanned his wide chest were gone. His manhood, which he had once made use of with such lusty efficiency, dangled wearily amid its nest of dense black hair. And small wonder Ruan MacKenzie had cackled like a rooster over his hairy, skinny legs!

Defeated, Tor slunk back to bed. Lying on his back, he closed his eyes and buried his face in the crook of his arm.

There was a knock on the door.

"Go away."

The door creaked open.

He didn't even bother moving his arm to see who it was. "I said, go away."

"I've brought supper."

Jewel, not Annie. Her soft voice was accompanied by the heavenly smell of hunter's stew. Tor's mouth watered. That and the sound of her sweet voice all but caved in his defenses. Unbelievably, he felt the sting of tears in his eyes. In a panic, he blinked and swallowed convulsively. Ye gods, what if Jewel saw him blubbering like a child?

In the doorway, Jewel halted uncertainly. Fighting down a rush of emotion at the sight of him, she squared her shoulders and crossed to the bed. Moving the candle aside, she set down the tray.

Tor didn't stir. His arm was flung across his face, but Jewel saw him swallow again. Her heart seemed to squeeze into a hard, aching knot. She forced herself to speak calmly, knowing how much he hated her pity.

"I wish you'd eat."

"Why?" The flinty gleam in his eyes when he took his arm away was so unsettling that Jewel couldn't help retreating.

"So—so you can recover, of course."

"Ah, yes." With difficulty, Tor pulled himself upright. His eyes burned in the hollows of his face. "I'd better get my strength back so your money won't go to waste. I'm no good in the distillery as a puking, crying weakling, eh?"

Jewel winced. Oh, why hadn't she sent the tray up with Annie? But how could she have known that he'd be in such a foul mood? For heaven's sake, what had set him off this time?

"Then again, perhaps you've been lying to me all along about the reason I've been brought here. Does rescuing and seducing condemned prisoners fill some perverse need in you?"

Jewel stared at him in disbelief. "What on earth are you talking about? Seducing you?"

"Your handsome friend seems to think that's the case."

"Ruan? You must be joking!" Jewel's hackles were rising. "Is that what he said?" By God, she'd tear him limb from limb!

"He didn't have to say a word."

"Oh, I see." She fisted her hands on her hips. "That was your interpretation, then. Or perhaps it was just wishful thinking?"

Tor could feel his manhood stirring to insistent life, fueled by her taunting and the furious thrumming of the blood throughout his body. The fact that he could desire her—at this moment, no less—enraged him.

"Black MacKenzie," he mocked. "What is he to you? Why do you ride off every day to see him?"

"I don't—"

But she got no further. Without warning Tor's arm shot out from beneath the blanket to capture her wrist. Up he rose before her, the blankets falling away to reveal his nakedness and the full arousal of his manhood, made huge from months of abstinence.

Jewel stared, aghast, and promptly turned crimson. Up swept her wide eyes to Tor's face. She quailed when she saw that his expression had gone rigid with desire.

In fact, he'd forgotten everything: his jealousy, his anger, his bleak despair. All he could think of was easing the physical need that pounded so fiercely through him. With a groan he curled his hand around Jewel's neck, spanning it with his fingers while his thumb came to rest against the wildly beating pulse at the hollow of her throat. Encircling her waist in a similar manner, he swept her up against him, bending her backward so that her skirts were crushed between them and she could feel the hardness of him pounding against her thighs.

She struggled furiously. "Let me go!"

"That pretty poppycock," Tor sneered, ignoring her. "All talk and swagger! Do you ever let him love you like this? Can he, I wonder?"

He tipped back her head, his control snapping at the thought of another man's hands on her. Her lips had parted, and now his dark head swooped down like a bird of prey's to capture that sweet prize. His kiss was brutal. Like a wild animal he ravaged her mouth, drawing the very breath from her body.

"Stop it! Let me go!"

Again Tor ignored her. His steely fingers captured her jaw as he drank in the sweetness of her lips. He was still holding her crushed against him, branding her through the folds of her skirts with his heat.

Panting, Jewel struggled to break free, and succeeded at last in working loose one of her arms. Making a fist, she punched him as hard as she could, and caught him square in the eye.

Howling, Tor released her and they stood glaring at each other, fighting for breath, like enemies on the battlefield.

Jewel was not a fool. She could see well enough that Tor's flinty eyes were glazed with passion. Tykie had been right in warning her in his own way never to find herself alone with this man. On the other hand, she had honestly thought him still too weak to do her any harm. How wrong she had been! He was a man too long denied, and his body had clearly betrayed him.

Well, it was time to let him know in no uncertain terms that this arrangement between them was nothing more than a marriage of convenience. If he wanted a woman, needed one, he'd have to look elsewhere.

But he only laughed the moment she told him as much. "Really? And where do I begin looking, here in this empty glen? Unless you'd care to lend me one of your chambermaids for a night?"

"You're disgusting."

His face changed. Before she could react he'd reached across the distance between them and jerked her to him. Once again she found herself crushed against his hard, insistent male body while he covered her mouth with his hand.

"Don't scream. This is between us, Jewel MacKenzie Cameron."

She twisted her head free, determined to regain the upper hand. "Then know here and now, Tor Ban Cameron, that I'll never lie with you be we wedded fifty years and more! The sooner you accept your place in this household, the better!"

How brave she was, like a spitting kitten. But Tor held her close enough to see clearly into her wide eyes and feel the pulse racing beneath his hand. "I could make you change that haughty tune," he said silkily. "Easily. Your position as mistress of this house, as my *owner*, doesn't change the fact that you're still a woman. And women," he went on, skimming his hand up her rib cage to her breast, "are made for certain things."

Jewel tossed her head scornfully, but Tor took her face in his hands and held her steady. Bending his own head, he kissed her, not at all like the last time. His lips were astonishingly gentle as they moved over hers, tasting, nibbling, seducing, while his dark eyes remained open, watching her.

"Don't!" she breathed, but the moment her lips were parted he slipped his tongue inside. His head dipped and his tongue grazed hers, and the heat and wetness made her gasp. She pushed away from him in a panic and was surprised when he let her go.

"You see?" he taunted softly, but Jewel was too caught up in her own angry shame to notice that his voice was not entirely steady either.

"You—you—"

Words failed her. As well, she could no longer stand there flaying him with the heat of her anger while he rose naked and gloriously male before her. She was out of her depth and it was awful to know that.

"If you need a woman," she spat, "there's plenty down in the village. Be my guest."

The door slammed violently behind her.

Chapter Seven

"Put that in here, will you? And try to get me an estimate by next week."

"Aye, miss."

Jewel watched from astride her mount as Sandy Sinclair slipped the soil samples into her saddlebag. Mist swirled around her, spangling her hair and spiking her long lashes into stars. Beneath the hem of her riding habit, her boots were caked with mud.

"There." Slapping his hands free of dirt, Sandy stepped back. With an air of satisfaction, he surveyed the newly plowed field in front of them. "Should be seein' summat pokin' through in a week or two."

"I hope so. Shall we go?"

"Aye."

Reaching down from the saddle, Jewel tucked the flap over the leather bag, then straightened.

"Pardon my askin'," Sandy said hesitantly, "but is aught amiss?"

Jewel went still. "Why do you ask?"

He flushed. "I—ahem—Ye seem rather distracted this morning."

She assured him that she was fine, that she had slept a little poorly last night, while inwardly she fumed. This was Tor Cameron's fault! He was the reason she'd tossed and turned all night; it was his fault that even now her lips felt puffy, as though a bee had stung them, and that she'd awakened in one of the worst moods ever—as Annie had so kindly pointed out to her at breakfast.

"Are ye certain ye're not gettin' ill, miss?" Concern made Sandy brave enough to persist, although normally he wouldn't have dared. But no one could fail to notice the smudges beneath Mistress Jewel's lovely eyes, or the fact that she went about without her usual buoyant step.

She did her best to give him a bracing smile. "I'm truly fine, Sandy, though I appreciate your concern. But I would like to take a look at this soil. You'll not mind if I ride ahead?"

"No, miss."

Jewel determinedly set the big drafter trotting toward the manor house, which was nestled in a copse of trees at the bottom of the glen. She could feel Sandy's worried gaze upon her and was glad that he had accompanied her on foot while she rode horseback. Sandy never rode because he was terrified of horses, and for once she was grateful for his annoying cowardice. It prevented her from having to answer any more of his questions.

She kept her head high although inwardly she was filled with a growing sense of hopelessness. What would have happened if she hadn't managed to defuse Tor's violent passions last night? Would he have raped her? In the sleepless hours of the night before she had come to the disturbing conclusion that, aye, he probably would have.

The likelihood didn't bear thinking about. Raped. Ravished by the husband of her own choosing, a filthy convict whom Jewel herself had released from prison. He wouldn't dare!

Would he?

There was no denying the dismaying truth that for a few awful moments yesterday evening the tables had been turned, and it had been Tor who had been in control of the situation, not her. Worse, he had proved himself a bold adversary, and a dangerous one. If he could be so now, still weakened by illness and the lingering effects of imprisonment, what would he be like when he recovered fully?

Jewel's heart skipped a beat at the thought, and she would have cried then if her tears hadn't been exhausted from the night before. Aye, she had actually wept after fleeing to her room last night; wept not with fear or anger but with humiliation, the sheer humiliation of knowing that, for the briefest of moments, she had actually responded—responded!—to Tor's tender kiss.

Not that first one, which had left her reeling and brutalized, but that other one, when he had held her face in his hands and let her know the shivery sweetness of taste and texture and mingling breaths so that her blood had heated in a strange, primal response. One kiss, only one, and yet it had sent her fleeing as his nakedness and his mockery had not, to spend the rest of the evening in her room, unable to face anyone, crying like a stupid, inexperienced lass and cursing him by turns.

She had slept eventually, uneasily, and gotten up in a thoroughly foul mood. There hadn't been a chance during breakfast to consider what she would do in the future to keep Tor in his place. She had had a hard enough time just keeping her wits about her so that Annie wouldn't suspect something was amiss.

But Annie was no fool, and Jewel quailed inwardly whenever she thought of the telltale bruises that darkened her wrist where Tor had grabbed her when he had first flung aside the blankets and gotten out of bed. Furthermore she didn't have to look in a mirror to know that her lips were swollen and that there were sleepless shadows beneath her eyes.

She didn't doubt for a minute that Annie had noticed and that she would be reaching some very disturbing conclusions of her own. There would be lectures forthcoming, Jewel knew, and warnings and accusations, but she was not about to listen to them or admit that Annie and Tykie had been right all along. This marriage was going to work; she'd make sure of that, because she wasn't going to give up Drumcorrie or her place at the head of the household no matter what her servants might think, or what that big, hulking beast in the Jacobite suite believed!

Through the larch trees below, the chimneys of the house came into view. As always, Tykie stood in the courtyard waiting, and Jewel smiled brightly as she halted her mount beside him. Tykie smiled back, unlike Annie sensing nothing amiss. Perhaps, for Tor Cameron's sake, it was just as well.

"I've brought samples," Jewel told him, patting the bulging saddlebag. "We'll look at them after lunch."

Tykie nodded. The MacKenzies of Glen Chulish were farmers of long standing. Their legendary skills lay in the use of the plowshare and hoe, not in the wielding of heraldic Highland weapons. As a child, Jewel had been taught that the soil's ability to repel the moisture of constant mist and rain affected the yield of the barley Drumcorrie harvested for its whiskey. She had learned the importance of putting back into the land the nutrients that the crops took out: cattle bones ground into meal, dung from the stables, and a yearly sprinkling of ash from the peat fires, as well as the importance of testing the soil to make certain that the percentage of clay and sand had not outstripped the rich, earthy loam.

But Jewel had no interest in her soil today. Two floors above the courtyard where she stood lay the dormers of Tor's bedroom, and she kept her head bowed as she hurried inside. As far as she was concerned, she'd prefer never to lay eyes on the horny goat again!

That other Goat, Annie's bad-tempered Scottish terrier, was pacing about in the hall. The moment Jewel came in he dragged his paws across her skirts and barked insistently for attention.

"What is it?" she demanded peevishly.

Goat raced ahead of her toward the library. Tapping the whip impatiently against her skirts, Jewel followed. The library door stood open. A peat fire burned in the grate. Jewel paused on the threshold to peer cautiously inside.

She saw at once what had agitated the terrier: a tall man with gaunt features who whipped about at the soft rustle of her skirts. The hand that had been reaching for a book fell quickly to his side.

Tor and Jewel stared at one another with mutual hostility. She had no way of knowing that he had only just worked up enough courage to step into this forbidden realm. He had stood on the threshold where Jewel now stood for countless minutes simply looking his fill, and not daring to step inside. But Jewel only noticed—with no small measure of resentment—that he looked cursedly well rested. Doubtless he had slept deeply the night before!

She had no idea that he, too, had paced the floor for hours after her furious exit, grappling with his own temper and the crying out of a male body too long unfulfilled. After an equally restless night he had bathed in the icy water of the basin and shaved the stubble from his jaw with the razor on the stand, and wondered what to do with the young hellion who was his wife.

He would have to exercise caution, for one thing. The first time he'd kissed her last night he'd been thinking with his loins, and that had availed him no more than a punch in the eye. But that second time . . . He smiled grimly, recalling how a mere kiss had changed everything between them, even if only for the briefest of moments. Whereas earlier he had been reduced nearly to tears by his own weakness, he had felt himself empowered simply by Jewel's reaction to that slow, tantalizing kiss. Aye, he was still a man, and it felt good to make that discovery.

Furthermore, he'd not be going down to the village to avail himself of the women there. No, when he finally appeased the long-denied needs of his body it would be with that poison-haired wench who'd been tormenting him from the moment he'd first laid eyes on her. Only the next time he had her alone in his room he'd not let his loins control his head.

That decided, he had found himself bolstered with enough courage to venture from his room and descend the stairs, this time without a trace of the weakness that had left him gasping on the bottom step the day before. Fortunately no one had been about and he had crossed to the library, where he had lingered on the threshold for some time before finally stepping inside. He had just reached for a volume of Chaucer's *Canterbury Tales* when the door had opened and Jewel appeared.

She was the last person Tor had expected to see. One look at her, and his newfound confidence vanished like mist over the mountains. Because just by looking at her, Tor wanted her again.

She had obviously been riding. Mud spattered the hem of her habit, and her cheeks were flushed with the wind and the cold. Her eyes, those maddeningly tilted eyes, glowed brighter than the fire, and the dampness in the air had left her reddish hair curling riotously about her head. Worse, Tor could see the stamp of his possession in the bruises on her wrist and in the swollen lips from which he had drunk so deeply the night before. Desire burned darkly through his veins. And with it, anger. He would not be imprisoned again, by God! Certainly not with lust for this snippet of a lass!

Jewel, too, was finding it impossible to stop thinking about last night. Looking at Tor's hands, she recalled how they had imprisoned her and boldly touched her breasts. She remembered how that carnal mouth had ravished hers, and how his body had betrayed his lust in a manner that even now left her burning with embarrassment.

At her heels, Goat whimpered. The sound stirred Jewel into action. "What the devil are you doing here?"

"I'm looking for something to read," he responded in a voice so ominous that Goat tucked his tail between his legs and slunk behind Jewel's skirts.

"I wouldn't have thought you the sort of man to care for books, Mr. Cameron."

"I thought you'd specified a prisoner who could read, Mrs. Cameron?"

He noted with satisfaction how the use of her married name struck a nerve. Jewel's little chin went up another notch while the color rushed to her cheeks.

"You are, of course, welcome to any books you find here. Only remember to return them when you're through."

As if he'd dream of stealing them! Tor glowered as the heat climbed to his face. Damn the bitch!

He whirled to tell her exactly that, but Jewel was gone.

* * *

It turned out to be a long and exhausting day. Jewel kept to her father's study, fingers cramped over the ledgers as she worked to update records neglected during her absence in Glasgow. But try as she might, she could not ignore the fact that everything had changed since she'd left. Even the house seemed different now that Tor Cameron was living under her roof. Despite the fact that he had withdrawn to his rooms after leaving the library and hadn't shown himself again, his presence somehow made itself felt by everyone in the household. Jewel had never known her staff to be so jumpy and irritable.

What bothered her most was the realization that she, too, had changed. Her peace of mind and her sense of well-being and safety had vanished forever with this man's coming. She had been wrong to bring him here, just as everyone had said.

Wearily she laid the pen aside and propped her head in her hands. Whatever shall I do now? she asked herself forlornly.

She thought of sending Tor back to Cowcadden, but just as quickly rejected the idea. She would never return him to a place like that, no matter how tempting the thought!

Perhaps she could give him a sack of coins and send him on his way? Surely he must have had some sort of life before he'd landed in prison. But what, and where, had that been? Jewel realized suddenly how very little she knew about him. Imprisoned for striking a nobleman, the Cowcadden gaoler had told her. What exactly did that mean? And why had he done so?

I don't know, Jewel thought angrily, and I don't care! All she wanted at the moment was to rid herself of the man. Now. At once, before another day could run its course. She wanted Drumcorrie back to herself, wanted to feel safe and secure in her own home once again.

But how could she? For better or worse, Tor was here to stay. There was no other way. The reasons that had compelled her to travel to Glasgow in the first place existed still. She needed a strong man beside her to help her hold on to Drumcorrie.

But only now was Jewel MacKenzie Cameron coming to realize at what cost.

Now it was evening, and a misty darkness was settling over the land. Tykie shivered as he drove the cattle into the byre and helped Piers MacInnis bed down the horses for the night. In the kitchen, Annie supervised the scrubbing of the floor and the big oak table, and dismissed the weary maids when they were through. Her terrier, Goat, and the house cats settled down to an uneasy truce before the fire, and high up in the garret, Drumcorrie's resident house mouse ate the cheese that Jewel had secretly laid out for it, and cleaned its whiskers with tiny paws.

Jewel herself had withdrawn to her rooms, which lay at the far end of the corridor from the Jacobite suite occupied by her husband. She had locked the door and had just removed the combs from her hair when a loud crash shook the floorboards. Reaching for the candle, Jewel hurried down the hallway and knocked on the suite's double door.

"Cameron?"

No answer.

"Cameron!"

A low moan, as though he were in pain.

Cautiously, Jewel pushed down on the latch and stepped inside. Her jaw dropped as she looked around her. Oh, the great idiot! Somehow he had succeeded in knocking over the armoire, and now he sat on the edge of the bed, nursing his battered head.

"What on earth were you doing?" Jewel demanded, stepping over the scattered drawers and halting in front of him.

Tor didn't answer. He just groaned.

Setting down the candle, Jewel pushed his hands aside. There was a cut on his brow from which the blood was oozing. Grimly she climbed back over the armoire and went to the washbowl. Dipping and squeezing out a cloth, she retraced her steps.

"Ouch! Leave me alone!"

"You're bleeding!" she snapped, pushing aside his hands once again. Seizing his jaw, she held him still while she cleaned the wound.

"You could at least be a wee bit gentle!"

"What for? 'Tis the least you deserve for wrecking the furniture!" But she obliged him by dabbing more carefully. "What on earth were you doing?"

"Chasing a mouse."

Her hand stilled. "What?"

"I said I was chasing a mouse!" His eyes bored into hers, as though daring her to laugh.

"Not a little brown one!" she cried with a catch in her breath.

"What other colors are there?" Tor snapped. "I caught him scurrying around in one of the drawers. Now leave me alone, will you?"

"Y-you didn't kill him, did you?"

"No, damn it! Next time I will."

"You can't!"

"Good God, why ever not?"

"Because h-he's a pet!"

"A pet?" Tor's eyes seemed to burn her with scorn. "Are you daft, lass? Why, in prison—"

But he broke off abruptly and turned away, and Jewel could see the tensing of his jaw and the way his Adam's apple bobbed as he swallowed convulsively. Her heart swelled with sudden understanding. Oh, God, what must things have been like in Cowcadden to leave this man with such an irrational fear of mice?

She had a sudden, piercing vision of Tor's dank prison cell swarming with rats that waited in the darkness with glowing eyes for the chance to wrest away the few scraps of food given to a weakened prisoner. Or even, driven by starvation, attacking more than the food . . .

She gasped and put her hands to her mouth.

"Don't," he said harshly. "Don't feel sorry for me! Haven't I told you that before? Leave me the hell alone, will you?"

Jewel had been kneeling in front of him as he sat on the edge of the bed. Now he seized her wrists and pulled her savagely upright. "Go on! Get out of here!"

Struggling to maintain her balance as he whirled her about, she tripped over her skirts instead and went crashing against him. "Now look what you've done, you great, braw idiot!" she raged.

Tor looked, and realized all at once that she had come to his room with her hair unpinned. The wild red-gold length of it spilled over her shoulders and down to her waist. He had never seen her that way before, and had to admit that it was a wantonly beautiful sight. As was the rest of her, which happened to be pressed very intimately against him. He cursed aloud as desire began burning a slow path through his blood. His fingers caressed the flesh of her wrists, where he could feel her pulse pounding with sudden fright, for she had seen the look that crept into his eyes and knew what it meant.

"Please don't."

It was barely a whisper. Ignoring it, he released her wrists and took her by the hips so that he could fit her more boldly to the length of him. Jewel could feel the heat of his erection burning through her clothes.

"Don't!" she repeated. It was a breathless plea.

With a forefinger, Tor tipped up her chin. His touch was surprisingly gentle as he caressed the slim line of her jaw, even though desire pounded through him. "What are you afraid of?"

"N-nothing!"

"Then kiss me. I won't hurt you."

"The hell you won't!"

She tried to wrench free, but Tor bent quickly to slip his arm beneath her knees. Lifting her against his chest he held her imprisoned while he lowered his mouth to hers. "No more punching." His breath gusted against her lips as he grated out his command. "No cursing, no kicking, no poking out my eyes."

So she bit him. Hard.

Yelping, he dropped her onto the bed, then threw himself on top of her as she tried to squirm away. Seizing her wrists, he trapped her arms high above her head.

"You'll pay for that."

Her eyes blazed. "I'll scream!"

His lip was bleeding. He turned his head and spat. "Go ahead, scream! Let the rest of the household know exactly what I'm doing to you! Let them know that every one of their fears has come dismally true. A man from Cowcadden is a man without scruples, Jewel MacKenzie Cameron; didn't they tell you that?"

Of course they had. In fact, his taunting words so accurately echoed everything that had been said to her that she sagged like a rag doll. Tears glittered in the corners of her eyes as she turned her face away.

"There's no need to scream," Tor added, bringing himself under control again. "Or cry. Let me show you. Let me—"

The kiss that followed drowned out everything he meant to say. Oh, God, he had only to touch his mouth to hers, to feel the rapid rise and fall of her breasts against his chest, and everything else was forgotten.

Groaning, he spread himself fully across her. Both of them were clothed, but it took no time at all for him to strip the gown from her body. He made short work of her corset and chemise, and his own clothing. When they were both naked, he pressed himself upon her so that his manhood throbbed against her belly.

Jewel turned her head aside, embarrassed by his nakedness, and her own. She wasn't about to cry out. No, she'd sooner die than summon help, sooner submit to this mindless lust of his than live with the shame of having Annie or Tykie rush to her aid and find her this way!

And yet . . . and yet . . .

There was something oddly exciting about feeling Tor's throbbing member against the skin of her belly. Her body was reacting in a strange way, her limbs growing weighted and her nipples rising taut. A drugging warmth seemed to invade her blood, spreading everywhere, so that the very core of her womanhood seemed to soften in response.

Above her Tor's dark head dipped to her breasts. Jewel gasped and jerked reflexively as his tongue laved one rosebud peak, then the other. His mouth moved lower, to her belly, his breath hot against her skin.

"There," he panted. "There, you see?" Transferring both of her wrists into one big hand, he skimmed his free hand down her rib cage. Practiced fingers found their way between her thighs, and as his mouth took hers again he slipped inside to stroke.

"Oh!" Jewel's eyes opened wide in shock. Her body

twisted like a leaf in the wind and she jerked and gasped as Tor continued his assault. She was trembling by the time he reared over her and released her wrists at last.

"Now," he said between ragged breaths, "now you'll see what all of them meant—"

Slipping his hands beneath her buttocks, he tipped her hips toward him. Jaw tensed as he strove to go slowly, he eased himself inside.

He was huge, and despite the silken slickness with which he had readied her, she gasped aloud. With his mouth covering hers the sound was muffled, but he heard it nonetheless. Panting, he levered onto an elbow and held himself still. His eyes were glazed and he trembled with the effort of holding back. Jewel lay quivering beneath him, and his harsh expression eased a little as he brushed the hair from her brow with a clumsy hand.

"Steady," he whispered. "Steady."

Drawing a shaky breath he moved slowly within her, burrowing deeply, then drawing back oh so carefully to fill her again. The pain had ebbed, but the fullness of him did not. Only when Jewel's taut body began accepting his possession did he lower himself fully upon her. The pace increased, an intimate stroking rhythm that fitted them belly to belly, thigh to thigh.

After a moment Jewel opened her eyes to look at him. She was astonished to see that his hard, frightening face had been transformed. The tension and the strain had eased so that he looked haunted no longer, but almost . . . tender as he moved inside her, filling her again and yet again. A feeling of wonder came over her as she sensed that she herself was somehow responsible for the change in him.

Even more unbelievable was the fact that what he was doing to her was no longer painful, not even remotely loathsome. The fullness of him, the strength and size of his maleness, was in some inexplicable way exciting. Still watching his impassioned expression, Jewel lifted her hips the next time he thrust into her.

Tor's face went rigid.

Jewel moved beneath him again, and this time her body reacted to his shuddering response. Something was happening inside her, something that was making her tingle all over, bringing a strange and wonderful ache to that very place where Tor was embedded. Her eyes drifted shut and she lifted her arms to run her fingers over the bunched muscles of his forearms.

The moment she touched him Tor's passion exploded. With an agonized groan he turned his face away as his body convulsed. Arching, he erupted within her, emptying himself in a raging tide that all but turned him inside out.

"Oh!" Jewel's eyes widened and she gasped and clung to him, but all too soon it was over. Tor collapsed on top of her, utterly spent, and the pinpricks of sensation that had begun dancing through Jewel's veins promptly disappeared.

He lay without moving, groaning a little, and Jewel felt the warm stickiness of his essence seeping between her legs. Her throat ached and tears stung the back of her eyes. While she'd been humiliated last night after he'd done no more than kiss her, then this feeling of having been used was worse than anything. The moment his throbbing member slipped out of her body she wriggled out from under him.

Tor shot upright as she rolled away. Seizing her wrists he pulled her back. That was when both of them noticed the blood. The bedside candle had been left burning, and there it was, darkening her thighs, marking his. Their eyes met for a shattering moment. Then Jewel uttered a strangled sound and fled.

She spent the night huddled beneath the meagre covers of a bed in an unused room at the end of the hall, hiding there in case he came looking for her. Fortunately he did not, but there was no comfort in that. The only comfort she had, in fact, was knowing that Tor hadn't noticed what had happened to her during his own overwhelming release, the way she had gasped and clung to him, straining toward something that had hovered just out of reach, something that she sensed would continue to elude her without him, only him.

She slept at last, fitfully, and got up long before Annie, who was always the first in the household to rise. Sneaking down to the kitchen barefoot and wrapped in an old plaid, she scrubbed her aching body clean in the icy pail by the door, and vowed that she would extract her revenge on Tor Ban Cameron in the most awful way she knew how.

Chapter Eight

Tor's expression was savage as he slammed the front door behind him and stepped outside for the first time since being brought to Glen Chulish. Bleak daylight was just beginning to brighten the mountain peaks, and an icy wind blew from the north. Pausing on the doorstep, he sniffed the scent of peat and pine and damp earth that was carried upon it. Abruptly he went still. His anger ebbed, and he inhaled again, drawing the scent deep into his lungs.

Oh, God. How long had it been since he had smelled such fragrant air? How long since the fetid stink of Glasgow had faded from his nostrils? Forgetting his anguish over last night, he looked around him, drinking in sights that he had last seen only in dreams.

Craggy mountains surrounded the glen, their peaks lost amid silvery clouds. On the hillsides, the winter grass was greening. A burn thundered near the house, the icy water swollen with melting snow.

The low stone stable that Tor had glimpsed so often from his rooms was nestled amid a copse of larches a short distance from the manor house, and further away, in the gentle cup of the valley, stood what must be Drumcorrie's distillery, with its numerous stone chimneys and outlying buildings.

Tor had no desire to explore any of them. He cared for nothing at the moment save the wonder of simply standing there and savoring the scents and sounds overwhelming his senses. No matter how foul his mood since Jewel had fled his room hours earlier, he had to admit that life had taken a turn for the better the moment he stepped outside. Last night he had experienced the piercing pleasure of being a man once again, and right at this moment, for the first time in far longer than he cared to remember, he was standing in achingly beautiful freedom. How could he not fail to let go of his anger?

Turning his back to the rising sun, Tor let his gaze travel southward. Somewhere over those mountains lay the city of Edinburgh. But how far? He had no idea. Jewel had never told him where, exactly, Glen Chulish lay.

Tor's jaw tensed the moment he thought of his wife. His elation faded. What was it about that bloody redhead that made him lose all sense of reason? That had made him pace his room for hours, sleepless, after he had pleasured himself inside her so completely?

A guilty conscience, believe it or not. And why? Because of the mere fact that he hadn't thought to pleasure her in turn. Oh, he had readied her, of course, but that had been for his own sake. He had behaved little better than a crazed animal in possessing her last night, and he had seen the loathing and disgust in Jewel's expression as she slipped out from under him and fled the room. It was obvious to him that she hated and feared everything he had done to her in bed.

Only, Tor knew perfectly well that a woman didn't have to be afraid. Not if she was loved with a gentle hand. He had always thought himself a considerate lover, had always managed to enhance his own enjoyment by making certain his women enjoyed themselves in equal measure. Surely it wouldn't prove impossible to be gentle with Jewel? Surely next time, the long months of abstinence would not come into play and he would not be caught up in a mindless passion that left him incapable of anything save appeasing the urgency of his own release?

What angered him, too, was the nagging suspicion that Jewel herself had somehow been responsible for inflaming his runaway passions. Bah! For most of the sleepless hours of the night just gone he had tried convincing himself that this was utter nonsense, that the same thing would have happened if he'd lain with any other woman, even an ugly one! Granted, Jewel MacKenzie Cameron was a tempting beauty, but she had lain rigid and unwilling beneath him, a quivering virgin who had fled in tears at the sight of her own blood. Was this a woman made for enticement?

Bah, Tor thought again.

Hands balled into fists, he strode away down the drive. His lungs burned with exertion as he crossed the rushing burn by way of a footbridge and started up the hill. He would stay here at Drumcorrie only long enough to recover his strength, he vowed to himself, and then he'd be off to Edinburgh, first to seek vengeance on the nobleman who had been responsible for landing him in prison, then to finish what he had started before that.

Out of breath, he halted at last amid a copse of larches halfway up the slope. Here, a low stone wall ran the length of a grassy meadow. Sighing, Tor settled himself on a boulder and turned his face to the sun. Closing his eyes, he sat without moving, listening to the distant bleating of sheep above the whistling of the wind through the grass.

Eventually his pounding heartbeat slowed. His breathing quieted. Gradually he became aware of someone singing in a lusty voice somewhere close by. Reluctantly he opened his eyes.

Not far down the slope a man in a kilt was repairing a crumbling portion of a stone wall. He had gathered a cairn of rocks together and was fitting them methodically one on top of the other. His shoulders were stooped as he worked, and the sunlight glinted on his balding head.

Accepting the inevitable, Tor rose and strolled over to see him. His presence did not seem to startle the older man, for he had obviously been aware of Tor far longer than Tor had been aware of him.

"Mornin'," he said, straightening. He was bearded and weathered and far older than Tor.

Tor returned the greeting warily.

"Rain's been heavy," the old man added. "Took awa' half the stones last week. I dinna want the beasties gettin' oot."

Tor assumed that he meant the sheep.

"Have a drink?"

Inclining his head, Tor accepted the flask and drank deeply. He had expected water. It was hot tea. Scalded and spluttering, he set the flask aside and met the laughing eyes of the bearded man. Rather than the flash of irritation he expected to feel, he found himself grinning back. "I think I've burned a path clear to my belly."

The other man laughed appreciatively. "Me missus always brews the tay too hot. Sorry. Name's Angus. 'Ee be?"

"Tor Cameron."

"Och, aye. Mistress Jewel's mon."

Tor warily accepted the proffered hand. "You've heard of me, then?"

"Och, aye. Mistress Jewel met 'ee in Glasgow, our Annie said."

"Annie Brewster?"

"Aye. She be cousin tae th' missus. Stands godmither tae th' grandchildren." Whistling, Angus turned back to his stones. That was all he seemed inclined to say on the subject of Jewel's marriage.

"Can I give you a hand?" Tor offered, relieved.

"If ye like."

As a matter of fact, Tor did. He could not remember when he had last indulged in something that was pure physical labor, although he had always enjoyed working hard. The long months in Cowcadden had softened him, however, and he found himself starting to sweat profusely even while Angus, at twice his age and more, enthusiastically hefted enormous stones beside him. Still, Tor welcomed the hard work, and they proceeded to patch the wall in companionable silence.

As the hours slipped by, the sun rose higher and the air warmed. Angus rolled up his sleeves and Tor removed his shirt. They shared what was left of the tea. When they were finished with the wall, Angus collapsed in the grass. With a groan, Tor stretched out beside him. Grinning, he gestured toward the older man's attire.

"I thought the wearing of kilts was illegal."

Angus grinned back. "Aye. But they dinna come here much nowadays, the soldiers."

"Glen Chulish suffered, then, after the forty-five?"

"Aye."

"The people at Drumcorrie, too?"

Angus's expression clouded. "We all did."

Thinking of Tykie's mutilated tongue, Tor said

nothing more. The '45 was not a subject one discussed like harmless gossip, even nowadays.

A piercing whistle sounded from the trees below. Angus sat up, brightening. "That'll be Jamie."

"Jamie?" Tor was still extremely wary of strangers.

"Aye. Oldest o' me first daughter's bairns. He'll be comin' wi' lunch. Ye'll share wi' me?"

Tor leaned back, relaxing. "I'd be honored."

They could hear singing now, a stirring tune that Tor recognized as one of those patriotic Highland ballads long banned by the English king. Surprisingly, there were two voices raised in song: one the unsteady warbling of a lad on the cusp of puberty, the other a soprano so sweet that Tor was moved despite himself.

"Never a serious moment, the two o' 'em," Angus complained with a grin.

Through the trees below, Tor could see the big, ugly draft horse that belonged to Jewel trotting smartly uphill. A curly-headed lad bearing a strong resemblance to his grandfather sat barefoot on the crupper. In front of him, skirts hitched scandalously to her knees as she sat astride like a man, rode Jewel MacKenzie Cameron. The two of them had been singing with gusto, but the moment she spotted Tor in the clearing above, Jewel's voice stilled. The animation left her face and her jaw tightened ominously.

Angus cast a probing glance at Tor but did not speak. Rising to his feet he brushed the grass from his kilt. "Ye be early, lad!"

"I met Mistress Jewel on the way," Jamie called back. "She gave me a lift."

" 'Twas kind of 'ee," Angus remarked as Jewel halted the big drafter beside him. "And good day to 'ee, too."

"Hello, Angus." Jewel glanced haughtily at Tor.

"Good morning, Mr. Cameron."

Tor didn't trust himself to reply just yet. He had seen the way the light had faded from Jewel's eyes at the sight of him, and he was annoyed by the fact that it could bother him so much. Still, his silence was obvious, hovering icily between them.

Angus brought an end to the awkward moment by stepping forward and helping his grandson from the drafter's back. "This be Jamie, me oldest grandson. Here, make a bow to Master Cameron, lad."

Jamie smiled and bobbed his head. He was barely fourteen, and his freckled face was unclouded by cares. "Welcome to Glen Chulish, sir."

"Thank you," Tor said gravely. No one else had ever welcomed him before.

"Will ye break bread with us, mistress?" Angus invited, smiling at Jewel as he helped her dismount.

She smiled back at him and there was no mistaking to the watching Tor that they were extremely fond of each other. "Sorry, I can't. I'm on my way home. I passed Jamie on the trail and offered him a lift."

"And where've ye been?"

Jewel's smile faded and she cast a sullen glance at Tor. "Taking the air."

At this hour? Fortunately Jamie stepped in to fill the silence by patting the bulging satchel he carried over his shoulder. "I've brought good things to eat, Grandfaither."

"I'm certain ye have. 'Tis just as well. Master Cameron has agreed tae join us."

"He has?" Jewel asked, astonished.

"Why? Do you object?" Tor demanded sharply.

She had the good grace to blush. "No."

"Then if you'll excuse us?"

She bristled at his arrogance, but was glad at the same time for the anger that coursed through her. It

111

gave her the excuse she needed to turn her back on him so that she didn't have to look at him anymore, because she didn't want him guessing how disconcerted she was to find him here with Angus, bare chested and disheveled and looking disturbingly handsome to boot. She hadn't failed to notice how much he had filled out in the last few days, thanks to adequate rest and Annie's good cooking. And she found the sheen of sweat on his naked chest profoundly unsettling. It made her think of him in a purely physical way—which was the last thing on earth she wanted, especially after what had happened between them last night!

Rutting stag! Why hadn't he left her alone? And why couldn't he remember the most simple of courtly manners right now and cover himself in front of a lady?

"Will ye be stayin'?" Angus was asking Tor. "Or do ye wish tae ride back wi' Mistress Jewel?"

"Aboard that elephant? Hardly."

Jewel bristled. "I'll have you know that Drum comes from a long and very noble line of destriers. And I'll bet you a guinea you haven't a clue what—"

"I know perfectly well what destriers are," Tor shot back. "They're horses that were bred throughout Scotland in medieval times to carry knights and their heavy armor into war."

"Drum would have made a grand warhorse," Jewel snapped, quelling the urge to stick her tongue out at him. Curse him, he seemed to have the knack of making her look the fool!

"Indeed. He's so ugly that he would have sent every last one of the enemy's mounts spooking in the opposite direction."

Jamie snickered. Jewel, glaring, looped the reins over the drafter's thick neck. Angus gallantly hoisted her into the saddle, and when she was seated, her habit demurely in place, she graced the old man with a warm smile. "Enjoy your lunch, Angus. And thank you. The wall looks grand."

"Thank Master Cameron. He lent a braw hand."

But Tor was not granted the same sweet smile. Jewel's eyes narrowed with hauteur as she turned her gaze upon him. "I'm very glad to see that you're good with your hands. You'll be needing them."

Tor scowled after her as she rode away through the trees. Sunlight torched her hair, and he had the sudden, unwanted vision of the way it had looked the night before, spilling down her shoulders and breasts and tangling in his hands as he pressed her back into the bed and loved her with a fury that even now bewildered him.

"Bloody brat," he muttered, but Angus and Jamie were laughing together as they unpacked their copious lunch, and so did not hear him.

Chapter Nine

By the time Tor returned from the fields, the sun was sinking toward the mountains. The stone fence had been mended and a friendship sealed, for Tor had told Angus more about himself in the course of the long day together than he had ever dreamed of revealing to his wife.

The chance to talk with another man had done him good. Enormous good. His mood was almost charitable as he crossed the footbridge and headed toward the house.

This was the first he had seen of the place from the outside—and perhaps his newfound friendship with Angus had something to do with it—but he could almost swear that the place looked welcoming. It was a half-timbered house, larger than Tor had originally guessed, and built of native gray stone. The roof was tiled rather than thatched, and the windows had been glazed with genuine glass, a rare luxury in this remote corner of the Highlands. A kitchen garden, well maintained by the meticulous Annie, stretched along the back, while the wing that held the library Tor so prized stretched off to the west.

A feeling of anticipation—the first in many a long year—quickened Tor's steps as he crossed the lawn and approached the massive front door. Lifting his hand to the knocker, he stopped himself in the nick of time. Ye gods, what was he doing? He didn't have to knock! Drumcorrie was his now; he had wed the woman who inherited it, hadn't he?

Turning the latch, he stepped boldly inside. A feeling of profound satisfaction rose within him as he did so. He was master of Drumcorrie now, not a starving, penniless prisoner.

Unfortunately, the feeling died the moment he crossed the portal and recognized the masculine laugh coming from the study at the end of the corridor.

Ruan MacKenzie.

And now Ruan's laughter was being joined by another's; a sweet laugh that cut to the core of his soul. Tor had never heard Jewel laugh before. He knew that he would never have the power to make her laugh himself.

Scowling ferociously, he stepped through the study door. In two swift strides he crossed to the desk, and before Ruan MacKenzie even knew what he was about, Tor had hauled him to his feet and subjected him to the most murderous look Ruan had ever experienced in his carefree young life.

To his credit, he reacted admirably well. "Am I forever to find myself dangling in your grasp, Mr. Cameron?" he asked calmly.

"As long as you dally with my wife, aye," Tor acknowledged blackly.

"Leave him alone," Jewel said sharply.

"Hold your breath, woman," Ruan told her irritably. "I can look after mysel'."

"Watch how you speak to the lady," Tor warned, giving him a shake.

"Jewel, a lady?" Ruan snickered.

"Cameron! Would you please put my cousin down?"

Tor released him so abruptly that he plummeted to his knees.

"Damn!" Ruan rose painfully and dusted off his finely tailored breeches. "There's no need for ye to play the jealous cad, Cameron!"

"I'm not jealous," Tor growled.

But it was true. He was. Just the thought of another man putting his hands on Jewel made the primitive urge to kill scorch through his gut. Seeing the scorn in her expression as she tossed her head at him only made the blood lust rise higher. Damn it, he had marked this woman, *made* her a woman, made her his. No one else had the right to touch her!

"I liked him better when he was ill," Ruan remarked from a safe distance.

"So did I." Jewel's eyes held Tor's as she spoke. She would not back down this time. Here in her father's study, where she had singlehandedly kept Drumcorrie going for the past year or more, she was mistress in her own right. She wasn't afraid of Tor or his temper here, and by now those dark, awful hours of last night were far, far away. He could not hurt, dominate, or ravish her here, and with his shirt back on and a sullen look in his eyes he wasn't half as overwhelming as he had seemed to her out on the moor with Angus.

Besides, she had just made a most startling discovery. She actually liked crossing swords with him. The act exhilarated her even while it frightened her a little. She felt as though she were doing something reckless and slightly dangerous, like jumping from the hayloft into the byre below, or climbing Ben Chulish, the highest mountain in the glen, with only a rope and a single metal pike nailed into the cliff face to keep her from falling.

Fortunately for Jewel, Ruan moved quickly to defuse the tension hovering in the air. Although he was rarely aware of anything that went on around him, thanks to his own self-absorption, he did feel the charge that crackled between his hotheaded cousin and her tall, black-haired husband.

"Ahem," he said. "Ye asked why I be here, Cameron. Well, Jewel asked me tae come. On account o' the distillery, ye ken."

"Oh?" Tor's expression was thunderous as he turned to look at Jewel. "I thought *I* was the one you wanted in the distillery."

"I wanted your muscles, not your brains," Jewel shot back.

"I suppose *he* has more than I do?" Tor countered, jerking his head in Ruan's direction.

"Hey!" Ruan protested.

Both ignored him.

"I need you for physical labor," Jewel continued tartly. "You've seen Sandy Sinclair. He's not exactly up to it, is he?"

"And I am? Two stone underweight and fresh out of gaol?"

"Annie's been fattening you up, hasn't she?"

"Are you certain I'm fat enough yet?"

A vision of his sweat-slickened chest rose before her eyes. She thrust it away with an angry toss of her head. "I surely hope so!"

"Do 'ee mind?" Ruan interrupted, hands on his hips. "I've better to do than stand here watchin' the two o' ye squabble like a pair o' banty roosters! I'd like an early start home, if—"

"Shut up," Jewel and Tor told him in unison.

Suitably cowed, Ruan slunk from the room. Jewel and Tor meanwhile, continued to stand there and glare at each other. Both were angry and defensive, and were itching to hurt each other.

"You're spoiled rotten, do you ken that?" Tor demanded at last.

"And you're a skinny weakling!"

"I've good reason for that!"

"Well, so have I!"

"Oh?"

Hot words surged to Jewel's lips, but she bit them back. She was too proud to tell him about her childhood, about her father and her aunt and the events that had led her to make the trip to Cowcadden. Besides, he'd never believe them anyway.

She searched for a better attack. "At least I'm not a filthy animal, the way you are!"

Tor's expression turned to stone, for he had understood at once what she meant. Slowly he moved toward her, reminding her of a panther stalking its prey.

"Filthy, am I?" he demanded roughly, halting in front of her. The heat of his big body enveloped her. His breath pelted her face. In that moment he really did seem untoward and feral to her. And menacing.

"I didn't mean—" she began, feeling slightly ashamed, but he wouldn't let her speak.

"If you find me so . . . filthy," he went on in a deceptively silky tone, "why don't you bathe me again? After all, you've done it before, and without suffering a qualm of conscience, I might add. Strange behavior for a supposedly sheltered virgin, don't you think?"

Jewel recoiled as though he had struck her. Her breath hitched and the color drained from her cheeks. She turned from him without speaking.

Tor was immediately sorry. Making fun of her in

that way was no way to humble her. "Jewel, wait."

He'd never said her name quite like that before, and it brought an odd constriction to her throat. But before she could respond, a shadow fell across the threshold. Both of them turned. It was Tykie, summoned by Ruan, rushing headlong from the kitchen to rescue his beloved mistress. Halting in the doorway, he immediately saw the tears glimmering in Jewel's eyes. With a soundless bellow he charged into the room. All of the pent-up frustrations, the doubts and hatred he felt for Tor Ban Cameron were unleashed in that single moment.

Tor saw it coming, but there was no way to stop Tykie Ferguson during a headlong rampage. There was time only to react with his wits, and fortunately Tor's had always been keen. Stepping aside at the very last moment, he put out his foot and sent Tykie sprawling.

The floorboards shook as Tykie went down. Jewel screamed and ran to him, but before she could reach him Tykie scrambled upright, shaking himself like a dog coming out of deep water. Lowering his head he charged again, like a bull maddened by the toreador's cape.

This time Tor misjudged the speed of the big man's approach. Sidestepping just a moment too late, he heard the bones of his rib cage crack as Tykie's head plowed into his chest.

"Oof!"

The breath whooshed out of him in a huge rush as he crashed against the desk. But he was up again instantly, fists at the ready. He might be weakened after long months in prison, but there was nothing wrong with his reaction time or his will.

Or, apparently, his strength. Tykie went down a second time as a well-aimed blow clipped him neatly on the jaw. Staggering upright, he wiped the blood from his lips. With a bizarre roar, he came at Tor again.

This time Tor met him halfway, blood lust boiling through his veins. Oh, God, it felt good, so damnably good, to vent his frustrations like this!

They rolled around the room, knocking over the furniture and smashing the bric-a-brac equally as often as each other.

It was doubtful that the fight would have ended before one or both of them were unconscious if Jewel hadn't put a stop to it by snatching an ancient fowling piece from the mantel. The weapon was old but the powder was dry and the flint in good order. The explosion as she fired it into the air was deafening, the flash all but blinding. Clouds of smoke wafted to the ceiling as Tykie and Tor fell to their knees, overcome by a fit of coughing.

Footsteps sounded in the corridor outside. A breathless Piers and Annie appeared in the doorway with a gaggle of wide-eyed servants behind. The clearing smoke revealed Tor kneeling by the hearth nursing his aching ribs while Tykie lay sprawled on the rug nearby cradling his throbbing jaw.

Ruan pushed his way inside. "Well, that be that," he pronounced, as pleased as though he himself had brought an end to the fighting. "Put the gun down, Coz, afore ye kill someone. Oh, and do ye suppose we could hae a bite to eat? I confess to a powerful hunger."

"Sit still!"

Annie's voice was little better than an imperious bark.

Tor, who had been trained as a soldier to obey orders, stiffened immediately. And sucked in his breath as Annie's probing fingers found the pain in his side.

"Leave be, woman!"

"Aye, 'tis cracked a'right. Mistress Jewel, the bindings."

In silence Jewel handed her the bandages. Retreating to the doorway, she watched as Annie removed Tor's shirt. He was sitting on a stool in front of her, his left eye beginning to swell and turn black.

"Lift yer arms."

Tor obeyed, wincing.

Unmercifully, Annie began to wrap the length of binding tightly about his ribs. Over her bent head, Tor's eyes found Jewel's where she stood amid the shadows.

"This is all your fault."

Her jaw dropped. "Mine? You've got some bloody nerve, Cameron! If you hadn't started in on Ruan—"

"If you had reined in your watchhound—"

"Are you calling Tykie a dog?"

"That, among other things."

"Why, you miserable—"

"Hush yer faces! Both o' ye!"

Annie's voice was like the crack of a whip. Tor found himself blushing like a schoolboy and dropping his eyes beneath her fearsome glare. Good God, the woman was a terror!

But Annie wasn't finished yet. "Clawin' and scrappin' like cats i' the henhoose!" she shrilled at them. "And I dinna mean Tykie, neither! I mean both o' ye, man an' wife, though ye be worse than a pair o' bairns! Mistress Jewel!"

Jewel straightened meekly. "Aye?"

"Fetch the ointment for me. Do ye ken the one I mean?"

Oh, aye, Jewel did. Annie meant the salve that she mixed in her stillroom, the one that smelled worse than something that had crawled under the floorboards and died. Oh, how she relished the thought of watching the expression on Cameron's face when

121

Annie smeared it on his swelling eye!

She tripped gladly to the kitchen to fetch it. Breathless, she knelt beside Tor's stool and offered it with a flourish.

He glared at her with his one good eye. "Nice to know you're so eager to nurse me."

"I wouldn't miss this for the world," she assured him smugly. Sitting down, she rested her chin on her updrawn knees to watch.

The three of them were in the Jacobite suite, where Annie was ministering to Tor after setting and binding Tykie's cracked jaw.

"Wish I were doin' the same to 'ee," she had informed Jewel tartly. "Tykie's no the one I'd like to silence for a bit!"

Jewel had waited until Annie's back was turned, then stuck out her tongue. Annie hadn't noticed, but Tor had, and he had tried hard to stifle his laughter, because of his badly bruised ribs.

Now he sat glaring at Jewel and wishing she didn't look so absurdly adorable sitting there with her legs tucked up beneath her like some chastened child. There certainly wasn't anything contrite in the mulish little chin that was hooked over her knees, though. What was she smiling about, anyway?

"Sweet heaven!" he bellowed as he caught a whiff of the fetid stuff that the harridan Brewster was slathering onto his face. With a roar he shot off the stool, ignoring the pain in his rib cage, ignoring the throbbing of his eye as he wiped away the ointment with the first thing handy—the hem of Annie's apron.

"Mr. Cameron."

The words dripped ice.

Tor looked up inquiringly.

Jewel hid her face on her knees. Her shoulders shook.

By God, Tor realized, the wench was laughing! At

him! He had taken enough abuse from both of these women today. He would not—he could not—take any more. Far better to return to the bowels of Cowcadden Prison, or face a horde of Ashanti tribesmen with razor-sharp spears than this pair of Highland witches!

"Mrs. Brewster," he said in a tone that nearly matched Annie's in iciness, although he did obligingly drop her apron. "I appreciate all you've done for me. You've gone out of your way to be kind. But I will not permit you to rub my face with pig manure, no matter how laudable its healing powers. Now, if you please? I'm tired and should like to rest. Will you close the door on your way out? And take that . . . that . . . baggage with you when you go."

Jewel lifted her face from her knees. All traces of laughter had been replaced by breathless anticipation. No one, simply no one, had ever spoken to Annie that way, not even Jewel's mother, who had been Annie's pride and joy, or Aunt Millicent, who was Ruan's mother and had always considered herself an empress in her own right. Jewel waited with bated breath. Would Annie kill him with her bare hands? Or would she make some sort of weapon out of a piece of furniture?

Annie didn't seem certain herself. For a moment she just stood there, opening and closing her mouth on incredulous words that for once refused to come. Then she did something utterly incredible—or at least it seemed that way to Jewel. Straightening her spine, she calmly gathered together her nursing basket.

"Very well, Mr. Cameron. We'll leave you to your rest. Come along, Jewel."

She swept out the door, leaving Jewel to follow, fully confident that her young charge would obey.

And she would have, if Tor hadn't caught her arm

on the way out and jerked her around to face him.

"What?" she demanded stiffly.

"I'll have to kill him next time. Let him know that, will you?"

Jewel drew in a quick breath. The look in her eyes made Tor aware of something he had doubted for a long time. He was still capable of feeling remorse.

"Go," he said wearily, releasing her. "Get out."

Now it was Jewel's turn to feel a sudden stab of regret. She realized that Tor was in considerable pain. He looked haggard and unwell, almost as bad as when he'd first come to Glen Chulish. She had no idea how to make amends.

"Can I—Do you need anything?"

Tor's jaw worked as he fought a rush of inexplicable yearning that overwhelmed him at her tone. "Nothing," he said harshly. "Get out."

And Jewel went, tears glimmering in her eyes.

I hate him, she thought, fleeing to her room. I hate him forever, and I wish I'd listened to everyone and never, ever brought him here from Cowcadden!

Chapter Ten

" 'Tis time we had a serious talk, ma'am."

Jewel laid aside her pen. She gasped as Tor stepped out of the shadows and into the study light. He looked awful. His eye was nearly swollen shut, and his jaw was badly bruised. He walked stiffly, as though he were an old, old man.

Halting before the desk, he looked down at her with a humorless smile. "No need to look so shocked. What else did you expect? You'll be pleased to know that it hurts. Bloody badly."

Jewel bit her lip. "Would it help to know that Tykie looks equally as battered?"

Strangely enough, it did. With a groan, Tor lowered himself carefully into the chair facing the desk. Jewel had been writing in a ledger, and there were ink stains on her slim fingers. A shawl was wrapped about her shoulders to ward off the chill, and wayward curls had escaped from the neat chignon she wore at the nape of her neck. Behind the big desk she looked like a child playing at being a grown-up. Tor thrust the image away with a grimace. He didn't want to soften toward her now.

"It's been long enough," he said curtly. "Time you told me why you brought me here."

Jewel tossed her head. "I suppose you deserve that much," she agreed haughtily.

He scowled. "Thank you."

She looked at him quickly, wondering if she had hurt him. But his expression was as hard and unapproachable as ever. She cleared her throat. "I think you've already gathered what Drumcorrie means to me. Certainly more than it ever meant to my father, curse his name."

Tor said nothing. He had already learned from Angus what sort of person Archibald MacKenzie had been.

"From the day I was born, my father mourned the fact that I wasn't a lad," Jewel went on with a shrug. "My mother died giving birth to a stillborn son when I was two, and he never forgave her for that. Or me, either. He always said I was the one who should have died."

"He wanted an heir."

"Aye."

"Then why didn't he remarry?"

"Oh, he did. But that one didn't last long, either. Nor did the second one, nor the third. They were Lowlanders, you see. I think our climate did them in."

"You had three stepmothers?"

Jewel smiled thinly. "Three stepwitches. Every one of them made Annie seem like a saint."

"Hard to believe." But Tor recognized the emotions behind those flippant words of hers, for he had seen glimpses of them when Jewel had first appeared at Cowcadden. It was obvious that her childhood had not been happy. Not by any means. And those awful years had apparently hardened her, made her cynical and wary, and killed a great deal of the joyous spirit he sometimes saw flashing in her eyes.

What would it take to bring it back? An exhausting amount of patience and time, no doubt, which Tor did not have to offer her—not that he wanted to, either, by God!

"And no heirs from any of those women, I gather," he said.

Jewel nodded, looking pleased all of a sudden. And hard beyond her years, although she probably wasn't even aware of it. "My father had a knack for picking poor breeders. Horses, cattle, and especially women. He always tended to choose looks over substance. Handsome women, all of them, but frail as hothouse roses." Her brow furrowed. "Why they were attracted to him in the first place is still a mystery to me. He was short, like I am, and a good deal overweight. But he had money and charm, and I suppose that matters to some."

"But not to you, apparently, judging from the match you made."

Jewel ignored that. "As it went, there was no one left to inherit Drumcorrie but me. The thought maddened my father. We'd never seen eye to eye, so when the last of his wives turned up her toes and he was too old to attract another, he tried to make the best use out of me. His intent was to marry me off to a suitable MacKenzie."

Tor leaned back in his chair. "None around that appealed to him, eh?"

"Oh, aye, plenty." Jewel shuddered, remembering. "But they didn't appeal to me. To give you an idea of how awful they were, the best of the lot was my cousin Ruan."

Tor scowled. "Why didn't you marry him?"

"MacKenzies don't marry their first cousins."

"Oh."

"My father tried his best to pair me off with someone, I'll grant him that. But in the end he couldn't sway me."

"I don't understand. You were underage. He could have married you to anyone he chose without your consent."

Jewel's eyes gleamed. "Let's just say that my suitors . . . umm . . . changed their minds once they got to know me a wee bit better."

Tor's lips twitched. Bloodthirsty savage. He could imagine well enough what awful things she had plotted in an effort to scare them all away. Was there no end to the things this flame-haired volcano was capable of doing to achieve her own ends?

He said arrogantly, "If I had wanted Drumcorrie, nothing you could have done would have swayed me from marrying you."

"Oh, I'm quite sure of that," Jewel answered tartly. "But you're nothing like the Glen Chulish MacKenzies. The forty-five did away with the best of 'em, you see. Naught but pimpled babes and inbred weaklings left in the lot. It didn't take much to scare them off."

Tor hid a smile by turning his head. He didn't want Jewel to see how easily she could amuse him. That was one weapon he wasn't about to drop into her lovely little hands! "If I'd have been your father, I would have left Drumcorrie to Cousin Ruan, if only to spite you."

Abruptly Jewel's expression changed. She stared down at her hands, which lay folded on the ledger. "That's what my aunt expected. Ruan, too."

"They weren't pleased when that didn't happen, I take it?"

"No."

Tor regarded her keenly. Jewel refused to look at him, which was not at all like her. He changed the subject. "Then where do I fit in? After you'd schemed for years to remain single, why did you marry at all?"

Jewel sighed deeply. "My father bested me in the end, I'm afraid. You can't exactly fight someone once · they get at you from beyond the grave. In his will, he stipulated that if I didn't marry within a year of his death, the distillery, the lands, the house, all of his holdings, would go to my cousin Ruan after all. He'd finally found a way to make me do his bidding. That's why I went down to Glasgow."

Tor sat back in his chair, filled with admiration for her. Clever lass, and how utterly simple a solution! Marry a convict, and keep Drumcorrie. Marry one with good, braw shoulders, and win a hard worker to boot. Even better, one who was so grateful for his freedom that he would be more than willing to trade the filth of Cowcadden Prison for the remote wilds of the Scottish Highlands.

Unfortunately for her, Jewel had miscalculated when she chose Tor Ban Cameron. Tor was neither willing to remain here at Drumcorrie, nor grateful for the chance to be her pawn. But Tor wasn't about to let her know that. He would let her go on thinking that she'd bested her father in the end. Once he had his strength back and the winter snows had melted in the upper passes, he'd be off for Edinburgh to pick up the pieces of the life he'd left behind.

But for some perverse reason, Tor couldn't let that be the end of it. Something about the matter needled him intolerably. "I still don't understand why you didn't marry your gay blade cousin. He certainly seems smitten, judging from the amount of time he spends here."

Jewel gave a tinkling laugh. "Ruan? He's not in love with anyone but himself. And he only comes here because he's hoping to see me fall flat on my face. It was a cruel blow to him when I married, you ken. He's wanted Drumcorrie from the very first."

Tor sat back, feeling extremely smug of a sudden. He'd disliked Ruan MacKenzie—Black MacKenzie, what a joke!—from the moment he'd first laid eyes on the pretty fellow. How delightful to know that he himself now possessed the one thing Ruan had always wanted. "Where does he live, by the way?"

"Oh, about five miles down the glen. In the gatehouse of the castle that used to stand at the bottom of Ben Chulish. His mother and sister live there, too."

"Why don't they ever come for a visit?"

"At the moment they're shunning me. They're furious that I got married without telling them. But I daresay curiosity will get the better of them eventually, so you'd best be prepared for a lookover."

Tor regarded her darkly. "Lord above, do you have no feelings at all, lass?"

Jewel's face closed up. "None. In my position, you can't afford to have them. You should know that as well as anyone, Tor Cameron of Cowcadden."

They looked at each other over the cluttered desk. In that moment each of them recognized in the other a fellow sufferer of old and bitter wounds. But rather than binding them together, the knowledge served to erect an ever higher wall between them. Jewel had already realized that there was danger in letting this enigmatic and devilishly handsome man get too close. Aye, he was handsome, despite his bruised and battered face, for he had been filling out in the last few days, and the prison pallor was rapidly falling away from him, thanks to Annie's skillful care. And what Tor Cameron did to her in bed was best left unmentioned as well. She would not, could not, let him sway her in any way from the path she had chosen!

And Tor? He, too, recognized the danger that Jewel MacKenzie Cameron presented him. She alone of all women understood a little of what he had suffered, for she herself seemed a survivor of similarly cruel abuse. Women, in Tor's former world, had never been anything more to him than the means of satisfying natural urges. Unfortunately, this one was different. This one had a way of worming past his defenses and opening old wounds without his quite knowing how. And that in itself was reason enough to keep her at arm's length.

There was a knock on the study door.

"Supper, miss," announced Annie. Her expression grew frosty as she became aware of Tor. "I'll set anither place." And she withdrew, muttering beneath her breath.

Jewel rose and carefully shook out her skirts. "Coming?"

Tor hesitated. He had not dined once with his wife since his arrival. In fact, he had never even set foot in Drumcorrie's dining room. But even as old inadequacies reared up inside of him, he thrust them savagely away. Those days were over. He was a free man now, and welcome to dine with his wife if he chose!

His wife. That thought in itself was laughable. Why, most times he couldn't even remember to call her by her bloody lawful name!

Jewel Cameron, he repeated softly to himself over and over as he went with her down the corridor. *Her name's Jewel Cameron now.*

There were three places set in the oak-paneled dining room. Jewel's look of surprise was not lost on Tor as he halted on the threshold beside her.

"Mr. Ferguson will be joinin' ye," Annie informed them tartly.

"Oh," said Jewel, and tried to behave as though this were perfectly natural.

131

Tor's mouth thinned as he followed her inside. So the great mute devil still intended to protect his innocent mistress from her big, bad husband, did he? Wouldn't the hulking fellow have an apoplectic fit if he knew that Tor had already bedded the young beauty and enjoyed himself thoroughly while doing so, thank you very much!

Tor glanced at Jewel darkly, remembering.

"Stop looking at me like that," she snapped.

"You're mistaken," he retorted. "I was trying to decide where to sit."

She recovered herself admirably. "At the head of the table, of course."

"My, my," he mocked. "Quite an honor, for a convict."

"Go to hell, Cameron."

He grinned. "Sorry. Already been there. I got kicked out for misbehavior."

Jewel couldn't help it. She had to laugh. Looking up, she met his amused gaze across the table and didn't look away immediately, the way she usually did.

Tykie's arrival ended the surprisingly peaceful moment. Looking at him, Tor could feel the hair at the back of his neck prickling like a dog's. His bruised rib cage throbbed and a pulse began pounding in his temple. God, how he resented this silent hulk for his unswerving devotion to Jewel! And he especially resented the way his wife always seemed to grow more relaxed and carefree whenever Tykie was near, as though he were the only man in the world she trusted.

His rivalry with Tykie had become a point of pride for Tor. All his life, his considerable charm and good looks had made an easy conquest of the ladies. He had come to take his talents with the opposite sex for granted, and used them whenever necessary to achieve his own ends. He would have been gratified to know that he hadn't lost his touch after his hellish experiences at Cowcadden.

That was why it was so galling for him to admit that even though he had already taken his wife to bed she still treated him worse than the lowly vermin beneath her feet—never mind, of course, that she hadn't particularly enjoyed it. In fact, even the rodent over which she'd shed genuine tears the night before got more sympathy than Tor did!

You're a curse, Jewel Cameron, he thought furiously, and it'll be a cold day in hell when you make me feel the least bit charitable toward you again!

Feeling Tykie's eyes upon him, he switched his scowling gaze to the other man's bruised face. They exchanged a long, bitter look, its meaning clear. A challenge had been issued, and Jewel lay at the heart of it.

The meal turned out to be nerve-racking for everyone, especially Jewel. Tor said absolutely nothing throughout, and ate with downcast eyes. Tykie, of course, was no help at all. The fact that he would have preferred eating in his own room was painfully obvious. That he blamed Tor for his need to act as a bodyguard was equally clear.

Looking from one bruised, stoic face to the other, Jewel had to fight the urge to scream. She almost wished that Ruan were here, for at least Ruan could be counted on to fill the silence with his brainless chatter.

Unfortunately, she was to discover a few minutes later that getting what one wished for could sometimes be a curse, not a blessing. Barely two minutes later the awful silence in the dining room was broken by the booming of the iron knocker on the front door. Footsteps sounded in the hall, followed by voices.

Jewel rose as Annie came in. "Who is it?" For the life of her, she couldn't imagine receiving visitors at this hour.

"Master Ruan an' his family."

Jewel's eyes widened. "All three of them?"

"Aye."

Jewel exchanged a swift, shocked glance with Tykie. Tor sat watching them, saying nothing.

She took a deep breath. "All right. Show them in. And you might as well set—"

But Annie was already gone.

"Dearest cousin!" Ruan swept in first, cold and windblown and fittingly handsome in a sheepskin coat and feathered cap. Bowing low, he kissed Jewel's hand in a courtly manner that set Tor's teeth on edge.

Jewel immediately slapped Ruan's fingers away. "Stop that! What's your mother doing here?"

"I told her what transpired earlier i' your library. She insisted on comin' tae see for herself if ye'd recovered from the shock."

Jewel's eyes blazed. "Liar! You goaded her into it, didn't you?"

Ruan laid a hand over his heart and looked deeply wounded. "Lassie, I swear I didna! In fact, I did my very best to—Och, now, will ye look at your bridegroom! An' Tykie! Tsk tsk." Ruan shook his head woefully. "Mauled each other badly, didn't they? Mother willna be pleased."

"About what?" came a chilling voice from the doorway.

Tor's heart sank as a handsome woman with the expression of a dried-up prune swept inside, her frilly skirts rustling. Lord, he knew the type. Nothing for it now but to try to keep his head above water.

"Seems Jewel's husband suffered a sound thrashin' at Tykie's hands," Ruan reported. "An' the other way around, as well."

Millicent MacKenzie looked piercingly from one bruised face to the other. Waves of icy disapproval seemed to radiate from her like a thick, black cloud. Tykie kept his gaze averted, looking as though he wished he were dead. Tor regarded her calmly, although he wondered fleetingly if maybe he wouldn't have been better off in his prison cell at Cowcadden. Lord above, these MacKenzies! Every one of 'em was worse than the last!

"I understand you're a convict, Mr. Cameron." Millicent MacKenzie was obviously English, and as haughty as a queen.

Tor nodded.

"Your crime?"

"Bludgeoning babies."

Tykie's brows rose. Ruan snickered. Jewel's eyes began to water as she tried to still her laughter. Relief washed over her. For once she was deeply glad of Tor's arrogance.

Aunt Millicent herself was looking rather uncertain. Should she believe the man or not?

"May I sit down, Mama? I confess I'm famished."

Cassandra MacKenzie, Ruan's younger sister, slipped gracefully into the empty chair beside Tor's. She had been educated at an expensive finishing school in London, and her accent was ripely upper class. So was the simpering smile she turned upon Tor, and it was instantly obvious to Jewel that she found her cousin's darkly handsome husband quite to her liking.

"I had no idea," Tor murmured, smiling back into Cassie's wide blue eyes, "that my wife's relations were so very lovely."

Cassie blushed prettily while Ruan chose to look

disgusted. Aunt Millicent radiated clouds of icy disapproval, while Jewel was hard-pressed to hide her astonishment. Flirting with a brainless chit like Cassie MacKenzie was the last thing she had expected from Tor! Perhaps it had been a mistake to nurse him back to such robust good health. He was turning out to be a difficult handful, not the meek and subservient fellow she had hoped to fetch from Cowcadden.

I should have picked someone else, she thought bitterly.

But of course it was much too late for that now.

While Tor and Cassie whispered together and her aunt and cousin began to look increasingly furious, Jewel sat toying with the ring on her wedding finger. The ring had been her mother's, and she had brought it to Glasgow more for appearances than anything else. The good Lord above knew it had never been the symbol of a happy union!

Annie brought soup and bread for the newcomers. Her expression was thunderous as she moved about serving and clearing away. Jewel, restless and angry, studied the faces around her. Ruan's expression showed that he was thoroughly bored. Tykie looked desperate to excuse himself, although he was much too loyal to abandon his mistress.

Finally, to everyone's relief, a smothered giggle from Cassie served to snap Millicent's control and bring her surging to her feet. "I think we'll be off."

"But Mama—"

"So soon?" Jewel asked, trying not to sound pleased.

" 'Tis far too late!" Ruan complained, changing tack as he thought of the cold drive back down the glen. "Couldn't we spend the night?"

"No!" Millicent and Jewel exclaimed in unison.

"Oh, please!" begged Cassie.

Aunt Millicent looked as though something slimy had lodged in her craw. "I said no! Tykie, fetch my coachman! Jewel, charming as always."

Jewel accompanied them dutifully into the hall. Much to her annoyance, Tor came along, too, and lingered far too long over Cassie's hand as he bade her farewell.

Annie stood waiting sourly with their wraps, and now even Ruan wasted uncharacteristically little time in slipping on his gloves. He kissed the top of Jewel's head.

"Ta, Coz. Lovely as ever tae see 'ee."

Jewel snorted.

The front door closed behind them. With a shout and the crack of the whip, the carriage rumbled off. Jewel and Tor were left alone in the hall. She whirled to face him.

"Why on earth did you do that?"

"Do what?"

"Oh, don't play stupid with me, Cameron! I know you're not that dim!"

His shoulders lifted. "Your cousin? Charming creature. I'd quite forgotten how enjoyable a harmless flirt can be."

"Harmless!" Jewel's eyes blazed. "How can you say that?"

Tor regarded her coolly. "Jealous, ma'am?"

"Jealous!" Jewel looked at him as though he'd lost his mind. "I—You—Why . . ." Her spluttering words faded into silence. With a harsh expletive, she lifted her skirts and stormed up the stairs. Tor watched her go, feeling enormously pleased with himself.

"She'll hae to pay for that, 'ee ken."

He turned slowly to find Annie Brewster standing in the shadows behind him. "What do you mean?"

"Only that ye dinna ken Millicent MacKenzie. If ye meant tae wound Mistress Jewel, ye've succeeded.

Only not in the way 'ee thought." Scowling, she turned to go.

"Just a moment, woman!"

Annie turned.

"That English harpy. Ruan's mother. What will she do?"

"We'll have tae wait an' see, won't we?"

"Theatrics, Mrs. Brewster? I didn't think you were the sort."

"Nay," Annie said emphatically, and for the first time Tor caught a flash of emotion on her cold, lined face. He was startled to recognize it as fear. He had never dreamed that Annie could be afraid of anyone, especially someone like Millicent MacKenzie.

"She'll no let this slip past," Annie predicted direly.

"What will she do?" Tor demanded.

"Ask Tykie," Annie snapped, and disappeared into the shadows.

Ask Tykie? A man without a tongue? What sort of bizarre household was this, anyway?

Ill-temperedly, Tor stalked outside. Icy wind lashed at him. He found Tykie in the tack room of the stable, closing up for the night.

"What does Millicent MacKenzie intend to do to your mistress?" he demanded, stepping inside.

Tykie didn't even pretend to misunderstand him. He glared at Tor with a look that clearly held him entirely to blame. Then he jerked his head in the direction of the whips and crops hanging in a neat row along the wall.

"Do you mean," Tor said disbelievingly, "that Jewel's aunt intends to beat her because I acted unseemly toward her daughter tonight?"

Tykie's shoulders lifted. *Who knows?* his expression said. *It's happened before.*

"And you let her?" Tor asked incredulously.

Tykie looked enraged, but also thoroughly helpless. Shrugging, he turned away.

Tor understood, or thought he did. Millicent MacKenzie had obviously beaten Jewel before, probably years ago, when Jewel had been a helpless child. And judging from the way everyone was acting, the woman still practiced some form of cruelty on the lass. Perhaps something more subtle nowadays, but significant enough to cow even the volatile Tykie, disturb the unflappable Annie Brewster, and bring a look of fear into his normally fearless wife's lovely blue eyes.

Tor's plan to torment Jewel by flirting blatantly with her golden-haired cousin had clearly backfired. He had somehow stirred up a hornets' nest without knowing it, and now he, like everyone else, was going to have to face the consequences. From the way everyone was acting, those consequences weren't going to be pleasant.

He growled out an expletive, running his hands through his hair. "This place is a veritable hotbed of intrigue! You MacKenzies are madder than I thought!"

Turning heel, he walked out before Tykie even had the chance to take a swing at him.

Chapter Eleven

Jewel was sitting at the window, elbows propped on the sill, when Tor stepped into her room. She was staring out into the darkness, and the reflection in the glass showed him her deeply troubled expression.

"I'm sorry I didn't knock," he said as she became aware of his presence and whirled to face him. "I didn't think you'd let me in."

"No need to apologize. It was my mistake. I should have slid the bolt."

But she hadn't. He'd never ventured into her room before, and she certainly hadn't imagined that he'd do so tonight. Coming to her feet, she lifted her chin. "Well? What do you want?"

"To apologize."

Jewel blinked. She hadn't expected that, either. "What for?"

"What will she do?" he asked.

"Aunt Millicent?" Jewel sighed and looked down at

140

her hands. "I don't know. She likes to keep me guessing. Nothing may happen for a time; then she'll fire both barrels when I least expect it."

Tor leaned against the doorjamb, arms crossed before him. "That's utterly ridiculous! What's gotten into you—and Tykie and Annie—anyway? The woman seems harmless enough. A prime example of moral English rectitude, to be sure, but not the type to send the three of you scurrying for cover!"

Jewel gave a bitter laugh. "You don't know her very well."

"Not at all, apparently."

Pushing himself away from the wall, he crossed over to her. For a moment he said nothing, only stood there searching her face, but Jewel could school her expression annoyingly well at times, and at the moment it told him nothing.

"What is it, Jewel? Tell me."

All of a sudden she found herself dangerously close to tears. She'd never heard Tor use that tone before, and the husky kindness of it undid her so completely that for one mad moment she was actually tempted to confide in him.

"Please," she said instead, "go away."

A muscle in his jaw worked in and out. It was the first time he'd offered her kindness of his own free will, and she had rejected it. It maddened him, the fact that her behavior could actually wound him.

"I was trying to make you jealous," he admitted harshly.

Jewel tossed her head, grateful to be on familiar ground once again. "Well, that was stupid of you, wasn't it? You can't make somebody jealous when they don't care a fat fig for you!"

"Touché," he said softly. But his eyes continued to blaze into hers.

Now it was Jewel's turn to fold her arms across her

chest. "I thought I asked you to go."

"So you did."

"Well, then?"

"Not until you tell me about your aunt."

Her face closed up. "There's naught to say."

"No?"

"No. And if you want to flirt with Cassie, be my guest. She's exactly what you need. All angelic blond looks and twittering brainlessness."

"Like her brother."

Despite herself, Jewel's lips curved. "Aye, like Ruan."

They exchanged a look of understanding. In this, at least, they were in agreement.

Tor withdrew obligingly. In the doorway, he turned. "Oh. You're wrong about one thing."

"What's that?"

"She's not to my taste at all."

Jewel knew she should let the matter drop, but she must have been beset by demons tonight. She couldn't help remembering the way she had raged inwardly at Tor's blatant flirtation with her lovely cousin, despite her vehement insistence that she was immune to jealousy. At the time she had yearned to claw out Cassie's innocent blue eyes and tear every golden hair from her head!

And Cameron! Smiling at the brainless chit with those curving, carnal lips, his smoky eyes heavy lidded, the light that burned within them so blatantly sexual! Aye, he knew how to use those good looks of his like a weapon!

"What exactly *is* to your taste, Tor Cameron?" she asked softly, aware that she was flirting with danger but unable to help herself.

His expression changed. Slowly he pushed the door shut and came back into the room. He towered over her, his shadow huge against the wall. There was something feral in his eyes, and Jewel shivered as she lifted her chin to stare boldly back into their gleaming blue depths.

"Witchery," he answered huskily. "I'm seduced by witchery, not porcelain perfection."

"Oh?"

"Aye. Poison hair and tilted eyes—like yours. You should be ugly, you know that, Mrs. Cameron? Nothing about you is the least bit conventional."

"Do you prefer that?" Now why was she suddenly so breathless? Instinct was telling her to flee while she could, and yet she was rooted to the spot, her eyes nailed to his.

"Oh, aye," Tor answered softly. "I do."

There was that look in his eyes again, a look she had come to recognize all too well by now. Desire. How innocent, how ignorant she had been the first time she had seen it!

But where there had been bewilderment and fear before, there was now a strange, shivery sensation flowing through her, warming her blood and bringing an odd weightlessness to her limbs. She remembered how it felt to have Tor kiss her, undress her, and touch her in places no man had ever dared.

"Do you know what I prefer the most?" Tor was asking.

Her eyes were drawn hypnotically to his mouth. "N-no."

"You with your hair unbound. Like the other night. Do you remember?"

"No."

Of course she did. They both knew it. The pupils of her eyes had dilated, turning them nearly black; huge, tilted eyes that a man could easily drown in.

"Like this," Tor whispered, holding those eyes with his own while he reached to pull the combs from her hair.

The chignon tumbled down, spilling a red curtain into his hands. He buried his face in its fragrant silkiness and breathed deeply. Only here, like this, did the memories of Cowcadden ever fade completely.

Jewel stood perfectly still. Her heart hammered so that she was certain Tor could hear it. His nearness made her feel faint. Why did she fear him so? Or was it really fear?

Tor drew back, but only enough so that he could look into her eyes once again. "A man would be mad to prefer pale prettiness to such vibrant passion." His voice was husky. Now he leaned even closer, his breath pelting her face. "Jewel," he murmured. "Close your eyes."

"Wh-what?"

"Close your eyes."

She did so, releasing him from their power so that he could tip her head back with his hands. His mouth swooped down and took her full lower lip, that maddening lower lip that had mesmerized him from the very first. He caressed it with his tongue.

Instantly Jewel stiffened and tried to jerk away.

"Oh, no," Tor murmured against her mouth. His arms slipped about her waist, trapping her. " 'Tis too late to run now, my poison-haired witch. There's more to love than you've ever dreamed, and tonight I'm going to show you."

"No!"

But the protest was lost in the swirling insistence of his kiss.

"Come, Jewel," he breathed against her temple, "there should be pleasure for both of us. Kiss me. Kiss me back."

Tor had stopped caressing her lower lip. Now he was molding her mouth to his, parting it with gentle pressure and then, when hers opened at last, slipping his tongue inside.

Jewel gasped as his tongue grazed hers. It was an explosion of sizzling heat, and Tor made it all the more erotic by cupping her buttocks with a wide-splayed hand and bringing her toward him until she fit intimately between his legs. Her thighs rested against his muscular ones, and at the vee between them his manhood throbbed insistently. She moaned and tried to shift away, but Tor wouldn't let her. Lifting her against him, he carried her to the bed.

"Jewel," he said roughly, "I asked you to kiss me. Show me what I've taught you."

The demon was back, that inexplicable part of her that craved this flirtation with danger. And Cameron had taught her some things well. From him Jewel had already learned the sensual beauty of taking a lover's face in her hands and pressing her mouth to his so that their breath mingled in wonderful gusts. Now she learned the heady pleasure of fitting her woman's body intimately to a man's, where the hard, angular planes of masculine muscle accepted perfectly her soft, feminine curves. And in learning, she found the pleasure he had promised—and the fact that pleasure in itself was not enough, not nearly enough. She pressed closer, wanting more, needing more.

Tor was unprepared for so swift a surrender. His senses swam as the kiss deepened and Jewel's slim arms twined about his neck. He ached for the contact of their naked flesh, and told her so in a husky whisper that shivered erotically through her.

And then, oh God, she was actually undressing him, undoing the buttons of the cambric shirt that had once been Tykie's and easing it from his shoulders. Tor groaned and caught her to him, his hands in her hair.

"Make me burn," he whispered against her lips.

145

"Little firebrand, make me burn."

And she did.

His manhood sprang free as she eased off his breeches. In wonder she looked down at the bold symbol of his maleness, then up into his face, and Tor bucked as her hand closed fearlessly around him.

Oh, God. His head fell back. He had forgotten the wondrous touch of a woman's hand, forgotten how she could reduce a man to shuddering mindlessness. Or was it because no other woman had ever inflamed him the way this fire-haired temptress did?

He knew he would forget himself if he allowed her to continue. And he did not want his control to be swept away just yet.

Leading her to the bed, he positioned her beneath him. He was completely naked now, and magnificent in his primal glory. Leaning over her, feral and strong, he showed her how a woman's pleasure could be heightened. For pleasure her he did, with experienced hands and drugging kisses. He undressed her slowly, worshiping the curves and hollows of all that he exposed. He laved her nipples so that they ached and grew erect, then suckled the fullness of those rounded breasts while she arched beneath him and caught her breath on a wondrous sigh. His hands slipped down her belly and skimmed her buttocks and thighs as his kisses deepened in intensity. Their breath mingled, as did the heady beating of their hearts. Then Tor's fingers found their way between her thighs, to touch very tenderly the bud of her womanhood.

Jewel gasped, and her eyes went wide.

Tor stroked and teased, and her head fell back as erotic sensations rippled through her veins.

"This," whispered Tor, working his magic relentlessly, "this is the sweet mystery you've been denied too long, little firebrand."

The sensations built, singing through her, and Jewel's hands clutched fiercely at the bunched muscles of Tor's arms.

"Cameron," she panted, "if you don't stop—"

"Let go," he urged hoarsely against her temple. " 'Tis as it should be. Let go, sweetheart."

And she did. And felt the explosion of her first climax ripple through her in a fiery crescendo of sensation. Up arched her body to the urging of Tor's hand as reality shattered into soaring pleasure. She beat against the flame like a helpless butterfly, all fire and ice, darkness and light. Her head twisted on the pillow and then, slowly, sweetly, her body went lax. She moaned and felt the tears seep from the corners of her eyes. She felt wrecked, destroyed, utterly spent.

But there was more.

Driven beyond the point of control by the force of his wife's release, Tor reared over her and built the flame a second time. Within moments she was writhing beneath him once again, his name a husky plea as it poured from her throat. She was his for the taking, and Tor took her, swiftly, urgently, sliding into the sweet passage he had made hot and slickly wet for his entry.

Jewel cried out as he filled her. Her nails bit into the flesh of his back as he reared and then bucked forward, stretching her with the very size of him. His nerves were taut and his desire pounded through him, and with only a few, fierce thrusts he, too, reached that razor-thin point of passion.

Jewel's name exploded from his chest as he peaked. His body convulsed as he poured himself into her, groaning out his agony as his hands clenched in the bright glory of her hair. It was a mo-

ment of mystical triumph, when ecstasy robbed a
man of his center and his will and his name. For both
of them, reality faded and was gone

What was passion? Jewel lay quietly in the darkness, considering. A fleeting moment of unbearable
delight, which one could grasp for only so long. It
did not last; nay, it could not last, but that, to Jewel,
made perfect sense. The human body, and the soul,
could take only so much.

But afterward? Ah, now therein lay the mystery,
bringing with it a host of questions she had already
considered at length and still could not answer to her
satisfaction.

How was it, for example, that a man she hated,
who had disrupted her world and made her so furious at times that she yearned to kill him, could reduce her to such weepy sentimentality simply by
taking her to a moment of shattering release? And
why, when her own passions had been so achingly
fulfilled, could she still find it in herself to share in
the glory of his?

Cautiously she raised herself up on one elbow,
afraid to awaken him. Dawn was graying beyond the
windows. Tor lay in heavy sleep, his handsome face
for once lacking its hunted urgency.

Holding her breath, Jewel traced a finger lightly
along the line of his nose. Down to his carnal lips she
went while her own lips curved and a strange
warmth seeped through her. How deeply he slept!
Aye, he needed to sleep, after having loved her again,
and yet again, throughout the strange, ecstatic night
that had passed. He had whispered things to her she
doubted he even realized, murmuring endearments
in Gaelic, a language Jewel hadn't even known he
could speak.

Darkly handsome, enigmatic stranger. How had

he come to mean so much to her?

And therein lay the greatest mystery of all. Jewel knew that she hadn't become so befuddled by Tor's lovemaking that she had lost all vestiges of reason. Quite the opposite. She knew perfectly well that men and women did what she and Tor had done all the time. Sometimes for money, sometimes for simple pleasure, often just to relieve their boredom. She also knew that people who went to bed together didn't necessarily love each other. Then how could she explain the fact that this rough and arrogant man had managed to steal his way through every pore and fiber of her being and ended up settling sweetly in her heart?

I shouldn't be in love with him, Jewel thought. But I am. I am!

Why?

She knew she wasn't so weak and weepy that she'd allowed her heart to be conquered merely by being loved for the first time in her life. But for some inexplicable reason she knew that if any other man had taken her virginity she would not have felt the same.

Her heart stirred again as she gazed down into Tor's unguarded face. A host of memories rose unbidden to her mind:

Tor glowering at her defiantly from the back of the warden's office while she made her choice of a husband.

Tor losing his supper on the Glasgow road and refusing to let the episode humiliate him.

Tor ill and cranky in the inn at Carlisle but still insisting that Jewel leave him the hell alone.

Tor trading blows with Ruan and with Tykie, and all because of her.

You're a grumpy man, Jewel thought, smiling down at him. But now I know that you're vulnerable, too.

She remembered the scars on his back. And the loneliness that was sometimes there in his eyes, even though he did his best to hide it from the world. But not from her. Because Jewel, too, knew what loneliness meant.

Was this the reason he had managed to work his way so subtly and completely into her heart?

Perhaps I don't love him at all, Jewel mused. Perhaps 'tis only because I understand a wee bit of what he's suffered.

Then again, she might simply be a victim of afterglow. No one had ever made her feel so warm and sweetly happy before, so why should she immediately assume that she had fallen in love with the first man who had shown her what passion was all about? Besides, Jewel thought grumpily, I don't really know what love is, anyway. How could she? She'd never had anyone to call her own before.

Sighing, she lay down beside him once again. In his sleep, Tor murmured and reached for her. Drawing her down against him, he hooked his chin over her shoulder and drifted back to sleep.

Strange, Jewel mused, how easily the chill could be chased from a person's bones simply by cuddling with another. Resting her cheek on Tor's shoulder, she closed her eyes.

I'll think about it tomorrow.

A moment later her breathing, too, became deep and even, and restful sleep claimed her again.

Chapter Twelve

"I'll have to get rid of that Cameron brute, of course. As quickly as possible."

Millicent MacKenzie sat at her secretary in the drafty sitting room of her apartment. Celeste, the maid she had brought with her from London nearly thirty years before, was doing her best to keep the peat fire from filling the room with smoke. But the gatehouse of the old MacKenzie castle was poorly designed, and the smoke curled to the blackened ceiling, making her cough and curse in French.

"I've already written the appropriate letter," Millicent added. "Hull can deliver it for me, by hand of course. That way I can be assured 'twill be received."

"Are you certain, madam, that you will find something useful when you write to this prison in Glasgow?"

"Unquestionably."

Millicent had that cunning look on her face that always warned the inhabitants of Drumcorrie to watch their backs. The look had been missing for quite some time, but now it was back in full force.

Life had by no means been kind to Millicent Childes MacKenzie. Oh, everything had started out grand enough years ago, when Sir Diamid MacKenzie, then the Scottish ambassador to the court of St. James, had first cast his eye on Millicent Childes, the lovely young debutante.

Despite her family's strenuous objections, Millicent had chosen Diamid over a score of equally qualified English suitors, and made a triumphant entry into Glen Chulish as his bride. But life in a Scottish castle, she had quickly learned, was not the stuff of romantic dreams. Castles were drafty places, and this one was so primitive that Millicent had been obliged to send away to England for the barest necessities of cloth, silver plate, furniture, and a properly trained staff.

Even then, and despite her formidable will, she had been unable to change the place into the genteel palace of her dreams. The Highlands were far too isolated, the people objectionable, clannish, and uneducated. Worse, the handsome, charming suitor who had danced with her in the ballroom at St. James's Palace and married her to boot had proved himself equally unsophisticated and rough. Before the year was out Millicent had learned that Diamid MacKenzie lived only for whiskey and deer hunting and that he deliberately shunned the fashionable salons of Edinburgh, even though Millicent herself was soon escaping to them to avoid the frigid winter months.

The Highland uprising of 1745 had brought an end to her unhappy existence. In its place, unfortunately, had come a time of even more wrenching misery. Unlike the Drumcorrie MacKenzies, Sir Diamid had decided to march into war with Bonnie Prince

Charles, and had promptly been executed for his troubles. His gloomy castle had been razed and his clan dispersed, and Millicent, spared only because she was English, had been forced to take up residence in the ugly little gatehouse that was all that remained.

At least she had taken the precaution of hiding her young son away with friends in Edinburgh. Cassandra hadn't been born as yet; Millicent had not even known when Diamid was beheaded that she was carrying a second child. After that difficult birth, she had returned to London only to discover to her horror that the society that had once embraced her so eagerly was closed to her now. She was an outcast, the penniless widow of a Scottish revolutionary, and as such, tainted for the likes of genteel company. Worse, her own family had closed ranks against her, and Millicent had been forced to use all of her considerable powers of persuasion simply to leave the infant Cassandra in their care before returning to Glen Chulish. Cassie, at least, had been raised in the proper English manner.

Indeed, in her children Millicent saw the only means of regaining something of the glittering life she had lost. Over the years that had followed she had schemed relentlessly to see Ruan inherit Drumcorrie, begging and pleading with Archibald MacKenzie to make the lad his heir. Several times she had even succumbed to Archibald's demands for gratification in bed, but all to no avail. After his death, the house and the distillery had gone to his daughter.

A conceited woman, Millicent had heartily despised her beautiful niece. The fact that Jewel had always been more like Sir Diamid, her handsome, charming uncle, than the pudgy little man who had sired her, had only served to increase Millicent's re-sentiment a thousandfold. Like Sir Diamid, Jewel had proved stubborn and impossible to sway, although Millicent had done her best to bring the girl to heel.

At first Millicent had been secretive in her plotting. Then, as her desperation mounted, she had become blatantly open as to her intentions. Too late she had realized that Jewel's determination to keep Drumcorrie for herself quite matched her own desire to wrest it away for Ruan.

It was a defeat Millicent had not accepted graciously. Though she cared nothing for the rustic hunting lodge and the sorry staff that inhabited it, she wanted Drumcorrie's distillery. In her opinion, Jewel and her idiot henchman, Sandy Sinclair, had always been far too stupid to realize that the distillery was a veritable gold mine waiting to be tapped. So enamored of Drumcorrie malt was the English Prince of Wales, in fact, that a regular shipment was sent to London every month—secretly, of course. Anti-Scottish sentiment was still so high in England even years after the war that the malt was consumed discreetly in the palace dining hall.

Millicent MacKenzie had plans for Drumcorrie that Jewel could not even begin to guess at. She intended to capitalize on Prince George's fondness for the drink to win her way back into English society. Millicent was convinced that with the proper presentation, the stigma of Drumcorrie malt's Scottish origins would be quite overridden by its outstanding taste. Even the most vehement Scottish-hating Englishman had a secret passion for malt, and Drumcorrie's was among the best.

Once she had won back the respect of her countrymen, Millicent intended to marry Cassandra off to an English aristocrat with a taste for the malt himself, a man so smitten with drink and with Cassie's beauty that her Scottish blood would not be seen as a social stigma any longer.

But all that wasn't possible now. All that had been planned before Jewel had stolen away to Glasgow and gotten herself a husband. Millicent MacKenzie was not a fool. She knew that Tor Cameron would pose a real threat to her plans once he regained his health—and his senses. At the moment he didn't seem to realize that Drumcorrie was the plum prize in his marriage. At the moment he seemed content to ignore everything but the mysterious power game he was playing with his wife—and the seductive one he had begun with Cassie, which Millicent intended to put a stop to immediately.

"From what I hear," Celeste was saying, "this Monsieur Cameron will not be so easy to dislodge."

Millicent gave a short, ugly laugh. "Don't be ridiculous! A minor setback. Please see that Hull takes the letter today. We'll be rid of the man before you know it."

Celeste didn't doubt it. She had been with Madam too long to think that anything would stand in the way of her schemes. If she considered the new husband of Jewel MacKenzie a minor setback, then so he was. A shame for the fellow. He had no idea what was about to hit him.

The distillery at Drumcorrie had been standing silent throughout the long winter months. Last year's barley harvest had long since been roasted and distilled into the golden liquid that now rested in oaken barrels deep in the cellars. Here it would remain undisturbed for the next twelve years, aging and perfecting its taste and perfume.

The cellars had always smelled strongly of oak and peat and whiskey. Today, after days of steady rain, the scent was also redolent of damp earth and stone. Jewel had taken the precaution of lifting the hem of her working gown as she crossed the wet floor to the arching doorway where Sandy Sinclair awaited her.

"There," she said, stepping into the light and dusting the chalk powder from her fingers. "All finished."

She had spent the last hour marking the casks intended for shipment and making a brief inventory of the rest. Sandy had walked beside her, scribbling notes on the pad he carried with him. "Weather's lookin' fine," he remarked now, following her back up the flight of ancient stairs.

"Then let's arrange for the shipment to go out tomorrow. Do you think you can manage?"

Sandy looked offended. "Aye, of course."

Jewel smiled at him. "I'm sorry. I can't help feeling of late that I've lost touch with everything."

It was the understatement of the year. From the moment Tor Cameron had come into her life, everything had literally been turned upside down.

"Don't fret, miss. 'Tis a' in order," Sandy soothed.

"I know. And I'm grateful. You've been absolutely wonderful."

Sandy blushed. Mistress Jewel was effusive in her praise this morning. Indeed, she seemed to be in extraordinarily high spirits. What on earth was the matter with her?

Jewel didn't know. By rights she should be slinking around with a fearful eye cast over her shoulder. Aunt Millicent would be striking soon, even though no one ever knew where or when. That in itself should be enough to leave her cowering. Instead, she was feeling quite bold, and almost cheerful. Surely it couldn't be because of the things Tor Cameron had done to her in bed last night!

Oh, but it could. Because there he was now, standing in the huge distilling room when Sandy and Jewel ascended from the cellar. Jewel's heart did a skittering dance the moment she saw him.

Tor hadn't noticed either of them as yet. He was looking up at the big copper distilling tuns with his hands clasped behind his back, his hair disheveled from the windy walk across the yard. He had obviously taken the time to shave this morning, and Jewel saw that the cleft in his chin was more pronounced than ever. His sensual lips were pursed in a thoughtful frown, and her eyes were drawn to them like a moth to flame. She remembered the way they had touched and teased and tasted the night before—everywhere, all over her body. And she remembered, too, how she had responded, without limits, without shame.

At that moment, Tor turned his head and saw her. He paused, the same way Jewel had done when she had first seen him, and his hands unclasped slowly from behind his back. With studied nonchalance, he strode toward her.

Jewel had long ago noticed that Tor moved quite soundlessly for a man of his size. Where had he come by that? Had he stalked deer in his youth, or perhaps honed the skill by eluding capture before being locked away in Cowcadden? Once, he had mentioned the fact that he had fought in the '45. Most of the Highlanders who had marched with the prince had been hunted mercilessly after Scotland's defeat. How had Tor managed to elude the vengeful English soldiers who had murdered and maimed so many of his fellow countrymen?

I know nothing about this man, Jewel thought suddenly. Nothing except the fact that he works pure magic in bed, and that I think I may be falling in love with him.

Which was absurd. And could only prove disastrous for her and everyone else at Drumcorrie.

Jewel had decided during breakfast that she must never let Tor suspect what lay in her heart. She could not afford to give him such a powerful weapon, especially not while he remained so secretive and aloof, and was plotting to flee Drumcorrie the moment he was strong enough.

Oh, aye, Jewel knew perfectly well that this was what he had in mind. For untold years she herself had been a virtual prisoner here—too long not to recognize the same drive in another.

Fortunately she felt trapped at Drumcorrie no longer. Her stepmothers were long dead, her father safely in his grave. She had married Tor Cameron and so kept her home out of Aunt Millicent's grasp. Where in her miserable childhood she had dreamed of nothing more than to leave this place, it was now dearer to her than life itself. And no one, especially not Tor Ban Cameron, was going to wrest it from her.

But those grim thoughts fled Jewel's mind as she watched Tor walking toward her across the wide expanse of stone and shadow. She had slipped out of his bed long before dawn that morning, and this was the first she had seen of him since he had gentled her to sleep following their numerous, soaring joinings the night before. Try as she might, she could not suppress the forbidden images that rose to her mind at the sight of him. She wondered if he was beset by similar demons. After all, his eyes were heavy lidded, which she knew was a habit he adopted whenever he wanted to shut his thoughts away from her. She was beginning to understand him a little, and she had learned to recognize those times when he did not wish to reveal too much of himself.

With great care she shook out her skirts and crossed the room to meet him. Though her heart was tripping like an impetuous girl's, her demeanor was that of the calm and self-possessed lady of the manor.

"Good morning, Mr. Cameron. What brings you to the distillery?"

Tor's lips twitched. Woman though she was—as he'd learned all too poignantly the night before—she still reminded him of a naughty child playing at being a grown-up whenever she tipped up her chin and assumed that haughty air.

"Curiosity," he answered obligingly. "I've never seen this place before, and yet it carries great significance for me. It is, after all, the reason you brought me here from Cowcadden."

"You're right, of course," she responded, annoyed. Trust the brute not to miss an opportunity to needle her! She struck back just as swiftly: "I'm sure by now you've had the chance to see just how much labor is involved in running the place. I hope Annie's brews and plasters have built you up sufficiently."

Tor's eyes burned into hers. "No need for concern. I'm up to any challenge."

Sandy, who stood awkwardly behind his mistress, cleared his throat. "Will you be wantin' summat else, miss?"

Jewel graced him with the smile that Tor had been wanting for himself. "Thank you, Sandy, I—"

" 'Tis Mrs. Cameron," Tor interrupted coldly.

They both turned to look at him.

"Strange how no one in this household seems willing to acknowledge that," he continued. "Strange, because you, Jewel, are my wife in name and *everything* else."

Jewel went scarlet. So did Sandy. Neither had to be told what "everything else" meant.

Stammering something unintelligible, Sandy withdrew so hastily that he nearly tripped over his own feet. Jewel waited until he had disappeared through the door before rounding on her husband.

"That was underhanded of you, Cameron! You've

no need to involve others in our feud!"

"Are we feuding? Faith, I thought we were negotiating—establishing my position in your household, as it were."

"You're not welcome in my household," Jewel shot back. "The sooner you remember that, the better."

"A pity," he countered harshly, "since we seem to get on so well in bed."

Jewel turned away, tears stinging her eyes. Right then and there she knew that Tor would always have the power to wound her, and with no more complicated a weapon than mentioning the sexual side of their marriage.

A feeling of despair overwhelmed her at the thought. Oh, why on earth had she ever allowed him to discover that he could bow her will and leave her like clay in his hands merely by bringing her to the edge of quivering fulfillment? It was dangerous, this hold he had over her, and she knew that she must bring a stop to it before it was too late. But it was already too late, because merely the thought of never lying with him again filled her with utter dismay.

Betrayed, Jewel thought bitterly. I've been betrayed by the one thing I've always known deep in my heart was my greatest flaw: my womanhood. I can't let him control me like this. But what on earth shall I do?

Work him, she realized suddenly. Work him hard. Exhaust him so that by the end of the day he'll be more than ready to collapse in his bed merely to sleep.

The idea came to her quite out of the blue, but she seized on it like a drowning sailor might a spar in heavy seas.

"So you've come to see the distillery," she said, lifting her chin in a manner that he had already learned spelled considerable trouble for him. "Come along, then, and I'll show you about."

Now why did the hair on Tor's nape prickle with a sense of danger? Why did he have this sudden, inescapable feeling of doom?

Jewel MacKenzie Cameron, he thought grimly, you've a plan up your sleeve. And I've the feeling 'twill spell disaster for me.

She was already waiting for him at the bottom of a rickety ladder. "Come on," she urged in a friendly tone that didn't fool him for a moment. "We'll start on the malting floor."

In his mind, Tor heard a heavy clanging sound, like the cell door at Cowcadden swinging shut.

By the time they'd finished their tour, he had unwisely forgotten most of his suspicions. Even though the distillery was currently inoperative, Jewel had explained the malting process so thoroughly that he came away feeling as though he had actually witnessed it. Despite himself, he had been deeply interested.

She had begun the tour by showing him the copper-floored malting room where the harvested barley was soaked in water until the rich golden grains germinated. Then she had explained the drying and roasting process, and the chemical changes that took place in the great copper kettles called the tuns, where the barley was heated and cooked into a gruel-like mash. Later, the mash was boiled into something called the wort in order to extract the liquid, which was then distilled and captured, drop by golden drop, in aged oaken barrels and taken to the cellar. There, in due time, it would become the heavenly libation known as Drumcorrie Single Malt.

A subtle change had come over Jewel as she led him through this lengthy but fascinating process. Tor didn't think she was aware of the change, but he

161

certainly was. The mistrust and arrogance had fallen away from her as she talked, and he had recognized the glow in her eyes as genuine passion.

No doubt about it: Drumcorrie was in her blood. There was no other way to describe it, and Archibald MacKenzie had been an utter fool to try to kill such a rare and wondrous gift in his daughter.

Later, when they stepped outside into a world of stunning blue skies and windless warmth, they stood admiring the scenery in a companionable silence heretofore unknown to them.

" 'Twould be a pleasure to work in your distillery with you, Jewel MacKenzie Cameron," Tor said unexpectedly.

Jewel whirled to look at him, an expression of wonder on her face. " 'Twould be a pleasure to have you," she responded honestly.

Their eyes held for a rare moment devoid of hostility. Then together they walked back to the house, the silence between them a companionable one.

Chapter Thirteen

Of course it couldn't last. Not when the antagonists were Jewel and Tor Ban Cameron.

Annie Brewster was chatting in the kitchen with Tykie when the first indication of trouble drifted to them through the walls of the adjoining study. First came the sound of angry voices, then something crashing to the floor, and then the unmistakable thud of Jewel's feet fleeing up the stairs.

Tykie set down the cookpot he was repairing and grunted in dismay.

"Truce be over," Annie agreed. " 'Twas too good tae last."

Tykie scowled at her.

"Oh, stop that, will ye? I'm no traitor! She's married tae the mon. The sooner ye accept thot, the sooner ye can help make their union work."

Annie propped her hands on her hips.

Tykie glared back defiantly.

"Go ahead," Annie snapped. "Tell me again I be a

163

traitor! Tell me I've no her best interest at heart!"

Tykie's shaggy head nodded in wild agreement. The gold earring he wore glittered. His expression grew even darker as he looked another accusation at her.

Annie snorted. "Bah! I've no likin' fer the black-haired bastard either, so stop lookin' like thot or I'll pull yer ears frae yer head!"

Then what is it? Tykie's look demanded.

"Ye be thicker than I thought! Think a moment, will ye?"

Tykie tried, but only ended up looking confused.

"Millicent MacKenzie. Remember? Would ye prefer takin' on Tor Cameron as yer enemy, wi' his simple man's needs an' the fact thot both of us ken he be no match for our Miss Jewel? Or would ye prefer tae battle Millicent MacKenzie?"

Tykie shuddered. The choice was not pleasant. But he had to admit that the memories of the difficult journey back to Glen Chulish from Glasgow, and the few times he and Tor Ban Cameron had come to blows over Jewel, paled in the face of other, far more disturbing images.

Mistress Jewel's beloved wolfhound writhing in agony after being poisoned by an unseen hand.

Mistress Jewel's chambermaid Lucy, falling to her death from the distillery roof, although no one could explain why she had gone up there in the first place. Granted, everyone at Drumcorrie knew that foolish young Lucy had been completely enamored of Master Ruan MacKenzie, but no one had ever believed for a moment that Ruan himself had been capable of instigating the girl's death. But his mother . . . ah, now that was another thing altogether.

And what about that wee mare Mistress Jewel had raised from birth and schooled so patiently for endless years? Destroyed of necessity after breaking her leg one night in a hole in the paddock where there had never been a hole before. So heartbroken had Tykie's mistress been that she had taken to riding the ugly workhorses kept in the stable for fear of risking a similar tragedy.

Annie was right. The enemy here wasn't Tor Ban Cameron. On the other hand, Tykie hated listening to Annie's talk about Tor's "simple man's needs." Tykie wasn't blind. He knew that his mistress was not a lass any longer. But that didn't mean he cared to think of her as a woman. Or to remember that she was married to that lusting piece of prison trash.

But there was no getting around the fact that Annie was right in one thing, the most important thing: everything else paled in the face of the threat posed by Millicent MacKenzie.

What'll we do? his abject look asked plainly.

Annie's expression grew equally troubled. Sitting down at the table, she pulled the squirming Goat onto her lap. "I been givin' the matter plenty o' thought. I think 'tis time we took Cameron into our confidence."

Tykie looked aghast. Then furious. Wordless threats burst from his throat.

Annie shook her graying head. "Nay, mon. Ye be protectin' the bairn frae the wrong thing. 'Tis only togaither, no brawlin' amongst ourselves, that we can put an end tae Millicent MacKenzie. And like it or no, we've an ally in Cameron. He's na fool. He's equally big and braw as ye—or will be, once I fatten 'im up proper."

Tykie shook his head, his expression still mutinous.

"He'll be spendin' much time wi' the bairn once work i' the fields begins," Annie argued. "More than ye, I'll wager. Better he kens the truth about Millicent MacKenzie, so he can keep an eye on the lass. An

165

enlightened mon be better armed than an ignorant one."

How could Tykie possibly argue with that? Annie was right. Oh, but it stuck in Tykie's craw, the thought of having to take that bastard into their confidence!

"I canna speak wi' him now," Annie was saying thoughtfully, sensing that Tykie was wavering. "No tellin' whot's brought 'em tae blows this time."

Tykie shrugged his massive shoulders. It could be anything.

And so it had been.

A matter as simple as clothing.

Ever since he had left his sickbed, Tor had been making do with the few items he had dug out of Archibald MacKenzie's trunks that fit him, as well as with the castoffs that Tykie had grudgingly donated. But now that he was putting on weight and standing taller, everything he had donned of late had grown uncomfortably tight.

Faced with the prospect of squeezing into something entirely unsuitable for dinner that night, Tor had taken the liberty of foraging through some of the other bedrooms after returning from the distillery. Much to his good fortune, he had stumbled onto a musty clothespress filled with a wealth of fine shirts and soft doeskin breeches, and a kilt woven of soft Cheviot wool in the lovely blue and green colors of the MacKenzie tartan.

Tor had decided then and there that he would dine with Jewel that night dressed as a MacKenzie laird. And he had certainly looked the part, dressed in a finely stitched lawn shirt with a hint of lace at collar and cuff, a waistcoat of dove gray silk jacquard, and a plaid about his shoulders to ward off the chill. At the very last, he had traded his breeches for a kilt, that ancient symbol of Highland tradition.

Although Highland born himself, Tor had never been able to explain why a kilt—which was admittedly no more than a knee-length, swinging skirt—should appear so very masculine when worn by the right man. But for some reason it was. Especially on him. He was tall, wide of chest, and black haired—the embodiment of the true Highland chieftain—and he had struck Jewel in precisely that way the moment he had appeared downstairs in the dining room.

Jewel had stared at him, stunned, as he paused in the doorway, grinning at her in a way that made her heart simply stop beating. This was the first time she had ever seen him as he must have been in the days before illness and incarceration had bowed him down. She could scarcely credit the change in him. The only thing about him that was even remotely recognizable was the gleam in his eyes, the spark of insolence and lusty hunger for life that had first caught her attention when he had glared at her from the back of the warden's office at Cowcadden. She saw, too, that he had shaved before dinner and used a brush to tame the windblown locks of his black hair. Now he stood before her, equally as magnificent as any of the portraits of long-deceased MacKenzie lords that graced the front hall.

Oh, how he had scared and exhilarated her, and made her realize why her cousin Cassandra had completely lost her head the night before! No woman could resist such a handsome young god, least of all Jewel Cameron, his wife, who had already learned from his own skilled hands what it meant to burn for him alone.

Jewel's reaction to such an onrush of feeling had been understandably defensive. Terrified that Tor would sense the betraying leaping of her heart, she had hastened to distance herself from him.

"Who in hell do you think you are?" she had demanded in a tone like frozen ice. "You've no right to wear the MacKenzie plaid, no right at all!"

The expectant light had died from Tor's eyes.

"And the kilt!" Jewel's voice rose as sudden fear grabbed her by the throat. "Don't you know 'tis illegal to wear the kilt, that it has been since the forty-five? You'll be arrested for treason should anyone catch you!"

"And who would turn me in?" Tor mocked. "You? I'd not put such an underhanded trick past you, ma'am."

That was when Jewel had lost her temper and thrown the lovely French decanter on the sideboard at him. Luckily she had missed, but Tor's expression had been so terrible that she had simply turned and fled from the room. In her heart, she knew that she had deserved his scorching accusation, but still it had hurt. Far worse than she had expected.

Now, as she paced her bedroom trying in vain to calm her agitation, she knew that she owed him an apology. Apologies had never come easy to a woman like Jewel. For most of her life, she was the one who had been victimized, and for that reason alone she had always found it difficult to squash her rebellious arrogance on those few occasions when the situation demanded it. But in this instance she knew she had been grossly unfair. And horribly unkind. She owed her husband an explanation as well.

But how to explain to Tor that the mere sight of him towering above her dressed like a Highland nobleman had turned her knees to water? How to explain that she had thought him the most devastatingly handsome man she had ever seen?

Perhaps she could say that she had been genuinely worried that he was risking arrest by wearing the kilt, which was forbidden by English law even in the privacy of a man's own home. But Tor would only counter that she couldn't possibly worry that he might wind up in prison since she didn't care a fig for him anyway. And Jewel wasn't so sure she could hide her true feelings from him, even in the face of his scorn.

"You're in love with him," she told herself aloud, and in a voice of doom. "And sooner or later he's going to find out."

But not yet. Please, not yet.

Being in love was so new to her still, and so unexpectedly frightening. All her life, she had managed to fight off her enemies simply by closing her mind and her heart to them. It was different with Tor, because she knew that she would never be able to shut away her heart from him now. And a person's heart, she was learning very quickly, was an easy thing to wound.

"Oh, what shall I do?" she demanded in frustration.

Apologize.

She had been blatantly unfair to Tor, and she had always prided herself on her fairness. And her courage. Still, it would take a lot of courage to apologize.

On the other hand, she couldn't forget the expression on Tor's face when she had lashed out at him so unfairly. She kept seeing the way his grin had faded and the jaunty light had died from his eyes. All because of her.

Did she, too, have the power to wound?

The thought spurred her as nothing else could have done. Making up her mind, she quickly left the room.

All was silent downstairs. The dining room was empty. She searched the library and the study. Both were empty as well. She tried the morning room and the parlor. Frantic now, she hurried into the hallway, and nearly barreled into Annie as she rounded a corner.

"Sorry," she gasped, smoothing her skirts in an effort to recover her composure. Then she cleared her throat. "Have you seen my husband, Annie?"

"He's gone out."

"Out? At this time of night? Where?"

"Back to Edinburgh, I imagine."

"Edinburgh!" Jewel's eyes were wide. "Why Edinburgh?"

" 'Tis where he came from," Annie replied, shrugging. "If he has any sense at a', 'tis where he'll return."

"How do you know? Did he tell you that?"

Annie snorted. "He didna have to! Have ye no listened to his speech, lass? Highland born, I'll wager me life, and Lowland educated. 'Tis there whenever he opens his mouth. Which, around you, he does rare enough."

Jewel ignored the barb. Her mind was reeling. She caught Annie's arm. Her voice rose. "You don't really think he's left for Edinburgh, do you?"

"Withoot money, withoot a horse, withoot so much as a coat? Bah!"

But there were horses in the stable. . . .

The night air was very cold. Jewel shivered as she hurried through the darkness. The stable was empty, the grooms retired for the night. And Tor was not there.

Frantic now, she hurried to the tack room and peered inside. Next she tried the feed storage and the toolroom, without success. By now her heart was pounding so that she could scarcely breathe.

"Jewel."

She whirled in the aisle, her skirts belling around her.

Tor was leaning against one of the stall doors behind her, his arms crossed before his chest. "Were you looking for me?"

"Yes—no! I . . . um . . . I was worried about the horses."

"Were you?" Tor straightened and came toward her. "Then let's take a look at them."

Jewel followed him mutely down the aisle. A lantern burned in a stone embrasure, casting a soft glow on his harsh features. She looked away quickly. No one had to tell her that he was still furious with her.

Drum, the big drafter, stirred as they halted in front of his stall. Recognizing his mistress, he came forward to greet her, whickering softly.

"I wasn't aware that you looked in on them," Tor said, watching Jewel closely as she stroked the drafter's velvety muzzle.

"I don't usually."

"Then what made you do so tonight?"

The moment their eyes met, she realized that there was no sense in lying to him. Her voice was barely a whisper. "I was afraid you'd left for Edinburgh."

"Edinburgh! Why?"

"Annie said that's where you're from. She—she said if you had any sense at all, that's where you'd go."

"Dressed in a kilt? With bare legs and no undergarments?"

Jewel stared at him, aghast. "Y-you've got nothing on under that kilt?"

"Only the things God gave me."

She looked so bewildered that Tor's lips turned up at the corners. "Jewel. I was teasing."

She swallowed hard. "Then—then you weren't really going to leave?"

His smoky eyes nailed hers. "Were you worried that I might?"

Blood rushed into her cheeks, but she made no

reply. She simply didn't trust herself to speak.

Tor stepped closer. His nearness, and the size and strength of him, overwhelmed her senses. "Would you be sorry if I went?"

He could see her swallow. He stepped closer, his voice husky now. "Would you? Answer me, Jewel."

"I . . ." She fell silent.

"Well?"

"Tor, please—"

"No!" He caught her arm as she attempted to push past him. "I want an answer, Jewel. I won't let you go until I get one."

The words were bursting in her lungs. Her love for him hammered through her veins, and it was all she could do not to shout the truth aloud. But even as she ached to do so, the bitter lessons of her childhood kept her still, and so the opportunity was lost.

As she hesitated, the light died from Tor's eyes. His fingers slid away from her wrist. A cold, implacable mask took the place of the urgency on his face.

"No need to worry," he said coldly. "I won't be leaving as yet. I've not had my fill of making you miserable."

With that he turned and walked out. The stable door crashed shut behind him.

Chapter Fourteen

Even the best-laid plans, Tor was soon to discover, had a way of backfiring on a person. Take his determination to make his wife miserable, for instance. A simple task, to be sure, and he had started out simply enough by avoiding her altogether. On the morning following their argument, he left the house long before even Annie was awake, and spent the entire day at the distillery. He carried his meals from the kitchen in a satchel, and did not return to the house until long after the evening meal had been cleared from the table and the downstairs lights extinguished.

It was a pattern that repeated itself on the following day, and the day thereafter, and on through the remainder of the week. His constant presence in the distillery quickly became a trial for Sandy Sinclair, but Tor made it clear that, if he had been brought from Cowcadden to work as a distillery laborer, then labor he would. And Sandy was going to teach him.

Over the next few weeks, in fact, Tor learned all he could about the art of distilling whiskey. It turned out to be a surprisingly difficult art. Although the basic chemistry of converting barley into malt was simple enough, the variables involved were not. There were no guidebooks to read or instructions to follow. The distilling temperatures, for example, were variable. So were the amounts of the ingredients used. Furthermore, an entire season's harvest could go to ruin simply by leaving the malted barley heating too long, or not long enough.

How then, Tor angrily demanded of poor Sandy, did one know what to do?

"Ye develop a feel for it," Sandy said. "And a nose. Both will tell ye what's right or wrong."

"A feel? A nose? Ridiculous!"

" 'Twill take time," Sandy soothed. But he was too timid to point out that no one had hired Tor Cameron to take over as Drumcorrie's master distiller. That was Sandy's job. Tor was expected to do nothing more than act as a common day laborer.

Surprisingly, he was proving to be a good one. Not only was he a fast learner and above average in intelligence, but as he continued gaining weight and filling out, his strength soon equaled Tykie Ferguson's, certainly a boon for a man as slight as Sandy Sinclair. Furthermore, Tor didn't seem to mind all the heavy lifting and carrying that was involved. In fact, he seemed to relish it. Over the long hours that both men worked together, Sandy lost much of his fear of him.

But while Sandy was coming to appreciate Tor's presence in the distillery, Tor himself was growing increasingly ill-tempered and resentful at finding himself there. The fault was his own, however, not Sandy's. His plan to make Jewel regret the day she had brought him here from Cowcadden was backfiring in his face. Because the more time he spent away from her, the more surly and combative he became.

The reason was simple.

He missed her.

Never in a million years would he have dreamed that he could. But as the long days went by, he found himself craving just a brief glimpse of her. Worse was the ache for her that never seemed to leave his bones, an ache that only worsened as the days melted into weeks and the weather warmed and became undeniably seductive. Spring was in the air, and Tor Cameron missed his wife in the most carnal of ways. Small wonder, then, that his mood was growing increasingly rancorous. Small wonder that an explosion was inevitable.

Not surprisingly, it began with a case of simple male jealousy, which grabbed Tor by the throat when he returned from the fields one evening to find Ruan MacKenzie in the library dancing attendance on his wife.

Though the study had remained Jewel's private domain, Tor had long since come to consider the library his own. It was here that he spent most of his time avoiding her whenever he was not at the distillery, and where he had found a measure of peace leafing through the pages of books that had long been denied him in prison and during his nomadic years as a mercenary soldier. Moreover, sequestering himself in the quiet room served to give him a feeling of control over his life, and a sense of belonging that the long months of imprisonment had nearly destroyed.

Here, among Archibald MacKenzie's fine collection of books, he had discovered that solitude could be healing, not destructive. Small wonder he was enraged to find Ruan MacKenzie invading the domain he had come to consider his own.

Tired and dirty after a long day in the fields, Tor had been on his way upstairs for a bath when the sound of laughter—Ruan's and Jewel's—had drawn him disbelievingly to the library door. Halting on the threshold, he had found the two of them seated together at the reading table, their heads close together.

"What's so funny?" he demanded now, in a menacing tone of voice.

Both looked up, their laughter stilling at the sight of him.

Tor had spent the day outdoors, learning how to plow a field. Because the weather was warm, he had rolled his sleeves past his elbows and stripped down to breeches and boots. Tall and lean hipped, he now stood in the doorway covered with mud, his black locks windblown and his rugged face sunburned and unshaven.

Jewel couldn't help thinking how devastatingly handsome he looked.

Ruan, however, thought that he looked no better than a peasant. "Good God," he said, wrinkling his nose. "Are ye sleeping i' the byre these days?"

It was the worst thing he could have said. Tor had been accused of many unpleasant things in his life, but smelling like manure had never been one of them. Now his intense dislike of Ruan MacKenzie, as well as the frustration of long weeks of sexual denial, boiled to the surface. With a growl, he sprang forward.

In Ruan's world, a gentleman always politely announced his intentions beforehand. Pugilism was left to the underclass. But not in Tor's world. Ruan yelped as he was dragged upright by his collar, and his chair went spinning out from under him. There came a sickening sound as a well-aimed blow caught him square in the jaw. The impact lifted him clear

Get Four Books Totally
FREE — A $21.96 Value!

▼ Tear Here and Mail Your FREE Book Card Today! ▼

PLEASE RUSH
MY FOUR FREE
BOOKS TO ME
RIGHT AWAY!

Leisure Romance Book Club
P.O. Box 6613
Edison, NJ 08818-6613

AFFIX
STAMP
HERE

off his feet and catapulted him backward into the bookcase. Several heavy volumes of Shakespeare spilled down on him as he landed, unconscious, on the carpet.

Jewel was on her feet, shaking and angry. "Have you lost your mind, Cameron?"

Breathing heavily, Tor dusted off his hands. "On the contrary. I think I've just regained my senses."

"Oh! So you're a boor *and* a blackguard now, not just a convict!"

That hurt, but Tor would be damned if he let her sense it. Furthermore, he wasn't about to let her spoil the moment for him. "You'll have to admit he had it coming."

Jewel said nothing. In a way, Tor was right. Ruan *had* been more than a wee bit insulting. But to hit another man like that, quite out of the blue . . . ! She knelt beside her cousin and worriedly shook his shoulder.

"Leave that!" Tor snapped, incensed by the sight of her touching another man, even if that man was her cousin. "That's Annie's job!"

Jewel rounded on him, truly furious. "You're hopeless, Cameron, do you know that? There's not a stitch of the gentleman in you! Barbarian, savage, that's all you'll ever be! God, am I sorry I brought you here!"

Getting up, she stormed past him, but Tor caught her by the arm. Spinning her around, he brought her hard against his chest. "You were never sorry in bed."

"That was low," she shot back. "Besides, there's more to life than bed."

"Is there?"

Her eyes scorched him with her scorn. "Now why did I know you'd say that? Could it be because everything you say and do is ruled by that objectionable thing in your breeches, not the brain in your head?"

Tor wanted to murder her then. Or carry her up

the stairs and make her eat every one of those words by forcing her to do his bidding with honeyed kisses. Oh, aye, he knew how to make this woman burn!

And she knew it, too, standing there pressed against his rock-hard chest with her breasts heaving and the blood pounding through her veins. Only a thin line separated fury from passion, and Jewel could tell that she was in the grip of both.

"Let me go!" Her words were a choked command. Tor still had her by the waist, and she felt as if she were on fire wherever they touched.

But Tor refused. He knew far too well what she was feeling. The pupils of her magnificent eyes had dilated and her nostrils flared. "Do you really want me to?" he asked huskily.

Just like that, Jewel's fury turned to ashes in her mouth. That silky, seductive voice of his had never failed to turn her knees to water. And it had been so long since he had loved her—or even looked at her that way!

"Let m-me go," she repeated tremulously.

"I'd rather not. I'd rather hold you even closer. Like this."

Curving his arm about her waist, he swept her toward him and tucked her impudently between his legs. His manhood had risen, and now it pressed insistently against Jewel's thighs through the thin fabric of his breeches.

He smelled of rich earth and the outdoors, a masculine scent that befuddled Jewel's senses. She could feel her head beginning to spin. She found she had to close her eyes against the smoky sensuality that burned in Tor's gaze.

The moment she did so, she felt him lift her so that she was standing on her toes. Leaning her backward against his arm until her chin tipped up, he kissed her, slowly and seductively. His full lips took possession of her mouth. His tongue grazed hers, seeking succor. His free hand found its way to her breast and cupped the quickening flesh there.

Jewel moaned low in her throat. Was it a sound of protest, or surrender?

Tor deepened the kiss, plunging his tongue between her lips. Encircling her shoulders, he pressed her fully to the heated length of him. Their bodies fused.

"Oh, God," he groaned against her mouth.

Jewel had forgotten everything, including the unconscious Ruan, who lay sprawled behind them. The long, lonely weeks of Tor's self-imposed exile at the distillery faded into the glorious welcome of reunion. How perfectly they fit together, like hand to glove, as Tor caught her up against him and deepened the kiss to a slow burn.

"Too long," he whispered, and Jewel's body echoed an aching agreement.

Would he have taken her right there on the library floor, with the unconscious Ruan behind them? Would Jewel have let him? Neither knew. Annie's arrival brought a swift end to any reconciliation. At least they were alerted to her coming by the scratching and whining of her terrier at the door. Quickly they broke apart.

"Bah!" said Annie, taking one look at her mistress's flushed face and Tor's disheveled attire. Her mouth turned down and her expression grew thunderous. By God, they didn't fool her for a moment!

On the floor near the bookcase, Ruan stirred and uttered a moan.

Annie's eyes widened. It was obvious that she hadn't realized she was interrupting something more serious than a stormy kiss.

Goat snuffled eagerly at Ruan's recumbent form.

"Go away," Ruan groaned, pushing at him. "Annie,

call off yer beast afore he lifts his leg on me!"

"I'll fetch Tykie," Annie breathed, backing out of the door.

"There's no need, Mrs. Brewster," Tor assured her quickly. "We've settled our differences."

"Be this true, Master Ruan?"

Although Ruan wanted to disagree violently, there was little he could do about it. His head was throbbing and he was trying hard not to be sick to his stomach. Tottering to the window, he breathed in the cold mountain air while Jewel hurriedly brought him whiskey.

"Good of you, Coz."

"Let it go," she begged in a whisper, handing him the glass. "He'll kill you next time."

"You may be right," Ruan said ruefully. "Bloody savage ye married, Jewel."

"I know," she said sadly.

Leaving him to Annie's care, she quit the room without a backward glance. She was halfway up the stairs before she heard Tor calling to her angrily from the hall below.

Resigned, she turned and tightened her hold on the banister. "Aye?"

"No need to look so sullen. I've only one thing to say."

She regarded him warily. "What's that?"

His expression was taut with fury. "If you dare deceive me with him, I'll kill you both."

She stared back at him, thunderstruck. "Wh-what? What did you say?"

"You heard me."

"Aye, I did. I just couldn't believe it at first!"

She came running down the stairs toward him, holding her skirts aloft so she wouldn't fall over them. She didn't think she'd ever been so furious in all her life. Literally itching to battle him, she halted on the last step, where her eyes were on a level with his. Her lack of height had always been a severe disadvantage whenever she confronted him, so she had no intention of allowing him to gain the upper hand this time. She was literally boiling with rage, and she wanted to make sure he knew it.

Aye, apparently he did, and the self-satisfied look on his face was so infuriating that her control snapped clean. Letting go of the railing, Jewel hauled off and slapped him as hard as she could. The sound cracked like a gunshot in the silence of the hall.

"You've got a hell of a lot of nerve to speak to me like that, Tor Ban Cameron!" she shrieked. "If you dare suggest anything like that again, I'll personally cut out your tongue! See how you'll like spending the rest of your life grunting and mumbling along with Tykie! Bloody Lowland git!"

Turning, she stormed back up the stairs, while Tor stared after her in utter amazement. His face burned where she had slapped him. His pride lay withered at his feet. But his heart, ah, his heart was filled with that odd, lighter-than-air feeling that always preceded laughter.

God, what a woman! If he wasn't careful, he'd end up falling in love with her.

Fortunately, the thought was like a dash of ice water in the face. Nursing his cheek, he sank slowly onto the bottom step. Sweet Judas! He didn't want to fall in love with a woman like Jewel MacKenzie Cameron! While he certainly didn't mind making love *to* her, he'd rather die than be in love *with* her.

Which would never happen anyway, he told himself furiously. Love was an alien word to him, so alien that he wouldn't know it if it hit him square in the face. So there.

Still nursing his cheek, which was hurting badly,

he got up and stalked to the door. Bloody Lowland git, was he? He'd show her, the damnable, hotheaded witch!

What the devil was a git, anyway?

Chapter Fifteen

For the next few days the air was so frigid at Drumcorrie that even Tykie Ferguson found himself wishing Jewel and Tor would hurry up and reconcile. In fact, the only one who seemed to enjoy the hostile atmosphere was Goat, who always took advantage of the preoccupation of the humans around him to relieve himself on the carpets.

"Let Cameron do that," Jewel snapped when she came across Annie on her knees one morning mopping up the latest of Goat's little offerings. "That's all he's bloody good for!"

" 'Twould do us a' a world o' good if ye'd make yer peace wi' him."

"That sounds to me like treason," Jewel snapped, planting her hands on her hips. "Have you switched alliances on me, Annie?"

"Tain't treason," Annie snapped back. " 'Tis common sense. Ye married the mon. Now ye maun live wi' yer choice."

"If you recall, I had no choice," Jewel said frigidly.

"No?" Annie's eyes sparkled with genuine anger. "Seems to me ye made a choice free and clear when ye turned doon yer cousin. And ye made the choice all on your ain to go to Glasgow. And ye chose him, did ye no?"

"Aye, more's the pity!"

But Annie was in no mood for her young mistress's sarcasm. " 'Tis time ye grew up, lass. Accepted the fact that ye've made yer bed, an' lie in it."

"I'll keep that in mind," Jewel promised, and swept away with a haughty toss of her head. Secretly she was angry and hurt by Annie's unfairness. And by the fact that, deep in her heart, she knew Annie to be right.

But how could she possibly lie in the bed she'd made when Tor Ban Cameron was the man who happened to be sharing it? He hated her. Hadn't said a word to her since that awful confrontation on the stairs last week, when she had slapped him.

The memory made her wince, for it shamed her deeply. She had never in her life lifted her hand to anyone, not a servant nor a crofter, not even the lowliest animal in the byre. But she had hit Tor.

But he made her so bloody angry!

And miserable.

And confused.

Just as he had promised he would.

Well, I hate him, too, she thought mutinously.

What was more, she wasn't about to follow Annie's advice and make her peace with the man. Why couldn't Annie mind her own business, anyway? Interfering old woman!

If she had had a choice, Jewel would have preferred spending the rest of the day sulking in her room and avoiding everyone, especially Tor. But that would have been cowardly, not to mention impossible. Planting time had begun on Drumcorrie's few arable acres, and Jewel was not about to leave such an important task to anyone else, least of all an unskilled laborer like her husband, God curse him!

Ten minutes later she was trotting Drum across the footbridge that led to the western slope of the glen, where a stretch of pine forest softened the bite of the wind and permitted the growing of Drumcorrie's barley. The weather was lovely. A warm breeze blew down from the peak of Ben Chulish, and early wildflowers had begun poking their heads through the moss.

Jewel, who hadn't ridden out in a number of days, could feel the tension ebbing away from her the farther she left the house behind. She was bareheaded, and the sun was warm on her shoulders and back. Drum trotted along at a spanking clip, and blew through his nostrils as though he, too, was enjoying the fragrant air.

Up ahead, where the trees thinned and the fields began, Jewel caught sight of Tor talking with Angus MacKenzie. Though she didn't get out much these days, she knew that Angus had, in his way, taken Tor beneath his wing. She had been secretly pleased by the fact, since Angus had always been something of a mentor to her as well. She had no doubt that he would prove a steadying influence on Tor during his difficult transition from prison life.

Emerging from the trees, she saw that Tor and Angus were seated on the stone wall enclosing the plowed field, laughing companionably together. She didn't think she'd ever seen Tor quite so relaxed before, and her heart filled with an odd gladness at the sight.

But the warmth bubbling inside her chilled the moment she saw that Tor and Angus were not alone. A fine pair of hunters stood saddled near the gate, and she recognized them instantly as Ruan and Cassie MacKenzie's. Cassie, looking beautiful in a trim habit of dark green velvet piped with black, was standing much too close to Tor, and she made no attempt to move away when Jewel appeared.

Jewel's expression was sour as she halted in front of them and slipped her foot from the stirrup.

"Still ridin' that prehistoric beast?" Ruan teased. "When will you buy yoursel' a proper mount, lass?"

"Och, Ruan," sniped Cassie, "you ken there's naught the least proper about our Jewel."

Jewel flashed her a look of utter dislike, then deliberately turned her back. "Good morning, Angus. How's the planting coming?"

"See for yersel', lass."

She followed the sweep of the old man's arm with her eyes. Pride filled her as she saw the fragile green shoots emerging from the soil. The low wall that encompassed the field had been laid with stones pulled painstakingly from that very earth. The task had taken years, and Jewel herself had helped with much of it, back in those difficult childhood years when it had been wiser for her to be outdoors and away from her stepmother's condemning eyes. Her friendship with Angus and his family had been forged back then, and it showed today in the fatherly way he draped his arm about her shoulders as he walked with her on a tour of inspection.

She was unaware that Tor watched them while he sat pretending to listen to Cassie's endless chatter. He hadn't seen much of Jewel in the last few days, and he thought she looked rather thin and hollow eyed. Hadn't she been getting enough sleep? Wasn't she eating enough? What the devil was the matter with her?

"What's that?" he said, suddenly aware that Cassie

had asked him a question. He didn't have a clue as to what she had said.

"I asked if you'd like to join us for tea on Sunday," Cassie repeated, annoyed.

Behind Tor's back, Ruan began to make desperate signals to warn her off. Cassie knew perfectly well what he was trying to say: Mama would be livid if Jewel's objectionable husband dared set foot in their house. But Cassie could be extremely stubborn when it came to getting what she wanted. And at the moment she wanted Tor. She'd never laid eyes on a better-looking man, or one who exuded such an exciting aura of brooding masculinity. Cassie didn't care that he was married to Jewel. In fact, the thought that she stood a good chance of stealing him away from her cousin only made the chase more exciting.

Not that Cassie wanted to marry Tor herself. She had every intention of obeying her mother's wishes and ensnaring an Englishman wealthy enough to assure her a fine home far away from the Highlands. But finding the right man wasn't going to be as easy as her mother seemed to believe. Not when Cassie wouldn't be bringing an untouched maidenhead to her marriage bed. Poor Mama! Protecting her daughter's virginity when it had been lost long ago!

In the meantime, there was no harm in dallying with a lusty longshanks the likes of Tor Cameron. Cassie had no doubt that Jewel was denying the man her bed, and surely it wouldn't take too long until he became thoroughly frustrated and turned his attentions elsewhere.

"We usually have tea around four," she said now, ignoring her brother's frantic gestures. "I'm sure Mama would be delighted if you joined us."

"Would she?"

"Of course," Cassie said innocently. "Why wouldn't she?"

Tor could think of a lot of reasons.

So could Ruan.

But Jewel and Angus came back at that moment, and the moment both of them were in earshot, Tor accepted Cassie's invitation with every evidence of keen anticipation.

"You're going to Chulish House?" Jewel asked, so shocked that the words burst from her.

"You're expected, too, of course," Cassie assured her sweetly.

But Jewel had long ago refused to set foot in Millicent's home again, and both of them knew it. Recovering her composure, she gave her husband a haughty glance. "I hope you'll give my best to Aunt Millicent."

"I most certainly will."

They glared at each other. So much for any attempt at reconciliation.

When it was time for Cassie and Ruan to leave, Tor invited them to join him for a late breakfast first. Cassie was eager to accept, but Ruan stepped in quickly to refuse. Some other time, thank you. They were expected home.

"Where is it that they live?" Tor asked, watching as the two rode off, arguing visibly.

"You'll find out on Sunday," Jewel pointed out frostily.

"Ah, that's right. I will."

She bit her lip. "Are you really planning to go?"

"Why shouldn't I?"

She didn't answer. When Tor turned to look at her, he was startled by the expression on her face. "Jewel, what is it?"

She longed to make some flippant retort, but the words stuck in her throat. She had no choice but to shrug her shoulders and hurry off to fetch Drum, who was grazing a short distance away.

The Enchanted Bride

"What is it about Millicent MacKenzie?" Tor demanded, turning to Angus in utter frustration.

Angus paused in the task of lighting his pipe. "There's bad blood i' the family."

"That's obvious. But why?"

Angus inclined his head toward Jewel. "Has she no told 'ee?"

"No. She acts bloody mysterious every time the subject comes up. You'd think the entire household was scared to death of that woman."

"We ain't fools."

"Oh, come on, Angus! Even you?"

The old man's expression darkened. "Especially me! Who's had tae look oot for the lass a' these years, eh? Me an' Tykie an' Annie! If no for us, she'd hae come to harm by now!"

"Because of Millicent MacKenzie? She seems harmless enough. A bit deluded, but certainly no match for Jewel."

Angus snorted.

Tor scowled at him. "Angus. You'd better tell me."

The old man sighed. "I suppose so. But ye'll no breathe a word tae the lass, or she'll have me head."

"My word on it."

Angus exhaled a cloud of fragrant smoke. Watching Jewel canter off through the trees, he lowered his voice and told Tor all there was to know about Millicent MacKenzie.

Twenty minutes later, Tor appeared in the tack room where Tykie sat polishing harnesses. Tykie took one look at his expression, laid aside the saddle soap, and lumbered quickly to his feet.

"No need for that," Tor told him harshly. "I'm not here to pick a fight. I've just been to see Angus, and I want nothing more than a yea or a nay from you.

189

Is everything he told me about Millicent MacKenzie true?"

Tykie hesitated.

"Well?"

The big mute shrugged.

"Damn it, answer me!"

Looking miserable, Tykie nodded his head.

Tor whirled and started for the door. Tykie stopped him with a hand on his arm, grunting in alarm.

"No need to worry," Tor snapped. "I know better than to let her know that Angus betrayed her confidence. The secret's safe with me. And I'll do what I can to see she comes to no harm."

The fear on Tykie's face eased somewhat. He let go of Tor's arm. For once there wasn't a trace of hostility in his expression.

"I've been invited to take tea with them on Sunday," Tor added thoughtfully. "Jewel doesn't want me to go, but I shall. 'Tis always wise to hold your enemies close, don't you think?"

Tykie's eyes gleamed as he considered the idea. For once, he and Tor were in total agreement.

As everyone else at Drumcorrie seemed to be. Everyone, of course, save Jewel. The thought of Tor socializing openly with the Chulish MacKenzies was enough to drive her mad. At first she tried to change Tor's mind by snubbing him. When that failed, she resorted to arguments and insults. Still no response. By the time Sunday morning arrived she had given up completely and had stopped speaking to him at all.

Tor had been surprisingly patient with her antics. He was quite used to Jewel's difficult temperament by now and inured to her insults—at least in this case, for he knew that fear lay at the bottom of her behavior. As well, it pleased him to believe that she objected so strenuously to the thought of his going because she happened to be the tiniest bit concerned for him. Of course, when he unwisely dared suggest as much a mere hour before his departure for Chulish House, her response was so vehement that he ended up losing his own temper after all.

"You're a spoiled brat, do you know that?" he demanded now, stung by her latest reference to him as a spineless toady. "All your life you've had your way, had everyone dancing attendance on you, and now 'tis driving you mad to know you can't have your say in this! Isn't that right, Jewel?"

What he suggested was so incredible that for a second she could only gape at him. All her life she'd had people dancing attendance on her? Spoiling her? Had Tor lost his mind?

She struggled to find the right words to crush him completely, but for once they refused to come. The two of them were standing in the great hall, squaring off against each other while Tor waited for Piers MacInnis to bring his horse from the stable. He had dressed with considerable care for his appointment at Chulish House, and this in itself had served to spark Jewel's already simmering temper into full-blown anger.

Someone—most likely that traitor, Annie Brewster!—had been sewing for Tor of late, and the altered breeches and finely embroidered waistcoat he was wearing for his visit made him look breathtakingly handsome. He had also brushed back his dark locks and tied them with a ribbon, which gave his hawkish face a roughly chiseled splendor. Not once since their marriage had he ever bothered to tie his hair in a queue for her, but he could do so for Cassie MacKenzie, the long-legged bastard!

Actually, it wasn't jealousy that riled Jewel so much as an almost tearful sense of betrayal. The fact

191

that Tor could willingly side with the Chulish House camp—whether he knew he was doing so or not—hurt her beyond belief. Perhaps if she told him all of the horrible things Millicent MacKenzie had done to her over the years?

But Tor would never believe her. He would accuse her of making them up, and call her petty and jealous. And that would be more intolerable than anything else.

So in the end she reacted by simply withdrawing into herself. Lashing out at him didn't seem to be doing much good. Even as he stood there waiting for her to counter his last, ugly blow, she retreated inwardly. The sparkling anger faded from her lovely eyes, and her expression became sad and watchful.

She reminded Tor of a sparrow, hiding in the hedgerow with a hawk circling overhead. He remembered suddenly that the same thing had happened to her when Millicent MacKenzie had arrived unannounced on their doorstep the other day. Back then, Tor had puzzled at length over the woman's odd effect on Jewel, for he had never until that moment seen her withdraw in defeat.

Now, recalling what Angus had told him, he felt an unexpected wave of tenderness wash over him. The urge to take her into his arms and smooth that troubled furrow from her brow was almost overpowering. Aching, he jammed his fists into his pockets. He knew better than to touch her.

The clopping of hooves sounded in the courtyard outside. Jewel cast a last, desperate glance at Tor. Gritting his teeth, he ignored her.

"Are you certain you won't come?" he asked, only because he felt the need to keep up appearances.

Jewel's chin tipped. "Thank you, no. I've too much to do at home."

"I understand."

They looked at each other, both of them stiff and unrepentant. Then Tor made a half-bow in her direction, as proper and distant as that of any gentleman to a little-known lady.

"Until this evening, ma'am."

She watched with her hands balled into fists as he crossed the hall and exited through the front door. She had to physically restrain herself from running after him and begging him to stay. Her lungs burst with the effort of keeping his name inside. Her throat ached with unshed tears. She would rather die than ask anything of him.

Outside, hoofbeats rang on stone, then faded on the packed turf of the path beyond.

"Good riddance," she said aloud, but the words were tremulous and she had to bite her lip to keep the tears at bay.

Chapter Sixteen

Far to the south, in the wild border county of Ayr, the dawn arrived to disperse a night that had been equally as tumultuous as the one in Glen Chulish. Along the vast corridors of Abercraig Castle, sleepy servants went about lighting the sconces and drawing back the heavy drapes. A grizzled steward stumped into the great hall to unlock the front door as part of his morning ritual. Behind him waited the housekeeper, her key ring jangling impatiently.

"I'll start i' the kitchen then, Mr. Bennish. 'Is lordship'll be wantin' breakfast shortly."

The steward grunted. The moment the housekeeper's footsteps faded on the cold stones, a bell jangled insistently from deep inside the walls. Mordart Bennish grunted again and shuffled off down the corridor.

The eastern wing of the castle was icy cold. Medieval rush mats failed to warm the stones, and the curtains shook with the draft. The wind along the border hills of Ayr was strong enough to break windows at times, and the lord of Abercraig had refused to indulge in such a risky expense as glass.

When Mordart Bennish shuffled into the anteroom, he found the present Earl of Abercraig completing his toilette. Finished with his shaving, he was toweling his jaw and shivering with the cold.

"Good morning, your lordship."

"Bennish."

"Mrs. Tweedham be fixin' breakfast. Tea be on its way."

"I know, I know. That isn't why I rang. I've been up half the night."

Bennish looked suitably sympathetic. "Your bowels again, m'lord?"

"No, it ain't my bowels! 'Tis that damned MacKenzie woman, the one who wrote me about my nephew! I've been awake since the wee hours giving it thought, and now I've decided what to do."

Malcolm Caulbane Cameron, fourth Earl of Abercraig, was a huge man, with powerful forearms and a head of thick black hair that showed no graying at the temples despite his advancing age. Like his nephew, Tor Ban Cameron, he possessed piercing blue eyes and a nose that could be called decidedly Roman. But where Tor's eyes were secretive and cool, Malcolm Caulbane's were cold and devoid of all life.

He was a hard man, and had made a point throughout life to show no one mercy. Not his servants, his wives (of which none survived), and especially not the last remaining member of his family, Tor, the only son of his long-deceased brother, Tarquin.

The letter Millicent MacKenzie had written him had taken Malcolm Cameron completely by surprise. He had thought his nephew safely transported to the colonies by now, and with any luck dead. The fact that Tor was not only still in Scotland, but had made what amounted to a brilliant marriage to some Highland heiress had come as a staggering blow.

Millicent MacKenzie had found out about Malcolm Cameron by making inquiries at Cowcadden. Indeed, she had apparently learned a number of interesting facts from the prison's talkative warden. While Jewel did not know the details surrounding her own husband's arrest, Millicent now did: the fact that Tor had been sentenced to the colonies for brawling in a Glasgow pub with the nephew of one Lord Carstairs MacLean, an old and powerful friend of Malcolm Caulbane Cameron's. That confrontation had been no accident. The drunken young MacLean had known exactly what to say to the returning Abercraig heir; insulting things that had goaded Tor into breaking the fellow's jaw and nearly killing him, just as Malcolm had hoped.

As planned, Tor had been thrown immediately into jail. With a generous greasing of the Glasgow magistrate's palm, Malcolm had made certain that his nephew was given the harsh sentence of transportation. Everyone had been sworn to secrecy, but now, thanks to that idiot Cowcadden warden, Millicent MacKenzie had managed to follow the trail of corruption from Glasgow to Abercraig Castle.

A devious woman, Malcolm had decided upon receiving her letter. Intrigued, he had responded immediately, urging her to write him again. Millicent had done so, explaining in detail the nature of her relationship with Tor, and suggesting that it would be in everyone's best interest to get rid of him once and for all.

Thus the sleepless night that had just ended. Malcolm had schemed for years to wrest Abercraig Castle and its rich dairy lands from his older brother,

Tarquin, and he wasn't about to see his ownership threatened again. After all, since boyhood he had been convinced that he should be Abercraig's rightful heir, especially since Tarquin had shown himself to be little more than a dreamer and a Jacobite sympathizer when he grew up. Nevertheless, as the older of the Abercraig sons, Tarquin had always stood first in line to inherit.

Malcolm, who had always fancied himself far more ambitious and clever, had been faced upon adulthood with the dreaded choice accorded second sons: the military or the church. Hating physical work of any kind, he had attempted religion, and actually made a small fortune by sinning his way up the hierarchy of the local church. Unfortunately, he had ended up losing everything by indulging in an ill-timed affair with the daughter of a bishop. Disgraced and stripped of all power, Malcolm had returned to Abercraig after years away to find his brother Tarquin married to the daughter of a wealthy Scottish earl, whose title he had been granted when the old man died. Abercraig's dairy herds had been greatly expanded during Malcolm's absence, and Tarquin now owned the finest Ayrshire bulls in all Scotland. He also had a son of whom he was rightfully proud, a sweetly lovely daughter named Cecilia, and another child on the way. His life had seemed every bit as settled and content as Malcolm's had been bitterly destroyed.

Then Prince Charles Edward Stuart had arrived from France to reclaim the Scottish throne in his father's name. Malcolm had immediately recognized the perfect opportunity to manipulate fate into giving him what he wanted; an easy matter, given his brother's naïveté and the violence of the times. With powerful friends in the English parliament, it had been a simple matter to arrange Tarquin's execution and the murder of his pregnant wife and daughter during the vengeful sweep by English troops that had followed the prince's defeat.

Unfortunately for Malcolm, young Torance Ban Cameron survived the massacre on the Culloden battlefield and eventually made his way back to Abercraig. But the lad had been forced to flee to the Continent, leaving Abercraig in Malcolm's hands.

For years thereafter, Malcolm had enjoyed his undisputed role as lord of Abercraig. Small wonder he had been staggered by the news that Tor had returned from the American colonies with a full royal pardon in his pocket. Malcolm had moved swiftly to stop him coming home, and had thought the matter settled when he'd had Tor imprisoned in Cowcadden. But apparently fate had once again intervened in his nephew's behalf. Now Malcolm was determined to take no more chances. He intended to see that this cursed infernal thorn in his side was permanently removed from earthly existence, and Millicent MacKenzie was going to help him do it.

"Bennish," Malcolm snapped now, tossing his shaving towel aside and regarding his steward with a jaundiced eye. "I've been up all night. Here." Handing his steward a sheaf of carefully penned papers, he outlined his plans.

The old man listened carefully, nodding from time to time. Then he straightened and tucked the missives into the folds of his coat. "I'll get 'em i' the proper hands afore noontime," he promised.

"See that you do," Malcolm responded curtly. "Ah. Here's Burford with my tea. What's kept you, you lazy sot? It had better not be cold, or I'll boot your arse clear back to the kitchen. Well, Bennish? What're you standing there for? Move, man!"

Mordart Bennish, scowling, turned and went.

* * *

The Enchanted Bride

In the breakfast room at Drumcorrie, Jewel rubbed her eyes and took another sip of tea. She was on her third cup, but she still couldn't seem to shed her weariness this morning. She had to face the fact that she was simply too old to go on sleeping in Annie's tiny trundle bed any longer. How many nights had it been now? Six? Seven? High time to get back to her own bed. Perhaps she'd be just as safe there if she slid the bolt on her bedroom door before retiring for the night.

Jewel grimaced at the thought. Safe? From what? The attentions of her husband? Why, the man was hardly home at all anymore! If he wasn't out in the fields from dawn to dusk, he was working in the distillery or disappearing for hours on end in the direction of old Angus MacKenzie's croft. Worse were the times he rode over to Chulish House, which Jewel knew he had been doing increasingly often of late. So often, in fact, that she had seen nothing of him since yesterday morning.

"I don't care!" she told herself aloud, but of course she did. More than she wanted to admit.

When Ruan had unwisely stopped by for a visit the night before, Jewel had hounded him incessantly for information. She had done her best to question him without appearing as though she were, but even so she had been unable to pry a single bit of information out of him.

Is he sleeping with your sister? she had wanted to scream at him, but pride—and a genuine reluctance to know the truth—had kept her silent.

Afterward, she had tossed and turned all night, up there in the attic on Annie's trundle bed. Oh, God, being in love was such a bloody awful thing! How she longed for a return to the days when she had hated Tor Cameron with all her heart, because hating Tor was far, far easier than loving him.

Annie had just brought in a second pot of tea and withdrawn to the kitchen when Tor appeared unannounced in the breakfast room. Jewel saw at once that he looked just as hollow eyed and poorly rested as she did. Instead of feeling satisfaction at this, however, she found herself growing more furious than ever. Served him right for spending so many hours at Chulish House!

With a curt nod in her direction, Tor slid into his seat. Jewel watched as he buttered a bannock and spooned on bramble jelly. Curiosity, and the wish to hurt him, burned through her veins, making it impossible to hold her tongue.

"I wasn't aware that you were back."

"I've been here since last night."

"Oh? I had no idea. What time did you get in?"

Tor thought a moment. "Twelve o'clock."

"Quite early for a change."

He scowled. "I wouldn't consider that early."

" 'Tis certainly earlier than three or four in the morning."

His scowl deepened. "Keeping track, are you?"

"You know perfectly well I am."

"Tut, tut. The role of harping wife doesn't become you, my dear."

"On the other hand, philandering husband becomes you very well."

Tor laid aside his knife.

Jewel set down her teacup.

They sat glaring at each other.

"If you must know," Tor said at last, coldly, " 'tis because of you that I'm spending all my time at Chulish House."

Jewel gave a bitter laugh to cover her hurt. "Oh, I'm quite aware of that, sir! You haven't warmed my bed for weeks now."

"Have you missed me?" he taunted.

Jewel made a very earthy sound of disgust.

Tor scraped back his chair and rose to his feet. "That does it," he said wearily. "I'm leaving."

"Back to Chulish House?"

His smoky gaze pierced her like a knife. "Is that what you think?"

"Where else would you go?"

"Oh, I don't know. Perhaps to Edinburgh."

Jewel caught her breath, although her face remained an expressionless mask. "You wouldn't dare!"

"No? It so happens that I'd far rather risk transportation, or even hanging, than to stay here another hour!"

Jewel hid her hands in her lap so that Tor wouldn't see how much they were trembling. "Do you mean that?"

"With all my heart."

She tossed her head defiantly. "Well, go ahead then. And good riddance."

"Are you giving me leave?" he demanded incredulously. "Dismissing me from your services?"

She bowed her head, saying nothing.

"Only a fool would pass up an offer like that," he remarked after a moment. "And I've never been a fool." Without another word, he strode from the room.

Ten minutes later he appeared downstairs wearing a heavy coat and gloves and carrying a small leather satchel. "I hope you don't mind," he said to Jewel, who was waiting for him in the great hall. "I need them to keep warm up in the mountains. I'll send everything back when I get to Edinburgh."

"There's no need," she told him stiffly.

"Oh, but there is. I came here with nothing, and that's how I intend to leave."

Her eyes flicked to his face, then slid away. "So you're really going."

"Aye."

"I thought so. That's why I asked Piers to saddle a horse."

"Kind of you. I'll return that, too."

She tossed her head. "If you wish."

"No sense in saying good-bye," he added, coming to stand before her.

"None at all," she agreed.

They glared at each other. Jewel's expression had never been so hard. In response, Tor's lips thinned. Jamming a tricorne onto his head, he turned and walked out.

Just like that.

Jewel stood in the doorway fighting back the crushing tears.

From the kitchen window, Annie Brewster watched Tor mount the waiting horse and gallop away. Fools! she thought furiously. Spoiled, stubborn fools!

In the stable doorway, Tykie stood watching as well. When Tor's mount had vanished in a thin cloud of dust in the glen below, he turned and went back inside. Silent, expressionless, he returned to his work.

Not five minutes later Jewel appeared in the tack room doorway. Tykie looked up and quickly hid a grin when he saw that she was wearing boots and a habit. She seemed to have dressed in haste, for some of her buttons were undone and her hat was askew.

"Tykie! Ready Drum for me!"

He was already reaching for the saddle.

Jewel knew perfectly well that Tykie intended to accompany her, so she didn't wait for him. The moment he tossed her onto Drum's broad back, she whipped the big drafter into flight and thundered across the courtyard.

She had no doubt that Tor had taken the westerly route through Chulish village. She would have to hurry if she were going to catch him. He was riding the only coaching horse that was broke to the saddle, a big bay who went by the name of Laddie, and Laddie was far swifter than the heavy-footed Drum.

"Come on, come on," she urged, leaning low in the saddle to whisper in his ear.

She was well aware that at the edge of the village the roadway forked. Although both of them led south toward the Aird mountains, they did so by different routes, and there would be no clue as to which one Tor intended to take. Fear made Jewel's heart beat faster. If she didn't catch up with Tor before he reached that fork, she'd never know which way he'd gone. There'd be no way on earth she'd ever catch him then.

The possibility didn't bear thinking of.

She had to whip poor Drum mercilessly before he broke into a grudging gallop. Even then, the village came and went and still there was no sign of Tor. Making up her mind in an instant, Jewel chose the southwesterly fork, and crossed the long moor at a dead run. Squinting into the wind, she scanned the narrow track ahead. Panic rose in her heart when she saw that the landscape remained empty. Where the devil was he? What if he had gone the other way? What if she didn't catch him?

Stubbornly she refused to consider the possibility. Leaning low in the saddle, she urged Drum onward. The moment she caught up with Tor, she intended to tell him how sorry she was. She would tell him that she'd do everything in her power to make their marriage better if he would only promise to come back.

Movement on the far side of the moor suddenly caught her eye. Through the dense firs that bordered the great, open expanse of land, she could see a rider approaching at a run. Tears of relief clogged her throat. He had turned around! He was coming back!

Drum pricked his ears and whinnied. At the same time, Jewel saw three more horses emerging from the shadows behind the first rider. Straightening in the saddle, she shaded her eyes with her hand. What the devil—?

Strangers were unusual in this part of the Highlands. After all, there was no reason for anyone to travel to a place as remote as Glen Chulish. As the riders neared, Jewel caught her breath, for she saw now that all four of them were wearing plaids, a tradition forbidden in Scotland since the '45 rebellion. And she could see the colors of their plaids as well: green and red interspersed with patterns of yellow and black. A Cameron plaid.

Jewel could feel her heart literally leaping into her throat. Straightening in the saddle, she drew sharply on Drum's reins to bring him to a halt. Something was wrong. She knew everyone in Glen Chulish. The only Camerons in the area lived a full three days' journey to the east, and their tartan echoed the colors of Cameron of Kintoch, to whom they were distantly related. Who, then, were these men, and why were they openly flouting the law?

Now they were close enough for her to discern their features. She recognized none of them, and her uneasiness grew. A big, bearded fellow was riding in the lead, and he waved to her as he approached.

"We're lookin' for Cameron of Drumcorrie!" he bellowed. "Know ye him?"

Jewel felt her heart squeeze with fear. "Aye! He rode out your way less than half an hour ago! Surely you must have seen him!"

Slowing from a gallop to a trot and then a walk, the riders circled around her, making Drum stamp nervously. The bearded fellow leaned close.

"How do ye ken Cameron of Drumcorrie?"

"He's my husband." Jewel tried hard to hide her rising panic. "What do you want from him? Is anything wrong?"

"As a matter of fact, there is," he told her forcibly. "We was on our way to fetch ye, ma'am."

"Why? Has—has something happened to him?"

"I'm afraid so, ma'am."

"What? Tell me, please!"

"Ye maun see for yersel', ma'am," he said gravely.

Jewel could scarcely contain her panic. "What do you mean? Has he met with an accident? Where is he?"

"Come this way, if ye please, ma'am."

She wasted no time on further questions. Whipping Drum into flight, she galloped after him with the others following hard behind.

Chapter Seventeen

Tykie was halfway through the village of Chulish when he spotted Laddie cantering toward him down the road. Quickly he spurred his own mount forward, and the two riders met in the shadow of the old stone kirk.

Tor was windblown and covered with dust. His expression was thunderous as he jerked hard on Laddie's reins. "So! Sent you to fetch me, did she? 'Tis too late, Tykie. I've returned on my own, though God alone knows why!"

Leaning back in the saddle, he wearily rubbed his eyes. "Do you see the depths she's reduced me to?" he demanded furiously. "I don't think I've run away from home since I was a lad! Nor come crawling back on my belly for anyone—let alone your pig-headed mistress! What's more . . . God Almighty, what's the matter with you, Tykie?"

"Oooh! Oooh!"

Tor sat staring, slack-jawed, as Tykie gestured

frantically and repeated that same strange word over and over.

"What in hell—" Tor began, thoroughly exasperated. Then all at once he understood. Reaching over, he grabbed Tykie by the collar. "Jewel? Are you telling me something about Jewel?"

Tykie nodded wildly. Tears of relief glimmered in his eyes.

"What is it? Has something happened to her?"

Again Tykie nodded. Sounds gurgled in his throat, but none of them made any sense to Tor.

"Slowly. Take it slowly, Tykie. You're no help to her this way."

Tykie expelled a shuddering breath. Pointing at Laddie, he then turned and pointed to the west.

"I know," said Tor. "I was headed toward the Galashiels road before I changed my mind and turned around."

"Oooh," said Tykie, nodding vigorously.

"Jewel followed me?" Tor guessed. "She was headed that way, too?"

Again Tykie nodded.

"And you're saying something happened to her?"

Tykie nodded, more agitated than ever. His earring bobbed wildly.

"What? Did she take a spill?"

Tykie grunted a negative.

Running his hands through his hair, Tor willed himself to remain calm. "Let's try it one more time. Slowly, if you please."

Tykie pointed at Laddie, then held up four fingers. With his hand, he mimicked a scurrying animal, then four others in pursuit. "Oooh! Oooh!"

"Someone followed her?" Tor guessed, even though he knew that the thought was ridiculous. "Four men on horseback?" He was thunderstruck when Tykie acknowledged this wild stab with vigorous nodding.

"What do you mean? Who on earth would follow her? Why?"

Tykie turned his palms up and looked utterly defeated.

"You didn't know them? They were strangers to Glen Chulish?"

Tykie nodded again. He was looking somewhat less panic-stricken now that Tor was on the right track.

Tor, on the other hand, was growing increasingly agitated. "Do you think they meant her harm? Where did they take her?"

Tykie pointed to the west. He indicated that he had been too far away to follow them. Then, brightening as an idea struck him, he thumped his shoulder with a fisted hand and traced the outline of a cape.

Tor understood immediately, although he had no idea how. "Plaids! The men were wearing plaids. Did you recognize the tartan? Which one was it, Tykie?"

Leaning from the saddle, Tykie tapped Tor's chest. His expression was accusing.

Tor was silent a moment; then a look of astonishment crept over his hard features. "Camerons? Are you saying they were Camerons?"

"Aye!" Tykie roared, or at least it sounded that way to Tor. And they had taken Jewel toward the west. . . .

"Oh God," he said softly. "It can't be!"

Tykie grunted a question, but Tor ignored him. He knew very well that it could. And he could guess, too, who was responsible. Taking up the reins, he said harshly, "I'm going to Chulish House. In the meantime, I want you to go back to Drumcorrie as fast as you can and—Oh, for God's sake, stop looking at me like that! I'm not paying a social call, man!"

Tykie looked at him doubtfully.

Tor gritted his teeth. "You said they were wearing Cameron colors, didn't you? Why in bloody hell would they be so blatant unless they wanted us to know that? My hunch is that Millicent MacKenzie's got a hand in this. She must have joined forces with my uncle, and now he's kidnapped Jewel."

Tykie's cry was that of a wounded animal's.

"Pull yourself together!" Tor said furiously. "You'll be no help to her behaving like an old woman! Now do as I say and ride to Drumcorrie. Round up as many men as you can. If my hunch is right—and Millicent MacKenzie will know for sure—we ride for Ayr immediately."

And with a savage blow to the unsuspecting Laddie's flanks, Tor galloped away, leaving Tykie alone in the dust of the kirkyard.

The long, wearying day had ended at last. The cold sun had slid behind the western hills, and the promise of rain—or snow—hung in the air. Jewel, so sore and tired that she could barely sit in the saddle, paid scant attention to the castle that loomed ahead of her through the twilight.

By her reckoning, they had traveled across the length of Strathclyde to Ayr. Her captors had stopped only to water their horses and snatch a few hours of sleep on the road. They had avoided Glasgow, Paisley, and the few villages along the way by sending one of their own off to procure food.

Jewel had been watched every moment, even when she had to disappear behind a tree to heed the call of nature. By now she was beyond caring of her modesty. She wanted only a hot bath and a soft bed, although the prospect of getting either seemed slim indeed considering the medieval look of the enormous castle that now rose on the skyline before them.

It was a magnificent edifice, and had obviously belonged to a powerful clan back in the long-forgotten days of Scotland's glory. Jewel, who had never been to Ayr, had no clue as to its history, but she had a good idea who owned it now. She had listened closely to the talk of the four men who rode with her, and had drawn her own conclusions from the things that they had said.

Now she straightened in the saddle and did her best to shake the weariness from her bones. She had been furious when she had first realized that she'd been abducted, and ready to murder the man responsible. But after six days on horseback over impossibly difficult terrain, she had lost much of her spunk and had resigned herself to the inevitable.

"If I could only get a decent night's sleep," she told herself wearily, "I'd be ready for anything!"

They entered the castle by way of an enormous stone gate. The icy wind that battered the treeless landscape was dulled here, and Jewel flexed her numb fingers with relief. Her knees buckled as she slid from the saddle, but a groom, hurrying from the stable, caught her before she could fall. She was ushered across the stone courtyard and through an arched doorway. Up several flights of stairs and down a gloomy corridor they went, and all at once Jewel found herself in a darkly paneled room where a tin tub stood filled with steaming water and a four-poster bed beckoned temptingly.

"We've been watchin' for 'ee," said a woman, stepping out of the shadows and into the firelight. " 'Tis Lord Cameron's orders ye're tae wash an' eat."

"Kind of him," Jewel murmured.

She needed help undressing, because she was too stiff to manage the lacings of her gown and corset.

Her body protested the steaming bathwater after the long, frozen ride. But Jewel leaned back, ignoring the pain, and rested her head against the rim of the tub. Within seconds she had drifted off to sleep.

Not a moment later she was awakened by vigorous scrubbing. The woman had unpinned her hair and was lathering it with scented soap. Another woman, much younger and with gentler hands, was doing the same to her aching limbs.

Jewel let them. She was beyond caring. Her body felt as if it were no longer supported by bones. As well, she allowed herself to be dried and dressed, then settled limply into a chair. She was brought something to eat. Meager fare, to be sure, but she tore into it hungrily. By the time she had finished every scrap, she was feeling well enough to take stock of her surroundings.

She found herself in a dark, uninviting bedroom. Mismatched furnishings from a long-ago age lined the walls. A tarnished mirror and worn rush matting were the only adornments. She noticed that the women had taken away her clothes and dressed her in a flowing shift of rough, homespun cloth. It smelled strongly of camphor, and itched horribly. They had left her hair unbound, and Jewel moved closer to the fire so that it might dry.

Sitting there feeling warm and with a full belly for the first time in days, she fell asleep once again. In no time at all, someone was shaking her.

"Get up, miss. 'Is lordship'll see 'ee now."

Jewel rose quickly and shook out the folds of the homespun shift. Stretching and yawning, she realized that she felt better than she had since her abduction. Thanks to that bath and the food, some of her spirit was beginning to return. In fact, by the time she was led along a dark, disused corridor, down a gloomy flight of stairs, and into a study lit

211

only by the glow of a peat fire, she was more than ready to take her abductor to task.

Days ago, Jewel had drawn the conclusion that the man responsible for her abduction, the one her mounted escort had constantly referred to as "Lord Abercraig," was somehow related to Tor. What she wasn't prepared for was the striking resemblance between the two. The man who rose from behind the desk as Jewel was shown inside was equally as tall as Tor, and just as darkly handsome. Jewel had no doubt that he had conquered many a feminine heart in his youth. But there was something unsavory in the blue eyes that studied her, and a dissipated softness about the mouth that was lacking in Tor's. And while her heart could squeeze at the resemblance to the man she so dearly loved, it could also exult in the fact that, his prison record notwithstanding, Tor was a far, far better man than the one who stood before her.

"So," Malcolm Caulbane Cameron remarked after they had measured each other for a long, hostile moment. "My nephew's wife."

"You might have sent for me in a less dramatic fashion," Jewel said accusingly.

The Earl of Abercraig looked startled; then he laughed. "Spirited. I should have known. Tor never did care for weaklings."

"You had me abducted."

"Aye. My apologies. I couldn't think of a better way of luring my nephew to Abercraig. He would not have come on his own."

"I can see why," Jewel murmured, looking around her.

Lord Abercraig scowled. "Thank you, Mrs. Tweedham," he snapped at the housekeeper, who hovered in the doorway. "You may go."

"You brought me here as a lure?" Jewel demanded

as the door closed on the woman's sour face. "Is that why your men were dressed in plaids? So Tor would recognize who they were?"

Lord Abercraig looked pleased. "Clever, wasn't it?"

"Medieval," Jewel retorted. "No one abducts helpless maidens in this day and age! What else do you do, I wonder? Raid your neighbors' cattle and burn your crofters' hayricks at harvest?"

"Sit down and hold your tongue!"

Jewel obeyed. She had underestimated this shabbily dressed, older version of Tor. It had been a mistake to goad him. She regarded him warily while he stood behind the desk grappling with his temper.

When he spoke, his voice chilled her, although the words were unfailingly polite. "We'll have no more of such talk. We'll be civil to one another until my nephew arrives."

"And then what?" Jewel whispered with a sudden sense of dread.

"I'll have to kill him, of course."

Jewel was glad she was sitting down. She couldn't have remained on her feet, not with the blood draining so quickly from her heart. "Why?"

He gave her an ugly smile. "Has he never told you?"

Jewel thought quickly, then answered honestly. "No. He's told me nothing about himself."

"Your aunt mentioned in her letter that you'd arranged for his release from prison."

"Aye. But that's the extent of my knowledge about him. I know nothing of his past." Inwardly she was seething. She should have known Aunt Millicent was at the bottom of this!

"So I've been informed. The marriage isn't exactly a love match, eh?"

Jewel shrugged.

Lord Abercraig laughed. Her honesty had obviously paid off. He seemed willing to keep on talking. "Your aunt considers my nephew's presence in that place—Glen Chulish, is it?—inconvenient. And I certainly consider his release from prison more than a wee bit inconvenient."

"Do you know why he was sentenced?" Jewel asked curiously.

"Oh, indeed. Striking a nobleman was the charge. Reprehensible, to be sure, although I can't really fault him for it. I'm the one who sent the fellow there to goad him in the first place."

Jewel's hands tightened around the arms of her chair. "Oh?"

"Your husband has been the proverbial thorn in my side ever since he was born," Malcolm said harshly. "Abercraig should have been mine from the first. I wasn't the oldest son, but I was the best. My father knew it, curse his soul, but he did nothing to change the situation. And do you know why? Because I was born with a caul. Do you know what that means, woman?"

Jewel did. Lord Abercraig had emerged into the world with the birth sac still covering his head. Here in the Highlands, the phenomenon was known as being born with a caul, and superstition had it that a baby thus born was enchanted.

"You should have been considered lucky, not cursed," she pointed out.

Malcolm gave a bitter laugh. "Hardly. It turned them all against me. Even my own mother had me sent away to England. She always maintained she'd done so for my safety, considering that Scotland was at war. Why, then, didn't she send my older brother, too? Because she was hoping I'd not survive the journey. Well, I did, and when I returned, I found my father had died and my brother Tarquin, that half-brained idiot, was in control of Abercraig. I spent the rest of my life trying to wrest it from him."

Jewel bit her lip, trying hard to hide her increasing anxiety. Lord Abercraig was obviously not sane. All his life he had lived under the delusion that he should have inherited Abercraig, even though it had rightfully gone to Tarquin as the firstborn son. He had apparently blamed the strange phenomenon of his birth for all of his ill luck and misery, although his parents had probably treated him justly and fairly. And Jewel very much doubted that Tarquin had been the idiot he described.

Tarquin Cameron. That would have been Tor's father. Which meant that Abercraig should have gone to Tor when Tarquin died. How had this evil man come to inherit it? And how had Tor ended up a penniless soldier imprisoned in Cowcadden?

Jewel was beginning to suspect that Lord Abercraig had masterminded some awful scheme to keep Abercraig out of Tor's deserving hands. It would explain so much: Tor's bitterness, his secretive ways, and his refusal to confide in her any details concerning his past.

Recalling how often she herself had belittled and insulted Tor because of his incarceration and his state of penury, Jewel felt a lump rise to her throat. How unfair she had been, and how she must have hurt Tor with her cruel remarks! As well, the irony of the situation was beyond belief. She had asked Cowcadden's warden for a prisoner who would never dare attempt to rise above his station, and had ended up choosing a man who was the rightful heir to an earldom! She knew in that one moment that she was never going to let Lord Abercraig use her as a means to hurt Tor again.

"You're wrong about one thing," she said coolly.

He looked at her sharply. "What?"

"Bringing me here isn't going to lure Tor back. As

a matter of fact, he doesn't even know what's happened. Last I saw of him, he was hard on his way to Edinburgh."

"Edinburgh! Why?"

Jewel had never been happier in her life to admit the truth. "He was leaving Drumcorrie. Leaving me. Our marriage was intolerable for him."

Malcolm rubbed his chin. "Aye, your aunt mentioned repeatedly that the union wasn't a happy one. Hmm. You're not lying to me, are you, girl?"

"No."

Clearly she wasn't. Even Malcolm could see as much. Turning his back on her, he cursed, paced, and cursed some more. "This changes everything, of course. You're useless to me now."

Did that mean he intended to get rid of her? Jewel lifted her chin and tried not to look frightened.

"On the other hand . . ."

He broke off and regarded her in silence. Jewel did her best to look back at him calmly.

Turning abruptly, he rang the bell behind him. When the housekeeper appeared, he said, "Take Miss—Mrs. Cameron back to her room." His expression was mocking as he turned back to Jewel. "You'll forgive me if I lock you in, ma'am?"

"Unquestionably."

He nodded, satisfied.

Two burly footmen accompanied Jewel and the housekeeper upstairs. The moment the key turned in the lock, Jewel flew to the window. Darkness had fallen, but she could still see the courtyard far below, and knew that she'd never survive a leap to the ground. No way of escaping by that route. She'd have to think of something else. But what?

Supper arrived a short time later, carried in by a hairy little man who stumped over to the table without giving Jewel so much as a glance. Jewel's heart leaped briefly, seeing that he was alone, but she knew better than to attack him and run from the room. She would never be able to find her way out of the enormous castle without being seen. Better to wait and see what Lord Abercraig had in mind for her, then lay her plans with care.

"I brought wine," the little man said.

Jewel thanked him, but her thoughts were elsewhere.

" 'Ee maun eat. Thin as a broomstick ye be."

Jewel glared at him. "I'm not hungry, thank you."

He surprised her by chuckling. "MacKenzies. Pigheaded, every last one o' ye."

Jewel's chin tipped. "I have good reason to—Wait a moment! How—how do you know who I am?"

He shrugged. "Na much gets past Mordart Bennish. Steward at Abercraig I been for nearly fifty years."

He certainly looked it. He was withered and wind honed and smelled strongly of mothballs. But his bright blue eyes burned with lively spirit. "I been here so long I ken every last thing what concerns Abercraig folk. Including," he added smugly, "what manner of lass our Master Tor up and married."

"Then you knew my husband when he was young! And Lord Abercraig, too, I imagine."

"Aye."

Jewel watched as the old man crossed to the door and peered left and right before closing it. She sat up, her lethargy gone, her heart starting to hammer with a sudden sense of hope.

"Na time to waste," he said, stumping back to the table and uncorking the wine. "But there ain't much 'ee can do withoot proper food i' yer belly."

Jewel was already pulling up a chair. "I understand." She looked at him searchingly. "What are my chances?"

He sighed. "I dinna ken. There be the servants, and ye'll have a hard time gettin' past 'em. Lord Abercraig brought 'em frae England when 'e came, an' they be loyal to him, curse 'em a' tae hell an' back. Now the auld ones, the ones what served Master Tarquin an' his lady, they be livin' i' the village an' elsewhere. 'Ee can count on their help. An' mine. But ye'll have tae get oot o' here first."

"But how can I help Tor after that? What shall I do?"

"Dinna worry about that now, lass! Leave this place first and get awa' frae that madman! After that, 'ee can warn Master Tor."

"There won't be any need for that," she said sadly. "He won't come here looking for me."

The old man glared at her. "Thot I willna believe."

No sense in arguing. No time to argue anyway. Jewel began to eat, hurriedly, even though she had no appetite. "How will you get me out of here?" she asked around mouthfuls of stew.

"I dinna ken yet."

Somewhere down the hall a door closed. Frowning, the old man whirled back to Jewel. "Eat," he commanded, then lowered his voice to a whisper. "An' be ready. Any hour, any moment."

"But—"

He shook his head curtly, then stumped to the door. The key turned in the lock as he let himself out, and then he was gone.

Chapter Eighteen

Jewel had resolved not to sleep at all that night. The steward had warned her to be ready, and she wasn't about to miss the only chance she might get of finding and warning Tor.

But weariness decided otherwise. After the sour-faced Mrs. Tweedham had taken away the supper tray, Jewel remained admirably alert. As the hours passed, however, boredom, and discouragement set in. So did fatigue. With heavy-lidded eyes she sat down on the edge of the bed—only for a moment, she promised herself—but within seconds her eyes had closed and her breathing quieted. She was asleep before she even knew it.

She dreamed of Tor. Dreamed that he had turned around before he left Glen Chulish behind, telling himself he was a fool, telling himself he didn't want to leave Drumcorrie for the distant environs of Edinburgh. Not because he had felt safe at Drumcorrie, and warm and well fed, but simply and solely because of Jewel.

In her sleep, she stirred and sighed, knowing it was impossible. In the next moment, she gasped aloud as someone shook her roughly.

"Whist! No sound, lass, or we're done for!"

She blinked and opened her eyes, and saw above her the grizzled silhouette of Abercraig's ancient steward. Quickly she sat up, brushing the hair from her eyes.

"Is it time?" she whispered.

"Aye. Here, put these on."

A bundle was thrust into her hands. There was no time for modesty. While Mordart turned his back, Jewel slipped out of her shift and into a pair of breeches and a boy's lawn shirt. A warm sheepskin vest covered her, and then her riding boots, which had been stored away in the armoire.

"They'll be standin' watch all around," Mordart told her in a whisper. "I ken 'is lordship, and 'e won't be takin' chances. We'll leave by way o' the cellar."

The cellar reminded Jewel in no small measure of Cowcadden Prison. It was equally as dank and spooky, and the stone hallway echoed with the scurrying of unseen rats. She kept close to the old steward, wondering all the while if perhaps this wasn't a trap and she'd be ambushed at any moment.

She wasn't. Even as her heart hammered and her courage began to falter, Mordart turned a corner, and all at once the sweet night air was wafting around her face. She had no idea how he had negotiated the twisting corridors in such utter darkness, but she was intensely grateful to him as he unlocked an arched doorway with an ancient key and led her outside.

"I oiled t'hinges," he whispered, pleased with himself for having thought of it.

He had, apparently, thought of everything. There were people waiting outside in the dark, a pair of shadowy figures who didn't speak, but gestured to Jewel to accompany them. She turned questioningly to the steward, who nodded and took hold of her hand.

"Do ye ken wha' tae do wi' this?"

She felt the cold steel of a dagger against her palm. Her fingers closed tightly around the carved horn handle. "Aye," she said grimly.

"God be wi' ye, then."

She wasn't given the chance to thank him. Instead she was pulled away by a tall man dressed entirely in black. Another, slighter figure hurried along beside him, no taller than Jewel herself. As her eyes adjusted to the dim light, she was startled to see that he was wearing her own riding habit, the same one in which she had been abducted. What was going on here? He was unquestionably a lad, for he lacked the curves that filled out the habit whenever Jewel wore it, and his short hair was tied in a definitely masculine queue.

Thoroughly bewildered, Jewel longed to ask questions, but didn't dare. They were hurrying along in the shadow of a high wall, and ahead of them loomed a rusty iron gate. This, too, had been recently oiled, and the door swung open soundlessly. A moment later, Jewel found herself standing outside. The force of the cold wind staggered her.

"Come on."

The tall man had her by the arm. As Jewel started after him, a pack of dogs set up a wild clamor from somewhere behind.

The man cursed. "Keith! Fly!"

The boy wearing Jewel's habit took off at a run. Seconds later Jewel could hear the drumming of hooves, and the howling of the dogs as they took off in pursuit. Now she could hear men shouting to one another along the castle walls. The flicker of torches sprang into view.

"Come on! We've just a few moments! Dinna waste them!"

Gasping for breath, stumbling over unseen roots and rocks, Jewel followed her rescuer through the darkness. The turmoil behind them grew fainter; not only because Lord Abercraig's men had gone in pursuit of the decoy Jewel, but because Jewel herself, along with her rescuer, had slithered down a rocky creek bed and were sloshing downstream.

"All right, lass?" he asked as Jewel stumbled and went down on her knees.

"Aye." She rose and slapped the icy water from her breeches.

"This way. We're almost there."

But more than an hour passed before he slowed their desperate pace. Cold and wet and thoroughly exhausted, Jewel followed almost blindly as they left the creek behind and crossed a field in which the huge shadows of cattle showed dimly in the starlight. They scrambled over the stone walls that divided the fields, skirted a darkened croft, and forded another rushing burn. Their footsteps were muffled by a thick carpet of pine needles as they passed through a glade of trees and emerged at last at the base of a hill where, far up the slope, a light showed wanly.

"Can 'ee gae on, lass?"

Jewel doubted it, but she gritted her teeth and nodded. They climbed in silence, saving their breath, the man in black leading the way. A tumbledown byre appeared ahead of them, and a cow lowed plaintively as they passed. The sound was answered by the barking of a dog, and in response a square of light appeared in the cottage farther up the hill. A woman in a shawl stood framed in the doorway. Lifting her lantern, she peered through the darkness.

"Alastair?"

"Aye," Jewel's companion responded.

The woman's relief was obvious. Gathering up her skirts, she flew to him. The question on her lips died as she caught sight of Jewel. Her breath caught.

"Old Mordart wasna lyin'!"

"Did ye think he was, woman?"

"I be Jeannie Morrisey," the woman said to Jewel, ignoring him. "Come inside, by the fire."

The cottage had but a single room and a loft. The ceiling was blackened by the peat fire, but it was cozy and warm. Jewel sank gratefully onto the chair that was offered her, and drank deeply of the water the woman brought.

"Thank you," she gasped.

"Why, ye're na more than a bairn!" the woman exclaimed, taking a good look at her.

"I'm nearly eighteen," Jewel countered firmly.

The man named Alastair chuckled. "There, Jeannie, ye see? Spirited she be. Quite enough for our Lord Tor."

Jewel turned to look at him. "Then—"

"No questions," he warned. "Up into the loft wi' ye. Rest now. And dinna come down unless I gie the word. Na matter what happens."

"Oh, Alastair! Ye weren't followed, were ye?"

"Nay, woman. Calm yer fears. Keith'll be leadin' 'em on a merry dance." Alastair chuckled again. "Wish 'ee'd hae seen him. As pretty a lass as Mrs. Cameron here makes a handsome young laddie. Ach, look at her, will 'ee? Fair droopin' wi' fatigue. Take her up tae bed, Jeannie, there's a good wife."

That was all Jewel remembered.

When she woke up, she knew that it had all been a dream. People didn't go about getting abducted nowadays, nor were they rescued in the dead of night by grizzled old men and boys dressed up like women!

But then how did she explain the age-blackened rafters that hovered directly overhead when she opened her eyes? Or the fact that she was lying on a pallet in a strange loft, wrapped in a sheepskin throw?

Groaning, she flexed her leaden limbs. She was still wearing the breeches and shirt she had been given the night before. Down below, she could hear the man named Alastair and his wife talking softly near the fire.

Not a dream, then.

Which meant that Tor was still in danger. As was she. If the youth named Keith had failed to fool his pursuers, or if he himself had been captured . . .

"Awake, are ye?" the woman named Jeannie inquired as Jewel's head poked through the loft railing to look down at them. She sounded friendly, not at all frightened or nervous.

"Is it safe to come down?"

"Oh, aye. Alastair's been to the castle and back. 'Tis bein' said ye vanished withoot a trace."

Room was made for her at the small table. Jeannie set down a bowl of porridge and fresh milk.

"Mordart says Lord Abercraig be furious."

"But he doesn't suspect a thing," Alastair added quickly as Jewel's face paled. "He thinks ye're headed back to Glen Chulish."

"What do you think he'll do now?" Jewel asked worriedly. "My husband—"

"Our Keith'll reach him first. Dinna worry, ma'am. He'll be proper forewarned."

"You've been so very kind," Jewel said, her eyes stinging with tears.

Jeannie reached over to pat her hand. " 'Tis i' our best interest, too, ma'am. We've a' been awaitin' the day Lord Tor returns."

While Jewel ate, the couple talked about Malcolm Cameron's gross mismanagement of Abercraig. They described the poverty of the last two decades and the harshness of his rule. Jewel, who had always treated her crofters fairly and believed passionately in their rights, was infuriated. Small wonder people like Alastair and Jeannie had been driven to the desperate plotting of the night before!

"How can I help?" she asked. "What do we do now?"

"We wait," Alastair answered heavily. "There ain't much else to do."

But waiting had always been hard for Jewel. She had never been a patient person, and the situation at Abercraig was intolerable. She knew that Alastair was right in counseling her to wait until Tor arrived. She certainly couldn't expect him to gather up the rest of the Cameron crofters and storm the castle as in feudal times—not without Tor, at any rate!

On the other hand, it was utterly nerve-racking to sit there and wait for news; to wonder if the boy, Keith, had found Tor and managed to warn him; to imagine Tor arriving to confront his uncle and, worst of all, to fret about the foul things Malcolm Cameron planned to do when Tor finally did show up.

The thought of Tor riding into danger was unbearable. To keep herself busy, Jewel offered to help with the housework. At first Jeannie refused to hear of it, but when Jewel insisted, she relented. Throughout that long, trying day, Jewel swept and aired linens, milked the family cow, and gathered eggs in the byre. She fetched water from the spring and helped Alastair mend a sagging gate. She carried peat and stacked it under the eaves and cleaned the ashes from the hearth.

Toward evening she found her patience at an end. After badgering Alastair and promising to be careful, she rode the couple's shaggy pony to the crest of the hill, where the turrets of Abercraig were visible in the distance. She rode astride, still dressed in breeches and boots, in order to pass as the Morriseys' son should she encounter anyone. Fortunately, the glen and the moors beyond remained empty.

As Alastair had predicted, she saw nothing unusual going on at the castle. There were no guards peering over the parapets, and no army massing in the bailey below. Lord Abercraig's herd of Ayrshire cattle grazed as ever on the hillside, and smoke poured from the chimneys of the distant crofts. The scene was a cursedly peaceful one.

Jewel rode back in a fever of impatience. She could scarcely sit still during supper. Alastair assured her that the wait was to be expected, but Jewel had her doubts. She couldn't stop thinking about Tor.

Where was he? What did his uncle have in mind for him? If only she could get away to warn him herself! She still had the dagger old Mordart had given her. It wouldn't be as if she were going unarmed. . . .

"Stay," Alastair urged, divining her thoughts with unsettling accuracy. "Ye'll be no use to Lord Tor if ye're captured again."

And Jewel obeyed, if only because she knew he was right.

She slept fitfully that night and was up long before the dawn. When Alastair went out to the byre to feed his livestock, Jewel went with him. They did not speak as they crossed the darkened yard. The air was cold, and their breath clouded before them.

Alastair handed her the bucket. She went obligingly to the grain bin to fill it, and started violently as a soft laugh came from somewhere behind her. Recognizing that laugh, she whirled, and the bucket went clattering across the stones.

Tor was leaning against the stall door, his arms crossed before his chest. He was windblown and unshaven, but otherwise fit and unharmed.

"I always suspected you'd make a dandy lad."

Jewel stared at him, speechless.

"Young Keith Morrisey warned me what to expect, but I confess I'm still surprised." Tor's gaze traveled lazily along the length of her shapely legs, which the tight-fitting breeches clearly revealed. "Quite a bonnie lad," he murmured, sauntering closer. "What's the matter, Jewel? Cat got your tongue?"

She gaped at him. She'd never been so happy—or so furious—in her life. "How long have you been hiding here?"

"Hiding? I was waiting for the household to stir. I know how much all of you need your beauty rest."

Oh, she wanted to fly at him then, to claw his eyes out and beat him senseless—and then throw herself into his arms and never let go!

"Tor . . ." she began in a choked little voice.

At that moment Alastair appeared in the doorway, gaping just the way Jewel had. Then, in two swift strides, he had crossed over to Tor, his eyes shining. The two men clasped hands, and Jewel saw the same glad expression of welcome on Tor's face. Even though neither man said a word, it was obvious that both were deeply moved by their reunion.

Jewel turned away, her eyes stinging. Tor hadn't been at all happy to see *her*. Indeed, he seemed to have forgotten all about her as he and Alastair began an urgent discussion of the current situation. Jewel busied herself with the livestock, since Alastair was ignoring their restive demands for feed. Once or twice she glanced at Tor, but he wasn't watching her at all. He was talking earnestly with Alastair, hands thrust in the pockets of his sheepskin coat.

I wish he'd never come! Jewel thought passionately, and quite illogically.

But of course that wasn't true. She was so deeply glad to have him here that it almost didn't matter how little he cared for her. Almost . . .

Up at the cottage, Jeannie had set out breakfast. She was clearly delighted to see Tor again, and blushed furiously when he complimented her on how kind the passing years had been to her. Keith was a fine, strapping lad now, he added. A son any parent could be proud of.

"Ye'll hae yer own soon enou'," Jeannie predicted emotionally.

"I very much doubt that," Tor answered, casting a dark glance at Jewel.

She glared right back at him. If he was going to revert to his combative old self, she'd keep right in step with him! But her heart seemed to shrivel, for she had so wanted to let him know how much she'd been worrying about him, and how glad she was that he was safe.

Only he wasn't, really. That much became obvious during breakfast, as Tor discussed with Alastair the best way to rid Abercraig once and for all of Malcolm Cameron's evil presence. There was a grimness about Tor that Jewel had never seen before, and it made him seem almost like a stranger to her. She had never realized before how deeply he could hate, and how much his past still tormented him.

"Mordart Bennish told me your uncle took Abercraig away from your father," she said after breakfast, when she and Tor were momentarily alone. "But he didn't tell me how. What happened?"

"I went off to war," Tor said curtly.

"War? Do you mean the forty-five?"

"Aye. My parents were against the Stuart Pretender, you see, but idealistic youth that I was, off I marched when the clans rose to fight for him."

"Just like Tykie did."

"Aye, just like Tykie. And like Tykie, I survived the massacre at Culloden and made my way back here, only to find that during my absence English soldiers had slaughtered my entire family. My uncle had wasted no time in declaring himself chief of the clan and lord of Abercraig. The appointment was sanctioned by King George himself, even though my parents had not declared for the Stuart king and so shouldn't have been considered traitors to the Crown. I, on the other hand, had no choice but to flee to the Continent to avoid being drawn and quartered at Carlisle."

A fate, Jewel well knew, that had befallen most of the brave Highlanders who'd marched with Bonnie Prince Charlie and survived the Culloden massacre.

"And then?" she whispered, aching for him.

Tor shrugged. "I offered my services to whichever government paid the most for able soldiering. The years passed, I grew older, and eventually I decided the time had come to confront my uncle and take back what was mine. When a royal pardon was offered those of us who'd fought for the prince, I did my tour of duty in the colonies as payment, and returned here a free man."

"Only to be set up in a taproom brawl in Glasgow," Jewel remembered. "Your uncle told me he'd been responsible for that. He was furious when I prevented your transportation back to America."

"I can imagine." Tor's eyes rested enigmatically on her face. "I'd always surmised he was at the bottom of my arrest. Now I know for sure. What else did he tell you?"

Briefly, Jewel described her abduction and her stay at the castle. She told him of her aunt's letters and the violent end Malcolm had in mind for him.

Tor listened without interruption, sitting back in his chair with his arms folded across his chest. He looked so calm that Jewel had no idea how close he was to exploding; that the mere thought of what Mal-

229

colm Cameron had done to her made the murderous rage rise like bile to his throat.

Jeannie Morrisey came back into the room just as Jewel finished her tale. She had brought freshly rolled oats from the mill, and now she set about baking bannocks. Alastair had not returned. Jewel suspected that Tor had sent him out on an errand, but she knew better than to inquire as to what it might be. Tor was so distant, so controlled and quiet, that she didn't dare ask him anything.

Jeannie had no similar qualms. While she stirred and kneaded and shaped the dough into bannocks, she asked bluntly, "What next?"

Tor sighed heavily. "We wait, much as I hate to."

"For what?"

"Weapons. And men."

Jewel gasped. "What on earth are you talking about?"

Tor said quietly, "You don't expect me to confront my uncle unarmed, I hope."

"I don't expect you to confront him at all!"

"Then how do you propose to get Abercraig back?"

Jewel had no idea.

"Ye'll hae plenty o' supporters," Jeannie assured him. "Though I fear na many weapons. They've been outlawed since the forty-five."

"That's why I sent Alastair out to look for some. I'll wager there are plenty of claymores and muskets hidden away in the haylofts hereabouts, Jeannie."

"Oh, aye! Depend on't!"

Jewel had been sitting there looking from one to the other. Now she jumped to her feet, sending her chair skittering backward. "Have you lost your mind?" she shouted at Tor. "Are you telling me you're planning to storm the castle? Arm your crofters with pitchforks and spades? The Middle Ages are over, Cameron!"

Tor said blackly, "I'll confront him first, of course. But if he refuses to back down, I'll have no choice but to fight."

"Does Abercraig mean so much to you?" Jewel asked wonderingly.

His expression was hard. "Aye."

More than Drumcorrie, obviously. More than his wife—who obviously didn't matter at all. Because if Jewel did matter in the least, Tor would have been satisfied with the fact that she was safe, and simply take her home with him.

Only home, for Tor, wasn't Drumcorrie, Jewel admitted wretchedly to herself. It was that brooding castle across the glen: Abercraig, Tor's birthplace and rightful inheritance. And he was obviously willing to go to war in order to win it back. Jewel could tell as much merely by looking at him. Was he willing to risk his life as well? The thought didn't bear thinking about.

With a choked cry, Jewel whirled and fled. The cottage door slammed behind her.

Wiping the flour from her hands, Jeannie cast a troubled glance at Tor. "Will ye no speak wi' her?"

Growling, Tor came to his feet. The cottage door slammed behind him as well, but Jeannie was saddened to see that he strode off in the opposite direction from the one taken by his wife.

Chapter Nineteen

Now it was evening, and Jeannie and Jewel left the cottage together to drive the cow back to the barn. Alastair had still not returned, and Jeannie kept peering anxiously into the gathering darkness. Neither of the women spoke as they went back to the croft. There was a coolness between them that hadn't existed earlier. Jewel suspected that Jeannie disapproved of her lack of support for Tor's plan to confront Malcolm Cameron.

In her heart, Jewel couldn't blame her. She had seen for herself how terribly Abercraig's crofters had suffered since Malcolm Cameron had come to power. Any lingering vestige of prosperity had been replaced by grinding poverty, and one had only to look at Jeannie's work-worn hands to know how difficult her life had been.

On the other hand, Jewel would not—could not—condone an outright attack on the Cameron stronghold. She knew as well as Tor did that Malcolm would not willingly step down, or even agree to talk things over with his nephew. And that made bloodshed inevitable.

As well, the fact that Tor's life could easily be the one forfeited during the coming confrontation made Jewel mad with rage. She wanted to shout at Tor, pull his thick black hair from his head by the roots, and tie him to the nearest tree to prevent his going.

Only she knew that she mustn't. Tor had made his decision. He wanted Abercraig, not her. There was little sense in standing in his way.

Jewel couldn't stop wondering what Tor intended to do with her if—when!—he won Abercraig back. Did he expect her to remain here and become mistress of his castle? Surely he must know that she would never give up Drumcorrie! After all, Drumcorrie was home to her. It might be modest, with only a handful of servants and very little acreage when compared to that enormous castle up on the hill, but Jewel would never give it up, not even for Tor.

Besides, he hadn't asked her to.

So there.

The tension between them was intolerable that evening. Jewel had to grit her teeth and physically will herself to sit and eat her supper without dashing her soup bowl at his head. Luckily, Alastair returned before the meal was over and so unwittingly prevented Jewel from losing control and murdering Tor with her bare hands. He was windblown and weary when he came back to the croft. He had walked a great distance that day and talked to a number of people. Though Tor was impatient to hear what he had to say, Jeannie refused to let either man speak until she had brought warm stew and a flagon of ale for her husband's supper.

"I've been to see every last man jack i' the glen,"

Alastair said once his strength returned. "Ye can count on 'em a', Master Tor."

"Praise God," Jeannie whispered, her eyes shining.

"And weapons?" Tor demanded.

Alastair smiled faintly. "No many, and rusted i' their hidin' places, but they're bein' oiled and sharpened even as we speak."

An excited light surged to Tor's eyes. "When?"

"Tomorrow, as ye requested."

"Then ye maun rest," Jeannie said quickly. "Alastair, ye're dead on yer feet."

"Aye."

"Ye'll take the loft wi' Mistress Cameron, sir?"

It took Tor a moment to comprehend that Jeannie was asking him to share the loft with Jewel. Dismayed, he realized that both Jeannie and Alastair would think it odd if he refused to sleep in the same bed with his lawful wedded wife.

"Aye," he growled, though it sounded deuced reluctant to the listening Jewel.

Fuming, she withdrew up the ladder after clenching her teeth and wishing her hosts a pleasant goodnight. Fortunately, Tor remained downstairs a while longer talking to Alastair. This gave Jewel ample time to strip off her breeches and shirt, and slip into the nightgown Jeannie had lent her.

Shaking the braids from her hair, she stood for a moment staring at the sheepskin-covered pallet that served as her bed. Lord, it was small! How was she supposed to share it with a man of Tor's size?

She heard the scraping of chairs below. Quickly she scrambled onto the makeshift bed and pulled the sheepskin over her head. The outer door closed as Tor went out to wash himself under the pump. Jeannie and Alastair remained below, talking softly together while Jeannie cleared away the last of the dishes.

Several minutes later the loft ladder creaked. Jewel squeezed her eyes shut and pretended to sleep. She heard the sound of Tor's boots hitting the floor. The whisper of clothing followed.

Holding her breath, Jewel stole a peek at him. He wasn't actually stripping naked, was he?

Aye, he was! He had brought no nightshirt from Glen Chulish, and Alastair had neglected to give him one. She caught a glimpse of his darkly furred chest and tapering hips before she quickly squeezed her eyes shut.

In the darkness, Tor cleared his throat and stretched wearily, then cleared his throat again. Jewel's heart hammered. Why, oh why hadn't she insisted on sleeping elsewhere? When Tor settled himself on the opposite side of the pallet, she lay perfectly still.

Down below, the candles were extinguished. Jeannie and Alastair had been sleeping in the barn since Jewel's arrival, although she had pleaded with them to take back their loft. Naturally, both of them had refused.

Now they gathered up a few things and went outside. The door closed behind them. The cottage quieted. Tor and Jewel were alone.

The minutes ticked by. The silence was oppressive. Jewel's arm was in an uncomfortable position and presently grew numb, but she didn't dare move it. She kept her breathing deep and even, so Tor would think she was sleeping.

He was quiet, too. So quiet that Jewel began to suspect that he himself had fallen asleep.

How could he? she wondered furiously. How could he lie there and slip off into unfettered dreams when tomorrow's threat of certain death loomed above him? More immediately, how could he lie so close to her for the first time in weeks, and not ache for her with every fiber of his being?

Because the fact of the matter was that Jewel herself was aching. Much as she tried to deny it, she was unable to ignore the bare inch or two that separated her from the naked body of her husband—a body that had, in the past, pleasured hers beyond all imagining. He had awakened a passionate side of her that Jewel could not control, and now she lay there and yearned for him no matter how hard she tried not to.

The silence gave way to tension. Every indrawn breath was torture. Nerves grew taut and limbs screamed for the blessed release of movement. Jewel ground her teeth together and willed herself to make no sound.

Useless.

With the gasp of a swimmer breaking the water's surface before her lungs burst, she choked out his name.

He was beside her in an instant, gathering her against him with an urgency that left her breathless.

"What is it, lass?"

"You know perfectly well!"

He withdrew instantly. After a moment, in a strained voice, he said, "I have to do what I must, Jewel. There's no way out of it. My people depend on me."

"I understand," she choked, because she did. Her sense of duty was strong, too. "But you could be k-killed!"

"I'd think that would make you happy."

"G-go to hell!"

He tipped up her chin with a finger and stared at her piercingly through the darkness. "Tears?" he said wonderingly. "Do you grieve for me, Jewel Mac-Kenzie Cameron?"

"N-no!"

He chuckled sadly. "Stubborn to the last, my wee witch. Well, come, then. If I'm to die tomorrow, love me one last time tonight."

He was ready for her after all. Jewel realized it the moment he took her into his arms and brought the throbbing length of his manhood against her naked flesh. She groaned and closed her eyes against the pleasure and the tears.

Turning her face to his, Tor covered her lips with his own, and Jewel wondered if perhaps he wasn't grieving a little, too. He had never kissed her quite like this before, with so much urgency and passion.

The sensation was newly magical and gloriously familiar all at the same time. Sobbing a little with the pleasure of it, she cast herself into his arms. Never had she come to him so willingly. The moment was erotic, charged with promise, and poignantly bittersweet.

Groaning, Tor pulled her hard against the length of his body. With hands and lips and seeking tongue, he learned anew every lovely inch of her. Committing to memory that which he might never savor again, he took his time to arouse her to that razor-sharp edge of ecstasy and pain. He worshiped her, molded her, loved her with touch and kiss and caress because he knew better than to do so with words.

This woman held his heart in her slim little hands. He knew that now, or at least he could admit as much to himself at last. His heart had never been so vulnerable before, despite how cruelly the past had hurt him. Although he ached to speak his feelings aloud, he knew that he could not risk his heart tonight, when tonight might well be all that was left him. With one single word, or even a glance, Jewel had the power to break him forever. He couldn't let her hurt him tonight. Too much depended on him tomorrow.

But the tenderness of his touch, and the gentleness of his kisses, did not go unnoticed by her. Aching, tears in her eyes, she lay beneath him and accepted his love, and waited breathlessly for him to say in words that which he poured into her with the actions of his great man's body.

But Tor did not. He said nothing at all. Even in that final moment, when his body convulsed and his hands fisted in her hair, he kept silent.

I love you, Jewel's heart thundered as his body emptied into hers. *Please, please, love me back.*

But Tor rolled away from her the moment he came to his senses. He was not about to let Jewel know how much this act between them meant to him, or to his vulnerable, yearning heart. But to Jewel, his hasty withdrawal seemed a sure sign that he could not get away from her fast enough once his passion was spent.

They lay side by side staring into the darkness, not touching, not speaking, hurting inside.

After a moment he said harshly, "If something happens to me tomorrow, you are, of course, free to go back to Drumcorrie."

"I'd already planned on it."

"I see."

Silence.

Jewel bit her lip and willed herself not to cry.

Tor stared at the ceiling, willing himself not to say anything foolish.

"You'll be happy to know that you won't have to worry about your aunt Millicent should you return to Glen Chulish a widow."

The word was like a knife in her heart. She swallowed. "Oh? Why is that?"

"I had a . . . chat with her before I came here."

Jewel rolled onto her side and came up on an elbow to look at him. He was staring up at the ceiling.

She could see nothing of his face.

"What did you do to her, Cameron?"

"Nothing."

"Nothing? You're lying."

Silence.

"Well? Are you going to tell me or not?"

"Jewel. I didn't murder her outright, if that's what you think. Though she certainly deserves it after the hell she's put you through."

A pause. Then Jewel said in a small, breathless voice, "Who told you?"

"Angus."

"But—" She broke off, overwhelmed. If Tor had known all along about the horrible things Aunt Millicent had done to her, then why had he continued to pay court to Cousin Cassie? The selfish bastard!

"I hate you," she said in a small, choked voice.

"I know."

He turned his back on her and said nothing more.

Jewel lay beside him, weeping into the sheepskin so that Tor wouldn't hear. Her thin shoulders shook and the tears rolled down her cheeks.

"Open the door!"

The command was accompanied by the sound of savage pounding.

"What is it?" Jewel asked, groggy with sleep.

Tor's hand covered her lips. "Hush!"

More pounding, then the sound of neighing horses. Fully awake now, Jewel sat up, Tor's hand still over her mouth.

"Tor Ban Cameron, if you're in there, come out!"

Jewel twisted away from him. "Who is it?"

"If I recognize the voice a'right, 'tis my uncle's valet. A scurvy little scoundrel if ever there was one." Tor rolled away from her as he spoke. Standing up, he began pulling on his clothes.

Jewel watched him, stunned. "You're not going out there, are you?"

"Of course I am. They'll tear the place down if I don't. I can't exactly leave Jeannie and Alastair homeless, can I?"

"Tor." Jewel scrambled out of bed and caught his arm with both her hands.

He shook her off. "I want you to stay out of this, Jewel. In fact, I insist on it. You'll only make matters worse."

"You can't expect me to stand by and just—just let you leave with them!"

"Why not?"

"Because . . . Because . . ."

"Well?"

Because I love you, you great daft fool! she wanted to scream at him. *And they'll murder you the moment you set foot outside that door!*

Tor's expression grew mocking as she stood there staring up at him, biting her lip with her eyes wide and frightened. "I can't think of a reason, either. So let me go, damn it!"

She had no choice but to obey, and watch in panic as he went down the ladder and crossed the room to slide back the heavy bolt. Instantly a crush of bodies descended on him. Tor fended them off with stunning strength.

"Get back!" he roared. "I'll speak to you outside!"

Incredibly, they obeyed. With a scowl, Tor followed them, pulling the door shut behind him.

Sobbing, Jewel scrambled into the breeches, shirt, and vest she had been wearing since her escape from the castle. Slipping Mordart's dagger into her boot, she shimmied down the ladder and crossed quickly to the window.

Her breath caught when she saw that the Morriseys' small yard was filled with men on horseback. All of them were armed with swords and muskets. Tor stood with his back to her talking with a man Jewel didn't know. Over near the gate, Alastair and Jeannie Morrisey stood surrounded by a menacing trio of riders. Jeannie looked terrified, Alastair grim.

Jewel finally understood what had happened. Tor must have been betrayed by one of the crofters.

The two men were still talking. Tor was nodding his head. Once or twice the other man gestured toward the cottage, then back at the castle. Finally a horse was brought forward. Jewel gasped as Tor swung himself into the saddle. Was he going willingly to his doom? By God, she wouldn't let him!

While the horsemen clattered out of the front yard, she climbed through the small window that led to the back. The Morriseys did not own a horse, only a sluggish little pony, but the McCallums, their nearest neighbors, did. If she could get over to their croft in time, and if the animal hadn't been confiscated by Malcolm Cameron's men, she just might have a chance to intercept Tor before he reached the castle and confronted his uncle.

She could hear Alastair calling to her frantically, but she ignored him. Lungs bursting, she crossed the field, vaulted over the fence, and splashed through the burn. Skirting the McCallums' house, she went straight to the barn. To her great relief, she found the horse in his stall. He was an elderly drafter accustomed to the plow, not to the presence of a panting young woman who insisted on bridling him long before he had been served his morning oats. He was stubborn, but so was Jewel. With heels and hands, she urged him outside and down the slope at a thundering gallop. Far across the moor she could see the trail of dust left by the other riders heading toward Abercraig Castle.

"Come on!" she yelled into the horse's ear.

Leaning low, her hands twisted in his shaggy mane, she set off across the turf at a dead run.

Chapter Twenty

Jewel did not know the castle's layout very well, but she had a good hunch as to where she might find old Mordart Bennish at this time of morning. No doubt she would find him in the castle's cellar inventorying the wine and the provisions that would be needed by his master for the coming day.

Sending the weary draft horse home with a slap on the rump, she made her way on foot the last quarter mile. Luck was with her, and she found her way to the cellar entrance without being seen. Though it had been dark when Mordart had brought her through this same gate and into the custody of the waiting Alastair two days ago, Jewel was able to retrace her steps without much difficulty. Easing open the gate, she prayed that she would find the elderly steward alone.

The echoing passage seemed even more frightening than on that recent, moonless night. Jewel could feel her heart thundering as she made her way cautiously through the gloom. Rats scurried and moisture dripped somewhere nearby. Candlelight flickered up ahead, and someone coughed and cleared his throat. Mordart?

Jewel's breath expelled in a long sigh of relief as she peeked around the corner and saw him shuffling between the barrels in the wine cellar. The moment he saw her, he dropped his chalk marker and hurried forward, wasting no time on foolish questions.

"They're bringin' 'im here, I warrant."

Tears filled her eyes. "Aye. They—they came for him just a few minutes ago."

"So Lord Abercraig said."

"How can I help him? What shall I do?"

The old man sighed heavily. "There ain't much ye can do, lass."

"How can you say that?" she flared. "You know perfectly well what his uncle has in mind for him!"

"And how will we stop 'im?" Mordart countered scathingly. "A wee lass and an auld mon like me?"

"I-I'm not sure. I just know that we have to do something, anything!"

"Haste and foolishness willna help Master Tor."

No, but neither would standing here arguing with the old beggar!

"At least take me upstairs!" Jewel pleaded. "You must have some idea where Lord Abercraig intends to confront Tor! If we could just listen in, maybe we can come up with some way of helping him."

The thought obviously did not sit well with the steward, but he had nothing better to suggest. Extinguishing the candle, he led Jewel upstairs by way of a little-used passage running beneath the kitchens. Muttering beneath his breath, he took her down a series of musty corridors far removed from the daylight and the commonly frequented rooms of the castle.

"Here," he said at last, leading her into a window-less anteroom that smelled strongly of camphor and mouse urine.

Disoriented by the gloom and the twists and turns they had taken, Jewel entered hesitantly. The room was barely big enough for the two of them. She turned to him questioningly, and Mordart gestured impatiently toward a narrow door that stood slightly ajar. Jewel looked through it, and was startled to find herself peering into the same study where she had first met Malcolm Cameron. Only this time she was standing at the opposite end of the room, behind Malcolm's desk, with a tapestry hanging from the wall to cover the doorway itself.

" 'Tis a private entrance," Mordart explained in a whisper. " 'Is lordship doesna use it much. He'll no think on't today. No with so much else on his mind."

Indeed, no sooner had he spoken those words than the door in the opposite wall opened and Malcolm Cameron strode inside. He headed toward them so purposefully that for one awful moment Jewel thought that the old steward had betrayed her. But Malcolm stopped at his desk, crossed behind it, and sat down. He didn't even glance at the tapestry to his back, or the figures crouching in the shadowed door-way behind it.

Scarcely a moment later, Tor was brought in. Jewel stifled a gasp as she looked at him. She had never seen that coldly murderous expression on his face before. It was hard to believe that this was the same man who had loved her so tenderly last night!

Although Tor was accompanied by an armed es-cort, he seemed wholly unaware of them. He had eyes only for the man behind the desk; the one who was so sure of himself that he did not even rise as Tor strode menacingly toward him.

"I intend to kill you for abducting my wife," Tor

ground out without preamble.

"My apologies," Malcolm answered, unruffled, "but it was necessary at the time. Seems she's been taking good care of you. You're looking well."

Tor was in no mood for such talk. Calmly and succinctly, he said, "I expect you to vacate Abercraig Castle immediately. You've no further claim to it now that I've returned."

Malcolm steepled his fingertips before him. He seemed to be enjoying himself. "Really? After I've worked so hard to gain it for myself?"

"After you had my family murdered, you mean."

Jewel bit her lip. From her vantage point, she could see Tor's face clearly. The challenge in his voice was unmistakable, but it was the barely leashed fury in his blue eyes that she found most frightening. Tor's uncle was calmer, more in control. She realized in that moment why he was behaving so coolly, so smugly. He was actually glad that Tor was angry, for he fully expected him to act impulsively, and thus make a mistake.

I'll have to be the one to stay alert for Tor, Jewel thought, because he clearly can't. 'Tis obvious that Malcolm intends to goad him into losing his temper, and when he does, when Tor explodes, Malcolm will have a ready excuse to kill him.

And the means to do so as well. As Malcolm kept on talking, the back of the room began filling with armed men. Jewel didn't doubt for a moment that they were merely awaiting a signal from their master to open fire. On the other hand, she suspected strongly that Malcolm intended to put an end to his nephew himself. He'd been denied the opportunity, and thwarted too often, to pass up the pleasure now. Furthermore, he was just arrogant enough to want that honor for himself.

Aye, he was the one who would bear watching,

Jewel thought grimly. Tor's life depended on it. Slowly, quietly, she reached down and drew the dagger from her boot.

"I sincerely hope that you needn't be reminded that I have a full royal pardon," Tor was saying icily. "Your claim to Abercraig is null and void as of this very moment. You could vacate peacefully, or—"

"Or?" Malcolm turned over his hand. "Be reasonable, lad. The place has been mine for more than twenty years."

"And a fine job you've done with it," Tor said furiously. "The crofters told me how you've run their farms into the ground. And I can see the rest for myself. Just look at this place! Not fit for dogs or pigs, is it?"

Malcolm's back was turned to her, but Jewel could see his shoulders stiffen. Her fingers tightened reflexively around the handle of her dagger.

"You've neither the money nor the skill to keep the place up," Tor went on, his anger barely under control. "You never did. My father was a far better administrator than you ever were, but you could never admit that to yourself, could you? Well, admit it now! Bow out gracefully. I'll not prevent your going."

"Kind of you," Malcolm sneered. "Unfortunately, you're not the one to give the orders here. Not by a long shot."

"You haven't a legal foot to stand on," Tor countered coldly. "No court in the land will grant you continued possession of the Abercraig title and lands now that I've turned up alive and fully pardoned. And as for that trick you pulled on me in Glasgow . . ."

"Stay where you are!" Malcolm warned as Tor moved closer to the desk.

The men in the back of the room made as if to charge, but Malcolm lifted a hand to stop them. Everyone froze and looked at him. He was silent for a long moment, grappling with his temper. Then he leaned back in his chair as though he hadn't a worry in the world. His tone was calm, his expression almost kind.

"My dear lad," he said to Tor, "surely we can discuss this reasonably, like the grown men we are?"

As he spoke, he eased open the middle drawer of his desk. Tor couldn't see what he was doing from where he stood, but Jewel and old Mordart could.

"Reasonably?" Tor was saying contemptuously. "The way you discussed matters so reasonably with my parents and my sister before you had them slaughtered?"

"Those were unsettled times," Malcolm countered with a shrug. "Everyone was suspect."

"A couple known to be loyal to the English king? A bonnie little girl no older than ten?" Tor's voice shook. "You can't possibly pretend you didn't have a hand in their deaths!"

The drawer was open now, and Jewel saw Malcolm's hand slide in, then emerge with a pistol so small that he was able to conceal it in the palm of his hand. She could tell from Mordart's indrawn breath that he had seen it too.

There was no need for her to ponder Malcolm Cameron's intentions; they were obvious. With only his faithful retainers as witnesses, he would have no trouble convincing the local magistrates that his nephew had attacked him outright and that he had had no choice but to shoot him in self-defense. Naturally his men would corroborate the story. It would be the perfect crime.

Only Malcolm hadn't counted on there being other witnesses. He hadn't counted on the possibility that his cleverness wasn't infallible, and that it wouldn't be so simple to lure his nephew to Abercraig, kill him, and still appear innocent of the crime. Because he hadn't counted on Jewel.

Malcolm was still talking, if only to hide the faint click as he pulled the pistol hammer back with his thumb. "What a pity," he said, shaking his head. "I had so hoped we'd be able to settle this without violence. It seems I was wrong."

"Violence?" Tor echoed. "Is that what you want? By God, I'll be glad—"

Malcolm's triumphant laughter drowned him out. Up swept the pistol, aimed straight at Tor's heart.

"Tor!" Jewel shouted, leaping from her hiding place and running to him. Counting on his lightning-fast reflexes, she thrust the dagger toward him.

Tor didn't fail her. Without hesitating, he grabbed the weapon by the handle. At the same moment he leaped aside, just as Malcolm pulled the trigger.

There was a roar of exploding powder as the pistol discharged. A blinding flash lit the room, and Jewel felt a searing pain in her arm. The impact spun her around and slammed her back against the wall. She stumbled and lost her footing, and the edge of the desk struck her a hard blow to the head as she fell.

And instantly the world, and everything in it, faded to black.

Consciousness returned slowly, in a misty blend of swirling images. Rain was falling, and a wood fire crackled in the hearth. Whispered voices sounded in the hallway.

Jewel stirred fretfully and moaned. Instantly a shadow fell across the bed.

Slowly Jewel opened her eyes. Disappointment brought a lump to her throat when she saw that it was not Tor. In the next moment, however, she gasped and struggled upright.

"Annie! What on earth . . . ?"

"Lie still!"

But Jewel had already fallen back against the pillow, groaning and clutching her head.

"Ye've a fracture," Annie said angrily. "Not enow tae kill ye, but bad enow that ye maun keep still."

"Aye," Jewel agreed. Gingerly she touched the lump on her temple. It was nearly the size of a goose egg, and cruelly painful. "Ohh, bloody blazes, it hurts! What happened?"

"Fell an' cracked yer head, ye did. On the desk int' study. Serves ye richt, I might add! Interferin' where ye had no—"

"Leave off, Annie," a masculine voice commanded from the doorway.

Again Jewel looked up with an eager expression. Again she was shocked by the identity of the speaker. "Ruan! What the devil? Has all of Glen Chulish come to Abercraig, then?"

"Just about. How are you, Cousin?"

"I suppose I'll—Oww! Stop bouncing the bed, will you? My head's about to burst!"

"Aye, ye're right, Annie, she'll live. Crabby as ever, more's the pity."

But Ruan eased himself off the bed as gently as he could and obediently pulled up a chair. Leaning forward, he took Jewel's hand and patted it awkwardly. "Ye gave us quite a fright, lass."

Us? Did he mean Tor, too? Where in bloody hell was he? Surely she'd given him plenty of warning before Malcolm Cameron fired his gun!

"Tor," she whispered in sudden panic. "He didn't—"

"The big lummox be unharmed," Ruan assured her.

"Then where is he?"

"Gone out wi' Tykie. I daresay they'll be back tonight."

"Tykie? You mean he's here, too? Will somebody

please tell me what's going on?"

"If Annie will permit it, aye."

"Five minutes," Annie snapped, and withdrew.

"I'll make it fast," Ruan promised. Giving Jewel no time to ask questions, he explained how he and Tykie had arrived from Glen Chulish with a number of armed men just as the confrontation in Malcolm Cameron's study had reached its awful climax. He described rushing into the room to find a scene of utter pandemonium: Malcolm Cameron lying bleeding to death behind his desk with a dagger embedded in his chest, Jewel lying bleeding and unconscious nearby, and Tor—in Ruan's words—literally tearing people limb from limb in an effort to reach her.

"But nobody was really putting up much of a fight," he added smugly. "I think there was no reason once Lord Abercraig—the former Lord Abercraig, I mean—was killed."

"Did Tor—was he the one who—"

"Aye," Ruan said grimly. "With the dagger Mordart Bennish says you threw to him at the last."

"Oh God." She put her face in her hands.

"Nay, lass. Everyone agreed 'twas necessary. Otherwise his shot would hae killed ye outright. This way ye suffered no more than a grazed arm."

For the first time Jewel became aware of a dull throbbing just below her left shoulder. Lifting the covers, she found her arm wrapped in thick bandages. Groaning, she leaned back and closed her eyes. Tears glimmered beneath her lids. "I bungled everything, didn't I?"

"Nay," Ruan said emphatically, his heart swelling as he looked at her, so small and defenseless in the big four-poster bed. She was pale and haggard, and even her glorious hair seemed to have lost some of its luster as it spilled unbound over her shoulders. It was a blessing that Annie had insisted on accompanying him and Tykie to Glen Chulish in order to care for her. Even though Ruan had done his best to convince her to remain behind, he was glad now that the stubborn old woman had refused to back down. If anything could nurse Jewel back to health, it would be Annie's magic potions.

Sighing, he looked again at Jewel. Her eyes had fluttered shut and her breathing had quieted. Pain and exhaustion had obviously taken their toll.

For a while Ruan sat by her bedside simply holding her hand. He thought she had drifted off to sleep, but after a long while she said, without opening her eyes, "I still don't understand what you're doing here. Why did you come?"

Ruan smiled sadly. "How could I stay away knowin' my own mither had done this to 'ee?"

Jewel opened her eyes and looked at him, astonished. "Then you knew? Who told you?"

"Mither hersel'. That's why I had to come. In all good conscience, Jewel, I never had the vaguest idea—"

"I know. I understand." She squeezed his hand, and was glad when he squeezed back.

"What happens now?" she asked sorrowfully.

"I dinna ken. Tor's gone wi' Tykie to Chulish House to see her. I imagine they'll be bringin' her to the magistrate's in Inverness. There'll be an inquest because o' Malcolm's death."

"Oh, Ruan!" Tears stung Jewel's eyes. "I'm sorry."

"Don't be. 'Tis time she was held accountable for a' she did. Tor said he'd speak on her behalf, but do ye ken, I dinna think she deserves that much."

Privately neither did Jewel. But she was grateful to Tor, if only because of Ruan's hurting. She squeezed his hand again to convey as much without words, and they exchanged a long, silent look.

It was an awkward moment for Ruan, who wasn't

used to serious moments. Squirming out of his chair, he muttered something about seeing to the servants. Giving his cousin a self-conscious peck on the brow, he stammered a few bracing words before beating an embarrassed retreat.

Jewel smiled after him, knowing how much he had always hated emotional scenes. Poor lad! This one had been particularly difficult for him, no doubt.

After a moment, she sighed and closed her eyes. She seemed to hurt all over, and she felt utterly, completely exhausted. A fierce longing for Tor, and worry for his welfare, nagged at her relentlessly. If only she weren't so cursed weak that she had to lie abed like a helpless invalid!

"Annie?" she called, but there was no answer.

Peevishly, she looked around for a bell. There was no bell, nor even a water pitcher that she might dash against the wall in order to summon the annoying woman.

"Bloody incompetence," she muttered to herself.

In the end, there was nothing left to do but close her eyes and fall asleep. Which was exactly what Annie had had in mind for her anyway.

Chapter Twenty-one

Tor stayed away from Abercraig for more than a
week. During that time, Jewel lay abed, sleeping and
mending, which perhaps was just as well. The rest
did her an enormous amount of good. The damage
inflicted by Malcolm Cameron's shot healed cleanly,
and the bruise on her temple faded rapidly. Her
headaches vanished, her appetite returned, and Annie was able to coax her into eating a number of
tempting foods.

By the time Tor returned on a blustery evening
nearly two weeks after the shooting, Jewel was feeling strong enough to spend a few hours after supper
reading downstairs in one of Abercraig's less shabby
parlors. On the night of Tor's return she happened
to be entertaining a trio of visitors: her cousin Ruan,
Jeannie Morrisey, and Jeannie's son Keith, whose
disguise had so cleverly lured Jewel's pursuers away
from the castle.

When Tor stepped, chilled and weary, into the parlor, he found his wife laughing gaily at something Keith Morrisey had just said. Her tilted eyes sparkled, and the color had risen high in her wan cheeks. Young Keith was looking decidedly pleased with himself, and Tor didn't have to be told that the lad was smitten.

His mood soured, and instantly worsened when he saw the smile fade from Jewel's lips and the light die in her eyes the moment she became aware of him standing in the doorway. A stillness came over her, and Tor was suddenly struck with the illogical urge to hurt her.

"Well," he said coldly, strolling inside. "I see you're no longer at death's door."

"Does that disappoint you?" she asked quietly.

Tor didn't answer. He just stood there glowering at her. She lifted her chin and boldly stared back, determined not to let him suspect how fiercely glad she was to see him.

"What happened at the magistrate's?" Ruan wished to know, as always unaware of any tension in the air.

"Come, Keith," interrupted Jeannie, who was not nearly so oblivious. "Lord Abercraig will wish to discuss the matter withoot us."

It took Jewel a moment to realize that the older woman was referring to Tor. Her breath caught. Oh, God, Tor was now the Earl of Abercraig. How on earth was she ever going to think of that title without affixing to it the evil image of Malcolm Cameron?

"Please stay," she begged as Jeannie prodded her reluctant son upright.

"Och, dearie, we canna. Alastair will be wonderin' what's become of us." Bidding them all a pleasant good-night, she all but pulled Keith from the room.

"Another conquest, I take it," Tor growled, looking after them.

Jewel stiffened but made no reply.

"Stop bein' so grumpy, man!" Ruan protested. "Tell us what happened! Did ye survive the inquest?"

"Obviously."

Tor collapsed in the nearest chair and rang for whiskey. Jewel's heart went out to him as she saw how drawn and weary he looked, but the moment his burning gaze fastened itself upon her, she stiffened and looked away.

"You'll be happy to know, ma'am," he said mockingly, "that I am rightfully installed as the Earl of Abercraig. The documents are on their way to London even as I speak. The circumstances surrounding Malcolm's death were ruled in my favor, and I've also been officially pardoned of any crime in connection with my incarceration at Cowcadden."

"So you're truly free now," she said tonelessly. She should have been delighted, but all she could do was sit there and blink back betraying tears.

Mordart Bennish brought whiskey, and Tor drank deeply.

"I assume," he added casually, "that you haven't changed your mind about staying here at Abercraig."

Jewel's chin came up. "No. I want to go home as soon as Annie says I'm well enough."

Tor looked down into his glass. "I see."

Jewel looked down into her lap. "I assume you intend to stay?"

"Of course. The place is a disaster, thanks to my uncle's neglect."

Ruan cleared his throat. "I was wondering if . . . um . . . if you'd mind me stayin' an' givin' 'ee a hand. Just for a while," he added hastily as Tor and Jewel looked at him in astonishment.

"You want to stay here?" Jewel demanded disbelievingly. "Why?"

"I like it here," he said with a shrug.

"Why, I'd be grateful," Tor said, meaning it.

"You won't be needin' me at Drumcorrie just yet," Ruan continued, speaking to Jewel. "The barley's no ready for harvest, and there's always Sandy to depend on."

"You're old enough to know your own mind," she replied stiffly. The traitor!

"What about me mother and sister?" Ruan asked diffidently of Tor.

"Aye, what about them?" Jewel added, for until that moment she had honestly forgotten all about them.

"I've arranged to have them sent to London."

"What!" they exclaimed in unison.

" 'Tis where she's always wanted to go, isn't it?" Tor asked, looking annoyed.

"Well, aye," Ruan stammered, "but . . . but I thought . . ."

"That I'd have her thrown in prison?"

Ruan nodded helplessly.

"I wasn't about to press charges against a member of your family," Tor said coolly. "No matter how much your mother may have deserved it."

"Then—then what did you do to her?" Jewel asked in a whisper.

Tor twirled the stem of his glass. "I sent her to England with the proper letters of introduction to ensure that she'll once again be accepted in the right places. She and Cassie will have a town house, and a servant or two, but the rest will be up to them."

"You mean ye've set them up? That—that was kind of 'ee," Ruan stammered inadequately.

Tor's lips curved into a humorless smile. "I can be kindhearted when I wish, Ruan."

Ruan had the good grace to flush.

"Besides," Tor added, looking again into his glass. "I've been in prison before. 'Tis not a place I'd care

257

to send anyone, not even your mother."

Jewel thought her heart would burst as she saw the pain of distant memories pass across his weary face. She had to hold tight to the arms of her chair to keep from springing up and going to him. Dear, kind Tor! Oh, how she loved him in that moment!

"And it really won't be that easy for them," he continued. "London isn't cheap. Life won't be a stream of endless invitations or glittering parties for them."

"Not at first. But they'll make out," Ruan predicted, scarcely able to hide his gratitude. "Ye ken Mother, Jewel."

" 'Tis what she's always wanted," Jewel agreed slowly. Once, she had prayed for a prolonged and painful death for her aunt. Now the thought of Millicent and her spiteful daughter far away in England building a new life for themselves filled her with profound relief. It had been kind—more than kind!—of Tor.

She finally found the courage to look at him. "How in the world did you manage it?"

He lifted his wide shoulders. "I have a number of friends in London."

Powerful ones, and very wealthy, apparently.

"They'll keep an eye on her, Jewel, I promise."

She fought back a sudden rush of tears. She knew that Tor was telling her that she would be safe from now on from the woman who had tormented and hurt her all these years. Furthermore, he had accomplished as much without resorting to violence or revenge, and with Ruan's full approval. How neatly he had tied up every last detail! 'Twas a happy ending for everyone, to be sure.

Then why did she feel so utterly miserable? Why did tears scald the back of her eyes and bring a lump like hot coals to her throat?

The parlor door opened just then and Tykie lumbered in. It was the first time Jewel had seen him since she had been abducted from Glen Chulish, because Annie had refused to let him visit her upstairs in her bedroom. Now she sprang up and threw her arms around him, her face wreathed in a joyous smile.

"Tykie!"

Unabashed, Tykie hugged her back.

Tor watched them darkly, recalling that he had not been granted the same loving welcome. "Your mistress informs me that she's more than ready to return to Drumcorrie, Tykie."

The big mute uttered a soundless laugh and swung Jewel into his arms. Mindful of her injuries, he set her down gently, but he continued beaming as he did so.

"Aye," said Jewel, smiling back at him as happily as she could. "Isn't it wonderful?"

Throughout the next day, and the next, Jewel continued to do her best to appear lighthearted so that no one—especially Tor—would suspect how much she was hurting inside. Despite outward appearances, she had never been more miserable in her life. Or bewildered and confused. While she wanted desperately to go home to Drumcorrie, she ached at the thought of leaving Tor. His continued pigheadedness made her furious. Why, oh, why couldn't he give up this gloomy castle and his grandiose plans for restoring it and come back with her? Couldn't he be just as happy in the modest surroundings of Glen Chulish?

Apparently not. The more quiet and sad Jewel became, the more Tor showed himself to be growing content. On his first day back from Inverness he took charge of his long-neglected castle with an energy and a sense of purpose that astounded everyone.

Those servants whom Mordart Bennish identified as having been loyal to Malcolm Cameron were summarily dismissed. A new staff was assembled from the inhabitants of the village and surrounding crofts who had been chased away so many years before. An ever-lengthening list was compiled of chores that needed doing in order to sweep away the long years of neglect and revert Abercraig to its former glory.

Naturally, a huge infusion of cash would be needed. Tor had expected as much, and was not at all surprised to discover to what extent his uncle had decimated the family coffers. No matter. He would write the necessary letters, attract investors, and take out loans, and before too long, the outstanding herd of Ayrshires that had formerly supplied Abercraig with most of its income would be producing milk and cheese and prizewinning stock once again.

As well, Tor intended to bring the barren fields into production, and thin the timber stands to increase the crop yield. Years of work lay before him, he knew, but he welcomed them with a sense of purpose that had been missing from his life for far too long.

The change in him was immediately noticeable. Hourly, he seemed to grow more mellow and approachable. The anger and the hunger that had driven him for so many years fell away from him like a stone, and the servants and the crofters who met with him nodded their heads approvingly. A new sense of purpose had come to Abercraig at last, and everyone rejoiced in it.

The Glen Chulish people were the only ones who didn't seem to share the general enthusiasm. Tykie and Annie chafed with impatience to leave for home. Both considered Abercraig Castle too hugely overwhelming, and Annie merely snorted when Tor asked if she would like to take on the responsibilities of chatelaine there. Tykie, though fascinated by the place, shuddered at the thought of the hard work to come. Daily he looked in on Jewel to mark her recovery, anxious to return to Glen Chulish before Tor had the chance to rope him into some difficult task or another. Even Ruan wasn't so sure anymore that he had been wise to offer Tor a helping hand.

Everyone seemed to take for granted the dissolution of Tor and Jewel's marriage. After all, Tor had regained control of his birthright and had no reason to return to Glen Chulish, while Jewel, as mistress of Drumcorrie, would no sooner give up her home than Tor would his castle. Besides, the marriage had never been more than one of convenience, and the situation that had made it necessary in the first place existed no longer. A peaceful parting was clearly in order.

Neither Jewel nor Tor behaved in a manner to indicate otherwise. Tor spent most of the daylight hours away from the castle, and evenings poring over ledgers and letters in his office. Jewel kept to her rooms for the most part, and if by chance the two met in the corridor or at the dinner table, they were politely reserved with one another.

No one suspected how much Jewel was hurting.

No one realized that beneath Tor's boundless enthusiasm lay an anger and frustration that he could scarcely hide.

On the morning of her departure, Jewel awoke to the clanging of cowbells. From her window, she watched the lovely herd of Ayrshires being driven to the fields by a redheaded lad and his collie. The sun was rising in a clear, rose-colored sky, and the hills were emerald with the full bloom of spring.

Ayr was a lovely place, but Jewel felt a strange emptiness every time she looked at it. She knew without a doubt that Drumcorrie would always be home to her, for it was the rocky mountains and the heather-purpled moors of Glen Chulish that called to her spirit. She had tried hard over the last few days to convince herself that she could be happy here, but deep in her heart she knew that she could not. Even if Tor had wanted her—which clearly he didn't—she would not have bloomed here had she stayed.

I would have withered and died over the long run, Jewel thought now, resting her cheek in her hand as she sat before the window. And so would our love.

Love?

Her lips curled contemptuously at her foolishness. Tor had certainly made no bones in choosing his castle over her! Deep down, Jewel couldn't really blame him. She loved Tor enough to understand the dreams that had driven him all these years, enough to let him go without making a scene.

But it wasn't easy. Her greatest fear lay in letting him catch wind of how she felt, and of shedding tears in front of him when the time came to bid him farewell.

Unfortunately, that time came far too soon. Already the stablehands were busy in the courtyard below cleaning and oiling the Abercraig coach. By the time morning brightened into an achingly beautiful spring day, it was ready, the horses standing in their traces, the snorting Drum tethered behind. Jewel's few belongings had been strapped to the roof, and sufficient provisions for the journey had been packed by the Abercraig kitchen. At the last, Tor had ordered a cask of ale to be loaded on for Tykie.

Now Jewel paused on the bottom step of the coach so that her eyes were on a level with Tor's, who stood on the ground below her. Annie was already sitting inside, clearly impatient to be off. Tykie was standing on the cobblestones awaiting his turn to board, although his path was blocked by Tor, who stood between him and Jewel, scowling at her in a manner that withered her heart.

"You'll not reconsider?" he asked now, harshly.

Jewel shook her head. She was afraid to speak because she couldn't trust her voice not to break.

Tor's lips curved derisively. "Forgive me for asking. I know what Drumcorrie means to you."

And Abercraig to you, Jewel thought, swallowing hard.

Tor drew in a deep breath. "Well, Mrs. Cameron, I suppose this is farewell. I must say, it's been very . . . hmm . . . shall we say *interesting* being married to you? Maddening, wearying, difficult, but never dull. In the future, should you wish to have the marriage annulled, I will not contest it."

Jewel nodded. She was glad Tor wasn't looking at her, because her eyes were brimming.

Without another word, he put his hand under her elbow and helped her up into the vehicle. When she was seated inside, he lingered for a moment in the doorway, looking down at her.

"Jewel." His voice was suddenly filled with urgency. She looked at him quickly. "If you ever need me for anything, anything at all, you need only write. I'll come immediately. I promise."

She nodded again, her head bowed, swallowing convulsively.

"And if you should ever change your mind about coming back . . . my door will always be open to you."

He stood there waiting, but when Jewel refused to respond or even to look at him again, he sighed and stepped to the ground. The coach rocked. Jewel clenched her hands into fists. Outside, farewells were exchanged between Tykie, Tor, and Ruan. Again the vehicle dipped as the big mute climbed inside.

Stepping back, Tor signaled to the coachman. With a crack of the whip, the vehicle lurched away. Jewel did not look up as it crossed the courtyard and disappeared through the gate.

Chapter Twenty-two

It turned out to be a singularly beautiful summer, that summer of '62. Week after week, the winds blew in from a southerly direction, keeping the North Sea rain and the cold at bay. The harvest promised to be bountiful, both at Glen Chulish and Abercraig, and by early August the grain was standing heavy in the fields.

At Abercraig, the castle and the grounds had undergone an astonishing transformation. Thanks to good care and proper nourishment, the dairy cows had dropped a record number of calves. The new housekeeper, a younger version of Drumcorrie's efficient Annie Brewster, had swept out the castle's dust and mildew and gloom. Long-unused rooms had been reopened, and the attics and cellars emptied of their debris. The stable had been given a new slate roof, and the tenant cottages were all neatly thatched and prosperous looking.

Everyone agreed that the new Lord Abercraig was

solely responsible for such wonderful changes. After nearly two decades of Cameron neglect, Tor's hands-on administrative style was decidedly welcome. Throughout the summer, no one had worked harder than the young earl himself. From dawn to dusk he labored in the fields alongside his workers, or in the dairy with his cowman, or busied himself mending stone walls and crumbling rooftops with his crofters whenever he was not doing the same to his castle. No amount of hard work seemed to daunt him. Sleep was not a requisite any longer, and he would have worked straight through the Sabbath if his God-fearing crofters hadn't insisted he stop and worship with them.

Old Mordart Bennish had never been happier. His duties as Abercraig steward had been minimal under Malcolm Caulbane. Now, with the farms in production and the land no longer fallow, his days were filled with bustling excursions from worksite to worksite, and poring over the ledgers long into the night, his fingers stained with ink from the blotter.

Often there were visitors. The local gentry, which had kept itself aloof from Malcolm, were quick to welcome the current earl back into their fold. Men came often to discuss administrative matters with him, and those ladies with marriageable daughters were quick to include the handsome young laird at every social event.

Few of the locals knew the real circumstances surrounding Malcolm Cameron's demise. Tor's crofters were a closemouthed lot, and his uncle's servants had been dismissed before they could spread any mischief. As well, Tor took care never to mention the existence, however far away, of a wife. In fact, Jewel's name was never uttered in his home, and his servants knew better than to ask after her. At first, indignant eyebrows were raised among the staff whenever a suitable young lady from the area was trotted out for his inspection, but the angry talk soon dwindled when it was seen that Lord Tor did nothing to encourage them.

Ruan MacKenzie traveled often between Abercraig and Glen Chulish. At first Tor had regarded his presence with considerable suspicion. When it became clear, however, that Ruan could make himself truly useful when he wished, his wariness had vanished. Tor gradually developed a grudging liking for the affable Ruan, for he had never forgotten that Ruan had, of his own accord, ridden after Jewel with Tykie and the Drumcorrie servants following her abduction at the hands of his uncle. The fact that Ruan continued to be grateful to Tor for his mother's banishment to England also served to ease the former tension between the two. By the time Ruan had established a regular pattern of monthly visits, Tor was actually looking forward to seeing him.

As for Ruan, it would seem that he was endlessly fascinated with Abercraig. The prizewinning herd of Ayrshires interested him in particular, and whenever he was in residence, he took over Tor's responsibilities with the Abercraig cowman. This suited Tor extremely well. He had already discovered that dairying was not one of his passions. Free to take on other chores, he preferred spending his time outdoors, particularly in the fields, where the grain was already turning the lush, golden color of late summer.

Most days, Tor didn't see Ruan until they met for dinner in the great banqueting hall, both of them sunburned and thirsty for a glass of wine. The talk between them was always lively. Tor had come to appreciate Ruan's wit, where once it had maddened him no end. They discussed the latest news from London, where Millicent was doing her best to marry

Cassie off to some elderly nobleman or another, and the newest developments in France. Ruan described the utter boredom of living alone in Chulish House, and how well the harvest was getting on at Drumcorrie.

But he never once mentioned Jewel. He knew better. The first time he had tried, Tor had made it clear that Ruan would no longer be welcome at Abercraig if he brought up his wife again. Besides, Jewel had made similar threats whenever Ruan went to see her, and since Ruan was an expert at protecting his own hide, he wisely learned to hold his tongue.

Arriving on horseback one morning for what he hoped would be a lengthy stay early in the month of August, Ruan approached the great castle of Abercraig by way of the westerly road. In the glen below, the harvest was in full swing. Workers were scattered throughout the fields wielding scythes while women in aprons and short-sleeved blouses bound the grain into sheaves.

The same bucolic scene could be found at Drumcorrie too, but where Jewel and her people were cutting barley for whiskey, the Abercraig workers were harvesting oats. Halting his mount at the edge of the field, Ruan was astonished when one of the workers, a broad-shouldered fellow he didn't recognize, lifted his scythe in greeting. The moment Ruan spotted that black hair and impudent grin, however, he cursed softly and rode forward.

"What on earth," he demanded, "are ye doin' out here?"

"Cutting grain," Tor answered, smiling and wiping the sweat from his brow with a shirtsleeve.

"Honestly, Tor! Workin' like a farmer! Don't ye know 'twill make ye coarse and common?"

"Too late. I already am. What's in the flask?"

"Water."

"Thank God. Hand it over, will you?"

Ruan dismounted and watched while Tor drank deeply. "Disgusting," he remarked. "You're burned dark as a blackamoor. Filthy, too, from workin' in the fields. 'Tis a pity Jewel canna see ye now."

"Oh?" said Tor. Carefully he capped the flask and returned it to Ruan. "And how is my lovely wife?"

"Well enou'," Ruan answered warily. He regretted the mention of her name, which had slipped out without his being aware of it.

"I suppose the harvest at Drumcorrie is almost over."

"Anither week, give or take a day."

"Hmm. Perhaps I'll pay her a visit when all's done."

Ruan looked alarmed. "What for?"

Tor leaned back against the stone wall surrounding the field, his booted legs casually crossed. "Why not? It's been nearly four months since I've seen her. Time to bury the hatchet, as they say in the colonies."

"Ye mean, make amends?"

"Good heavens, no! I've had enough of Jewel to last me a lifetime, thank you."

"Then keep it that way," Ruan advised. He fiddled with the buttons of his vest while Tor looked at him sharply.

"What's the matter, Ruan?"

"Eh?"

"You're jumpy as a cat now that Jewel's name's been mentioned. Not hiding anything from me, are you?"

"Dinna be silly!"

"I'm not. What's wrong at Drumcorrie?"

"Naught, I tell ye!"

All of a sudden an odd look crossed Tor's face. It was almost as if he'd taken an unexpected blow between the eyes. He said in a strangled voice, "Not pregnant, is she?"

Ruan looked so shocked that there really was no need for an answer. Tor didn't know whether to be elated or disappointed. No matter. The point was moot. Ruan had made it clear that Jewel wasn't expecting.

Thank God.

"Come on," Tor growled, feeling suddenly, inexplicably angry. "I'm done for the day. I need something stronger than water, and you could use some time out of the heat, old man. You're pale as a ghost."

Indeed, Ruan did look rather out of sorts, and he remained uncharacteristically subdued for the remainder of the day. Tor soon became convinced that he was hiding something from him, but no amount of prying earned him more than a cagey response.

I'll have to go to Drumcorrie myself, Tor thought, annoyed. Find out what the devil's going on.

He should have known that marriage to a woman like Jewel would continue to be bothersome even though the two of them lived nearly a week's journey apart. Damn it, Tor could see perfectly well that Ruan was sitting on a secret where Jewel was concerned! An unsavory one, given the way he was acting: as though someone had put fleas in his breeches, for God's sake! Tor wasn't sure how much of his squirming behavior he could tolerate.

Fortunately, Ruan spared him a great deal of aggravation by cutting his visit short. He announced that he would stay no more than four days, which was not at all like him, and that he intended to while away most of those in the dairy with the cowman.

This suited Tor well enough. Still, he hadn't taken into consideration the fact that Ruan had become a great favorite among the locals. When word of his presence traveled through the glen, a number of invitations promptly appeared on Abercraig's doorstep.

"Sorry, old man," Tor remarked, leafing through them as they sat at breakfast on the last day before Ruan's departure. "You won't be here long enough to accept any of these."

"Are any worthwhile?" Ruan asked curiously.

"Not really. The usual obligations. Tea with the Farquarsons. Supper at Barriemore Hall. A birthday party for Heather Menzies. Summer games at—"

"Wait a moment. Isn't she the one with the gray eyes?"

"Who?"

"The Menzies lass."

"Are her eyes gray? I confess I've never noticed."

"Oh, come, Tor! She's got the bonniest eyes i' the country! Like pewter, or minted silver, or—or clouds on the loch . . ." Ruan broke off, scowling. "What's so funny? Why are ye laughin'?"

"Waxing poetic, Ruan?" Tor countered with a smirk. "That's never a good sign where a woman's concerned."

"What d'ye mean?"

"Only that a gentleman never notices the color of a young lady's eyes unless his feelings are somehow engaged."

"My feel—What!" Ruan went scarlet. "That be the stupidest thing I've ever heard!"

"At any rate," Tor went on, scribbling something on the bottom of the embossed invitation, "I'll have to send Mrs. Menzies our sincere regrets. I shall be out in the fields working during Heather's birthday, and you will be back at Glen Chulish."

"When's the ball?"

Tor glanced at the invitation. "Thursday next."

Ruan cleared his throat. "I wonder—"

"Hmm?"

"How old will she be?"

Tor looked again. "Eighteen."

"Er . . . 'tis something of a milestone, don't ye think?"

"Oh, indeed. A person turns eighteen only once in her life."

Ruan didn't even rise to the bait. He merely sat there toying with his fork and looking miserable.

Tor decided to take pity on him. "Actually, it is something of a milestone, now that I think on it. And rather rude of me to refuse to attend. I wonder, Ruan, if I might call upon you for a tremendous favor?"

Ruan regarded him suspiciously. "Aye?"

"Would you represent Abercraig at the party for me? Personally deliver my felicitations to Mistress Menzies in my stead."

Ruan looked positively speechless.

"I know 'tis an enormous sacrifice," Tor continued, looking down at the invitation in order to hide his grin, "especially since you'll have to cool your heels here for another week. You mentioned pressing matters at home—"

"Ach, no!" Ruan had finally found his tongue. " 'Twas Jewel who insisted I return quickly! There's much to be done on the maltin' floor, you ken, and I promised I'd help."

"Did you? Here, now, don't look so woebegone. I'll go in your stead."

Tor might just as well have suggested that he'd eat dog liver for dinner. Ruan looked so astonished that his jaw literally dropped.

"No, no! Ye canna!"

"Why not?" Tor demanded, annoyed. "I can do your work as well as the next man, perhaps even better. You forget, I apprenticed under Sandy Sinclair when I was there."

"Aye . . . but . . . it isna—You and Jewel—"

"We're still married, for God's sake! It shouldn't be so difficult for us to tolerate each other for a week or two, should it? Especially when Jewel's precious malt is at stake?"

"Nooo . . ." Ruan agreed in a long, drawn-out, unconvincing way.

"Then what is it?" Tor demanded, rapping his fist on the table. "Are you getting all secretive on me again, Ruan? Better tell me now what the devil's going on!"

Ruan tried to oblige him, he truly did. For a moment Tor actually believed he'd blurt out whatever secret he was keeping, but in the end loyalty to Jewel—and a keen sense of self-preservation—kept him silent. Laughing a little nervously, he shrugged his shoulders dismissively. " 'Tis naught, really. Just my cousin up to her usual tricks."

"Hmm," said Tor. "That could mean anything. Illness, chaos, another disaster at the distillery, or an involved scheme to alleviate her boredom with some tasteless prank or another, most likely aimed at me."

"Tor—"

"No. 'Tis quite all right. Keep your silence. I'd rather find out for myself. That way you can't be accused of betraying her."

"But ye canna—"

"Enough! Do you want to attend that birthday ball or not?"

"Aye," Ruan said hastily. "Though ye maun tell me one thing, Tor."

"About Jewel? I'd rather not gi—"

"Nay, 'tisn't that. 'Tis only . . . umm . . . what do ye suppose I should wear?"

Tor threw back his head and gave vent to a roar of laughter. No doubt about it, the lad had it bad for Miss Heather Menzies!

"We'll speak to Jeannie Morrisey," he promised as Ruan, crestfallen, turned away. "She's fair gifted with the needle. And there's plenty in the way of fabric and the like up in the attic."

Ruan promptly forgot all about Jewel. Beaming, he lifted his teacup and toasted his host.

Tor's spirits had risen as well. He could hardly wait to return to Glen Chulish in Ruan's place and confront Jewel without her knowledge. Whatever secret she was keeping from him had to be a good one, judging from Ruan's jumpy behavior, and Tor relished the thought of making her squirm.

"Come on," he said, scraping back his chair and looking more boyish and carefree than he had for weeks. "Let's see what's up in the attic. I confess the suspense is killing me."

Chapter Twenty-three

The long summer twilight had drawn to an end. A faint glow lingered to the west, but the glen, and the manor house of Drumcorrie, were plunged into darkness. Windows and doors had been left open due to the warmth, and squares of light splashed across the grass. On the mountainside, the smoke from numerous cooking fires curled from the croft chimneys while sleepy sheep bleated in their pens.

It was a scene of peaceful domesticity, and one that unexpectedly touched the heart of the weary rider who had drawn rein at the edge of the clearing. Tor Ban Cameron had ridden hard all day in order to arrive at Drumcorrie before nightfall. Unfortunately, his horse had cast a shoe, and he had waited more than an hour at the nearest smithy until a new one could be fashioned.

He had made the long journey alone, ignoring the protests of everyone at Abercraig. Traveling light, and sleeping only a few hours each night, he had managed the distance in less than four days.

If asked, he would not have been able to explain what drove him so forcibly. All summer long, he had managed to put every thought of Jewel from his mind, and had even come to convince himself that she no longer mattered to him. He had thrown himself into the restoration of his castle and his lands with an energy that had left him exhausted at night— and too deliberately tired for any thought.

For a long time, Tor had actually come to believe that he was content. For more than twenty years he had dreamed of avenging his family and reclaiming the lands and the title that his uncle had taken. It was that dream alone that had sustained him throughout the bitter cold of his Turkish campaigns; the misery of endless months spent in tropical swamps; the years of searing heat endured in the African deserts. Nor had the war in the colonies or imprisonment at Cowcadden served to dim those dreams.

For a long while, Tor had honestly believed that he had finally attained those dreams. For a long while it had been enough to wake each morning in the bed in which he had been born, and meet with his crofters in the same study where Cameron lairds had dispensed wages and justice for centuries on end. The backbreaking labor of repairing the crofts and bringing the farms back into production had satisfied him as nothing else could have done.

But gradually, without Tor's even being aware of it, a sense of discontent had begun to creep into his life. He found himself growing increasingly restless, and irritated with the people around him. Somewhere along the way, Abercraig's endless problems had been subtly transformed from a challenge into an outright annoyance. Worse, he soon found himself growing lonely—lonely in a way he could not explain although he had never in his life been surrounded by more people.

The inevitable realization that Jewel was at the bottom of all this had enraged him. In desperation, he had thrown himself even harder into his work, and for a while had managed to keep all thoughts of her at bay. But he still hungered for news of her, and whenever Ruan arrived from Glen Chulish, it was all Tor could do to keep himself from asking about her.

One night, sleepless and pacing in his room despite his fatigue, Tor had realized that he could no longer deny the obvious. His hunger for Abercraig was as nothing compared to his hunger for Jewel. His dreams were meaningless without her. There was little point in working himself into an early grave without someone to work *for*.

And so he had set out for Drumcorrie—but only to keep his promise to Ruan of helping Jewel in the distillery. At least that was what he kept telling himself. Now, as he gazed down at the sleepy manor house with its welcoming squares of light, a host of memories rose unbidden to his heart, making a mockery of his intentions.

He remembered Jewel laughing at him when she caught sight of him in his nightshirt. He remembered her singing long-banned patriotic songs with Angus's son as they rode across the moor on that monster of a drafter, Drum. He remembered watching her tapping the newest barrel of Drumcorrie malt, her lovely face a study of concentration as she savored the aroma, the clarity, and, finally, the taste.

He rode quickly down to the stable. He supposed he would find her eating supper at this time of night. A fierce longing for the quiet of the firelit dining room filled him, reminding him of how hungry and tired he was.

Strange, but it felt like a homecoming, riding into the deserted stableyard. How could a modest little place like this, where he had spent but a few tumultuous months of his life, call to him more strongly than the magnificence of Abercraig, where the spirit of his ancestors lingered all around him?

Because Abercraig was too big and gloomy. There was little warmth in its soaring halls and empty salons, and Tor had developed a hearty dislike of being alone there.

Drumcorrie was different. It was a home with a heart, a place where a man could rest his weary bones after a long day in the fields, and find within its cozy rooms the renewal he so desperately needed.

Why hadn't he realized it before?

You're a fool, he told himself irritably. Surely it was only his weariness, and maybe his unfulfilled desire for Jewel's lovely body, that was making him feel this way.

But his spirits rose nonetheless at the warm welcome of the stablehand who came out to take his horse.

"We weren't expectin' ye, sir," the lad said happily.

"I know. That's why I came. Is your mistress in?"

"Aye, sir. She'll be havin' dinner now."

Tor's footsteps quickened as he stepped through the small service entrance just off the kitchen. No one was about. Candles sputtered softly in their sconces. Pausing in the butler's pantry, he washed away the dust from his journey.

A patter of feet sounded behind him. Annie's black terrier, Goat, appeared in the doorway. Man and dog eyed each other suspiciously. Tor risked the first olive branch.

"Hello, old fellow. I'm back."

The terrier hesitated, then, unbelievably, began to wag its tail.

"One down, one to go," Tor muttered with a grin. Quickening his pace, he went down the corridor. The dining-room door was open, and a murmur of voices came from within. Jewel was sitting at the head of the table, slicing a huge roast, and so did not see him right away. Tor leaned against the door to watch her, wondering how he could ever have fooled himself into believing that this woman didn't mean everything to him.

The summer had been kind to her. She had gained weight, and the long days in the fields had brightened the golden highlights of her glorious red hair. She was wearing a frock of blue homespun that matched the color of her eyes. A simple frock, with unadorned sleeves and a crisp white apron, but in it, Jewel could easily have rivaled the silk-clad beauties Tor remembered seeing in the court of the Turkish sultan. Crossing his arms before his chest, he looked his fill, his heart at rest.

Jewel had spent the day working on the western slope with old Angus MacKenzie. The harvest was the best that anyone at Drumcorrie could remember. Cart after cart of golden sheaves had rumbled off toward the barn, and Jewel had happily threshed and bundled alongside her crofters until the daylight was gone.

Returning home, she had soaked her aching body in a wonderfully hot bath, then hurried downstairs feeling ravenously hungry. There she found that Annie—bless her!—had prepared an enormous roast, and it was this succulent meat that she was in the process of cutting when she suddenly became aware of eyes upon her.

Looking up quickly, she found her gaze locking with Tor Cameron's. He was leaning against the doorjamb watching her, his arms crossed casually before his chest, apparently feeling perfectly at ease with the fact that he had strolled into her dining room unannounced. Jewel almost didn't recognize him, because he had changed considerably over the summer. He had filled out in her absence, and gained unsettling strength in his shoulders, chest, and arms. Windblown, deeply tanned, and dressed in the tailored vest and buckskin breeches of a true gentleman, he looked positively gorgeous to her.

Aye, there was no other way to describe him. Tor had always been darkly handsome, but now he was truly magnificent, a man in his prime: tall and strong, and exuding a heady lust for life that was almost sexual in its pull. Gone forever was the haunted look that had made him seem so wild eyed and driven. He looked arrogantly confident standing there in the doorway with a devastating smile curving his sensual lips. As well, he had never seemed so happy before. Or so content. Why, 'twas almost as if his every need and want had been fulfilled beyond his wildest expectations.

There was no doubt in Jewel's mind that Abercraig was responsible for the change in him. And the moment she realized as much, all the breathless joy that had begun bubbling inside her died. A wary look crept across her face.

"No," Tor said quickly, straightening and coming forward. "Jewel, please don't—"

"Well, well, who's this?"

The strange voice made Tor halt in his tracks. Until that moment he hadn't realized that he and Jewel were not alone. He didn't recognize the iron-haired gentleman seated across from her at the table, and instantly his mood soured. The last thing he wanted was a witness to the moment.

"I'm Tor Cameron," he said with a half-bow, struggling to remain polite. "I didn't realize you had a visitor, Jewel."

Meanwhile the man had risen, revealing that he was nearly as tall as Tor, although he was clearly getting on in years. "I'm John Chisolm," he responded affably. "And I'm not a visitor."

"Oh?" Tor glanced questioningly at Jewel. She was sitting there as if frozen, like a doe caught in a hunter's line of fire.

"Would you care to join us, Mr. Cameron?" John Chisolm asked politely.

Before Tor could reply, Annie Brewster bustled in with another chafing dish. A disbelieving oath burst from her when she saw him.

"What the de'il's *he* doin' here?"

"Charming as always, Mrs. Brewster," Tor said with a grin. " 'Tis pleasant to see you, too."

Annie was not amused. The look she sent Jewel shouted volumes of accusation.

"Look here," Tor began, annoyed, "I have every right—"

"I told ye!" Annie interrupted, ignoring him and glaring fiercely at Jewel's bowed head. "I told ye there'd be trouble! What will ye do now, eh? Will ye tell him? Should I?"

"Tell me what?" Tor demanded.

Annie rounded on him. "Ye'll no—"

"Annie, don't!"

The old woman glared. "Well, then?"

Jewel said nothing. She just sat there, white faced.

"Bah!"

Jewel's eyes lifted helplessly to Tor's. "Why did you come?"

Oh, God, what could he tell her? The truth? With Annie and that Chisolm fellow looking on?

"Jewel—"

"Lass—"

"Mrs. Chisolm—"

They had all spoken at once: Tor, Annie, and John. Now they all stopped. A charged silence filled the air.

Slowly, Tor turned to face Jewel. "What did he say?" His voice was filled with silky menace.

"He called me Mrs. Chisolm," Jewel answered wearily. "Sit down, Tor. I'll explain."

He sank into the nearest chair. "Aye, I think you'd better."

She drew a deep breath. " 'Tis simple enough, really," she said, although she still refused to look at him. "I'm married to him now."

Tor awoke with a pounding headache. Bleary eyed, he crept to the washbowl and splashed water on his face. The room reeked of whiskey. Disgusted, he drew back the drapes, then turned slowly to survey his surroundings.

Where the devil was he? He didn't recognize a thing. Not the oil paintings on the walls, not the heavy oaken bed in which he'd slept, not the faint trace of perfume that lingered in the whiskey-laden air.

Oh, lord, he hadn't spent the night in drunken debauchery, had he?

Relief filled him when he saw that the bed was empty. He'd half expected to find a painted woman lying there. As the fog in his brain began to clear, he remembered where he was. Chulish House. *That's right.* He'd ridden over the night before in a fit of murderous rage, awakened the servants so that they'd admit him, and then drunk himself to sleep in Millicent MacKenzie's former bedroom.

"Laudable behavior," he told himself aloud, then groaned and clutched his throbbing head. His stomach churned. He'd be better off getting some breakfast into it soon, especially if he wanted his mind clear before returning to Drumcorrie to confront Jewel.

His mouth thinned grimly at the thought. Aye, he'd confront her all right, and if he didn't strangle her before the day was done, she should consider herself lucky!

No one was about when he arrived later in the day. The weather had turned during the course of the morning, and now a heavy mist hung over the fields. The same groom hurried from the stable to take Tor's horse, but his welcome today was decidedly subdued. There was no doubt in Tor's mind that he had heard all about his stormy exit from the house the night before.

Aye, it had been unpleasant. Tor didn't really recall the details. All he could remember was Jewel's white face as she sat with her head bowed while he ranted and raged above her, cursing her, shouting at Annie, and threatening that iron-haired Chisolm fellow, who'd actually had the gall to try to reason with him.

Reason! There was no reasoning where Jewel MacKenzie Cameron—nay, Chisolm—was concerned! The woman was poison from the top of her lovely head to the tips of her dainty feet! Heartless, opportunistic witch! Dump him just like that and choose herself another man, would she? Well, Tor Ban Cameron was going to show her that he was not the sort who could be discarded at a whim!

No doubt the Drumcorrie chambermaids had seen him coming, because the front door already stood open and Tykie had been summoned from his room. There he stood beneath the portal waiting, looking so undecided that Tor had to laugh as he ascended the steps.

"Don't know whether to murder me or let me in, do you, old fellow?"

Tykie nodded woefully.

"I'm not sure, either. I suppose you really ought to chase me off, considering the things I said to your mistress last night. On the other hand, if I go, who'll talk her out of this insanity?"

Tykie responded with a heartfelt sigh.

"Because I warn you, Tykie, I intend to try," Tor went on. "I'll not have her married to some English lecher old enough to be her father! I'd much rather—"

"—see her married to the likes of you?"

Both men turned as Annie Brewster appeared in the hallway behind them. Though she was barely half Tykie's size, she was doing a far better job than the big mute of blocking the entrance so that Tor couldn't step inside. Her withered face was cold with fury.

"Think she was better off wi' ye? What did ye ever do for her except make her miserable? Shout at her, threaten her, see her kidnapped and nearly killed!"

"For God's sake, woman, I'm aware of that!"

"Then what do 'ee want?" Annie demanded.

Tor glared at her. He wanted Jewel back. But that was none of the old crone's business!

"I'll tell ye one thing, Lord Abercraig," Annie continued scathingly. "She's been fair settled these few months past, settled and calm and, aye, even happy! And Master John be kind to her, kinder than Tor Cameron ever was! Ye've na richt tae come here unannounced and destroy her peace o' mind! Na richt at a'!"

Slowly, Tor turned to Tykie. It was some time before he trusted himself to speak. "Is this true?"

Tykie stared down at the ground.

"Well?"

The big mute fumbled in his coat pocket and withdrew a handkerchief, which he began to work be-

tween his fingers. After a moment he gave a faint
shrug.

"Answer me, damn it! Is she better off with him?"

Tykie nodded.

A soft expletive burst from Tor. He took the steps
two at a time until he stood towering above Annie.
To give the woman credit, she neither flinched nor
moved aside.

"Where is she?"

"I' the library."

"Alone?"

"Aye."

"Then let me pass."

"Nay."

"For God's sake, woman, I only want to talk to her!
Will you make me heave you over my shoulder?"

Annie, looking as though she had swallowed a
prune, stepped reluctantly aside. The moment Tor
was gone, she took Tykie by the arm and gave him a
mighty push. "After 'im! And fetch yer pistols! If
there be any trouble like the night before, ye'll storm
the library and shoot him, do ye hear?"

Looking as though he'd rather eat live earth-
worms, Tykie turned and went.

Chapter Twenty-four

Ever since her return from Abercraig, Jewel had taken over the library as her own. She had had her father's desk moved out of the study and into an alcove between a tall window and several shelves of books. She had convinced herself that the library was more conducive to work than her father's austere study, but deep in her heart she knew that she preferred spending time here simply and solely because of Tor.

Memories of him lingered everywhere. She could never step inside the cozy, book-filled room without remembering how often he had withdrawn here to regain his sense of dignity and self-worth after both had been so badly battered in prison. She remembered how angry he always became whenever anyone failed to take proper care of the books and manuscripts, and how he had sent Ruan sprawling against that bookshelf there after one of their more heated confrontations. And who could forget how often she and Tor had faced off against each other here themselves, shouting, trading insults, and even coming to blows?

Maddening, arrogant, selfish Tor.

But life had never been dull with him.

Sighing, Jewel laid aside her pen. Rising and stretching, she went to the window and stared out across the misty landscape. Last night's confrontation between the two of them had been the most painful one ever. And it was all her fault. She should have listened to Ruan and notified Tor the moment she'd married John Chisolm. For once it seemed that Ruan had been right, because it had been unfair and unkind of her to let Tor find out this way.

I was too cowardly, Jewel thought, and now I'm paying the price.

Behind her, the door opened, then softly closed.

Scowling, she turned around, resenting the intrusion of a witness to her private pain. Her heart froze when she saw Tor standing before her, tousled, handsome, and obviously angry.

She had been a coward last night, cringing inwardly at the things he had said to her, saying nothing to defend herself nor even trying to explain. But she could make up for that now. She would give Tor the explanations he deserved, and be dignified and kind about the situation, too.

"You're wet," she said suddenly, noticing that he was. "Would you like dry clothes? How about tea?"

"Spare me the charming hostess act. I'm not in the mood."

Jewel's expression remained outwardly calm. She supposed she had deserved that. "I understand. Then would you—"

"Why did you marry him?"

Her chin tipped. "For the same reason I married you. I needed help in the distillery."

"Don't be ridiculous! When you married me, you were complying with the conditions in your father's will. You didn't have to do that this time, and both of us know it. Why didn't you turn to Ruan? He's become quite decent, actually, since his mother's left the country."

Jewel said frostily, "You know as well as I do that no one can work side by side with Ruan for long."

"Perhaps so. But you could have hired any number of workers to take my place. You didn't have to find a new husband."

She said nothing.

"Why did you do it, Jewel?"

She shrugged.

"Why, damn it?"

"I didn't want to be married to you anymore," she mumbled, not looking at him.

"What's that?"

"I said I didn't want to be married to you any-more!" Jewel shouted, glaring.

"Ah. I thought that's what you said." Tor sauntered over to the window where she stood, and looked down at her pityingly. "Too proud to stay married to a man who rejected you, eh?"

She bit her lip to hide her hurt. In the past, Tor had told her often how much he despised her pity. Now she knew why.

His gaze bored into her. "Where is he now, your Englishman?"

"I don't know. In the study, perhaps."

"And has he shown himself to be suitable? Compliant, hardworking, polite? All the things I never was?"

Her eyes flashed. "Aye."

"And does he please you better in bed?" he taunted.

Her eyes slid from his so that he wouldn't see them

fill with tears. "I—He—We don't—that's why I chose him. He's too old."

"Ah. I see." Tor turned away from her and thrust his hands into his pockets. "This time you opted for the fatherly sort. Clever lass."

"Tor, please—"

"Where did you find him? Not Cowcadden. No Englishmen there, as I recall."

"Carlisle," she answered sullenly.

"You went all the way to Carlisle?" he demanded, rounding on her in surprise. "I can't believe you managed to keep all of this a secret! What was his crime?"

"He committed no crime. I found him in debtor's prison."

Tor was secretly relieved. He had stayed up half the night imagining Jewel married to some depraved criminal who would sneak into her room and rape and strangle her. He'd considered more than once riding over to rescue her, but he'd been much too drunk to sit in the saddle. Besides, she didn't need rescuing, especially by the likes of him! Annie was right. She did look well rested, well fed, and happy. Or at least as happy as she could while being confronted by her furiously angry husband.

Former husband.

His eyes went to her left hand. He saw that the ring he had put on her finger in the gaoler's room at Cowcadden was gone. In its place was a simple band of gold adorned with a single pearl. A lovely little ring that Jewel had no doubt received as a young girl and which had probably lain in the bottom of her jewelry box until she'd taken it with her to Carlisle.

He turned away with an oath.

"I'm sorry, Tor," Jewel whispered haltingly. "I should have written sooner. Ruan said it was wrong of me not to let you know."

"Ruan's been wearing himself out trying to keep

your secret. You owe him a lot."

"He—he has? You mean he never told you?"

"No."

"Then how—how did you find out?"

"I didn't know until I met your bridegroom personally last night," Tor answered grimly.

"That's what you said, but I didn't believe you."

"Well, I hope you believe me now."

"Aye." She looked down at her hands. "If—if you didn't know about John until you got here, then why did you come?"

There it was, the simple question that touched upon a wellspring of explosive emotions. What on earth was he supposed to tell her? Certainly not the truth! Everything had changed. He'd been cast aside in favor of a penniless Englishman, and he'd be damned if he let Jewel suspect that he was anything more than heartily relieved about it!

But Jewel was standing there waiting for an answer. He had to tell her something. But what? It was bloody hard to think clearly with her looking up at him with those damnable blue eyes of hers, their expression so solemn and sad that Tor wanted to close his own just to get away from them.

He said the first thing that came to mind. " 'Tis ironic, in truth. I was coming to annul the marriage myself. Abercraig needs an heir, you see, and I've found a woman perfectly suited to take your place."

Jewel moved behind the desk and steadied herself against the back of her chair. "Oh?" she said casually. "Anyone I know?"

"Doubtful. An old childhood acquaintance of mine, a Cameron herself. Our families will make an admirable union."

"A political match, then."

Tor regarded her keenly. "Should it be anything else?"

Jewel gave a mocking laugh. "I had thought . . . sometimes people get married for love."

"Do they?" He laughed, too, as though the thought were absurd. "That was certainly never the case with us, was it?"

She made no reply. Only her hands tightened around the back of her chair.

"Was it, Jewel?"

"No."

"Good. I wouldn't want to marry someone else while worrying that you still have feelings for me."

"You arrogant bastard!" Jewel exploded. "I never had feelings for you, never!"

"Is that so? Then why did you ride after me when I left for Edinburgh the day you were abducted? Tykie told me you did."

"I was worried about Laddie. He wasn't used to being ridden so hard."

"Hah!"

"And why did *you* turn around and come back?"

"I—I forgot my hat."

"Hah!"

"What's more, I had Abercraig to think of. I needed money, and able-bodied men like Tykie to help me win it back."

"Well, I had Drumcorrie to think of, for much the same reason."

They glared at each other.

Jewel had never fought so hard to keep the tears at bay. Her throat hurt with the effort, and her love for Tor filled her heart to bursting. Her very bones ached with want of him and with the hurt of his leaving.

Because leaving he was. Even as she stood there, frozen, he gave her that rare, devastating smile of his, nodded his head, and started for the door.

"Tor!"

He turned questioningly.

"You—you aren't really planning to get married, are you?"

He regarded her suspiciously. "Why? Did you lie to me about our annulment?"

When she didn't answer, he forged ahead.

"Why shouldn't I marry?"

"Because you—because I—"

"Jewel. In all the months of our marriage I've never known you to stumble over words. Get on with it."

Damn him to hell and back! She would not grovel!

"Please go," she said wearily. "And don't come back."

His mouth twisted. "Don't worry. I won't."

The door closed hard behind him. Jewel's head fell against the wood and the tears she was holding inside erupted in a wrenching sob. She heard Tor's footsteps halt outside as though he'd heard. Quickly she mastered the tears. A long silence fell. Then she heard him turn and walk away, down the hall, through the front door, and out of her life.

Ruan had prepared himself for Tor's ill-tempered return to Abercraig, and Tor did not disappoint him. The long summer twilight was still lingering over the glen when Mordart Bennish brought news that his lordship was back.

"With my cousin's blood on his hands?" Ruan inquired anxiously.

The old steward growled in disgust. "Nay. Though the look be i' his eyes."

"I imagine he spent the whole journey here wonderin' why he didn't kill her," Ruan agreed, secretly relieved. "Is he joinin' me for supper?"

"So he said."

"Good. Make sure there's plenty o' brandy."

Mordart growled again as he shuffled from the

room. He had already planned on it.

Ruan leaned back in the chair where he had been reading by the fire and, sighing happily, propped his arms behind his head. So, neither one had killed the other, eh? Good. He couldn't wait to find out what had transpired between them at Drumcorrie, but knew better than to ask right away. Besides, he already had a pretty fair idea. An unpleasant scene at best, with tears and hurtful words and bitter recriminations. At worst, a goodly deal of violence, with vicious blows from each of them. Since he'd not put either scenario past Jewel, it wasn't surprising that Tor had returned home in the blackest of moods.

On the other hand, supposing that Tor was furious with *him* for keeping Jewel's marriage a secret? If so, Ruan had better forget about asking nosy questions and watch out for his own hide. His newfound friendship with Tor hadn't completely erased the memories of all the times the two of them had come to blows.

Fortunately Ruan needn't have worried about his personal safety. Tor didn't look the least bit angry when he appeared in the west parlor an hour later, freshly bathed and shaven and wearing clean clothes. But he didn't look particularly happy, either. In fact, he looked more tired and dispirited than Ruan had ever seen him. Was this a good sign or a bad one?

Going in to supper, Ruan waited until the first course had been served and Tor had managed to appease some of his hunger before finding out.

"So. All was well at Drumcorrie?"

Tor shot him a black glance. "You know bloody well it wasn't."

"Aye. And I—"

"Save your words. 'Tis done. We'll speak no more of your cousin in this house."

"Good enough."

Ruan watched as Tor poured himself another brandy. "But I was wondering—"

Tor lowered his glass, glaring.

"Sorry. 'Tis just, well, this Chisolm fellow. How did he strike ye?"

"I hardly said two words to the man."

"Then he's still alive? Phew! I thought—"

"I'd killed him?" A glimmer of black humor showed in Tor's eyes. "My quarrel isn't with him. 'Tis that mulish cousin of yours I'd rather string from the nearest tree."

"Ah."

"And that's all I have to say."

"Very well." Nodding in agreement, Ruan leaned back in his chair. Tor's behavior was a good sign.

Encouraged, Ruan helped himself to another slice of beef. After a moment he went on, "I think he's a good man at heart, though clearly no match for Jewel."

"Who?"

"Chisolm, of course."

Tor laid down his fork.

"I'll let ye in on a secret," Ruan added, ignoring this obvious warning. "He's soft on Annie Brewster."

"W-what?"

"Aye." Ruan grinned. "Soft i' the head, more like. Now, which'd be worse, I wonder? Marriage tae Jewel or tae Annie? The choice makes me shudder."

"Ruan. What on earth are you talking about?"

"Are ye deaf? I said, John Chisolm has a yearnin' for our own Annie Brewster."

"Good God. Did he tell you as much?"

Ruan tapped the side of his head. "He didna, but I ain't dumb, ye ken. I've eyes in me head."

"But he's married to Jewel!"

"Aye, and grateful that she got him out o' gaol, no

doubt. But Tor, she's young enou' tae be his daughter! He's got a fatherly fondness for her, na more. And they get on well enou', as father an' daughter should. Annie, on the other hand, be—"

"Do you mean that?"

"What?"

"About Chisolm and Jewel."

Ruan hid a triumphant smile. "Aye. No cause for worry there, old man. He told me so himself, na long after he came tae Drumcorrie. Quiet, kindly fellow—for a Sassenach. Lost his fam'ly tae the fever somewhere in Northumberland years back. Made his way north lookin' for work, but didna find better than a prison cell, poor sod. 'Twas kind o' Jewel tae give him anither chance."

Tor made no response.

Unconcerned, Ruan rambled on. "As for Annie, she'll hae no truck wi' the fellow. Doesna surprise me, considerin' she's never liked anither human being save Jewel. Still, I'm thinkin' mayhap she ain't indifferent. Meaner than ever, she be. Jewel says 'tis like livin' wi' a volcano. Tykie's fair ready tae tear oot his hair, an' the rest be walkin' on eggs."

"That doesn't sound like being in love," Tor said dryly.

"No? Reminds me a bit o' yersel', it do. Grumblin' an' growlin' like a maddened bear if only tae cover up the truth o' yer feelings."

Tor sat back in his chair. "Is that so?"

"Aye, 'tis so! Will ye no come out wi' the truth, Tor? 'Tis i' love with our Jewel ye be, and have been from the first!"

Tor's expression darkened. "You MacKenzies are a brash-mouthed lot. And you've become too bloody cheeky for your own good, young fellow."

"Will ye thrash me again?" Ruan demanded, hiding his sudden concern behind a show of bravado.

"By God, I ought to."

" 'Twill only prove my point."

"What? That I'm in love with your cousin?"

"Aye."

"Bah!"

"Then prove to me ye ain't."

Tor propped his elbows on the table and wearily massaged his temples. "MacKenzies," he muttered beneath his breath. "It doesn't matter anyway," he added, looking blackly at Ruan. "Jewel doesn't care a pig's ass for me."

Ruan made a rude sound.

"Is that supposed to signify disagreement? Well, then, would you mind explaining why she ended our marriage?"

"Why, 'tis obvious. Because she loves ye back."

Now it was Tor's turn to make a rude sound.

" 'Tis the truth, by God! If she didna care for 'ee, ye'd no have been able tae hurt her by choosing Abercraig o'er Drumcorrie. She would hae been cheerin' aloud tae be rid o' ye."

He had a point there. Nonetheless, Tor said blackly, "That still doesn't explain why she got rid of my wedding ring and found herself another man."

"Tae show us a' how little ye do mean. First husband didna fit the bill? Then throw him out an' take another."

"Ah, but this time she didn't have to take another. Drumcorrie's safe, and she knows that bloody well. She could have hired anyone to work the distillery and not had to marry him to boot. Why, then, such haste to marry again?"

"I already told ye! Tae show the world she doesna care for ye. And tae convince hersel' as well."

"Bah," repeated Tor.

"Lord, ye're stubborn," Ruan grumbled. "Ye an' Jewel both! I give up. Wash my hands o' ye."

"Where are you going?" Tor demanded as Ruan folded his napkin and came to his feet.

"Home."

"To Chulish House?"

"Aye."

"Ruan."

The younger man turned in the doorway. "Aye?"

"Stay."

Ruan looked suspicious. "What for?"

Tor propped his head in his hands. He looked utterly defeated. "What else? To help me get her back, of course."

Ruan's grin could have lit the gloomy night. "Hallelujah," he said, returning to his seat. "I thought ye'd never ask."

"Do you know what?" Tor demanded, glaring.

"No. What?"

"I liked you a damned sight better when I hated you."

"I strike most people that way," Ruan agreed happily. "Now, then. I've gi'en the matter plenty o' thought, and here's whot we'll do. . . ."

Chapter Twenty-five

Old Mordart Bennish, resplendent in a kilt and a Cameron plaid smelling strongly of camphor, personally opened the front door. His demeanor oozed hauteur, which was not surprising considering that he had been given the unprecedented honor of officially receiving the Earl of Abercraig's guests. It had been years since Abercraig Castle had held such a grand ball.

Realizing who stood before him on the doorstep, he broke into a rare smile. "Welcome, welcome! We didna think 'ee'd come."

"I thought the same myself, Mr. Bennish. Thank you."

Shivering with the cold, Jewel stepped past him into the hall. Here the bleak winter daylight was dispersed by the warmth of candles and a crackling fire.

"Did 'ee have a pleasant journey?"

Nightmarish, Jewel longed to say. Filled with doubts and heartache and the constant urge to turn around and flee. "Lovely, thanks."

"Yer rooms be ready, ma'am, and a fire lit. Mairi will show ye upstairs." Mordart peered over her shoulder toward the door. "Ye came alone?"

"Mr. Ferguson accompanied me. He's in the stable seeing to the horses."

Mordart nodded, hiding his relief. She'd come alone, then. No husband in tow.

"Is my cousin here?" Jewel added casually, drawing off her gloves.

"Aye. His lordship will begin receivin' guests at six."

"I'd better go upstairs, then. We'd hoped to be here yesterday, but the roads were awful."

"Aye, ma'am. Winter be no time for travelin'."

Unless you'd been invited to the Christmas festivities at Abercraig, the first to be held in almost thirty years. Mordart gleefully suspected that a lot of folks would brave the cold and the mud to attend. "I'll see to Mr. Ferguson an' yer luggage," he added, then turned to the waiting maid. "Mairi, take Lady Aber— eh . . . Mrs. Chisolm tae the red room."

"Aye, sir."

And I, Mordart thought, watching the cloaked figure of young Lady Abercraig cross to the stairs, will tell his lordship she's come.

Jewel had never been inside the red room before. She had no idea that it lay in the western wing of the castle, where only members of the Cameron family traditionally stayed. True to Mordart's words, a fire had been laid, and Jewel warmed her hands before the blaze while Mairi went about closing the wine-colored drapes and smoothing the counterpane on the enormous bed.

"Will 'ee be wantin' a bath before dinner, ma'am?"

"Oh, yes, please."

"I'll see to it, then."

"Thank you."

The maid scurried off with a final, curious glance at Jewel. Jewel had no doubt that the girl had heard quite a bit of gossip concerning Lord Abercraig's absentee wife.

They've probably been laying bets below stairs, Jewel thought wryly, wondering if I'd come or not.

Until the last minute, she hadn't been sure if she would herself. The invitation to spend Christmas at Abercraig and partake of a formal ball as well as something mysteriously labeled the Kirkwall Ba' Game had arrived more than two months ago. Jewel's initial reaction had been to ignore it. Flush from the most bountiful harvest Drumcorrie had ever seen, she had been far too busy at the distillery to consider going anywhere. But as the long, golden autumn gave way to the mists of November, she had found time beginning to weigh heavily on her hands.

Ruan had left for Abercraig long before the holidays began, but not before urging Jewel to come after him. John, too, had said he thought the idea splendid, adding that Jewel would benefit enormously from a change of scene. He hadn't mentioned going himself, even though the invitation had been addressed to both of them. Tykie and Annie had added their own reasons as to why Jewel should attend, and Jewel, who secretly longed to go more than anything in the world, had finally allowed herself to be swayed.

But that had been long before her coach had put miles and miles between herself and the safety of Drumcorrie, and before her reunion with Tor loomed unavoidably on the horizon. Nearly four months had passed since that awful day when he'd come to Drumcorrie to tell her he planned to get married, and Jewel had heard nothing from him since then. Day after day from that moment on, she had dreaded the arrival of the official engagement announcement, but the fact that it never came had only served to increase her torment.

For once, Ruan had ignored Jewel's insistent demands for information. As well, he had spent far too much time that autumn away at Abercraig. Miserable traitor! No doubt Tor had sworn him to secrecy concerning his forthcoming marriage, and Ruan, spineless toady that he was, had blithely obeyed him. Why, the fellow no longer deserved to be called a MacKenzie!

The arrival of her luggage put an end to Jewel's agonized remembering. Mairi and another girl accompanied the footmen inside and began unpacking her things with surprising speed and efficiency. Jewel knew that Tor had dismissed Malcolm Cameron's servants and hired his own, but the realization that he had done it so efficiently filled her with an illogical anger. It made her furious to see how smoothly he kept his household running. How stupid of her to think that Tor could be a failure at anything!

While soaking away her weariness in the bath, she tried valiantly to keep her thoughts from Tor. But how could she? She hadn't been able to stop thinking about him even far away at Drumcorrie, and here, in his own home, it proved impossible. She had expected to relive a lot of unpleasant memories concerning her abduction by Malcolm Cameron, but it turned out to be Tor alone who filled her every thought. Just knowing he was somewhere nearby made Jewel's heart beat faster. Anticipation quivered through her every nerve, making her furious.

Damn his long-legged hide! She'd missed him more than she would have thought possible!

I hate you, Tor Cameron, she thought, stepping

hastily from the tub. And I'm going to show you to-night that I'm getting along just fine without you!

By the time Mairi returned, Jewel was sitting by the fire drying her hair. As her ball gown, shoes, and jewelry were being laid out, arriving carriages could be heard rumbling into the courtyard below.

"Lord Abercraig must be planning quite a party," Jewel observed dryly.

"Aye, ma'am."

"And Mr. Bennish in a plaid and kilt! Tsk, tsk. Does he know he's breaking the law, or simply not care?"

"Mr. Bennish be more excited than a' of us, ma'am," Mairi said with a laugh. " 'Tis the first time since the old laird's death that we've had Christmas at Abercraig, ye ken."

"The old laird?"

"Aye. Lord Tor's father. There be many what remember him fondly."

Jewel looked away, feeling ashamed of a sudden. How could she possibly begrudge Tor a holiday like this? Memories of boyhood Christmas celebrations had probably sustained him during the long, grievous years that had followed his family's deaths. She had no right to set foot in his home as an invited guest and behave in a manner that would ruin this important night for him!

As a matter of fact, she had better stop nursing her resentment and anger now, before it was too late. Tor had made it clear months ago that it was Abercraig he wanted, not her. If she truly loved him, she would respect that choice and graciously let him go.

I won't be like my father, or Aunt Millicent, cling-ing to something I've already lost, or perhaps never really had, Jewel thought suddenly. I may have let Tor out of that prison cell at Cowcadden, but until now I've never really set him free.

"Is anything wrong, ma'am?"

"No, nothing," she said quickly. "I'm a bit nervous, that's all."

Indeed, it was not easy for Jewel to descend the grand staircase when the time came, no matter how firm her resolve. Not only would she be facing Tor for the first time in months, but also subjecting herself to the curious stares of his guests, who would no doubt have heard all sorts of wild tales surrounding the couple's brief and stormy marriage.

But for Tor's sake she held her head high and adopted a smile that was beguiling in its charm. Jewel had matured quite a bit over the summer, although she remained unaware of it. Oh, there was still a great deal of the mischievous imp about her, and she would never lose that playful side no matter how old she became. But there was a lovely, womanly allure radiating from her as she descended the stairs that night that drew admiring eyes no matter how unobtrusive she tried to be.

She had not meant to cause a stir. Her gown of gray watered silk was modest in cut, but the contrast of her willowy figure and the rich glow of her red hair in a gown of such simple, classic style was striking. Heads turned and voices stilled as she was announced in the doorway of Abercraig's long-unused grand ballroom. In the minstrel's gallery, the fiddlers kept on playing, and those guests who hadn't seen her yet continued laughing and chattering together. But those closest to the door, the men in particular, turned to look again and yet again at Tor Cameron's former wife.

The facts surrounding the earl's brief marriage were unknown to most of them, and they would not have mattered much had they been revealed. Everyone in the area had a strong sympathy for the Camerons of Abercraig, who had endured more than their fair share of tragedy. No one had thought ill of the current earl when it was recently learned that he had once been married. Indeed, the scandal had actually served to enhance his rather mysterious reputation.

But everyone wondered now why the earl had dreamed of ending his marriage to such a stunning beauty.

"Lady Abercraig."

A tall man with curling whiskers was bowing over Jewel's hand. Jewel opened her mouth to correct him, then closed it again. If Tor had neglected to mention to his friends that she had remarried, then she wouldn't be the one to provide them with fodder for gossip.

"I'm an old friend of Tor's. Known him since he was a bairn." The man said his name, but Jewel scarcely heard. She was looking for Tor.

The ballroom was crowded. Guests in bright attire conversed in small groups on the dance floor or were gathered in the alcoves laughing and flirting. An enormous Yule log burned in the hearth, and ropes of evergreen were twined around every column and window and along the fireplace and walls. Cinnamon pots simmered and candles burned brightly.

"Jewel!"

She whirled, breathless with expectancy, but it was only Ruan. Still, she was so relieved to see a familiar face among the crowd that she cast aside all thought of decorum and embraced him fiercely.

"Hey, watch the waistcoat," Ruan warned with a grin.

"Oh, Ruan!"

He looked at her closely. "What's this? Tears? Since when have ye become so weepy, Coz?"

Without waiting for an answer, he tucked her hand beneath his arm and made their excuses to the bewhiskered gentleman. Quickly he led her to the far end of the room, where servants in green velvet livery stood waiting to serve refreshments.

"Here. A stiff dram's what ye need." He handed her the glass, then stood grinning as she tossed down the contents in a single swallow and immediately requested another. By the time this, too, had been consumed, Ruan was satisfied to see that the threat of tears had passed.

"Do ye ken," he began conversationally, "I was half worried ye'd refuse to come. Not yer cup o' tea, I realize, but on the other hand, a Christmas ball isna just another—"

But Jewel wasn't interested in small talk. "Where's Tor?"

Ruan shrugged. "Not come in as yet. There's an office full o' menfolk wantin' tae see him on some matter or anither."

Jewel exhaled a breath of relief. More than anything, she had wanted to confront Tor for the first time far away from the crowded ballroom. "Ruan, how do I look?"

He surveyed her critically, although she should have known that she was heart-stoppingly beautiful. "Hmm. I suppose ye'll do."

"Thank you. Where's the office?"

"I' the library. Tor didna wish tae use his uncle's study."

Jewel shuddered. "I can understand that." As for the library, she should have known he'd choose to spend his time among books. "I'm going to find him. I'll see you shortly."

"Jewel, wait."

She turned unwillingly.

"There's summat ye should know."

"What?"

"It's about Tor."

She eyed him warily.

"The reason he's holding this ball."

"Ruan, 'tis Christmas. Why else would he . . ." She stopped, scowling at him. "What is it? You've got that look on your face. What's Tor up to? What's he plotting?"

"Now, Jewel, I only wanted to warn ye so ye'd no be so shocked when the announcement's made."

"The announcement? What—" She broke off as the blood drained away from her heart. She knew. She *knew.* Tor had made as much clear the last time she'd seen him and now Ruan had that ghastly look on his face!

"Jewel, believe me when I tell ye I've no—"

But she swept away, her jaw set with determination.

It doesn't matter! I don't care! Nothing's changed. Nothing!

But she was already wondering how to manage a private moment with Tor in view of his pending engagement. What should she say to him once they were face-to-face? What *could* she say? Congratulations and the best of luck? Her heart was pounding so that she could scarcely think.

"Lady Abercraig?"

Jewel hurried on without stopping.

"Lady Abercraig! Please wait!"

Jewel whirled, almost weeping with frustration.

It was a slim, pretty girl in a tarlatan ball dress who came running toward her from the direction of the ballroom. Her hair was a soft ash blond and her eyes were wide and as dark as pansies.

She halted breathlessly in front of Jewel. "May I speak to you a moment, Lady Abercraig?"

"Yes, of course." Jewel motioned her into an alcove. "What is it?"

The girl smiled shyly. "I've been wanting so to meet

you. I hope you don't think me forward by not waiting to be introduced?"

"Not at all."

Jewel waited, but the girl said nothing more. She just stood there biting her lip and blushing.

"What did you wish to say to me?" Jewel prodded at last.

The girl looked surprised. "Why, surely you should know? I-I thought . . . That is, I-I'm Heather Menzies."

Was the name supposed to mean something? Jewel searched her memory.

"I hope you don't mind my being so forward, but I just had to speak to you," the girl rushed on, noticing Jewel's confusion. "I know the engagement isn't official as yet, but I'm so very happy that I want everyone to be happy. Especially you!"

"Me?" Jewel asked blankly.

Heather nodded eagerly. "Tor—Lord Abercraig—told me about your father's will. He explained about the marriage, and about Drumcorrie, and so I wanted to make absolutely certain there aren't any hard feelings."

Her father's will? Drumcorrie?

"I refused to get married thinking for one moment that I was coming into the middle of something," Miss Menzies went on. "I couldn't help worrying even though I know his feelings for me are genuine. 'Tis silly, I know, but now that I've been told about the two of you and, well, especially now that I've seen you . . . You're so very beautiful, so naturally I thought—"

She broke off, twisting her hands together, and looked at Jewel with anxious eyes.

"You refuse to get married unless . . ." Jewel echoed in a whisper. "Then you're . . ."

Color flamed high in Heather Menzies's cheeks.

" 'Tis premature, I know, but only by a little, really, as Tor—I mean Lord Abercraig—plans to make the announcement . . ."

Her words trailed off. She put a hand to her cheek. "I—I'm sorry. Maybe I shouldn't have said anything."

"No," Jewel said quickly. " 'Tis quite all right, Miss . . . Miss Menzies, is it?"

A relieved smile brightened the girl's face. "Aye. But please, Heather. I've been so hoping we'd be friends."

"Of—of course."

"Then you don't mind? About our getting married, I mean?"

"No," said Jewel. "Why should I?"

Heather took Jewel's cold hands in hers and squeezed them joyously. "Thank you!"

And she danced away, so obviously in love that it hurt Jewel's heart just to watch her.

Chapter Twenty-six

The library was crowded. A murmur of masculine voices came from the alcove where Tor's desk stood. He was surrounded by a group of laughing and animated men when Jewel entered, and she caught no more than a glimpse of his startled face before he rose and came toward her.

He was dressed far more grandly than Jewel had ever seen him, in satin breeches and a cutaway coat of burgundy silk. Unlike his guests, he wore no wig, but he had tied his black hair into a queue that emphasized the rugged features of his handsome face. Gone forever was the filthy, unshaven prisoner Jewel had married at Cowcadden. His blue eyes burned as he approached.

"Mordart told me you'd come. I didn't think until the last moment that you really would. My God." His voice dropped to a husky whisper. "I scarcely recognize you. I never thought—Jewel, what is it? Are you unwell? They told me you seemed fatigued when you arrived, but not—"

"I'm fine."

Turning his head, Tor issued a curt dismissal. The door closed on the retreating men, and suddenly the two of them were alone.

I should have stayed home, Jewel thought wildly. I should never have come.

"Jewel, what is it?"

She tried to pull free of his grasp, for he had taken her hands in his as he spoke, but Tor wouldn't let her. She had never seen that expression on his face before, so tender and filled with concern. Any moment now she was going to humiliate herself by bursting into tears.

"I can't possibly stay," she told him shakily.

His sensual lips curved. "Stubborn as ever. Of course you can."

"I won't."

"Aye, you will."

"Give me one good reason."

"All right. I'll owe Ruan fifty guineas if you don't last the night."

The thought that they had been laying bets on her made her furious. Twisting free of his grasp, she glared at him, her eyes flashing. "You've got some bloody nerve, Tor Cameron!"

"So you've told me often enough."

"Be serious for once, will you?"

"I am." His eyes were very intense as he leaned toward her. "More serious than you realize."

His nearness was making it hard for her to breathe. A pulse began pounding in her throat. She retreated a step only to find her path blocked by the desk.

Tor had followed her. Now he stopped. Tipping her chin, Jewel stood her ground. "Why did you ask me here?"

"Why did you come?"

"Annie thought it might be a good idea."

"So did Ruan. That's why I wrote."

"Ruan! Do you do everything he says nowadays?"

"Not at all. Sometimes he obeys me. It depends on who wins the coin toss."

"I'm going home," Jewel snapped, attempting to brush past him.

"What for?" Tor mocked. "Do you miss him so much?"

"Who?"

"Chisolm. Your husband."

"As a matter of fact, I do."

"Liar."

Her eyes widened. "How dare you tell me—"

But Tor wouldn't let her speak. Leaning down, he laid a finger against her lips. "Hush. We'll not talk about him tonight. Tomorrow maybe, but not tonight. Right now there's so much we—"

A knock sounded on the door. In response, a look of utter defeat crept across his face. "Aye, what is it?" he called out wearily.

"Excuse me, sir." Mordart Bennish was peering hesitantly around the door. "They be callin' for 'ee. They want 'ee tae open the dancin'."

Tor was silent for a moment. Then he chuckled. All at once he seemed unbelievably free of cares. "I wouldn't dream of disappointing them." He turned and smiled into Jewel's startled eyes. "Are you coming?"

She was too confused to say a word. At any rate, he didn't give her the chance. He just tucked her arm beneath his and led her back into the ballroom.

They were surrounded the moment they stepped inside. Jewel tried to slip away, but Tor refused to relinquish his hold on her arm. In fact, he held her so tightly that Jewel couldn't wriggle free without causing a scene. For a moment she considered doing exactly that, but then she remembered the promise she had made to herself not to do anything to shame or embarrass Tor tonight.

So she stood there and simply accepted her fate. She smiled dutifully, traded friendly words with the guests who came to meet her, and behaved as though it were the most natural thing in the world to stand at Tor's side and help him receive his guests while he was engaged to someone else.

It was exhausting. She longed for a quiet moment in which to slip away, but Tor still refused to let her go. Being the evening's host, he was obliged to speak to everyone, and engage in all of the necessary small talk that was expected of him. But he did so with a charm and a grace that could not fail to impress, and it soon dawned on Jewel that he had been born to the role.

He left her at last, to open the dancing. As tradition demanded, the laird of Abercraig took the first dance for himself with the lady of his choice, and Tor did so with Heather Menzies. He said nothing about it to Jewel, only left her side to lead Heather onto the floor while the music began and Jewel looked on, frozen inside.

She could not fail to notice the approval on the faces of the watching crowd as the pair swept past. Heather Menzies was a tall girl, and she and Tor made a striking couple. When the dance ended, Tor led her from the floor with his arm about her waist and an indulgent smile upon his lips.

I should be glad for him, Jewel thought numbly. He seems so happy. Far happier than I ever made him.

She had never made him anything but miserable. And by turns humiliated, cold, and furiously angry.

Why had he asked her to come here tonight? To show her how little she mattered to him? To remind her of how much she had given up by returning to Drumcorrie?

"Jewel! You're not leaving, are you?"

Ruan caught up with her in the doorway. He had to raise his voice above the din of the music and laughter.

"I'm tired," she replied. "I want to go to bed."

"So early? We've only just started!"

"I don't care."

Ruan regarded her searchingly. Jewel bit her lip and willed the tears away.

"Tor would be sorry."

"He wouldn't even notice! Look at him!"

They both watched as Tor led Heather over to a smiling couple who could only be her parents. His strong, sun-browned hand still rested intimately in the small of Heather's back, and she was smiling up at him sweetly as he said something that was obviously meant for her ears alone.

"She's lovely, isn't she?" Ruan asked, watching them.

"Aye."

"Tor's been smitten for months."

"I have to go, Ruan."

"No, ye don't."

"Try and stop me."

"I will."

And he did.

A moment later Jewel found herself whisked onto the dance floor, where a new set was forming for a rousing country reel. She tried to kick Ruan in the shins, but he knew her too well, and managed to twist out of reach before she could. His laughter made her furious.

"Ruan, let me go!"

"Och, come, lass! Relax for once i' yer life, will ye? When's the last time ye heard the scrape o' the fiddles? When's the last time we danced together, eh?"

"I said, let me go!"

"Whist! They'll hear ye!"

By now other couples were flocking onto the floor, laughing and calling impatiently for the dance to begin.

Ruan turned emphatically to Jewel. "Life's too short, lass! Come, now. Show me what ye remember!"

Tykie had taught Jewel to dance when she was just a little girl, and she had forgotten how much she loved the traditional reels of the Highlands. Despite her misery, she couldn't help feeling her heart stir to life as the familiar music rang down from the gallery. Her eyes lost their angry fire and she stopped trying to break Ruan's legs.

Grinning down at her in his irresistible way, Ruan swept her through the rousing steps, whooping as he went.

Naturally they created quite a stir. As her inhibitions fell away, Jewel hitched up her trailing petticoats and followed Ruan's lead, her trim little ankles scandalously exposed. Her eyes still sparkled with the remnants of her tears, but to everyone watching, they seemed to glow with all the vibrant joy and beauty of youth.

"What a lovely child, Tor," Heather Menzies's mother said, watching them.

"Aye," Tor agreed softly.

"And such a gifted dancer."

"She seems to get on well with her cousin," remarked another guest, overhearing them.

"Too well," murmured Mrs. Menzies.

Tor had to agree. Ruan and Jewel looked much too happy out there, and they made a far prettier couple than he cared to acknowledge. When the music ended he waded toward them, catching Jewel's elbow as she stood there with Ruan, breathless, glowing, momentarily freed of the urge to weep.

"I had no idea you could dance so well, ma'am."

"You never asked," Jewel countered, turning toward him, her smile fading.

Tor's gaze scorched her. "Would you dance with me if I asked?"

"Would you dare ask?"

They challenged each other with their eyes. Ruan, an unwilling witness to plenty of such scenes in the past, wisely withdrew.

"Well?" Tor persisted.

"Well, what?"

"Will you give me this dance, Jewel MacKenzie Cameron?"

"Chisolm."

He looked as though he wanted to kill her right then and there, but at that moment the fiddlers in the gallery sounded the blood-stirring notes of one of the Highland's most beloved dances. As a special treat, the strings were joined by old Mordart Bennish, who had been tippling long enough at the whiskey barrel to work up sufficient courage to dust off his ancient bagpipes. Now, wheezing, wailing, the sound of the pipes, unheard for decades in the great hall of Abercraig, echoed to the rafters.

The effect was electrifying. A great roar went up from the crowd, and there was a mad rush for the dance floor. Within seconds, Tor and Jewel were surrounded, their pathway completely blocked.

"Well?" Tor demanded again. But he no longer sounded coldly challenging, and his eyes were no longer bright with anger but sparkling with a great lust for life. "Will you dance with me, Jewel MacKenzie Cameron Chisolm?"

She could not have denied him even if she wanted to. Her blood was singing just as his was with the thrill of the pipes. For a magical moment she knew what it was to be young and free of cares and utterly, completely happy. Smiling, she put out her hands and Tor took them in his own.

All her life, Jewel would remember that glorious dance. All her life she would remember the stirring melody of the long-forgotten music, the joyous shouts of her fellow dancers, and the look in Tor's eyes whenever they shared a knowing smile.

I belong here, Jewel thought suddenly, here with this man, who belongs to me, even though he doesn't know it. It goes far beyond love, this belonging, and 'tis a knowing without words. I can't understand why it is. I just know that it is. I can't lose him now. Not to Abercraig, and certainly not to Heather Menzies.

When the music ended, there was thunderous applause. Some of the younger men stomped their feet and roared for an encore, but the fiddlers were parched and needed a break. Besides, old Mordart was purple from blowing so hard.

With Jewel's hand in his, Tor signaled for another cask of ale to be tapped. Another approving roar went up, for there was nothing a Highlander loved better than his ale. In the mad rush to drink, Jewel and Tor were separated. In a way, she was relieved. It gave her racing heartbeat the chance to still and cleared her mind of the fanciful emotions that had gripped her out on the dance floor.

Fanciful. That was all the moment had been, really. Just an intangible dream she'd not be able to grasp any more than she could capture the mist outside the window.

I have to leave, Jewel thought numbly. Tonight. There's no reason for me to stay.

She turned to go, but all at once Ruan was beside her, perspiring, grinning, sipping a tankard of ale. "I canna believe ye, lass, dancin' circles around the rest of us that way! Nearly did me in! What's come over ye, anyway?"

Jewel smiled sadly. "I wish I knew."

"Never seen Tor act that way, either. Ye've bewitched him, I think."

"Have I?"

"Aye! For a moment there I thought—Hey! Where are ye going?"

"Home. I never should have come."

"Jewel!"

But this time she ignored him, slipped beneath his outstretched arm, and was gone.

Chapter Twenty-seven

But of course there was no thought of her leaving, any more than there was a chance that she could have persuaded the grooms to quit the festivities and harness the carriage horses for her. Tor had not neglected his servants, and when Jewel hurried into the stable, she found a scene of merriment there that rivaled the one in the glittering ballroom.

Quietly she went back inside, leaving the men to their laughter and their ale. Not even Tykie, usually so sensitive to his mistress's presence, saw her go.

Besides, I'm not leaving, Jewel thought stubbornly, for once again she had illogically changed her mind. I fought for Drumcorrie even when all seemed hopeless, and now I'm going to fight for Tor.

Only, did she really want to make things difficult for him when he seemed perfectly happy here at Abercraig, and was betrothed by choice to Heather Menzies? Did Jewel really have it in her heart to pick a fight with that shyly smiling lass?

It was a question that haunted her for the remainder of the night. She kept to her rooms because she couldn't bear to see Tor together with his fiancée again, and refused to unbar the door no matter how many times people came knocking. Ruan was the most persistent, returning every half hour to threaten and plead, and even old Mordart put in a convincing argument that Jewel found difficult to ignore.

Only Tor stayed away. She told herself that she was relieved, knowing that she would never have been able to resist him had he come himself. Inwardly she tormented herself with the thought that he simply didn't care. No doubt the lovely Heather was keeping him well occupied!

She knew that she was being jealous and childish, but she just couldn't seem to help herself. Dawn was but a few hours away when the last of the carriages rumbled out of the courtyard, and still she sat wide-eyed in front of the fire.

She must have dozed off at last, without even realizing it, because she was awakened suddenly by a loud banging on the door.

"Lady Abercraig!"

So insistent was the call, and so befuddled with sleep was Jewel, that she forgot her vow not to let anyone inside. Stumbling over her skirts, she reached the door and drew back the bolt. Astonished, she stared at the crowd gathered before her.

"Wh-what is it?"

Mordart Bennish elbowed his way to the front of the pack. " 'Tis dawn, ma'am! We be waitin' for the football!"

"The football?"

"Aye!" they all shouted in unison.

She stared at them. Had they lost their minds? Just how much had they been drinking? She turned, bewildered, to Mordart. "I'm afraid I don't understand."

" 'Tis dawn," he repeated helpfully. "Time for th' game. 'Tis the lady o' the manor what throws i' the ball."

One of the footmen who had carried Jewel's trunks upstairs the day before now pushed his way forward and thrust an inflated pigskin into her hands. She stared at it, still mystified.

"Hurry, ma'am!"

"They be waitin' downstairs for 'ee, m'lady!"

"Who?" asked Jewel.

"Why, the teams. The Uppies and the Doonies."

Jewel's expression cleared a little. Was this the mysterious Kirkwall Ba' Game mentioned in Tor's invitation? "You're wanting to play football? Now? But most of you haven't even been to bed!"

They hooted in response, and assured her that this made for better play.

"And when does the game end?" Jewel asked, looking down at the ball in her hands.

"When the kirk bell chimes two."

Two o'clock in the afternoon? Jewel shook her head. She was familiar with the Shrovetide ball games that the villagers in Glen Chulish played, but this madcap plan defied understanding.

"Are ye ready, then, ma'am?"

Good-naturedly, Jewel allowed herself to be escorted down the hall while the rules of the game's commencement were explained to her in a jumbled chorus of eager voices. More confused than enlightened, she halted at the top of the stairs while a loud cheer went up from below.

Looking down, she saw that the hall was filled with people, many of them guests from last night's ball. But there were others as well: homespun crofters and shepherds from remote huts and outlying farms, servants from other noble houses wearing embroidered armbands to signify their affiliation to their teams, as well as every single one of Abercraig's groomsmen, cooks, and field-workers. The stable-hands were gathered around their newly chosen team captain, the grinning, earringed Tykie.

At the foot of the stairs, surrounded by friends and fellow teammates, stood Tor. He was looking up at her with a smile on his lips, and all at once Jewel was very much aware of her appearance. She was still wearing her silk ball gown, its petticoats crushed from having been slept in. Her hair had worked its way loose from its once immaculate chignon and now spilled in an unruly fashion down her back.

"Have you been informed of the rules, ma'am?" Tor called up to her.

"I'm supposed to throw down the ball from the northwest tower," Jewel called back.

A loud protest went up from the crofters. Cries of "cheat" and "unfair" could be heard above the din.

Tor held up his hand for silence. Mounting the stairs, he paused on the landing just below the railing where Jewel stood. He, too, was still dressed in the elegant attire of the night before, although he had traded his embroidered waistcoat for a worn leather hunting vest over which he had slipped on a warm sheepskin coat. Jewel's heart turned over as his glowing eyes met hers.

"I'm sure you've been told that there are two teams playing."

"Yes," said Jewel. "The . . . wait a moment. The Uppies and the Doonies."

The corresponding teams cheered wildly as their names were mentioned. Tor grinned up at her.

"Each team takes its place at the far end of the courtyard, the Uppies near the north gate, the Doonies to the west. You'll stand on the bailey wall between them and toss the football directly into the middle." He spoke loud enough for everyone to hear, and his eyes danced as he looked at her. "Will you do it, ma'am?"

Jewel's nod brought forth another round of cheers, and then everyone made a mad dash for the ball-room, where servants stood ready to dole out mugs of warmed grog.

" 'Tis tradition," Tor explained to Jewel, wading into the stampede that had swept her along, and pulling her into the safety of an alcove. "We never start the Kirkwall game without the equivalent of a stirrup cup."

He chuckled as he saw the confusion in her eyes. "I was going to explain it to you last night, but you left the ball early."

He paused as though expecting an explanation, and Jewel said lamely, "I was tired."

"So Ruan said. Was it true?"

Jewel bristled. "Why shouldn't it be?"

He stood there towering over her, tall and handsome and utterly masculine. "I don't know. I like to think your disappearance was more the result of panic than fatigue."

Her chin tipped. "Panic! Now why on earth would I panic? What was there to be afraid of?"

Tor leaned close, his eyes locking with hers. "Me, perhaps?"

She tossed her head, laughing. "I'm afraid you value yourself too highly, m'lord!"

"So you've told me time and again." His voice grew husky. "I came up a time or two myself to check on you."

"You did not!"

"Oh, aye, I did. But I prudently retreated once I heard all the muttered curses coming from behind your door."

She didn't know whether to be furious or pleased.

She only knew that her heart was filled to bursting because of the way he was looking at her, and smiling that crooked smile of his, as though he couldn't get enough of her, as though he truly cared.

"Jewel," he said suddenly, perhaps discerning some of her thoughts.

"Wh-what?"

Instead of answering, he leaned closer, so close that he had to prop his arms against the wall on either side of her head in order to keep his balance. The familiar, manly scent of him enveloped her like a heady drug, and she could feel her breath hitch in her throat and her lips part on a soft gasp.

Slowly, Tor took her chin in his hand. With his thumb, he stroked her jawline, sending shivers down her spine. "Defiant as always, my wee Highland gem. Why can't you simply admit that you left the ball last night because—"

"M'lord!"

Tor cursed softly beneath his breath. Wearily, he bowed his head and massaged the bridge of his nose. "Aye?" he demanded without looking up.

" 'Tis time."

"Very well."

Straightening, he pushed himself away from the wall. With him he took the warmth of his big body, which had been surrounding Jewel like a physical caress. She found herself aching for it, and for him, as she followed him back into the hall.

Ruan caught up with her in the doorway. He was tousled and hungover, but otherwise eager to play. Seeing the football she held, he grinned broadly. "So they've talked you into it, eh?"

"Hardly. Coerced is more like it."

"Just make sure ye throw the ball straight, Coz, otherwise ye'll be accused of playin' favorites."

"Why would I want to do that?" Jewel was genuinely puzzled.

"Oh, I dinna ken. Perhaps because your husband be captain o' the Uppies?"

Jewel planted herself in front of him, the football tucked beneath her arm. "What, exactly, are these Uppies?"

It was Tor who answered, having come up behind them in time to overhear her question. "I see a bit of history might be in order. Morning, Ruan. Awakened from the dead, are you? You'll excuse me if I borrow your cousin for a while?"

"Do I have a choice?"

"As usual, no."

Jewel looked from one grinning face to the other. Why, the way they were acting, the two of them could well be the very best of friends! Were these the same men who had literally torn each other apart whenever they met at Drumcorrie?

"The game was brought here from Orkney when one of my ancestors took a Kirkwall bride," Tor was saying. "At the time, the Uppies were selected from the local aristocracy and the Doonies from among the crofters and laborers. My great-grandfather, so the story goes, thought the practice unfair, and one year declared the Uppies to be all those players at Abercraig born north of the castle bailey, and the Doonies those born below. He was a most democratic man."

"And how did you come to be an Uppie?" Jewel asked.

"I was born in the bridal suite. The bedroom lies just north of the bailey. Damn it, be careful there!"

"Sorry, your lordship!"

A pair of burly locals had pushed their way between them, jostling Jewel and nearly knocking her down. Tor moved quickly to put a protective arm around her.

"Are you all right?"

She gazed up at him in wonder. He sounded so concerned that she could almost believe . . . But no, that was ridiculous.

"You've got quite a restive crowd here," she remarked quickly, watching the noisy men swarm around the punch bowls.

"They're more than ready to play. We haven't had a Kirkwall Ba' Game since the uprising. Be forewarned," Tor added. "It may turn violent."

It already had. Over in the corner, two farmers who had been disputing each other's place in the grog line, now came to blows. Tor, Tykie, and a pair of strapping groomsmen moved quickly to separate them, but not before one of them had had his nose bloodied. No one seemed to care, however, least of all the protagonists. If anything, the gathering became even more boisterous as a result.

"I hope it won't be too dangerous," Jewel said fretfully as Tor rejoined her, dusting off his sleeves.

"I'm sure it will. We never get away without a few broken bones."

Jewel looked at him quickly. Tor had been smiling down at her as he spoke, but when he saw the expression on her face, he grew still.

"Surely you aren't worried about me, ma'am?"

"I—no! Why would you think that?"

He leaned toward her, his eyes glittering. "Why don't *you* tell me?"

Jewel looked back into his eyes, mesmerized. "I—I—" Then, over his shoulder, she caught sight of Ruan coming toward them with Heather Menzies in tow. The girl had obviously gone home early last night, for she looked far better rested than Jewel, and coolly beautiful in a green woolen gown and a shawl woven in the Menzies colors.

Tor had turned to follow Jewel's gaze, and now he straightened and went to them, Jewel obviously forgotten. As Jewel saw the welcoming smile that lit his face, inwardly her heart seemed to die. She did her best to continue looking cheerful, however.

At that moment someone in the crowd shouted that it was time to begin the game. The cry was taken up immediately, and before Jewel could protest, she was spirited away by the housekeeper and a swarm of giggling maids. With the football tucked beneath her arm, she was escorted across the courtyard and up the outer steps to the bailey. Mordart Bennish accompanied them, blowing hard on his ancient bagpipes to produce a reedy but otherwise recognizable rendition of the Camerons of Abercraig's battle march. An air of expectancy settled over the crowd.

It had rained the night before, and an icy wind blew from the north. Clouds scudded across the sky and Jewel shivered as she took her place near the parapet. Far below, the courtyard was a scene of mass confusion as the teams took their respective positions at the north and west gates. Tykie, as captain of the Doonies, towered head and shoulders above his teammates. So did Tor. Jewel saw them exchange a mock salute from each end of the courtyard. She turned to the housekeeper.

"What happens now?"

"Once ye throw the ball, the game's begun. They'll hae until two rings o' the kirk bell tae score three goals. The first team tae do so be the winner."

That didn't seem too difficult to Jewel. "Where are the goals?"

One of the maids pointed. "The Uppies score at Midden Moor. Ye can just see it past the trees there."

"But that's almost two miles away!" Jewel exclaimed. "And most of it's swamp!"

The Abercraig women laughed at her ignorance. Getting muddy was part of the fun.

"And the other goal," the housekeeper added, "be at the Morrisey croft, halfway to their sheep byre."

Also quite a distance away, and most of it uphill. Jewel remembered the difficult trek she had made there after escaping from the castle with Mordart's help. Shivering, she thrust the awful memory away and soothed herself with the reminder that Malcolm Cameron was months in his grave. Tor had worked miracles in making the people of Abercraig forget that he had even existed. She must try to do the same.

"I haven't seen Alastair Morrisey today," she said quickly. "Will he not be playing?"

"Oh, aye. There he be, near the gate. And there be young Keith. He's one tae watch, m'lady. A good, swift runner he be."

"No doubt he'll be leader in a' the hugs," added young Mairi, looking down at him with admiring eyes. "His mither said she'll be watchin' frae Midden Moor. She says he'll probably score the first goal."

Her companions hooted. Loyalties were obviously divided.

"What's a hug?" Jewel wanted to know.

But there was no time to explain. The players were shouting impatiently to begin.

"Go on, m'lady," prodded the housekeeper.

Jewel slowly crossed to the edge of the catwalk. A roar went up as she lifted the ball high over her head. Taking a deep breath, she tossed it down exactly where Tor had told her: into the center of the courtyard, unleashing as she did so a mad scramble that was nothing short of a riot.

Jewel couldn't even tell who got to the ball first. All she saw was a massive tangle of bodies as the opposing teams collided. Arms, legs, and red, shouting faces became a seething blur as the players fought for possession of the ball.

Spectators rushed across the courtyard for a better view. Some of them were trampled when they got too close, and one or two were even carried away like injured players, dazed, bleeding, but seemingly uncaring. No wonder the majority of spectators had chosen to watch the game from the safety of carriages and on horseback outside in the open air! This was nothing short of a free-for-all!

But it was impossible not to be caught up in the excitement. When the Doonies finally managed to take possession of the ball and headed in a huge mass out of the gate and uphill toward the Morrisey croft, Jewel followed behind with the rest. She ran on foot, holding her skirts aloft, and cheering along with the other Abercraig women when Ruan MacKenzie snatched the ball away during an ill-timed Doonie pass.

The seething tide of players followed in pursuit as Ruan headed back downhill. In the middle of the crush, Jewel caught a glimpse of Tor. Disheveled and windblown, he was fending off a trio of attackers who were trying to get at Ruan. Catching her eye as the group swept past, he tossed her a grin.

Jewel waved back at him. Strangely, she had never felt so close to him before. She knew him so well, this man whom she had married against all better judgment. She understood his exhilaration, his lust for victory, and his pure enjoyment of such an intensely physical game.

It turned out to be a bone-crushing event. Players were carried from the field by the dozen, battered and bruised, some of them unconscious. Jewel never once actually saw the football. She only knew where it was by following the hugs, which turned out to be wild tangles of attackers and defenders crushing each other as they tried to put their hands on the ball.

At noon it started to rain. Midden Moor, where the Uppies had already scored two goals and were desperately fighting for their third, became a battlefield of mud. Some of the spectators had given up and gone home, but Jewel had remained behind with the rest. Never mind that most of the players were unrecognizable by now, covered as they were with thick, peat-colored ooze. She would stay until the third goal was scored.

It came sooner than anyone expected. Tykie Ferguson was in possession of the ball, even though he was trapped in the middle of a violent hug with half a dozen Uppies clinging to his back. Giving a mighty heave, Tykie knocked them aside, but as he turned to run, he slipped in the mud and went down on his knees. Immediately a swift-footed Abercraig scullery lad seized the soaking pigskin and splashed triumphantly across the stream that served as the Uppie goal line.

A cheer erupted from the victors, a weary groan from the losers. The game was over.

A triumphant procession of Uppies escorted the football back to the castle. Mordart Bennish, who had been waiting for hours on the north tower wall, hastened to fire the cannon after learning who had won. The cannon was an ancient thing, no doubt left over from the Middle Ages, and Mordart's kilt was nearly ignited as it went off, showering him with sparks and blackening his face.

Jewel was swept along in the middle of the cheering crowd. A wild welcome was accorded the victors by those who had remained behind. They were surrounded, congratulated, joyously pummeled. Someone thrust a heavy silver loving cup into her hands.

"For the Uppies, m'lady! Gie't to the captain!"

A path was cleared for her, and the jubilant cheering became a roar as Tor waded toward her to accept the trophy.

Jewel beamed at him. He was covered with mud, but he had never looked more dashing and dear to her.

Taking the cup from her, he held it aloft as he returned her smile. The roar grew deafening.

"Kiss 'im, m'lady!" someone cried.

Shouts of agreement went up all around.

Jewel shook her head and tried to back away, but the crowd pressed close, forcing the two of them together. Tor leaned over her, his face only inches from hers.

"Scared?" he taunted with a grin.

To prove that she wasn't, Jewel rose up on her toes and planted a kiss on his cheek.

Just as quickly, Tor slipped his arm about her waist. Bringing her close against his soaking, mud-covered body, he pressed his mouth to hers.

The kiss was searing in its passion, and the crowd went wild. Jewel couldn't have escaped even if she'd wanted to. Tor's arm held her like a vise and, oh, but it was heavenly to be held that way again, to feel his heart thundering against her own while his lips boldly ravaged hers!

She could feel her head starting to swim. The sights and sounds around her melted away until nothing remained but Tor and the dazzling wonder of his kiss.

She wavered a little when he set her down at last, and thought she saw regret in his eyes as she opened her own to look at him. He did not release his hold on her, and as his teammates swept him from the courtyard and into the hall, she was carried along. Barrels of ale had been brought up from the cellars, and the hot, thirsty players drank deeply. Everyone crowded around to congratulate Tor, and he acknowledged them graciously, a tankard of ale in one hand while he continued holding on to Jewel with the other.

Dazed and smiling, she clung to him, happier than she had ever been in her life because it was obvious that Tor wasn't about to let her go, that he was as reluctant as she was to break the warm contact between them.

"You've ruined my gown," she said at one point, for her skirts were streaked with mud, and he had left dirty handprints wherever he touched her. Not that she minded in the least.

"Then come upstairs with me," he said, looking deeply into her eyes, "and let me help you out of it."

Desire, darkly intense, burned in his gaze. It shivered through Jewel's blood, making her breath come faster.

Tightening his hold about her waist, Tor drew her close against him. "What do you say, Mrs. Chisolm?"

His hot breath fanned her brow. Jewel was crushed against the hard slab of his chest, but she made no attempt to break away.

"What about your guests?"

"They're enjoying their ale. They'll never notice our absence."

Tor's voice was husky with desire. The heat of his body enveloped her, making every other thought impossible.

Jewel wavered, her knees like water. "I—I—don't know. . . ."

"Go on," he murmured. "I'll follow you shortly."

She did as he asked, although it was an effort to pull herself free from his grasp. She felt his eyes upon her, hot and lustful, as she made her way out of the hall. By the time she reached the stairs she was almost running. Hitching aside her petticoats, she hurried to her room, her heart hammering.

At the end of the corridor, a sudden commotion made her whirl. Gasping, she saw her cousin Ruan being escorted to his rooms by a pair of footmen who were supporting him with their arms beneath his shoulders. His head was bowed and his feet dragged behind him. Heather Menzies was with them, clutching Ruan's hand.

"What's going on?" Jewel demanded, crossing quickly to them.

"Oh, Lady Abercraig!" Heather choked, near tears.

" 'Tis nothing," Ruan added harshly, although he was pale and sweating profusely.

"Nothing!" Heather cried. "Have you lost your senses?"

"Well, Ruan?" Jewel demanded, planting herself in front of him.

He looked at her, exasperated, while the footmen propped him up. "If ye maun ken, I've broke me collarbone. Snapped clean durin' the last tackle. 'Tis nothin', I swear!"

"Nothing!" Heather cried again. "How can you say that?"

Jewel motioned the footmen to carry Ruan into the nearest room and lay him across the bed.

" 'Twill delay the wedding," Heather fretted, following behind. "I just know it!"

"No, it won't," Ruan insisted. He groaned loudly as Jewel eased off his coat. "Have a care, there, Coz!"

"I told you not to play!" Heather persisted, white faced and frantic. "Oh, Ruan, how could you? What about the wedding?"

"The wedding?" Jewel echoed. "But Ruan's getting hurt shouldn't delay that! Unless . . . unless he's to be the best man?"

"The best man?" Heather wrung her hands, weeping openly now. "How can you say that when you know he's the bridegroom? Only, how can we go on with the wedding now that he's broken his bones?"

Jewel's hands stilled on Ruan's shirt buttons. "You and Ruan? But—but I thought you were betrothed to Tor!"

Heather looked at her, horrified. "What? Marry *Tor*? Why on earth would I want to do that?"

Jewel didn't know what to say. She sank back on her heels, her face drained of color.

"Ahem," Ruan said into the silence.

Both women turned to glare at him accusingly.

"You told me Miss Menzies and Tor—" Jewel began furiously.

"Why on earth would she think—" Heather said in the same breath.

"Mayhap I should explain," Ruan interrupted meekly.

"Aye, you'd better!" both women exclaimed in unison.

" 'Twas my idea," Ruan went on, looking sheepishly at Jewel.

"What?"

"Lettin' ye think Tor was marryin' anither."

"Me?" Heather cried as Ruan turned his eyes upon her.

"Aren't you?" Jewel demanded, rounding on her, too.

"Why would you ever think that?" Heather repeated helplessly.

"When you spoke to me last night at the ball, you said you wanted to be sure there were no hard feelings," Jewel explained in a rush. "You were worried that I might still be in love with . . . with your betrothed."

"Oh, for heaven's sake!" Heather cried. "I was talking about Ruan! I was worried you might hold a grudge against me because you were once betrothed to him yourself!"

"I was?"

"She was?"

"Aye!" Heather was obviously on the verge of tears. "Tor told me your father insisted in his will that you marry within a year or you'd lose your home. He said you'd been considering Ruan and that . . . that the two of you—"

"Good God!" Ruan exploded.

"I'd sooner marry the Devil!" Jewel cried.

They glared at each other.

"Oh," said Heather weakly.

"I was sure you were talking about Tor," Jewel went on, struggling to make sense of everything. "You called him by his Christian name, and he'd told you some very personal things about me."

"I'm sorry," Heather said, reddening.

"And you!" Jewel whipped around to confront her cousin.

Ruan gulped.

"You made out that Heather . . . that Tor . . ."

"Lady Abercraig, please. He's no well."

Jewel put her head in her hands. She didn't want to talk about this anymore. All she wanted was to tear her cousin's limbs from his body.

"Jewel?" Ruan said hesitantly.

"You—you liar!" she repeated. "All this time you let me think—"

"Now, lassie," he soothed, " 'twas in your best interest. I only wanted to make you realize that by losing Tor—Ow! Jewel, let go!"

"I'll break your shoulder as well as your collarbone, you deceitful, lying, two-faced git!"

"Jewel, I swear 'twas all—Ow!"

"Lady Abercraig, let him go!"

"Not until I've broken his other bones as well! All of them!"

"Jewel, don't. He's not to blame. I am."

Jewel froze. Heather gasped. Everyone turned to see Tor striding through the doorway.

The footmen melted away at the sight of him. Heather put her hands to her lips and backed against the bed. Jewel straightened slowly while Ruan fell back against the pillows, groaning.

"I should have known," she said heatedly. "You've always been at the bottom of every plan to make me miserable!"

Tor winced. "That wasn't my intention. Not this time."

"God, I'm sorry we ever laid eyes on each other!"

"You can't mean that, Jewel," he said softly.

"Oh, aye, I can." She came to stand before him, her head tipped back in order to look fully into his face. "I'm sorry I ever met you, Tor Ban Cameron. What's more, I hope I never lay eyes on you again. Ever!"

"Jewel—"

She retreated as he reached for her, but that didn't stop him. So she uttered a savage curse and spat at his feet. Whirling, she fled from the room while an awful silence fell in her wake.

Chapter Twenty-eight

I meant what I said that day. Every word of it. If I lay eyes on him again, 'twill be far too soon!

How often had she repeated those words in the days and weeks that followed? A hundred times? A thousand? Did it matter?

Spring had come to Scotland, and with it the time of planting. The days were full for the people at Drumcorrie, and the season a good one, for the weather was mild and there was talk of a harvest as bountiful as the last one. The sheep on the hillsides had dropped a record number of lambs, and there were new infants in many of the crofts as well. Jewel was asked to stand as godmother to nearly all of them, and during those halcyon days she was invited to at least half a dozen weddings.

Indeed, it was a bountiful spring for Glen Chulish, and no one could recall a happier time. Tykie Ferguson was rumored to be courting a lass in the village, and even Annie Brewster was behaving for all

336

the world like a blushing young maid. If only Mistress Jewel could be as happy!

But she was not. Everyone knew it, although they took great pains to hide their knowledge from her. She worked as hard as ever, and took part with enthusiasm in the many celebrations that marked the passage of that lovely spring, but it wasn't the same. Gone was the spirit that had always sparkled in her eyes, while her laughter lacked the youthful gaiety that Tor Ban Cameron had managed to bring to it.

"Lovesick," Angus's wife pronounced sympathetically.

"Pining for her man," her daughter agreed.

"She's made her bed and now she doesna care tae lie in't," Annie Brewster stated accusingly.

Tykie only grunted sorrowfully.

Jewel was aware of the talk, but chose to ignore it. She knew better than to argue with anyone about her supposed feelings for Tor. She knew better than to mention Tor at all. Still, he was always there, in the concerned glances sent her way and in the well-intended but tiresome advice that people always seemed to be giving her.

I wish they'd leave me alone! she would think furiously, and then take to pushing herself harder than ever in the distillery and the office, and spending more time out in the fields, where she could at least trust Angus MacKenzie to offer her companionship while keeping his mouth shut.

Toward the middle of April a wedding announcement arrived from Ayr. Heather Menzies and Ruan MacKenzie were to be united in marriage on May the thirty-first. A huge banquet and numerous festivities were planned, and the couple would embark on a long tour of the Continent before returning to Chulish House to live. Would Jewel be so kind as to attend?

Although it hurt her deeply, Jewel declined. She had no doubt that her aunt Millicent and cousin Cassie would be coming up from London for the nuptials, and she couldn't bear to see them again. Worse was the thought of enduring Cassie's snide remarks when it became obvious—as it surely would—that Jewel's marriage to Tor had gone permanently awry. Although Cassie was married now herself, Jewel didn't doubt for a moment that she would resume her past flirtation with Tor, and that in itself wouldn't bear watching.

I can't go, she told herself over and over, in the face of stern opposition from her disapproving household. How can I face Tor after what I did? How can I ever look him in the eye again when I spit on his boots in front of his servants?

She was convinced that Tor had never been so humiliated in all his life, not even during his long months of incarceration in Cowcadden. The thought tormented her for countless sleepless nights, and even now, months afterward, she could not remember the incident without bowing her head in shame.

And so May came and went, and the wedding took place without Jewel. Those in Glen Chulish who did choose to attend returned with stories of a fabulous feast and a bride who had charmed everyone with her beauty. No one remembered ever having seen Master Ruan look so happy, and if the nuptials had been marred by his cousin's absence no reference was made to it, but Jewel could tell as much from everyone's accusing expressions.

"I'll make it up to him, and to Heather," she promised herself. "When they return from Italy. They'll see."

It was not like Jewel to go back on her word. Scarcely a week after the wedding she took Annie with her on an inspection tour of Chulish House.

Shocked by the neglect she found there, she rolled up her sleeves and went to work. While Ruan might not object to living like a pig, she was determined to make his home a pleasing place for Heather. It was not a simple task, however, and before too long she was spending most of her waking hours there. Sometimes she was gone for days on end, and it was during one of her lengthy absences that Tor Ban Cameron rode unannounced into the stableyard of Drumcorrie.

The weather had been bitter all week. A gale had blown in from the north, muddying the roads and uprooting the larch trees below the house. Sandy and Angus had feared for the barley, but when the storm blew itself out at last and an inspection was made of the fields, the damage was revealed to be minimal. The sun had even managed to emerge briefly from the roiling sky when Tor dismounted outside the stable and nodded to the smiling groom who hurried out to take his mare.

"Rub her down well, Ian," Tor commanded, drawing off his soaking cloak. "And see to that foreleg. I think she may have cast a shoe."

"Aye, m'lord. Happy to oblige, m'lord. We weren't expecting 'ee."

"I know. That's why I came. Where's your mistress?"

"At Chulish House, m'lord."

Tor's brows rose. "What's she doing there?"

"I dinna ken, m'lord."

Perhaps Annie knew. But Annie was away as well, and the girl who admitted Tor to the house could only blush and stammer and shake her head at the sight of him. Shrugging, Tor ordered a bath and headed up the stairs to his former rooms.

Memories overwhelmed him the moment he stepped inside. Little had changed during the long months of his absence. He stood in the doorway recalling the illness and the demons that had tormented him in that huge, dark bed, and the long, difficult road to recovery that he had been obliged to take. He remembered the nasty gruels that had been force-fed him so that his strength would return, and the reeking mustard plasters that had been clapped on his chest to draw the prison poisons from his lungs. He remembered the endless hours when he scarcely had the strength to move and would lie on his back staring at the ceiling and listening to the sounds of the household below.

But most of all he remembered Jewel. The way she had argued with him, annoyed him, belittled and chided him, all in a tireless effort to recall him back to health and sanity by the sheer force of her will.

Oh, God, and the way she had loved him . . .

He turned away, his jaw clenching.

Two footmen he didn't know brought in his bath. They had little to report when he asked after John Chisolm, except to say that he worked as hard as the mistress. Annie Brewster's name brought a more heated response. Aye, they said, she still had Goat, and they were happy to inform him that she had taken the cursed terrier with her to Chulish House. Tykie Ferguson? He was away in the village helping the farrier mend a wagon wheel. With numerous winks and grins they made him understand that it was the farrier's daughter more than the work that had drawn Tykie to town.

The thought of Tykie actively courting anyone amused Tor no end. Smiling, he stripped off his filthy clothes and slid into the tub. Sighing blissfully, he closed his eyes and let the hot water soak the ache of the journey from his bones.

Down below, the familiar sounds of clanging pots came from the kitchen. Outside, the stable door creaked as the grooms went about their business. The plaintive bleating of sheep came from the hillside. Tor sighed again. 'Twas good to be home.

Jewel did not return until late the following evening. She and Annie had spent long hours washing and mending linens, and both had been too weary to brave the dark road back to Drumcorrie. Clearing weather had greeted them at breakfast the following day, and they had resolved to finish their work while the weather was favorable. Not until the sun had slid below the horizon did they return home.

"I'm starved," Jewel announced, appearing in the kitchen after leaving her horse at the stable. "Would you please bring me tea and scones? And see what Mrs. Brewster would like."

The maid working there bobbed a curtsy. "Aye, ma'am."

"I'll be in the parlor."

"Oh, if it please ye, ma'am—"

But Jewel was already gone, unpinning her hat and drawing off her gloves as she went.

The parlor was bathed in the glow of a peat fire. Sighing appreciatively, Jewel tossed her hat onto a nearby chair and crossed to the hearth. She drew up short, gasping, as someone rose from the settee before her. A tall man, bareheaded and in shirtsleeves, who had made himself comfortable with a book fetched from the library.

"I thought you might show up here," he said, coming toward her.

Jewel stood frozen.

"Did you have a pleasant ride back? I was disappointed when you didn't return yesterday. How are things getting on at Chulish House? Has Ruan . . . Oh, come, come, lass, don't stand there gawking. I've never seen you at a loss for words."

"What," Jewel said disbelievingly, "are you doing here?"

"Why, reading."

"Tor. Why did you come?"

"I had to. I've nowhere else to stay at the moment."

"I don't understand."

He clasped his hands behind his back and looked down at her, grinning. "The weather's been so awful in Ayr that Ruan and Heather postponed their departure for Italy. I invited them to stay at Abercraig for the rest of the summer. Since they're newlyweds, I thought it only proper to give them some privacy. That's why I'm here."

Jewel stared at him. "You left Abercraig before the harvest?"

"Spoken like a true farmer. Aye, I did. Ruan said he'd oversee the thing for me. As a matter of fact, he was delighted to volunteer, though I have the feeling 'twill be more work than he bargained for. Heather's aware of it, sensible girl, but she told me Ruan should benefit enormously from acting responsibly for a change. Which reminds me. They were both extremely hurt that you refused to come to the wedding. Ruan thought perhaps you wanted to avoid his mother, and you were right to do so. She was there, along with Cassie and her husband, and I confess I was deuced glad to see them leave. They expressed a desire to visit again in the fall, which is another reason I thought it advantageous to let Ruan stay on at Abercraig a while longer. That way they'll have no reason to come to Glen Chulish, and you'll be spared any confrontation."

"But what about Chulish House? It shouldn't stand empty so long."

"Ruan suggested you ask Annie and John to move in and keep an eye on the place. 'Twould suit them well enough, I imagine, since I've been given to understand that they're planning to be married in the very near future." Tor broke off and wagged a finger at her. " 'Twas deceitful of you, Jewel, to let me think all this time that you and Chisolm were wed."

"We were! I—I mean, we are!"

"Come, come, be truthful. You had all of us fooled and you know it. John, too, I imagine, since he didn't strike me as the sort to marry under false pretenses. Had he known that you'd never officially annulled *our* marriage, I seriously doubt he would have taken vows with you."

Jewel's chin came up. "I don't know what you're talking about."

"No? Well, let me tell you something. The day Ruan and Heather agreed to stay on at Abercraig, I departed for Inverness. I spent nearly a week poring over court books and records. At Kirkfeld Priory I finally came across the rector who'd married you. He remembered you quite well, and obligingly showed me the proper documents when I asked. Interesting, the way you signed the register."

"Tor—"

"Jewel Elizabeth MacKenzie, bold as you please. Your maiden name, which you had the right to use only if your first marriage had been annulled."

"It had!" she insisted stubbornly.

"Really? That's not what I found out when I went to Glasgow to investigate. Strange, but there was no record of an annulment in any of the records I checked. And believe me, I checked them all."

"I don't doubt it," she said bitterly.

Tor's eyes burned into hers, holding her prisoner. "Do you know what I think? I think you married John Chisolm without telling anyone you were still married to me. I think you let everyone here in Glen Chulish believe that you had annulled your first marriage, when in truth you'd done no such thing. No one would have been the wiser anyway, since Glasgow and Inverness are miles apart."

"And what if I did?" she demanded defensively.

Tor seemed to be enjoying himself hugely. It made her want to claw his eyes out. "Why, Jewel," he chided. "You know as well as I do that your marriage to John Chisolm was a sham from the start. 'Tis null and void and always has been. Scotland may have some extremely lax marriage laws, but no court in the country recognizes bigamy. You and I are legally man and wife, and have been all along."

"So what?" Jewel snapped.

"So, here I am. With Abercraig occupied at present, I've come to Drumcorrie to stay."

"You don't honestly think I'll let you!"

"You don't honestly think you have a choice?"

"By God, Cameron, if you think for a moment—"

"I'm sorry, my dear, but 'tis late and I'm tired. I'm in no mood for a fight, even though I can see you're clearly spoiling for one. So, if you don't mind, I'm off to bed."

Oh, but she did mind. She minded plenty. But even as she opened her mouth to tell him so, Tor leaned down and planted a brotherly sort of kiss on her cheek.

"Good night, my dear. We can talk again in the morning."

And with that, he sauntered out the door.

What followed was the strangest week Jewel had ever experienced. Everyone at Drumcorrie was thoroughly delighted to have Tor Cameron back. What was more, he settled into the place as though he'd never left, taking his meals at the table with her, spending his days in the distillery with Sandy, and relaxing in the evenings in the library. At bedtime, he was unfailingly polite as he took his leave of her before withdrawing to the Jacobite suite. At least he knew better than to dare suggest that he share his bed with his wife, which suited Jewel just fine!

Annie Brewster made no effort to hide her pleasure at Tor's return. Neither did Tykie, much to Jewel's disgust. Even John Chisolm gladly gave up his place in Drumcorrie's household to take up residence in Chulish House. Once there, he immediately began a physical relationship with his beloved Annie, showing no trace of the shyness that had marked his relationship with Jewel.

It all made Jewel want to scream.

"I know what you're doing," she said accusingly to Tor one night.

"Oh? What?"

"Ingratiating yourself with all of them so that they'll plead with me to let you stay. Only I won't."

"Ah. So you intend to send me away. How will you do that? With brute strength? You'll have to, I'm afraid, because I don't intend to go willingly."

"Oh, you needn't worry. I'll think of something clever."

"Aye, I'm sure you will."

This conversation took place on a balmy evening early in June, after the long, difficult week had finally drawn to a close. Jewel had been simmering all day over a number of offenses commited by Tor, including several decisions he had made at the distillery without consulting her. Never mind that they had all been sound; she had finally lost her temper and confronted him at dinner.

Now she set aside her fork and glared at him across the table. If looks were lethal, this one would have slain him on the spot.

"It won't take brute strength to get rid of you, Cameron! I'll simply make your life so miserable that you'll be happy to go."

"I've never doubted your abilities in that respect," Tor agreed.

"Then make it easy on yourself. Go back to Abercraig. Tomorrow. Better yet, tonight."

"No."

Jewel switched tack. Her angry expression became mellow, and she smiled at Tor in a manner that made him grit his teeth. "Surely you have enough money to set yourself up in fine fashion elsewhere for the interim. Why Drumcorrie? 'Tis a backwater for the worldly Earl of Abercraig, don't you think? I can't imagine why you'd want to stay here."

"To be honest, I've developed a fondness for the place."

"But what about me?" Jewel countered, all wide-eyed innocence. "Surely you realize that I much prefer living alone! I'll never welcome you back, even on a temporary basis!"

To her fury, Tor merely chuckled. "My poor, wee Jewel. I know you'll never forgive me for the way Ruan and I plotted behind your back. I know how much you despise being taken for a fool. On the other hand, I have every reason to be optimistic about our relationship."

She tossed her head and gazed at him pityingly, as though he'd lost his mind. "Oh? And why is that?"

"Because I happen to know you're still in love with me."

"Hah!" Jewel's wineglass skittered across the table as she sprang to her feet. "Now I know you're utterly daft, Tor Ban Cameron! Love you? I'd sooner love a swine!"

He seemed totally unperturbed by her outburst. Rising himself, he blotted the spill with his napkin and then settled back in his chair. He was smiling when he looked at her, that mocking half-smile that was so devastating in its charm. Damn the long-legged blackguard!

"I've suspected for quite some time that you were in love with me," he informed her calmly. "As early as that first week you brought me here, in fact. My suspicions were confirmed when you returned of your own free will to Abercraig Castle to confront Malcolm Cameron, after Mordart had helped you escape. If you'd truly hated me, you would have gladly left me to my fate."

"Oh, don't be ridiculous! I came back only because I felt an . . . an obligation to you after getting you out of prison."

"I see. Then what about the fact that you didn't show up for Ruan's wedding?"

"That had nothing to do with you! I had no desire to see my aunt."

"I can understand that. But more than your aunt, I think you wished to avoid me."

"Too true," she said nastily.

"Ah, but don't you see the obvious in that? If you were indifferent to me, truly indifferent, you would have come to the wedding anyway. I don't think you're afraid of Millicent any longer, and it's not in your nature to do Ruan such a bad turn simply because you wished to avoid her. You've come a long way in laying old ghosts to rest, and knowing you as I do, I think you would have actually enjoyed confronting her."

Jewel said nothing. In a way, it was true.

"What, then, bothered you so much that you couldn't bring yourself to attend Ruan's wedding? I know how close the two of you are, and I couldn't imagine Millicent being enough to keep you away. But what about me? Why was the thought of facing me so abhorrent that you hurt Ruan and Heather the way you did? Was it possible that you were worried I'd find out how you feel?"

"Don't be stupid!"

"Are you going to tell me again how much you hate me? Save your breath. I've already heard it enough."

Jewel tossed her head. "As a matter of fact, I *don't* hate you, Tor Ban Cameron. I simply don't care about you one way or the other. Go ahead and stay here, if that's what you want. It doesn't matter a fig to me!"

"Is that so?"

"Aye, that's so!"

And with her chin held high, she headed for the door, banging it shut behind her.

Chapter Twenty-nine

For the next few days Jewel did her absolute best to pretend that Tor did not exist. She ignored him at the supper table, and spoke to everyone else in the room as though he weren't there. If they happened to meet in the corridor, she walked past him with her chin tipped skyward. If he settled himself in a chair facing her desk while she worked, she went right on working as though she were alone. If he brought a book to the parlor where she sat reading by the fire, she kept reading, and the sound of turning pages was all that broke the stillness for hours on end.

It was excruciating. It made her want to scream. She knew she'd not be able to endure much more of it. He was trying to wear her down with his patience and his affable smile, and she was certain that before he lost interest in doing so she would end up utterly mad.

Worst of all was the fact that there was no one she

could turn to. Annie thought she was being pig-headed for refusing to make her peace with him. Even Angus, to whom Jewel turned at last in a desperate need to pour out her misery, pointed out that there was absolutely no reason why she couldn't accept Tor back into her life—permanently, no less!

But Jewel could think of plenty of reasons:

Because he had lied to her.

Because he had made her the butt of a joke with Ruan.

Because she had no idea what he really wanted from her.

Because he had never once told her that he loved her, damn his filthy hide! If he had . . .

"But he didn't, and he won't!" Jewel whispered aloud. "Because he doesn't! He just bows to me when we meet for supper, and kisses my hand when he goes to bed, and asks me politely if I slept well when we meet again in the morning. 'Tis no different from the way he treats Annie or the maids or . . . or anyone else!"

As if she really gave a damn.

On the other hand, life would be so much easier if they could just stop all this nonsense. But Jewel had learned early in life to be stubborn and hard, and so the frosty silence continued unabated at Drumcorrie.

Until one morning, when Jewel awoke to find the weather windy and gloomy and threatening rain. Sighing, she turned her face into the pillow. No doubt about it; while it might be going on high summer now, all too soon that glorious season would wane and autumn would come, and then winter, clamping down on Glen Chulish with all its usual ferocity.

The thought of winter, however far away, filled her with dread. The long, snowbound nights were always so lonely, and they would seem even more so once Tor went home. Back to Abercraig, as eventually he must.

But wasn't that what she'd been wanting all along?

She felt utterly weary as she slipped out of bed and splashed her face with the chilly water in the ewer. Dressing in a warm velvet frock of green trimmed with gray, she went slowly down the stairs to the breakfast room. Tor was already there, and she paused in the doorway at the sight of him. He was casually attired in buckskin breeches and a leather vest, his sleeves turned back at the wrists. Since he had been spending a lot of time outdoors, his face was deeply sunburned and his raven dark hair had been bleached to chestnut. How different he looked from the gaunt prisoner she had brought home so many months ago! She had never dreamed then how devastatingly handsome he really was, or how much she would come to love him . . . or at least fool herself into thinking she had.

Becoming aware of her presence, he looked up, and his expression grew wary. He, too, must have been feeling the effects of the weather, because he didn't even bother pretending he was delighted to see her, the way he normally did.

"Good morning," she said coolly, stepping inside.

He inclined his head.

"It doesn't feel much like summer today, does it?" Tor remarked.

"No."

She bit her lip, almost wishing he'd pretend to be kind, because his surliness only made her feel more woebegone than ever. Not that she was about to let him know. Clearing her throat, she sat down across from him and reached for the bread basket. "I thought I'd ride to the Cowarts' today."

"Who?"

351

"The Cowarts. They're crofters of mine. Mrs. Cowart just had another baby."

"I didn't think you were interested in babies."

"Tor, they're my crofters. I'm expected to offer my congratulations. Besides"—she spread butter on her scone—"I like babies. And it's time I started learning about them."

"Oh? Why?"

"Because I—I—" She didn't know what to say. She'd spoken without thinking and now she lowered her gaze, blushing. The subject of babies was not one to discuss with Tor.

"Not expecting one of your own, are you?" he asked suddenly.

She looked at him, her jaw slack. "Wh-what?"

"You heard me."

"For God's sake, how could we? We haven't—"

"Of course not! But you wouldn't have someone else's bastard just to drive me off, would you?"

Jewel recoiled as though he had struck her. Leaping to her feet she ran to the door, but Tor got there before she did. Catching her by the arm he whirled her around.

"Jewel, I'm sorry."

"Let go!"

"Listen to me! That was unfair. I'm just in a foul mood. I know you'd never—"

She twisted out of his grasp and stormed away. She would have reached her room in time to bar the door against him if she hadn't stumbled over her skirts on the landing. It gave Tor time to catch up, and to wrestle with her on the threshold as she tried to slam the door in his face.

"Jewel, for God's sake, I didn't mean it!"

"Aye, you did! Now go away! P-please!"

She was crying now, no longer angry but defeated and hurt. Putting her face in her hands, she turned away from him and slumped onto the bed.

The mattress sagged as Tor sat down beside her. Without a moment's hesitation he drew her into his arms and held her tightly. "I'm sorry," he whispered. "I swear I didn't mean it."

She knew instantly that he spoke the truth, but she wasn't about to relent. Not even while he held her like this, whispering endearments into her hair. But, oh, how good it felt to lay her head against him! She wondered if he had ever noticed how perfectly she fit against his heart. Did he even realize that his hand was threading ever so gently through her hair?

I can't let him do this, she thought. I mustn't!

But where was the harm, if only until her hurt faded?

Perhaps Tor was thinking the same, for he made no move to set her from him. They were silent for a while, neither wishing to see the moment end. Then, slowly, his hand came down to cup her chin so that he could turn her face toward his. As she looked at him questioningly he saw the tears that lingered on her lashes. A muscle in his jaw worked in and out, and without warning he lowered his head and kissed her. A wordless apology, nothing more, but it soothed her pain in a way she hadn't dreamed possible.

"Ah, Jewel," was all he said, sighing and gathering her close.

A tremor fled through her and fresh tears stung her eyes. With this one show of tenderness Tor had managed to batter down her defenses in a way that all his charm and devilment had not. She found herself wishing, fiercely, that he would tell her that he loved her, although only recently she had prayed he would confess his hatred for her and leave her alone.

"Jewel," he whispered into her hair.

"Hmm?"

"I'm sorry."

"I know you are," she said into his chest.

Down below, Goat's annoying bark sounded dimly from the kitchen. The sound startled both of them back to reality. Hiding her reluctance, Jewel slipped out of his arms and off the bed.

They looked at each other for a wordless moment, Jewel with longing in her heart. Please, she implored silently, it's not too late. Say it. Say what I want most to hear. . . .

"You've got jam on your dress."

So she did. "I must have spilled some at breakfast. I'd better change." She didn't want him to know that she was close to tears again. "Would you mind?" she added brightly.

His mouth thinned. "Not at all. I'll see you downstairs."

She changed quickly, without help, thinking about the expression that had been on Tor's face just after he had kissed her. He'd looked . . . miserable. Not just sorry about what he'd said, but as if . . . as if . . .

Jewel's hands stilled as she stood in front of the mirror repairing her hair. As if he, too, were weary of pretending. Did that mean he *had* been pretending? Acting unruffled by her stony silences not because he didn't care for her but because he wanted to hide his real feelings from her?

She was shaken by the thought, and in the next breath by the possibility that she could well be mistaken. But supposing she wasn't?

Tor had a great deal of past experience with women; she knew that. But supposing he'd never actually been in love before? Would that be the reason he had sat there holding her just now and not saying one word even though his eyes had shouted volumes? Was it too much to hope that he simply didn't know how to admit what was in his heart? Or even realize what was there?

But I could show him.

She turned to her reflection and saw that all the lingering uncertainty had faded from her eyes, while a becoming blush had crept into her cheeks. She scarcely recognized the self-assured woman looking back at her.

"I love you," she said suddenly, in a calm, steady voice. "I love you, Tor Ban Cameron."

There. She'd said it, and the world hadn't ended. She hadn't screamed or fainted or caused the walls around her to collapse. Laughter bubbled inside and she picked up her skirts and ran from the room. She didn't think she'd ever been so happy. It was as if a great weight had been lifted from her shoulders and all the gloom of the morning and the pain in her heart had fled as well.

She prayed that Tor had waited for her, that he'd not gone down to the distillery or out into the fields. But no, he was there in the breakfast room, and the moment he saw her in the doorway he set aside his cup and went still.

"I'm back," she said, feeling unexpectedly shy.

"So I see."

"Could we try breakfast again? Without fighting this time?"

"If you like."

"Oh, no, you don't, Tor Cameron," she said quickly. "You'll not get away with that sort of tone, not anymore."

"What tone?" he asked, scowling at her.

"You know. The one you always use whenever things affect you in a way you don't want them to."

"Is that so?"

"Aye." She pulled out a chair and plunked herself down across from him. "You retreat, and act surly and enormously difficult whenever you find yourself out of your depth."

"And when, pray tell, did this happen, this out-of-depth thing?"

"Upstairs in my bedroom."

He made a rude sound. "Nonsense."

She propped her chin on her hand and smiled at him lovingly. "No, 'tis not."

"Aye, it is."

"So you deny that something happened between us?"

"Jewel, something always happens between us. We quarrel and then we make up. Sometimes."

"But this time it was special."

"Apparently so, since you're acting so sweet and loving for a change. Have you got a dagger in your pocket? Intend to use it now that you've caught me off guard?"

She wanted to yank his dark hairs out by the roots. Or throw her arms around him and kiss that stubborn, scowling mouth of his until it kissed her back. She wasn't going to give up now, no matter what! "Liar."

"Jewel—"

"Jewel nothing," she countered, scraping back her chair and coming around the table to stand behind him. "You always say my name like that whenever you think I'm being utterly daft."

"Well, you are."

"No, I'm not."

He refused to turn around and look at her, so Jewel laid her hands on his shoulders and began to massage them, ever so lightly and lovingly. She felt the shudder that went through him, even though he kept himself admirably still.

"Was kissing me upstairs really so daft?" she whispered in his ear. "Was it so wrong to open your heart just for a moment and let me look inside?"

"I came upstairs to tell you I was sorry. That's all that happened. You imagined the rest."

No, she hadn't. In that one moment she was more sure of it than she'd ever been of anything in her life. She knew him; ah, she knew him so well by now! She leaned forward once again to whisper in his ear. "You can tell me the truth, Tor, really you can. Whatever you think of me, whatever I've done to you in the past, I've never betrayed a single one of your secrets. And I never shall."

She kept on massaging his shoulders as she spoke, and all at once Tor groaned and his head fell forward. He seemed so vulnerable in that moment that her heart cramped inside her. Those difficult months following his release from Cowcadden had indeed forged something special between them; she knew it, he knew it, and there could no longer be any pretense. Never had Jewel loved him more than in that one moment. Never had she wanted so much to assure him of her love.

"Tor—" Her voice shook with all that was inside her.

But it was not to be. In that same moment a knock sounded on the door and Sandy Sinclair peered hesitantly inside.

"Oh." He blushed. "I didna mean—"

" 'Tis quite all right, Sinclair." Tor came swiftly to his feet, his relief obvious. "My wife and I were just finishing breakfast. Care for tea?"

"Th-thank you, no."

"Then what are we standing around for?" He gave Jewel a thoroughly dispassionate look. "If you'll excuse us, ma'am? We're off to the distillery."

"You're not going to get away with this so easily," she warned as he brushed past her.

He cocked his head at her. "Oh?"

"Aye," she vowed.

And because she had always been as good as her word, and stubborn once she made up her mind about something, her assault was immediate and unrelenting. When she returned from visiting the Cowarts, she appeared at the distillery with hot tea, cheese, and bread. With Sandy looking on, openmouthed, she fussed over Tor as a mother would a baby—or a woman her lover.

"I can do that myself," Tor snapped at one point when she would have fed him a slice of cheese with her own hands.

"Of course you can." And she smiled at him so sweetly that he gritted his teeth, while behind him Sandy's brows rose to the roots of his hair.

"What's gotten into her?" Sandy burst out the moment she had collected what remained of the luncheon and danced out of the building.

"Midsummer madness," Tor growled.

"I see," said Sandy, who clearly didn't.

Tor scowled at him. "Let's get back to work, shall we?"

Sandy was only too happy to comply.

When Tor returned to the house that night he was thoroughly spent. It was going on eleven o'clock and the entire day had been given over to dismantling and cleaning the enormous copper distilling tuns. That, coupled with his lack of sleep since his return, and his baffled musings as to what Jewel was up to, had reduced him to utter exhaustion. He wanted nothing more than a hot meal, a hot bath, and bed.

The thought of Jewel had him scowling as he crossed the courtyard and ascended the steps. The daft piece of baggage! If only he was certain of her feelings for him! He'd told her he knew she loved him, but in his own, wary heart he was less sure. She had thrown him off balance so many times, he was afraid to trust her.

Never mind that in his secret heart of hearts he had come back to Drumcorrie hoping for just such a reunion between them. Never mind that her behavior in the breakfast room and later in the distillery had tugged at his heartstrings in a way that was difficult to ignore.

Oh, but he was too tired to think about that now, or to puzzle out this new and admittedly delightful Jewel. His heart surged as he entered the dining room and found her waiting there for him, looking far too lovely in a muslin frock the color of moss with her hair spilling in an unruly fashion from a careless knot pinned to her head.

She rose as he came in, but he shook his head at her. He'd been denied his heart's desire for so long. Now that love seemed within reach, he was afraid to grasp it.

"Jewel, don't. I'm not in the mood."

She didn't make the chirpingly sweet reply he expected. In fact, she didn't say anything at all. Instead she helped him off with his jacket and silently steered him toward his chair. She signaled Annie to begin serving the meal and sat there silently watching while he ate, her chin in her hand.

"You can tell me what you've accomplished at the distillery tomorrow," she said at last, "after you've had a good night's sleep."

He grunted. She poured him more ale. When he was through eating, she went with him upstairs. A bath had already been drawn and he stripped gratefully while she stirred the ashes in the hearth to life. As the room warmed, Tor leaned his head against the back of the tub and wearily closed his eyes.

He heard her take up the soap and the washcloth. "I can do that," he mumbled.

"No, you can't. You're too tired."

He felt her hands on his body, lathering him. There was nothing seductive about it. She washed him gently but quickly, and afterward shampooed his hair. Tor found himself drifting in a blissful state between sleep and wakefulness, soothed by her touch. He remembered, dimly, how she had cared for him like this when he had first been brought to Drumcorrie. Then, as now, he had marveled at the fact that a woman could touch him in a way that wasn't sexual but comforting, even healing.

"Come on," he heard her whisper in his ear.

He shook his head. "You'd better go, lass. I'm too tired for that."

She chuckled, a low, pleasing sound. "I'm not after 'that.' I want to dry you off."

Groaning, he stood up and let her towel him dry. After she had slipped a freshly laundered nightshirt over his head, he allowed himself to be put to bed like a child. He grunted when he felt her fumbling with the blankets.

"I said I can't. Go away."

"Hush. Rest now."

The covers were drawn over him. He felt her lips brush his brow and heard the rustle of her skirts as she retreated. The lights were extinguished and the room grew still. He was asleep before she even closed the door.

Chapter Thirty

"What the devil was that all about last night?"

Jewel looked up from her breakfast as Tor stalked into the morning room, fully dressed, wide awake, and clearly spoiling for a fight. She put down her cup and smiled at him innocently.

"What?"

"You know damned well what I'm talking about."

"Oh. The bath and all. Well? Could you have managed on your own?"

"Maybe not," he admitted, scowling. "I was tired, but that doesn't mean I appreciate being treated like a child."

"I know you don't."

"I prefer getting ready for bed myself."

"I know you do."

"Stop agreeing with me!"

"I'm not."

"You are! Oh, never mind." He sat down at the table and put his head in his hands.

Jewel, hiding a smile, poured tea and pushed the bread basket toward him. His hand shot out as she did so to capture her wrist.

"I liked you a bloody sight better when you weren't so obliging," he said, his head still bowed.

"Oh?"

"Aye." Now he was looking at her—or glaring, actually—with a smoldering intensity that could have melted stones. "I know why you're doing it, too."

"Oh?"

"You want me in your bed again. To do the things I did to you once."

Jewel's laughter held a trace of wistfulness, although Tor didn't notice. "Is that what you think?"

"Aye. 'Tis exactly what I think."

"Poor Cameron." She pushed back her chair and came around the table. He drew back suspiciously, but she merely laid her hands on his cheeks and brushed his mouth with hers. "Go on believing that. 'Tis wonderfully cute."

"By God, woman . . ."

She returned to her chair and said nothing more. She knew better than to push him. His wounds had always been deeper than hers, and they would take longer to heal. As well, she would have to convince him that he could trust her, a task that wasn't going to prove easy in view of the way she had been treating him.

But I'll wear him down eventually, Jewel thought happily. Last night was merely a start.

A delightful start, as it had turned out, because spoiling Tor had proved far more satisfying than she had ever dreamed possible. Certainly more satisfying than feuding with him or scheming to be rid of him. Why hadn't she realized as much before?

She watched him stir his tea. Watched those big, capable hands and remembered despite herself how they had once touched her, everywhere—very gentle, very sure. . . . Blushing, she lifted her eyes to his face and realized that she had been caught staring. She coughed and cleared her throat. "What are you planning today?"

"There's more to be done in the distillery."

"But you did so much yesterday!"

"We're not finished yet." He eyed her grimly. "Why? Did you have something else in mind?"

Her blush deepened but she made no answer. She heard him curse softly and then scrape back his chair. Halting in front of her he waited until she'd gathered the courage to look up at him. Reaching down, he twined a bright red tendril of her hair about his forefinger. Tugging gently, he pulled her to her feet, his eyes intense.

"Am I to take that the way I think I should?"

"How do you mean?"

"Don't be coy with me, Jewel. Not now."

She found she couldn't tear her gaze from his. A pulse began beating in her throat. "If—if you like."

He shook his head. "One minute you're ready to throttle me and the next you want me upstairs in your bed. What are you playing at?"

"Nothing. It's been a long time, Tor."

Too long. She swallowed hard, scarcely daring to breathe as she realized as much.

"Just like that?" he asked softly.

She nodded, so filled with emotion of a sudden that she couldn't even speak. He was going to kiss her; she was sure of it. Any moment now that wonderful, sensual mouth was going to sweep down to claim her own, and she lifted her face, yearning for him with every fiber of her being.

"And after we make love, Jewel, then what? Will you scald me with your tongue? Freeze me with your silence? Or simply toss me out on my rear?"

"I—I want you to stay, Tor."

"For now, aye. But after?"

"N-not just for now."

His big body went still. A stunned look crept across his hard face. "Do you know what you're saying?"

She nodded. Her eyes clung to him desperately as he straightened and turned away. When he ran his hands through his hair she saw that they were shaking.

"You don't have to answer right away." She was suddenly terrified that he was going to refuse. "Go to the distillery. Tell me tonight. When you've had time to consider."

"I don't know, Jewel." His smile was sad. "We've hurt each other so many times. Our marriage hasn't brought joy to either of us."

"Tor." She peered into his face with tears in her eyes. "It was wrong of me to take you from Cowcadden and simply expect you to work for me. Everybody told me so, but I refused to listen. I was so scared of losing Drumcorrie that I didn't even think about your feelings in the matter. I'm sorry. Deeply sorry. I've been wanting to make it up to you, b-but I've only ended up bungling badly."

"What is it you're trying to say to me, Jewel?" His eyes were heavy lidded now, the way they always were whenever he wanted to hide his thoughts from her.

She clasped his wrists with trembling fingers. Her voice shook. "I-I'm telling you that I want you to stay. Drumcorrie isn't the same without you. If you stay, I promise never to curse you or shout at you or s-spit on your boots again. I'll never do anything to m-make you angry. I know I've been hurtful before, but it doesn't matter. Not if you—"

"Doesn't matter?" He pried her fingers loose. "Doesn't matter? Of course it matters! Can't you see how futile a reconciliation between us would be, Jewel?"

She swallowed hard. God, how she hated crying! "If you'll help me, I'll change. Tor, please. You and I together—"

"Together?" He laughed bitterly. "So you're on my side now, are you? And how long do you wager that will last?"

"Oh, God, Tor—"

"How can you expect me to believe you?" he went on savagely. "You've always been impossible to trust, always blowing hot and cold, loving me one moment, clubbing me to my knees the next!"

He started to pull away but she clung to him. "Not anymore, I swear it! I love you, Tor, with all my heart."

He rounded on her furiously. "I'm beginning to realize that's not enough, Jewel." He shook her off and slammed through the door.

"He can't forgive me, Annie, nor trust me either."

"And why should he?"

Jewel sighed tearfully. "I know. At least he didn't go home to Abercraig this time!"

"You're lucky he didna."

"I would have gotten him back even if he had," Jewel said stubbornly.

Annie snorted.

"Well, I would have!"

"In chains, na doubt."

The two of them were in the kitchen, Annie baking tea cakes while Jewel sat on a footstool watching, her hands in her lap. She looked drawn and weary and miserably unhappy. Outside, a relentless summer rain was falling. Tykie and Tor had ridden to Chulish House to repair a leaky roof.

"He doesn't talk to me at all," Jewel went on in a

whisper. "Doesn't look at me or even acknowledge that we live in the same house. It's been days, Annie!"

Annie snorted again. Had there ever been two people more intent on making each other miserable? Too stubborn to admit that they had both grown weary of the game?

Not a game, a ridiculous charade, Annie thought wrathfully. Stealing a glance over her shoulder she saw that Jewel was sitting with her head bowed, fat tears plopping unheeded into her lap. Annie's anger vanished and a rare feeling of tenderness overwhelmed her. She said gently, " 'Twill be Midsummer's Eve in a few days. Time for celebratin', no cryin'."

"I don't care."

"Och, lass, that ain't true! 'Tis one o' yer favorite holidays!"

"Not this year."

"Come now, dearie. Why don't ye put your heartache aside for a time? Join in the festivities as always. Mayhap when 'tis over things won't look quite so bleak."

"Do you think so, Annie?" Jewel asked, as piteous as a child.

Annie's reply was an earthy snort. She'd had enough of being bracing and kind.

Behind her Jewel scrubbed furtively at her eyes. "I'll give it some thought."

For centuries the people of Glen Chulish had celebrated the summer solstice with the traditional feast of St. John the Baptist, which included the lighting of bonfires high in the hills after darkness fell. This particular June, with its temperate weather, was promising a harvest of fantastic proportions, and gave the local folk even more reason to celebrate.

The Enchanted Bride

Not long after dawn on Midsummer Eve morning, Jewel accompanied the Drumcorrie footmen and maids in the traditional search for firewood. They were joined by a number of crofters and village folk, for legend had it that not contributing one's share doomed a person to ill luck for the remainder of the year.

Even though Jewel's father had always frowned upon celebrations of any kind, she had slipped away from the house every year to join in the festivities and watch the huge bonfires burn. She had cheered with everyone else as the young men of the village bravely leaped over the fire in order to bring themselves good luck, and helped the young girls weave their blooms of St.-John's-wort together down in the kirkyard at midnight to see which of them would be the next to be married.

It was a mystical, magical time without the aura of doom that marked some of the festivities held elsewhere in Scotland, for the people of Glen Chulish had never been overly superstitious. No one believed in witches or morbid premonitions of death (at least not anymore), and Midsummer Eve was now welcomed as one of the more joyous holidays of the year.

Indeed, coming back from the larch copse with an armload of branches, Jewel felt her troubles slipping like a weight from her heart, just as Annie had predicted. She found herself managing to smile at the antics of the maids and crofting girls she had accompanied, and for a time everyone forgot that she was mistress of Drumcorrie and the wife of the Earl of Abercraig.

There would be bonfires throughout the glen that night, and Drumcorrie's, by tradition, was built on the hillside that nestled along the westerly end of the barley fields. A small crowd had already gathered there by the time Jewel and her companions arrived. Their contribution of resinous larch wood was acknowledged with enthusiastic cheers. Angus, smiling, crossed over to clap Jewel on the shoulder.

" 'Tis good ye've come."

She looked at him, surprised. "Why wouldn't I? I've never missed a Midsummer Eve."

"Nay, but wi' yer husband here . . ." Angus's voice trailed away, and Jewel's gaze followed his to where Tor was standing among the crowd of villagers. In shirtsleeves and a vest, he was helping the menfolk pile the latest contributions of sticks and branches onto the growing pile of fuel. Everyone seemed to have accepted his presence gladly, if a little shyly, and he looked so fit and handsome as he worked alongside them that Jewel's heart turned over.

She made a point of approaching Tor with a friendly smile on her lips. At the same moment he turned and saw her, and she could tell that he was immediately suspicious of that smile. Frowning, he came downhill to meet her.

"I didn't expect to see you here," she said.

"Nor I you."

"I wouldn't dream of missing Midsummer Eve."

"No more than I would."

They fell silent, both having run out of things to say.

Do you know how hard it is to resist you? Jewel ached to tell him, gazing up at this handsome, windblown man whom she loved with all her heart.

Tor was looking down at her with an equal amount of intensity, and all at once she became aware of the fact that she was as disheveled as he was, and that her hair had come loose from the combs that held her heavy braids, and that there were grass stains on the frock she had pulled on that morning.

"Did your family celebrate Midsummer Eve at

Abercraig?" she asked in a self-conscious effort to break the silence.

"Aye. Though the holiday always began with a common riding, not the gathering of firewood."

"We don't do that here." She smiled thinly. "Drumcorrie doesn't have enough land to justify border inspections."

" 'Tis a small place," Tor agreed, looking about him. "But cozy. When I was in prison—" He broke off abruptly, a shadow crossing his rugged face.

Jewel hadn't seen him do that for quite some time. The pain she knew the memory evoked for him cut her to the quick. She laid her hand on his arm.

"Tor, don't. 'Tis over now."

"Is it?" He glared at her, his gaze accusing.

"I'm sure you're aware that there's talk about us at home, and elsewhere in the glen."

He gave a bitter laugh. "The state of our marriage is no secret to anyone."

"I know. That's why I was wondering . . ."

"Aye?" he asked when she hesitated.

She looked down at her grass-stained slippers. "Tonight will be the first time since your return from Abercraig that you and I . . . that both of us will be . . . um . . ."

"On display for the locals?" he guessed.

"Aye." She traced the toe of one slipper through the grass. "Would you . . . do you suppose you and I could be . . . kind to each other?"

"Fie, madam. I'm always kind to you."

So he was. Unfailingly polite. Treating her as though she were some remote and highborn lady made of the finest porcelain—when he was speaking to her or acknowledging that she was even alive, that is!

"That's not what I meant," she hissed, though she

knew he had understood perfectly well what she was asking.

"Well, then?"

She gritted her teeth. "Do you suppose, just for tonight, we could behave as though our marriage was a happy one?" Her tone grew wistful. "If only to scotch rumors. You know how people talk, and exaggerate, and spin wild tales."

"I didn't think your reputation was so important to you," Tor countered coldly.

Jewel's gaze faltered. "No, it isn't," she confessed in a small voice. "It never has been. But—but these people . . ." She gestured toward the crowd gathered around the unlit fire. "They—they mean so much to me." Tears sparkled in the corners of her eyes at this unexpected and quite honest confession.

Tor had forgotten her devotion to Drumcorrie and its people and her fierce love for the home in which, from all accounts, she had spent such a miserable childhood.

"Very well," he said coolly, if only to hide the fact that he was softening. "For today, at least, we'll give them no reason to believe there's aught amiss with our marriage."

She smiled at him through her tears, a smile for once devoid of all deception. "Thank you."

But Tor merely turned away without speaking. She waited until she had gained control over her tears before joining him again. It took a lot of courage, but she was determined to show everyone that there was no merit to the rumors of discord in their marriage. She smiled at Tor as she halted beside him, slipping her arm companionably through his.

At that moment they were approached by a family that had just arrived from one of the outlying crofts. Since Jewel had recently visited them on the birth of their youngest child, she greeted them with genuine warmth, her sadness fading. Tor was introduced and names said all around, and the children were trotted forward to be exclaimed over. The new infant, colicky and crying, was held out for Jewel to admire.

" 'Ee allus fusses thot way," the father, Jamie Cowart, explained apologetically.

" 'Ee's been fussin' since we left hame," Mrs. Cowart added wearily. She bounced the baby on her ample bosom, but that only served to make it cry harder.

"Can ye no stop the caterwaulin'?" one of the older Cowart offspring demanded, covering his ears.

"Give him to me," Tor said.

Though obviously surprised, Mrs. Cowart did so.

Jewel watched in amazement as Tor dandled the wailing bundle with none of the clumsiness one would expect from a man unfamiliar with babies. Then, laying it facedown across the length of his arm, he massaged its back before quickly lifting it upright and laying the tiny, wrinkled face to his big shoulder. The baby responded by emitting a loud burp. Instantly the crying stopped.

"How did ye do that?" Mrs. Cowart demanded, wide eyed, as he handed her the now placid infant. "He's allus gassy and we can never get 'im tae burp!"

"An old trick taught me by a Turkish beldam," Tor answered, winking.

Eagerly they asked to hear about his travels abroad, and Tor obliged them with more information than he had ever revealed to Jewel. But for once she didn't mind. She was watching him with a strange, possessive ache in her heart, for he had taken the infant back from Mrs. Cowart as he spoke and was once again holding it in that relaxed, confident way.

Babies had always mystified Jewel, and she was ashamed to admit that she felt clumsy and timid whenever she was asked to hold them herself. But watching Tor as he talked about his travels while swinging the baby on his arm, she felt the ache inside her grow into a breathless longing. What would it be like, she wondered suddenly, if Tor were able to forget the past and they became man and wife in every sense of the word, and had children of their own?

She had never considered the matter of a family before, but now the longing blossomed in her heart until it became unbearable. She found that she had to look away and bite her lip to hold back the tears.

" 'Tis time we went home, ma'am," Tor said suddently, making her wonder if he had noticed. "There's much to be done before the feast. Will you excuse us, Mr. and Mrs. Cowart?"

They were only too happy to do so. Obviously they had taken a strong liking to him and were eager to permit him any liberty. Handshakes were exchanged all around, and then Tor took Jewel's hand and led her away.

"Time you went to bed," he growled in her ear.

"Bed! But 'tis barely noon!"

"Aye, and you've been up since dawn. A nap won't do you harm. You look tired, and much too pale."

She glanced at him quickly. Was he concerned about her?

But he wasn't paying attention to her anymore. He had halted suddenly, and an odd look had passed across his face.

Her breath caught. "Tor, what is it?"

"What the devil?"

He was fumbling in his vest pocket. Jewel's eyes widened as he removed something small and squirming. With an expression of extreme distaste, he disposed of it in the bushes. As it scampered away, she saw that it was a field mouse.

"That Cowart lad!" he bellowed, storming back to

her. "I should give his backside a good paddling!"

But Jewel could tell that he wasn't really angry. Quickly she covered her mouth with her hand to hide her grin. "Here at Drumcorrie we play pranks on Midsummer Eve."

"Aye," he growled. " 'Twas the same at Abercraig."

She was instantly intrigued. "Did you ever play tricks on anyone?"

"Once or twice."

"Such as?"

He shuffled his feet like the small boy he must have been then. "Ah, well, sometimes I joined the village lads in misbehaving."

"And what do you mean by misbehaving?"

"One year we salted the food the Abercraig cooks had prepared for the banquet."

"You didn't!" Jewel was enchanted. "What else?"

"Another year we fed whiskey to Alastair Morrisey's pigs and released them, drunk, on the village green. Oh, and I nearly forgot the time we poured glue into the vicar's shoes. Unfortunately we were caught out for that and caned."

"A well-deserved punishment."

"Is that so? I'll have you know—" He broke off as a giggle escaped Jewel's tightly compressed lips. "So you think it funny, do you? Would you still laugh if I were to put a mouse down your frock tonight?"

"Oh, I like mice," she assured him.

"Ah, that's right. You've a pet up in the attic, don't you?"

She sobered quickly. "Do I?"

His eyes sought hers. "Surely you haven't forgotten?"

Of course she hadn't. But she didn't want to be reminded of the night she had hurried into Tor's room after he had sent the furniture crashing in an effort to catch the tiny rodent, and how she had ached for him once she came to understand his fear of mice and rats after all that he had suffered at Cowcadden. And she certainly didn't want to be reminded in any way of what had happened between them afterward. . . .

"Jewel."

The way he said her name made a shiver flee down her spine. She didn't have to look at him to know that he, too, was remembering. Desire, hot and dark, poured through her blood. She had gone too long without his kisses, his touch.

"Give me your hand. I'm taking you home."

Scorching him with her eyes, she laid her hand boldly into the one he held out to her. Could it be that he was really relenting?

Oh, but how her blood sang the moment his strong fingers closed around hers! He must have been aware of it, but he only stood there looking wordlessly down at her.

"A favor from you, Mr. Cameron," she said at last.

"What?" he countered suspiciously.

"I want to call a truce tonight, a real one. Not just for the crofters, but for us."

He tried to let go her hand, but she wouldn't let him.

"Just for tonight. A promise, Tor. No more feuding. No calling names. No treating the other like the dirt beneath one's boots. Please trust me not to hurt you. Just for tonight."

"Very well," he said, tipping her chin up to him. "A truce."

"A real one," she insisted tremulously. "I want you to behave as though you're in love with me."

Their faces were so close that their lips were almost touching. Curling his fingers around her hand, Tor brought it against his chest. Jewel could feel the wild drumming of his heart beneath her flattened palm.

"I'll do my best," he whispered huskily.

He led her down the hillside and left her briefly while he went to talk with Angus. Jewel, watching him hungrily, saw the other lasses turn their blushing faces toward him in much the same way. Her heart swelled with a fierce, possessive joy. Tonight, just for tonight, everyone would know that he was hers.

Chapter Thirty-one

The feast of St. John the Baptist began at sundown with an invocation by the local vicar. Since it was a fine night, the service was held outdoors on the front lawn of Drumcorrie. This was the only solemn moment of the evening, and everyone gathered there tried to look suitably pious even thought the coming festivities were foremost on their minds.

During Archibald MacKenzie's long tenure as Drumcorrie's master, the feast of Midsummer Eve had been notoriously lean. A mean-spirited man, Archibald had always withheld the bounty of his table from his household and the tenants who farmed his land. Not so his daughter. When gout and increasing age began keeping Archibald confined to his rooms, the task of managing the house, the farms, and the distillery had fallen more and more to Jewel. Far more generous than her father, she had made certain that the food served at every public occasion was sufficient to fill everyone's belly. As well, barrels of fine

Drumcorrie malt were rolled out and broken open, and while Archibald might howl and thump his cane at such extravagance, Jewel had stubbornly continued the practice until the day he died.

And afterward. Already the tables set up beneath the trees were groaning with tempting dishes. The Drumcorrie kitchen had been a beehive of activity all week as Annie and her crew churned out countless hams, sides of beef, roasted fowl, and all of the wonderful side dishes that accompanied them. Tykie had gone down to the distillery cellars numerous times to select the whiskey, and now the barrels stood among several others filled with ale just waiting to be tapped. Small wonder the folk gathered to hear the vicar speak were so restive! And no one, not even the vicar, objected when a mad rush for the refreshment tables broke out the moment the sermon was over.

As the sky overhead darkened and the first stars sparked into light, the sound of fiddles filled the air, mingling with the laughter of the company. The celebration had officially begun.

A roar went up from the crowd as, with tapers and torches, the menfolk set the enormous bonfire ablaze. Other fires were already burning in the hills farther down the glen, and the effect was magical. As if on cue, the bagpipes joined the fiddles in a rousing country reel, and soon everyone was dancing.

Jewel and Tor stood in the darkness near the refreshment tables watching. Already everyone had drunk too much whiskey and ale, and inhibitions had been thrown to the wind. Why, there was John Chisolm cavorting with Annie, who had hitched up her skirts to reveal a scandalous length of her pale, skinny legs as she kicked and twirled beside him. Tykie, too, had bravely asked the farrier's daughter to dance, and Jewel smothered her laughter as she watched him lumber like a huge bear around the slim little thing.

"I think she likes him," Tor said, smiling.

"I hope so. He's been agonizing over her for months."

"Is he courting her?"

"Aye, though he denies it. Come midnight, we'll know."

"What happens at midnight?"

"All of the lasses here will walk twelve times 'round the kirk, scattering hempseed as they go. If they're lucky, their true loves will appear, and legend has it that they'll be married within the year."

"Bah."

"Oh, don't be such an old grump. Didn't the Abercraig lasses do any such thing?"

"Yes, yes," he said impatiently. "Picked orpine roots, twined St.-John's-wort into wreaths, and gathered fernseed before dawn—all that nonsense in the hopes of winning themselves a husband."

" 'Tisn't nonsense," Jewel protested. " 'Tis magic."

He looked at her closely, but her face was hidden by the darkness. "Do *you* believe in magic, Jewel?"

"I've tried," she said with a sad little catch in her voice.

He looked at her for a long moment, saying nothing. She had dressed simply that night in a pale blue muslin frock with only a hint of lace edging the collar and sleeves. Her hair was twisted into a braid that was held off her slim neck by a pair of tortoiseshell combs. She looked enchantingly lovely and innocent, like one of the village lasses whose fresh, pretty faces were lit with animation as they gathered around the tables on the lawn below.

"Come," he said impulsively, taking her hands.

"Where?"

"You're going to dance with me."

The other couples greeted their appearance with whoops of delight.

Oh, and to dance with Tor! Here was all the magic that she had assured him abounded on Midsummer Eve, springing up to surround them while the music of the pipes stirred her soul. Tor's smiling face so close to hers showed her that he, too, was realizing life could be good, and fun, and free of cares, if only they would let it. Somehow, when she danced with this man, he was able to coax from her all of the heartache she had suffered in the past.

Did he sense what he did to her as he led her through the joyous steps of a true Highland reel? He must have, because he, too, looked uncommonly free of cares for once. His arm about her waist was strong and very sure, and when the steps of the dance brought them close together he held her to him with a bold familiarity that he had rarely dared show before.

He swung her into his arms and twirled her around so that her skirts belled around her. Then he released her so slowly that she slid sensuously down the length of his body before her feet touched the ground. She did not step back right away, but stood there looking up at him, her hands twisted in the lapels of his vest. Both of them were breathless.

"Who taught you how to dance like that?" they asked each other in unison.

"Tykie," Jewel said with a laugh.

"My mother," Tor said with a bittersweet smile.

"Will you tell me about her?"

"Aye. But not tonight."

She tried not to look disappointed. "Why not?"

He tipped her chin with a forefinger. "How can I talk about my mother when my wife is pressed against me like a second skin?"

Jewel blushed. "Cameron! 'Twas you who put me here."

"Aye. And I've a mind not to let you go."

His husky voice shivered through her blood. She felt her lips parting as he gazed hungrily into her upturned face. She yearned for him to kiss her, and perhaps he would have if they hadn't become aware just then of the hooting laughter rising around them. Turning her head, Jewel realized with a start that the dance had ended and everyone else had withdrawn from the circle, leaving her and Tor standing there alone, their bodies meshed together.

Crimson with embarrassment, she broke away. Tor infuriated her by acknowledging the laughter and catcalls with a grinning bow. Keeping her tightly by his side, he fetched them both an ale, and Jewel drank thirstily from the mug he handed her.

Another dance began, and Jewel was whisked away by John Chisolm, who ignored her protest that she was much too tired. Afterward it was Tykie who led her out, then Sandy Sinclair, blushing furiously all the while and stepping clumsily on her toes.

Breathless, her head spinning, she was released at last. In the glow of the bonfire she searched the crowd for Tor. Unable to find him, she started back toward the house only to be surrounded by a sea of giggling girls who blocked her path.

"Mistress Jewel, 'tis almost midnight!"

"Will ye come wi' us to the kirk?"

"Time to find yoursel' a lover!"

She laughed aloud. "Oh, no, I couldn't possibly—"

They didn't give her a chance to finish. Laughing and cheering, they captured her arms and swept her away.

Drumcorrie's tiny stone chapel had been erected centuries ago by some pious MacKenzie ancestor.

The vicar toiled up the mountain path from the village every Sunday to deliver a sermon for the benfit of Jewel's household and to perform any of the rites of passage, such as baptisms and burials, that its inhabitants might require. Jewel had watched two of her stepmothers marry her father here, and as a young girl had dreamed of being married someday herself. Never in a million years would she have imagined that she would end up being wed instead in the office of a prison warden and then again to another man in a remote rectory far beyond the town of Inverness!

But Jewel wasn't thinking about either of her marriages as the laughing girls swept her off through the darkness. She was listening to their gay, untroubled talk, and finding her own spirits rising because of them. How long had it been since she had last enjoyed the company of her own sex?

A reverent silence descended as the spire of the whitewashed kirk came into view. The moon was a heavy sickle in the sky, and its pale light reflected eerily on the slate roof. The sagging tombstones were dark shadows against the grass.

"Who'll go first?" someone asked in a hushed voice.

No one volunteered.

"Have ye got cold feet, then?" demanded Fiona, Angus MacKenzie's youngest daughter, crossly. Jewel knew Fiona well. She had six older brothers. Nothing, not even the magic lurking abroad on Midsummer Eve, could scare her. "Here, give me the seed. I'll start."

The others watched with bated breath as she scooped a handful of hempseed from the burlap bag they had brought with them. With a bold toss of her head, she started for the kirkyard. Those watching counted in electrified whispers as she circled the tiny building twelve times without stopping, scattering the seeds as she went. No sooner had she finished than she was joined by a tall young man who emerged from the shadows on the far side of the gate. They laughed softly together before melting into the darkness.

" 'Twas Charlie MacBride!" whispered one of the girls crouching beside Jewel. "I just kenned 'ee were courtin' her! Do ye suppose anyone else followed us here?"

"Your turn to find out," said another girl, giving her a push.

When this girl, too, found herself similarly spirited away after performing the prescribed ritual, there was no lack of volunteers among those remaining. Jewel knew perfectly well that there was no magic involved in any of this. Every last one of the girls had obviously made her intentions known to the lad in whom she was interested prior to leaving the bonfire. Still, it was fun to watch them pair off, one after the other, with their intendeds, and Jewel graciously refused to give the rest of the young men away when by chance she spotted them hiding in the shadows behind a massive vault at the back of the graveyard.

"Good luck to 'ee, Mistress Jewel," said the last of the girls when she hurried off to meet her fate with her hempseed tucked in an apron pocket.

Jewel laughed in response. She had enjoyed watching this ancient ritual tonight, but she wasn't about to indulge in it herself. She didn't need to coax a husband out of the darkness, thank you very much. She already had two too many.

By now the last of the girls had been spirited away by her waiting beau, and Jewel found herself alone in the kirkyard. Although the hour had grown late, she did not leave right away. Instead she stood savoring the sweet night air and the welcome silence after the noise of the crowds back at the bonfire. As well, she felt warm and sleepy, and wondered if perhaps she hadn't drunk too much ale.

Turning to go at last, she nearly tripped over the sack of hempseed that sat forgotten at her feet. As she bent to pick it up, she was seized by a mischievous impulse. Scooping up a handful of seed, she stepped through the gate and began to circle the walls of the kirk. Giggling, she repeated the ancient rhyme:

> "Hempseed I sow,
> Hempseed I hoe.
> Let him that is my true love
> Come after me and mow."

The last of the seeds whispered into the grass. Dusting her hands, Jewel turned back toward the gate. As she rounded the corner of the church, she bumped squarely into a tall man who had stepped out of the shadows in front of her.

She went still. The moonlight cast shadows on Tor's craggy face. It was too dark for her to read the expression in his eyes, but she could see that his mouth was curved into a smile. She swallowed.

"You followed me here."

"Aye."

"You were hiding with the others."

"No. I've been down by that larch tree there, watching alone."

"All this time?"

His smile deepened. "All this time."

"Oh. Then you saw—"

"No need to blush, Jewel. 'Twas a charming sight, watching you trying to conjure up a lover."

She glanced at him quickly, but he was no longer teasing. His lips still had that soft tenderness about them, however, and Jewel, filled with wonder, could not seem to help herself. Slowly, very slowly, she came up on her toes and brushed her fingers across them.

With a groan, Tor caught her by the elbows and lifted her toward him. Down came his mouth to hungrily claim her own, and Jewel gasped as the wonder of that long-desired kiss swept over her. Her knees seemed to give way and Tor caught her by the hips just as she threw her arms about his neck to keep from falling. Breathing heavily, he brought her fully against him.

He was ready for her, more than ready, for she could feel the massive hardness of him quickening where she stood trapped between his legs. She whimpered low in her throat.

"Jewel, ah, Jewel," he said hoarsely, "I can't wait. It's been too long."

She couldn't wait either. They sank onto the grass, still locked together, their mouths tasting and teasing, their tongues mating in a furious dance. Tor leaned into her, drawing her frock from her shoulders and exposing her breasts to the warm night air. His dark head lowered as he coaxed the rosebud nipples into straining attention with his circling tongue.

Jewel arched beneath him, her hands burrowing under his shirt. Beneath the hard muscles of his back she could feel the wild hammering of his heart.

"Oh, God," he breathed, echoing her own aching sentiments. "It's been too long. Too long. I've dreamed of this for weeks, for months. . . ."

With feverish haste he stripped off her gown. Taking her by the wrists, he pulled her upright so that she was kneeling before him. While he kissed her she undressed him as well, taking pleasure in his shuddering delight as she caressed and teased the naked flesh she exposed. The moment she drew off his breeches he sprang full and heavy into her waiting hands. The moonlight played off his glorious male body, and she gazed at him with worshipful eyes, loving him, wanting him so much that it hurt.

Still on her knees, facing him, she slipped her arms around his neck. Their naked bodies came together, the long months of denial fading into the wondrous rush of reunion, of the sensuous feel of skin to skin, muscle to feminine curves, of lovers who fit with the sweetness of easy familiarity.

Cupping her buttocks in his big hands, Tor fitted her tightly against him. Now they could both feel his manhood throbbing against her belly. Jewel went still, frozen by the poignant ache of anticipation, by the sweet torment of wanting the moment never to end and knowing that she would die if Tor didn't take her now.

When he did, it was not a moment too soon. Cupping her face in his hands, he kissed her with all the heated promise of the glory to come, then laid her back slowly, slowly into the grass. For a timeless moment he hovered over her, his dark eyes burning into hers, his carnal mouth twisted with longing, while Jewel looked back, her gaze starry with all that she wished to say and didn't have to.

Then Tor groaned and came down on her swiftly, urgently, and Jewel cried out at the stabbing ecstasy of possession. A sob rose in her throat as Tor burrowed deeply, then reared back before filling her again. Her fingers bit into the bunched muscles of his forearms as he leaned into her, stroking in and out and building within her the great fires of their passion.

Fulfillment came for both of them after little more than a few fierce thrusts. Groaning out her name, Tor buried himself inside her while Jewel swirled up to meet him, sobbing, as the force of their climax swept them up and out of themselves. For a wrenching moment they soared together, teetering on the brink of consciousness, not knowing where one began and the other ended, only that in this sublime moment they were one and the same. Together, entwined, they found the ultimate ecstasy.

Chapter Thirty-two

The kirkyard was silent for a long time afterward. Tor lay above her, thoroughly spent. Jewel lay quietly beneath him, utterly shattered. Neither spoke. All they could do was lie together and wait for their tortured breathing to still.

At long last Tor came up on his elbows and tried to shift away from her. Jewel wouldn't let him. When he looked at her questioningly, she wound her arms tightly about him.

"I don't want to crush you," he protested.

"You're not."

"Good." He laid his cheek against her temple and closed his eyes.

She could feel the sting of tears in her throat. She had never felt so devastated, so weepy. Perhaps Tor felt the same, because his hand shook noticeably as he reached to brush the hair from her brow.

"My God," he whispered.

He kissed her, without the wild passion he had

shown her earlier, but fiercely nonetheless. Then he slipped out of her and, before she could protest, rolled onto his back, taking her with him. Splayed across his chest, Jewel laid her head on his shoulder and blissfully closed her eyes.

"Mmm," she murmured after a while. "I could stay like this all night."

She felt him shake with silent laughter, and looked at him accusingly. "What's so funny?"

"I could, too, but 'twould be rather scandalous, don't you think, if the vicar found us like this in the morning?"

"To hell with the vicar."

"Is that how you speak in a kirkyard, lass? Fie."

"What does it matter? I think we've already sinned here enough."

"Do you call this a sin, Jewel?" he asked huskily, shifting so that she could feel the muscled length of his naked body.

"No," she said dreamily, moving sensuously in response.

"Now you've done it," he complained as his manhood stirred in response. "You've bewitched me for sure, my fiery enchantress. I'd not have thought I could do this again so soon."

"Do what?" she murmured innocently.

"This," he said, taking her face in his hands and kissing her deeply. "And this," he added, rolling her beneath him on the grass.

"God, I want you," he whispered against her mouth.

Indeed, he seemed unable to get enough of her. Touching, stroking, caressing, he took possession of her again. With lips and hands he told her how much she was revered and desired. Slowly, slowly, he built her budding passion into something that promised to be an act not only of love, but an affirmation of life as well.

Jewel had never felt so cherished before. She had never known Tor to be so tender. Though he burned for her, his touch was gentle. Though he craved to overwhelm her with the sheer force of his need, he took his time in bringing her to the edge of fulfillment.

"No," he said urgently as Jewel, inflamed and teetering close to that edge, moved invitingly beneath him. "For you, my love. Only for you."

And he drove her up, with his kisses and his magic touch, up and over that wondrous edge while she clung to him, writhing, sobbing, and gasping out his name.

There were tears in her eyes when she opened them at last. She was lying in the grass with her arms locked about his neck while he leaned over her, his strong, capable hands still splayed across her belly. Everything that she was, everything that she felt, was there in her magnificent eyes as she lifted her face to his. Her cheeks were stained with the lingering glow of passion, her lips swollen from his kisses.

He smiled at her, a tender welcome back to reality. Before he could speak, she lifted her head and slowly drew his mouth down to hers. Her arms tightened about his neck and she eased him onto his back so that she was now above him, the aggressor in their glorious game.

Pressing soft kisses upon his lips, she leaned tenderly over him. He shuddered as she took him into her hands, inflaming him with her bold caress. Her unbound hair spilled across his chest, her silky legs tangled with his. Her hands, so delicate and small, worked their own magic upon him, leaving him groaning with pleasure and want.

"Jewel, ah, Jewel," he murmured, "do you ken what you do to me?"

"Aye," she whispered against his mouth, her breath mingling with his. Slowly she slid her body along the length of his, nestling her hips in the curve of his outspread thighs, satin against steel. Lifting herself, she took him into her, and Tor moaned her name as the velvety warmth of her sheathed him tightly.

"For you, my love," she echoed. "Only for you."

It took no more than a few sensual movements of her swirling hips to have him erupt within her. Hands fisted in her hair, he arched beneath her, giving her his very essence in a moment of wrenching splendor.

"I love you," she whispered against his brow while he shuddered and came. "I love you, Tor Ban Cameron."

At long, long last, he groaned and went slack beneath her. She lay with her cheek pressed against his jaw, her fingers threading through his dark, thick hair.

"I love you," he whispered raggedly. "I love you, Jewel MacKenzie Cameron."

Her hands ceased their wondrous stroking. Her breath caught in her throat and he felt her grow still above him. Then she lifted her head and looked down at him. Their eyes met in a long, silent look of dawning wonder, a naked truth in which each finally dared to welcome the other home.

"I almost lost you," he said, his voice breaking. "Over and over, with my distrust and my pride. I've been a fool to deny what you mean to me. How much I love you."

"Aye," she whispered simply, and lowered her mouth to his.

They kissed, softly, a tentative reunion. The future

shimmered before them, ripe with promise. A man's heart, sorely battered by time and fate, need hurt no longer. A woman's heart, left lonely since childhood, needed filling no more.

"Will you tell me again that you love me?"

Tor obliged without hesitation. He didn't think he'd ever get tired of saying it.

"I love you, my beautiful, stubborn wife. Though you'll doubtless drive me to an early grave, I can't seem to help myself."

"I know."

"Ah. Modest as well as beautiful."

She came up on one elbow and peered deeply into his eyes. "I love you, too, my strong, stubborn husband. But I think we'd better be practical now."

"Oh? Since when have you ever been practical?"

"Tor. Stop teasing. I want to know what you're going to do when we get back."

"Home, you mean? I've decided that already. Breakfast, a hot bath, and"—he grinned, not at all practically—"bed."

"And after that?"

"Why, more bed, of course. I thought 'twould be . . ." His grin deepened as he looked into her eyes. "Very well, I'll be serious. What do you want to know?"

"If—if you intend to go away."

He gathered her close, shaking with silent laughter. "Do you think I could after this?"

She couldn't share his humor. Too much was at stake. "You've done it before."

"I was a coward then," he said, the laughter fading from his voice. "I've faced imprisonment, torture, cannons, muskets, and swords during my lifetime, but I couldn't face the way I was beginning to feel about you. Knowing that you represented everything I'd ever dreamed of scared me so badly that I ran.

Like a mewling schoolboy, I turned and ran, time and time again." He said this wonderingly, as though he still couldn't believe it, and not without a certain measure of self-contempt.

"I always have that effect on men," Jewel said, dimpling. "Dinna fash yersel', Cameron. 'Tis perfectly natural."

Ah, his Jewel. Had there ever been another like her? Always, always, she knew just what to say to make the moment right. And a weightier moment there had never been in his life, because he knew right then as he gazed into her upturned face that he had indeed lost his heart to her and that he no longer cared. He knew now that she would always keep it safe.

"I ran, too," she reminded him softly. "Over and over, the same way you did."

"We're scarred warriors, my love, and always will be."

"Ah, but MacKenzies have always been warriors." She leaned over to trace her lips along his jaw to his ear. "But the war's over at last, Cameron."

"Thank the good Lord for that." He grunted.

She tried to swat him, but he caught her arms and held her tight.

"There's one more thing I'd like to know," she said when he finally stopped kissing her, tracing her finger across the muscles of his chest.

He was instantly on guard, alerted by the subtle change in her tone. "What is it?"

She hesitated, and he gathered her close against his heart. "You can tell me, Jewel. Don't be afraid."

"Abercraig," she whispered, as though reluctant to say the name aloud.

"Oh." He was silent for a moment. "What do you think we should do?"

"I—I don't know," she replied, close to tears.

"Well, I've been giving the matter some thought."

She turned her face into his shoulder. "Y-you have?"

"Aye."

He felt the tremor that ran through her, and he lovingly stroked her back. "Supposing we were to give it to Heather and Ruan? As a wedding gift from the two of us? I'm certain they would love dividing their time between Ayr and Glen Chulish. And Annie and John would probably be delighted to keep up Chulish House in their absence. As for you and me, we could visit them whenever—What is it, love? Why are you looking at me like that?"

"Do you—do you mean it?"

Aye, he did, for he had come to realize that she meant far more to him than Abercraig ever could, that wherever she was would be home to him. And so it would be Drumcorrie that beckoned to him for the rest of his days, because Drumcorrie was so much a part of the woman he loved that he could not help but love it in turn.

It was an enchanted place that had begun the healing of his wounded heart, and reunited him with his enchanted bride.

WHITE HEATHER

Helene Lehr

Bestselling Author Of *The Passionate Rebel*

She is a fiery clanswoman who can wield a sword like a man, a sharp-tongued beauty with the courage to protect her people. But when rival clan leader Thornton MacKendrick takes Diana captive, nothing can protect her from the sinful pleasure that awaits her.

Although Diana is determined to return to her beloved Highlands, her heart betrays her will, and she finds herself drawn to the rippling, tartan-clad body of her captor. But it will take more than Thorn's heated caresses to make Diana his own. Only with a love as powerful as her pride can he hope to win her trust, to conquer her heart, to make her his love's captive.

_3795-5 $4.99 US/$5.99 CAN

NEVER CALL IT LOVING GAIL LINK

"An enthralling tale!" —Jayne Ann Krentz

A royal ward of Charles II, Marisa Fitzgerald doesn't meet her betrothed until they are standing at the altar—and then the young bride gets the shock of her life. For after a villainous temptress betrayed him, her husband's enemies had savagely tortured him, scarring his body and soul. But Marissa is no simpering beauty ready to submit to an overbearing ogre. Somehow, some way, she will tame Cameron's brutish demeanor and turn the mighty beast into a loving man.

_3519-7 $4.99 US/$5.99 CAN

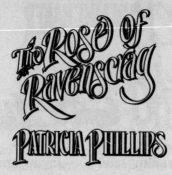

The Rose of Ravenscrag

PATRICIA PHILLIPS

Bestselling Author Of *The Constant Flame*

The daughter of a nobleman and a common peasant, Rosamund believes she is doomed to marry a simple swineherd. Then a desperate ruse sweeps the feisty lass from her rustic English village to a faraway castle. And even as Rosamund poses as the betrothed of a wealthy lord, she cannot deny the desire he rouses in her soul. A warrior in battle, and a conqueror in love, Henry of Ravenscrag is all she has ever dreamed of in a husband. But the more Rosamund's passion flares for the gallant who has captured her spirited heart, the more she dreads he will cast her aside if he ever discovers the truth about her.

_3905-2 $4.99 US/$6.99 CAN

Dorchester Publishing Co., Inc.
65 Commerce Road
Stamford, CT 06902

Please add $1.75 for shipping and handling for the first book and $.50 for each book thereafter. NY, NYC, PA and CT residents, please add appropriate sales tax. No cash, stamps, or C.O.D.s. All orders shipped within 6 weeks via postal service book rate. Canadian orders require $2.00 extra postage and must be paid in U.S. dollars through a U.S. banking facility.

Name _____

Address _____

City _____ State _____ Zip _____

I have enclosed $_____in payment for the checked book(s). Payment <u>must</u> accompany all orders.☐ Please send a free catalog.

MADELINE BAKER

Beneath A Midnight Moon

Winner Of The *Romantic Times* Reviewers Choice Award!

He comes to her in visions—the hard-muscled stranger who promises to save her from certain death. She never dares hope that her fantasy love will hold her in his arms until the virile and magnificent dream appears in the flesh.

A warrior valiant and true, he can overcome any obstacle, yet his yearning for the virginal beauty he's rescued overwhelms him. But no matter how his fevered body aches for her, he is betrothed to another.

Bound together by destiny, yet kept apart by circumstances, they brave untold perils and ruthless enemies—and find a passion that can never be rent asunder.
_3649-5 $4.99 US/$5.99 CAN